FRANCO

NOW READ HER MOST GLORIOUS BESTSELLER YET—*PRINCESS OF FIRE!*

They met on the field of battle. He was Alaric, a Norman knight sworn to the service of William the Bastard. She was Fallon, a Saxon princess who dared to take up arms to save her country. They were enemies—and yet, these two people were destined to be much more than that to each other. In the year 1066, the clash between Normans and Saxons threatened to tear the whole world apart. Their love was a battle as fierce as the war. . . .

PRINCESS OF FIRE!

Taylor—made Romance From Zebra Books

WHISPERED KISSES (3830, $4.99/5.99)
Beautiful Texas heiress Laura Leigh Webster never imagined that her biggest worry on her African safari would be the handsome Jace Elliot, her tour guide. Laura's guardian, Lord Chadwick Hamilton, warns her of Jace's dangerous past; she simply cannot resist the lure of his strong arms and the passion of his *Whispered Kisses*.

KISS OF THE NIGHT WIND (3831, $4.99/$5.99)
Carrie Sue Strover thought she was leaving trouble behind her when she deserted her brother's outlaw gang to live her life as schoolmarm Carolyn Starns. On her journey, her stagecoach was attacked and she was rescued by handsome T.J. Rogue. T.J. plots to have Carrie lead him to her brother's cohorts who murdered his family. T.J., however, soon succumbs to the beautiful runaway's charms and loving caresses.

FORTUNE'S FLAMES (3825, $4.99/$5.99)
Impatient to begin her journey back home to New Orleans, beautiful Maren James was furious when Captain Hawk delayed the voyage by searching for stowaways. Impatience gave way to uncontrollable desire once the handsome captain searched *her* cabin. He was looking for illegal passengers; what he found was wild passion with a woman he knew was unlike all those he had known before!

PASSIONS WILD AND FREE (3828, $4.99/$5.99)
After seeing her family and home destroyed by the cruel and hateful Epson gang, Randee Hollis swore revenge. She knew she found the perfect man to help her—gunslinger Marsh Logan. Not only strong and brave, Marsh had the ebony hair and light blue eyes to make Randee forget her hate and seek the love and passion that only he could give her.

PRINCESS OF FIRE

SHANNON DRAKE

ZEBRA BOOKS
KENSINGTON PUBLISHING CORP.

Prologue

Hastings, October 1066

"The Norman duke is dead! Duke William is dead!"

The cry had begun as a murmur, but it rose like a shrill wind at the least opportune moment. Among the left division of the Normans, the knights had broken. A chaotic and horrible retreat had begun, and the horses slipped and fell in the marsh. Men and animals alike shrieked, but the Saxon line remained unbroken.

"Fools!" Alaric thundered over the cacophony of clashing battle-axes and swords. "William lives! There, see! He casts his helmet aside to prove he is alive!"

Alaric's emphatic declaration stilled the panic, but the situation remained bleak. The damned English! They were a mob—a disorganized but stalwart body. William, leader of the Normans, attacked with horsemen; Harold and his English forces had none. But if William's forces were fewer, his battle plan was superior. His weaponry was more advanced and deadly, whereas a number of the Saxons fought with nothing but crude slingshots—and desperation. They fought for their homeland and for Harold, their king, Alaric realized, and they would probably do so bare-handed if necessary.

William rode before his troops; Harold was afoot. How order could be sustained, Alaric did not know.

But in spite of it all, the English were holding the day upon the battlefield of Hastings. William had come in with arrows and missiles to break and confuse the ranks; his knights followed on war-horses to trample down those broken ranks, and foot soldiers finished the grim task. Yet for all William's military finesse, nothing went right. The horsemen moved before all the arrows had flown, and Norman arrows had downed Norman fighters. The Saxons' shields had created an impenetrable wall, and little damage had been done.

Caught in the melee with the retreat in abeyance, Alaric paused and stared at the line of Saxons upon the ridge of their defense. Thousands had died; more men came to replace them. England was being defended by a wall of flesh and blood. And by God, for all that Alaric would lay down his life for William without hesitation, he was heartily sorry for the bloodshed. Harold Godwinson was a good man and a fair one—an excellent king. Somewhere among his troops he fought, barely returned from battle with Viking scavengers in the north. He had fought with genius, it was said, and with mercy; he had proved himself both a man and a king. Now, today, he fought again; fought with raw men, and raw weaponry, fought in desperation—and Alaric was one of those invaders he must fight.

Among the Norman banners was that of the pope—and Alaric suspected that this pennant was the most potent weapon on the field. For he knew Harold, and he shuddered to think of the Saxon's feelings when he believed that even God had turned against him.

"God's will," Alaric muttered between his teeth, and drew his sword, for a Saxon defender was upon him, swinging a crude ax and letting out a horrible cry. Savage blows rained on him, but Alaric was well trained in the art of warfare, and the Saxon fell before him in a pool of blood.

"Alaric!"

He turned his horse around. William was calling to him—tall in his saddle, tense, and still bareheaded, to assure his troops that he lived.

"They come; the English are attacking. Hold the ranks and cut them down as they come!"

Perhaps the counterattack was the Saxons' first mistake, for they were cut down. The Norman retreat was halted; horses trod upon screaming Englishmen where they fell in the mire. Chaos reigned again, but at last the tide was turning.

"By God, 'tis Harold! Harold is dead! The Saxon king is dead."

It began as a murmur; it rose to a chant. And this time, the news was true. After the long and bloody battle, Harold lay dead. The shouts of victory rose. It seemed that no one near Alaric really knew how Harold had died—some claimed he had been wounded in the eye by an arrow, then hacked to bits by the Normans. But he was dead.

And the Saxon wall of defense, which had been unbroken by arms and carnage, blood and death, now scattered like autumn leaves in the wind. Harold Godwinson, the Saxon king, was dead.

Alaric smiled bitterly. He had liked and admired Harold; now he felt no victorious joy—only pain. He knew that this moment was only the beginning. This bountiful land of forests and fields would fall, too, before William's pillaging troops.

William did not advocate rape or murder or mayhem. But he had promised riches to those who rode with him, and riches were attained through plunder. Like the Saxon king, the land would bleed and scream . . .

"Alaric! Count Alaric!"

Falstaff of Boulogne, heavy in armor, was riding his charger over the corpse-strewn battlefield toward Alaric.

"A large group of Saxon swine retreated down the ravine, and our men went in chase. Their horses tumbled and fell, and the Saxons fell upon our men, slaying them. They are fighting fiercely still, led by one who knows nothing of surrender or retreat."

Alaric swung his horse around and cantered toward the ravine. He did not make the mistake that had killed his men, but dismounted and made his way downward on foot, drawing his sword to join the battle.

Sheer force of numbers brought the Normans and their Breton supporters to triumph as swords clashed and axes fell. The Saxons began to flee and beg for mercy.

"My lord!"

With a heavy, shuddering sigh, Alaric strained to retrieve his sword from the fallen form of his latest foe. Falstaff—great, bearlike Falstaff—was behind him again, calling for his attention.

"The men—they pause—there, by the oak! 'Tis a Saxon swordsman so adept that our men can only circle about him. They ask if he seeks quarter—he asks none! He fights like a madman gone amok—like a Viking berserker, by God! My lord—"

Alaric waited for no further explanation but sped up the ridge. The climb was difficult for him, for he was in full armor—so heavily clad that nothing of him showed but his thunderous, brooding gray eyes.

At the ridge he mounted his horse, spurring the well-trained steed to hasten, and quickly came upon the scene at the tree.

Like many of the Saxons, this warrior was clad in leather armor, a tunic that protected his body, a mask to shield his face. Alaric was annoyed to see that ten armored and well-armed Normans were still circling this one fighter. The position had been a fine choice for the

Saxon warrior; his show of bravado had surely allowed many of his men to escape into the forest.

Alaric watched one of his own men move in; he saw the defender's prowess with the sword, and his mouth tightened.

"Stand back!" he ordered grimly. "The fight is mine."

Perhaps it was not fair, for the defender was surely exhausted, yet so were they all, for it had been a bloody day. Nor did Alaric intend to fight to the kill, for he admired the brave show and would rather have had him a prisoner. But he moved in with a measured fury, for by God, he would see no more of his own men slain or crippled.

Alaric was mounted; the Saxon was on foot, and yet prepared. As Alaric moved in, the defender's sword came up and caught his own.

But Alaric's strength was greater, and he was aided by the speed of his mount. The Saxon's sword flew high into the air like a silver bird or a comet with a flashing tail— foreshadowing doom for the defender. That same force sent the Saxon to the ground, flat upon his back. He did not rise, but lay there—panting, gasping for breath, awaiting the death blow.

Still grim, Alaric rode in a circle around the fallen swordsman. His great steed paused with his hooves just a foot from the Saxon's head.

Alaric leaned down and pressed his bloodied sword against the Saxon's throat. "Surrender and live," he said quietly.

No answer came his way. With great agility he leapt to the ground, graceful despite his armor. He reached for the leather mask that concealed the Saxon's face.

"Nay, leave me be!"

Alaric started. A wave of astonishment seized him, and a fiery sizzle cascaded along his spine. The voice was soft; it was English, naturally, but melodic and fluted . . .

And it was no man.

Alaric's senses told him who the woman was. Just as he had known Harold, so, too, he knew her. Disarmed and fallen, she still fought, struggling viciously with her bare hands against his hold.

He felt vicious himself as he grappled with her with clenched teeth and bulging muscles. She was strong, but she was not his equal hand to hand.

He caught the tie at the back of her head and furiously wrenched the mask away.

She paused at last in her struggle and tried to stand.

Smiling grimly, Alaric planted his foot on the tress of midnight hair that had fallen free. She was forced to stare up into his face, into his eyes.

He spoke English to her—bitter, biting English, for she had sworn herself his enemy and proved it many, many times before this battle had been joined.

"Cease, Fallon! You are beaten!"

"No! Never!" she choked out. "Never!"

With a startling and desperate surge of force, she lunged at him, tearing her own hair beneath his boot in her frenzy to attack him and free herself. He saw her eyes dart, and he knew she sought to escape into the trees, as her mates had done. She flew against him, seeking his weakness, his inner thigh where the armor did not protect his flesh. Her teeth hit him and in exasperation, impatience, and raw ire, he swore out an oath and released her for the briefest moment. She tried to spin and run, but he lunged after her and threaded his fingers through her hair, dragging her hard against the cold steel that covered his body.

"Bloody Saxon bitch! You are beaten. Surrender!"

"To the bastard henchman of a bastard duke?" she retorted, as tears of pain filled her eyes. But her courage was unshaken. "Nay, William will not have England!"

Even then—ill clad and muddied with the filth of the

battlefield—she was strikingly beautiful. Eyes as blue as the crystal sky over the northern realm of her Viking ancestors, hair as black and glistening as ebony night. Her face, a delicate heart, lips as red as potent wine. Beneath the dirt her skin was as fair as cream, her cheeks like rose petals. Her brows were high and arched like a pixie's and, laughing, she was more stunning still, like a playful goddess, more enchanting. Like a princess . . .

She *was* a princess—if not by birth, then by the acclaim of the English people. Harold Godwinson's daughter by his "Danish marriage," she was as proud as any queen and as English as the earth on which they stood.

She was a beauty, yes—a great and enchanting beauty. This Alaric could acknowledge, for it was as simple as the grass being green, or the ocean blue.

She had been a thorn in his side since the day he had met her, and standing there he knew she had to be subdued if ever William was to rule all of England. Fallon was Harold's cub, and she had to be tamed.

Alaric released her, then removed his helmet and ran his fingers through his hair. "Fallon, you are done. You are my prisoner—"

He halted, gritting his teeth as she spat in his face.

He wiped his face with a gauntleted hand, watching her defiant blue eyes. Then he caught her wrist in no subtle grasp and wrenched her back to him. "Lady, you are done! England is done!"

Her head fell back and she stared into his eyes, her own still gleaming rebelliously. "England, sir? This is but a battle, and England is a big country. My father's country."

"Your father is dead!"

She suddenly seemed to wilt, as if consciousness were leaving her and she would fall. He reached out to steady her; furiously she wrenched her arm from him.

"No!" she denied hoarsely. "My father is not dead! He cannot be dead!"

"Fallon, I tell you the truth. Harold is dead."

"No!" She stared at him, seeking some word. He knew that she longed for him to deny himself, to tell her that Harold lived. "Please! For the love of God, Alaric . . ."

Alaric stood as stiff and cold as steel. He longed to reach out to her and soften the blow, for she had adored her father. He did not wish to be cruel, yet for Fallon just now, perhaps, swift cruelty was the greatest kindness. He was too busy to spend time tangling with her, but she had to be handled.

If she kept fighting, she, too, would soon be dead. She was lucky she did not lie among the dead now, after the fool's stand she had taken to save her friends.

She had to be beaten, Alaric realized wearily. She had to be beaten so thoroughly that she could not rise again and bring about her own end.

"England is not lost!" Fallon cried out. "Surely my brothers live! Edgar Atheling lives, and the English will turn to him! William will never, never be king—"

"Take the—uh—princess back to camp," Alaric told his men, interrupting her, his tone a cool dismissal of her. "See that she is kept under guard until we determine what we shall do with her."

Two of his armored knights stepped toward Fallon, each taking one of her arms. Thank God for armor; she struggled against them still, biting and kicking. But sadness clouded her voice when she spoke again. "The bastard will not be king! The lords of the witan meet together to choose the king in England. The law creates the king! The witan made my father king, and my father—"

"Get her out of here!" Alaric commanded his men. He turned away, clenching his jaw, glad that few of his Breton horsemen spoke English, for they would surely take exception to her calling William a bastard—true though it was. He was Duke William to those who loved him, and that was that.

Alaric started back to the center of the field. The Saxons were gone—slain or dispersed. Night was falling. It was time to separate the wounded from the dead, to pick up the pieces and plan further strategy.

Falstaff, carrying Alaric's helmet and the gauntlets he had pulled from his hands, followed as Alaric went from one fallen soldier to the next.

Alaric had known many battles; he had fought at William's side for years to retrieve the duchy of Normandy from the hostile barons who had tried to steal William's inheritance. Alaric had fought—but he had seldom felt as he did this night. Bodies were entwined with bodies. Men cried out for water, for God, for life, and for death.

The priests had arrived and were quickly giving last rites. The surgeons and barbers and the whole men hastened to the wounded.

Alaric watched these ministrations and inhaled sharply. Just before him lay a boy with arm outstretched—dead beneath the body of a heavy Norman horseman. The sight of the youth hurt him. A young lad, fresh from his wheat fields, battling with nothing grander than a stick.

"He promised us rewards. Right, Alaric?" called a voice.

"What?" Alaric turned with a frown.

"Nothing, Alaric, nothing. I'll speak when we've seen to the men."

The grisly chore took them well into the night. William sent for Alaric, who made his way to the duke's tent. As he entered, William clapped him enthusiastically on the back and handed him a silver chalice of wine.

Alaric downed the wine quickly, eyeing William. Somewhat shorter than Alaric and broad in the shoulders, William was handsome at forty years plus. He still shook with excitement and emotion.

"Alaric, we've done it. In one day! Harold is dead, Alaric. We've taken England."

"We've not taken England," Alaric said bluntly, knowing their twenty-year alliance gave him the right to speak his mind. "William, 'tis a big country. Harold is dead, but the land stretches before us."

William stalked across his tent, frowning. "I know. But God is with us—destiny has spoken. Alaric, my mother felt it when I was conceived; I was to be like a giant tree spreading its limbs across the Channel." He paused, taking his comrade by the shoulders. "England will be mine! And you shall have any of it you desire."

"Ah, yes, I shall be rewarded," Alaric murmured. He walked to the rough wooden camp table in the center of the tent and pointed at a dot on the map.

"London, William. We must reach London; we must get the witan to proclaim for you and not for Edgar Atheling."

"Bah! He's just a boy."

"William, you know as I do that the witan must proclaim the king. You must be crowned in London."

"We'll march for London, then," William said, falling into his chair wearily. "We'll battle all the way if we must. We'll move carefully, but I will prevail. I had hoped . . ." He slammed his fist on the table. "By God, Alaric! England was promised to me! I meant to be a good king, a fair king, and now—"

"And now," Alaric continued for him, "you owe a pack of French and German mercenaries half of your new kingdom—not to mention what you owe your loyal Normans."

William clenched his jaw. "You are right; I am in debt." He glanced at Alaric sharply. "The people will despise me."

"Perhaps."

"There is no question about it," William said flatly. He sighed long and deep, shaking his head. "I will prevent what plunder I can. But the people must be broken, and my hold on this country must be like an iron fist. I shall prevail."

"Yes, I believe you will."

William rose. "I'm going back out. We must find Harold's body. Christ in heaven, so many dead—'tis near impossible." His voice softened. "He was an honorable adversary. I shall find him and bury him with all honor."

"I wonder if the Saxons will appreciate it."

"I do not do it for them; I do it for myself." He smiled. "Ah, Alaric! My right hand. When I found you battling all alone on that ridge so long ago, I did not know that such a ragged scrap of boy could grow to be my strength. But then, you were a bastard, too, young but fighting for life and rights, as I had always done. We won those battles, Alaric, and we shall win the ones that await us. I shall be king."

"William, Harold's sons fought today. You know they will rise against you. There is more slaughter coming."

"There were times when I wondered if we would ever see this shore," William said softly. "I tell you it was destiny. We shall prevail."

"Yes, I believe we shall," Alaric agreed. "I just pray that it is not a wasteland of corpses and scorched earth that you rule."

William lifted a hand. "I did not seek Harold's death; he died on the battlefield as I might have done. If his sons are captured, they will not be slain—unless they refuse to surrender. They will, I assure you, eventually swear an oath of loyalty. Harold's family I will respect—"

"Oh, my God, family! William, I have his daughter, Fallon."

"Fallon!" William said sharply, his teeth grating.

"We captured her on the battlefield, where she was fighting."

"Fighting? I'm sure her father did not know," William brooded.

"What shall I do with her?"

"She is still hostile, I imagine?"

"Aye, that she is."

"Keep her prisoner, under tight guard." He hesitated, and Alaric could see that William was remembering Harold's daughter, too. He stiffened his shoulders and said coldly, "Take her yourself or give her to one of your men." William's words were harsh and bitter. He could be a merciful man when he chose. He could also be as hard as stone. "Or give her to all of your men. Her tongue is more dangerous than the strongest sword. She must accept that I will be king. She must swear an oath of allegiance."

"She'll never do that."

"If she insists on fighting me, she will lose her head. Alaric, the battle will be long and hard. I will not have her at my back through it all! She is yours. Do with her what you will, but control her. If she will bend, she will have my love and protection; if she will not, she will have nothing, perhaps not even her life."

William stood again and clamped a hand on Alaric's shoulder. "Go, the night is yours. I will finish with the death detail this night and tomorrow. Then we will forge ahead, and I will pay heed to your strategy, as I did this day, and trust in your sword arm, as I have these past two decades."

Alaric nodded and left. He was weary, having been awake all the previous night, awaiting the morning and the battle.

Outside the tent, Falstaff fell in behind him. Alaric smiled at his faithful follower, this great hulk of a man, deadly in battle, as gentle as a kitten to his friends and

loved ones. Many times, with hostile swords at their
backs, each had been saved by the other's prowess and
loyalty. When Alaric had first joined William, Falstaff had
decided to protect him, and he had followed Alaric into
battle ever since. He was a huge man, dark and grizzly,
with pudgy cheeks and flashing dark eyes and a quick
smile. He was not born to lead, but created to follow well.
Alaric was the leader to whom Falstaff gave his allegiance;
yet theirs was a fine friendship. Where Falstaff was eager,
Alaric was wary. Falstaff was sympathetic, and his heart
was easily won. But the years had made Alaric hard. His
emotions did not show, and few knew what went on
behind the steel-gray mirrors of his eyes. The hostile
barons who had fought William in Normandy had
learned that Alaric's sword meant death; those who had
come to honor their duke had then given Alaric their
respect and their friendship, having learned, too, that he
gave his gravest concern to his men, offering justice and
a quick wit and careful use of his power.

"Wine, women, and song!" Falstaff declared, smiling
broadly. "Alaric, William will be king! The country lies
before us. . . . Which of our camp followers will you have
tonight, my lord? The buxom redhead? The blonde? Or
will you choose a Saxon wench from the towns we took
upon arrival? Will you drink and dance and laugh?"

Alaric arched a dark brow. "I wish a bath and a good
meal. Then I shall study the countryside we must traverse
in order to reach London. And then——"

"Then?"

"Then perhaps I shall share some good wine with the
redhead with the huge smile——"

"And the huge breasts!"

Alaric chuckled softly. They had reached their horses
and they mounted, then started off at a brisk trot for their
base camp.

"Alaric, William will give you anything you ask for, won't he?"

Alaric shrugged. "He has little to give me as yet."

"Alaric . . . ?"

"What are you trying to say, Falstaff?"

The great man gave him a sheepish smile, then leaned across his horse to grip Alaric's arm. "I am a man in the deepest throes of agony. I have fallen in love; I wear my heart upon my sleeve."

"For God's sake, Falstaff, what are you talking about?"

"The girl, the lady, the princess! Harold's cub. Never have I seen eyes so blue, hair so rich, flesh so fair! A face finer than an angel's! A body—slender, supple, curved, and trim. Ah, but her lips are like roses; she's as splendid as the rising sun, as glorious as the twilight, as—"

"Enough, enough!" Alaric laughed, looking at his friend curiously. It was true; the man was enamored of Harold's beautiful little shrew.

"Alaric, please. I beg you! Ask William if I might have her. I will love her, I will be good to her. I will honor her and cherish her, and if she will have me, I will marry her. Alaric, if you would grant me any small favor, grant me this! At least speak with William."

Alaric was silent, feeling a hammer thud against his heart. Nay, he could not do it. He could not give her to anyone, for he could not untangle his own emotions regarding the minx.

He spoke at last. "She is a witch! She despises Normans. She will fight you tooth and nail. She can be dangerous; she can rouse the people. And you saw her today; she knows how to wield a weapon. Friend, I grant that she is beautiful. But she is proud and knows nothing of bending. If you take her, you win only trouble."

"You know her so well?"

"Oh, aye. I know her well." For Alaric knew the sweet taste of her kiss, and the bittersweet fury of her heart. He

knew what it was to want her beyond sense and logic
. . . "I met her when she was a child, Falstaff. You must
remember when she came to Normandy with her father."

"Aye, I do! I adored her from afar!"

"When I came here this year as William's messenger to
Harold," Alaric said, "I saw her again." Touched her
again, felt her fire and her wrath, and nearly lost his soul
before it!

"Falstaff, before we came here as invaders, she had
good reason to hate and mistrust us. She thinks us barbarians, rough and uncouth. 'Norman dung,' I believe, is her
favorite epithet."

"I will be so gentle and tender!" Falstaff declared
nobly. "I love her, you see."

Something about Falstaff's passion rankled Alaric. Perhaps Fallon could spark in any man this deep emotion,
this fury like a living blaze. How many times had he felt
it himself? How often had he touched her and thought he
was lost?

A strange feeling slid along his spine as he remembered
battling her today. William thought it was fate that would
give him England. Alaric thought it was fate that had
decreed his struggle with Fallon today. Their feud seemed
ancient; she had been a child when it began. Years and
years had passed before he had seen her again, yet it had
been there, between them, instantly—a hostility that filled
the air with tension.

Alaric shook his head. He knew he had to answer
Falstaff's request. Aye, he should give her to the great
bear who adored her! Alaric did not trust himself near
her. Whatever it was, passion or pure hatred, it burned
too brightly between them. Alaric had the duke's business
at hand. There was a whole country before them to conquer; he dared not find himself weakened by his efforts to
save her from her own temper and wounded pride. She
was beaten. She was conquered.

Alaric inhaled sharply. He wanted to wash his hands of her. He wanted to see her locked in a tower far, far away. He did not want to see her, or feel the ravaging desire she elicited from him.

William had given Fallon to him; she was his property now, to do with as he would.

She was Harold's daughter, he reminded himself. And Harold had been his friend, a man who did not deserve dishonor in death. And still, wouldn't he seek her life above all else?

He cocked his head at Falstaff, glad of this chance to so please his good friend. "Falstaff, she is yours."

"Bless you—"

"Take care!" Alaric raised a hand cautiously. "Love her, cherish her, be tender—but *take care*, Falstaff. Fallon must be imprisoned and well guarded until she swears an oath of loyalty to William. You must watch your back!"

"I shall! I shall!" Falstaff chortled, a happy man. "Hurry, can you ride no faster! I'll have her bathed and perfumed. I'll order wine and have a minstrel play, and I swear, I'll make her love me!"

"Umm," Alaric murmured. He clenched his teeth and swallowed. He would have to forget her; she was Falstaff's worry now.

His brow furrowed, and he forced his mind to other things. He wanted to bathe the blood of battle from his body. He wanted a drink, and he wanted to study the roads and determine what route they should take to London.

Fallon . . .

Unbidden, her name came to his mind. He pictured the rose-and-cream softness of her flesh, and he remembered a cabin in the rain where they had reviled each other, and shared a single kiss.

He remembered the touch and taste of her . . .

"Oh, be damned, haunting witch!" he swore out loud.

Falstaff stared at him curiously, and Alaric shook his head. "Friend, ignore me. I am battle-weary. Come; let's hasten to our rewards."

"Aye, let's hasten!" Falstaff readily agreed.

William had ordered a wooden fortress built at the center of Hastings, and it was here, in a room sparsely furnished with a cot and a crude desk, that Alaric sat, studying the maps of England and the roads to London.

Harold was dead, but the country still had great resources of manpower. And in London it was most unlikely that the witan would proclaim for William, a foreigner. Edgar the Atheling—last surviving grandchild of Edmund Ironside—had come to England years ago to stand in line to inherit the throne, if necessary. Surely the English were hoping that William's quarrel had been with Harold and that he would honor their wish to be ruled by Edgar.

Alaric shook his head. William believed that King Edward the Confessor had honorably bequeathed England to him. For fifteen years he had lived with the belief that England would be his upon Edward's death. His connection to the crown was a shaky one—the king of Denmark and the king of Norway both had better claims to the throne—but William believed in Edward's bequest and for years had dreamed of ruling England.

Alaric understood the Saxon people better than William did. He had spent more time among them. The Confessor promised William the throne at a time when Edward was at odds with Harold's father, Godwin. That quarrel had ended, and Edward—who was unstable at best—had surely forgotten his bequest to the Norman duke.

Harold himself had made a similar promise to William. But how seriously could that vow be taken? William had cunningly extracted it while Harold was a prisoner in Normandy, at William's mercy.

Harold, of course, had known that no one could make promises about the English crown. The witan had to approve the choice, even after that choice had been stated by the ruling monarch on his deathbed.

The witan had proclaimed Harold king, and Harold was not free to keep a promise to William, even if it had been made in good faith.

William had spent half his life fighting to secure his hold on Normandy. He did not condone wholesale slaughter, but he would accept it in order to secure this inheritance.

Alaric stared at the map, then sipped some spiced wine from his chalice and gazed idly across the room at the smoky fire that burned in the hastily constructed grate.

What would happen now?

Edgar the Atheling could be proclaimed king. Or perhaps the witan would choose one of the two surviving northern earls of England to be ruler. They were young men, but they had proved themselves in battle. Then there were Harold's brothers who might rise to power. His sons, too, although they were very young.

An Englishman would ascend the throne in one way or another. William had to reach London and see what the churchmen and the lords of the witan would do, for their decision would carry great weight.

Alaric stood and stretched, thinking that they would not take the main Roman roads, but go by a more circuitous route. He winced, for where the army went, the army would conquer, and the land would lie devastated.

He walked to the mantel and leaned against it, glad to be free of his armor. He had bathed in the river and wore a clean shirt and tunic, and clean woolen hose. The smell of blood about him had been nauseating; no amount of wine could have washed it away.

There was a hesitant tap on his door; it opened a crack. He grinned slightly, glad of the interruption. Margaret, the redhead, stood there.

She was a "lady" of Matilda's court, and she was, of course, a camp follower. Margaret was no great lady in truth, but she was lovely and voluptuous. She claimed a certain pedigree, and she "followed" only for him. Women always came along with the armies in such fashion, Alaric thought dryly. The Normans had scores of "laundresses" with them; they, too, were whores, offering a service much welcomed by weary warriors.

Margaret smiled warmly at Alaric and sauntered into the room, eyes sparkling, breasts billowing against her clothing, spilling over her bodice.

"Ah, my great, brave conqueror!" she told him, slipping her arms around him. "Already the minstrels are telling tales of your prowess upon the field. They say the Saxons shuddered and gave way where you walked."

He caught her hands and held them, ruefully meeting her eyes. "Margaret, I rode most of the day. And the Saxons did not shudder; they fought bravely."

"Ah, but you rode and you conquered!"

She spun from his arms, moving with her fluid, swaying walk toward the cot. She looked back at him, her red hair a flame of glory in the firelight. She lifted an arm to him. "Come, Alaric, comte d'Anlou. Come, my love. Ride me, conquer me."

He chuckled softly and went to her, ready to join her, ready to forget the day. He took her into his arms and she was soft and giving and her lips parted hungrily to his, her breasts swelled into his cupped hands.

"Hurry," she urged him, and together they fell to the cot, fumbling with each other's clothing.

A furious thundering came then at his door, startling them both.

"What the hell—"

"Count Alaric! Milord!"

"See to it," Margaret told him. "I shan't go anywhere."

Swearing irritably, Alaric stamped to the door and swung it open. One of the Norman knights was standing there, stripped of his armor, but he held his sword tensely at his side.

"What is it?" Alaric demanded.

"Sire, 'tis—'tis Falstaff and the Saxon cub. The girl. She's—she's stabbed him!"

"What!"

"Come quickly, my lord. He calls for you!"

Alaric grabbed his mantle, swept it around him, and hurried through the darkness to Falstaff's large tent out on the field. He threw open the flap and gazed at the scene within.

Three candles burned in grounded sconces; two armored knights stood within. From some pillaged manor Falstaff had taken linen sheets and with them had created a most welcoming bed, draped and pillowed, in the center of the tent. A small table stood there and, on it, a silver chalice of wine, a loaf of bread, and a hunk of cheese, and something delectably baked. The corners of the tent were in shadow.

Falstaff lay on the floor in a pool of blood.

Fallon—the Saxon bitch!—stood white and grim in a corner, her back pressed against the canvas, blue eyes huge, rose lips silent.

Alaric barely gave her a glance; he rushed to Falstaff. So silent there, so still.

The great friendly giant groaned softly, and Alaric bent his head low to him, listening for his breath. He tore at the man's tunic and shirt then, seeking out the wound, feeling his own heart beat like thunder.

"Falstaff . . ."

He found the wound—surely not so deep!—beneath

the left rib. Blood poured copiously from it, though, and Alaric could not judge if he would live or die. He looked to the two Normans standing guard.

"He will die," one of them whispered.

"Fools, aye, he *will* die if you stand there like idiots! Come, take him—gently, I implore you. Find the duke's most trusted physicians. See that they attend him instantly."

The guards obeyed, reaching for the heavy man as tenderly as if he were a babe. Falstaff let out another groan, and a fury like lightning raged through Alaric, burning away all thoughts of mercy and reason.

As Falstaff was carried out, Alaric turned to Fallon. Ah, yes! She was bathed and perfumed and beautiful—just as Falstaff had wanted her! Black hair freed and brushed to a gloss, perfect young body adorned in a flimsy garment of virginal white that scarce concealed her lush young form.

"You murderous bitch!" he spat out at last.

She stared straight at him. She did not waver, yet her eyes remained as great as misted pools and it was several seconds before she answered him.

"I had no wish to kill him, or even harm him." She spoke softly and with cool precision. "He attacked me, and I fought back."

"He adored you. He was hopelessly enamored of you!"

Her eyes flashed and her temper broke. "I was not enamored of him!

He was afraid to approach her. Falstaff! Great bear, best of men, and most loyal of friends! He—Alaric, comte d'Anlou, known for his careful judgment and cool wisdom—was afraid to go near her; he had no control whatsoever now. If he went near, he would grasp her beautiful swanlike throat; he would squeeze and twist until . . .

He took a breath and said hoarsely, "You might have killed him!"

"He shouldn't have attacked me!"

"Attacked you! You are his property! I gave you to him!"

The candlelight flickered between them. It seemed incredible that she could have wounded the great Falstaff so—she was slim and lovely, deceptively fragile. In the sheer white garment of softest gauze she was totally feminine, her young breasts full and curved, the nipples like cherries—red as roses—in the glow. Ribands of ebony hair fell over her shoulders, over her fair flesh, soft and smooth as cream.

"I am the king's daughter, a princess of England," she said regally. "The daughter of Harold Godwinson. I am no man's property!"

"You are a murderess, Fallon. Bitch!" he swore again, taking a menacing step toward her. "Princess, as of this day, your father lies dead, and you are mine. Mine, lady! And I chose to bestow you upon Falstaff. Mother of God! What have I done!"

"He was a Norman invader!" She cried, suddenly passionate. "A thief, a ravager, a vulture, a viper, out to attack me! I care not what you say! I am not yours to give or take! I do not recognize the authority of the Norman bastard."

"English law allows free men to own slaves, Princess!" Alaric thundered. "Whether criminals condemned in court or prisoners of war!"

"English law! English law! You foul barbarian! Don't speak to me of murder or English law! You slew innocent men on that field today! I am not your property or William's or anyone else's. I am an English princess, my lord count," she hissed scathingly. "I will not be pawed by a Norman animal while I draw breath into my lungs!"

Alaric clenched and unclenched his fists. A pain, swift and violent, like lightning, seemed about to split open his head. "Fallon, you refuse to comprehend the situation. We have come; we have conquered—"

"You have conquered nothing! You own nothing. You have slain my father, but that does not give you England!"

"Fallon, if all of England should fall tomorrow or if your people should fight on for a decade, it means nothing where you are concerned. You have been conquered. You have fallen. You are a prisoner—*mine*. And by God, girl," he warned, his words barely a whisper, "you should have bowed before him!"

Falstaff! Had the last heartbeat pounded through that massive chest yet?

"Nay!" she cried. She stared into his eyes and knew that his soft voice held a deadly menace. "What would you have me do? Should I say, 'Aye! Come! Burn our villages, steal our food! Murder our farmers, plunder, pillage, ravage—and we, like lambs, will scurry out of your way? I tell you once again, bastard count, that I am the daughter of a king, whether that king be dead or alive! Never, never, will I submit to the foul and filthy touch of a Norman vulture!"

Alaric crossed to her at last with long strides. He had no thought and no feeling except the pain. All of England was about to know rape and pillage and tragedy, and Falstaff had meant to set her upon a pedestal.

He saw her eyes dart about as she desperately sought a means of escape. There was none, for he blocked her way. "You are a princess of England, eh? And so you must murder a man who would love you. You are too clean and pure for the likes of us Norman swine?"

She stared at him for a moment; he saw that she quivered, but whether with rage or fear he knew not. Nor did he care. He hated her, despised her at that moment. And all that filled his mind was the terrible physical constriction of his wrath, like a rushing sweep of the wind.

"Perhaps you should slay me now, for I shall always fight you!" she warned him suddenly.

"Hear this, Fallon: If Falstaff dies, you will beg for mercy."

Her chin went up. *"Mercy*, Alaric—from you? Beg? Never, vulture."

He moved slightly away from her—confident now, for he saw in her eyes the fear that belied her words. Yet even as he grew certain that he had bested her, she moved with the speed of wind. Her arm rose to strike, and he saw in her hand a small dagger dripping with blood.

"Saxon bitch!" he shouted, and with a sweep of his hand sent the knife flying across the tent. "By God, you will be humbled!"

She cried out, but that was not enough for him. He threaded his fingers into her hair and locked an arm around her waist, lifting her off the floor. The pounding pain in his temples was ferocious now; it filled his body with passion and a need for vengeance. She had gone too far; this night, so help him, she would break. She would plead for mercy or feel his wrath.

"No!" She raked her nails along his arms, drawing blood, but he didn't notice. He threw her down on the bed that Falstaff had prepared so lovingly.

And he fell upon her, cupping her exquisite chin in his palm, speaking in a deathly quiet tone, even as she writhed and flailed, twisting, trying with all her might to fight him.

"William could well decide that your throat should be slit, my princess. I am to extract an oath of allegiance from you, lady, one way or another—or see to your execution."

"See to it, then!" she hissed at him. "Bastard! Slay me, but—"

She caught her breath, and he wondered if she meant

that. But even his wonder was brief, for it was his anger that ruled him, and fury shuddered through him.

"Bend!" he raged at her. "Bend, lady! Ask my mercy. Beg for your life! Fallon, by God—"

She spat in his face.

He smiled grimly. With one hand he secured her arms high above her head. He wiped his face against her gown and with swift purpose ripped the gauze garment from hem to thigh, ignoring the allure of the beautiful shape that had plunged Falstaff to his demise, aware only that the shrieking inside him demanded satisfaction.

Her eyes widened further—those splendid angel's eyes—as she saw his intent. Her struggles and oaths began to increase in earnest, but her struggles were in vain, for his passion was beyond reason, beyond control.

As he stood she tried to scramble from the bed, but he caught her with one strong hand and flung her back, and as she gasped for breath, he calmly doffed his scabbard and tunic. She swore and attempted to rise again, but he fell upon her with the full strength of his hard, muscular weight.

"No!" she shrieked, and like a fox cornered by a hound, she struggled desperately to free herself from his hold. His anger was so great that he was barely aware of her wild flailing. With cold precision he held her wrists high above her head with one hand while he boldly passed his other hand down the length of her body, then wrenched her knees apart and wedged his weight between them, stripping her of all power to elude him.

She saw his eyes but briefly as he hovered over her— dark gray eyes, full of thunder. She shook her head vehemently, even now refusing to be conquered. Even now when he, the knight, hard as alien steel, rose with brutal determination above her.

"Pray, Fallon! Beg quarter!"

"Quarter! From you? I swear I shall die first—"

Her words were curtailed by her own cry as he
slammed his weight menacingly against her. It was meant
as a show of strength, but he felt a storm of passion burst
free inside him and he wondered distantly if he had loosed
a tempest he could not control.

"Bastard!"

She struggled furiously against his hold, gasping as she
felt his body nearly cleave to her own. She fought desperately to dislodge him, to escape the threatened invasion.
She dug her nails into him instinctively, but she could not
free herself. Nor could he release her then—or even find
the strength within himself to make gentle his assault.

Now fire sang in his very blood, and instinct came like
a sweeping tempest, telling him he could not cease what
he had begun. He had wanted her too long; he had been
a fool to think that giving her to another would still the
desire within him, and now he was touching her too
closely; he was nearly a part of her. The tempest came
unchecked, invading his body with heat even as he
thought to invade her body with his own.

The violence he felt created a burning tension within
him. He felt it in his hands as they traversed the softness
of her flesh, felt it in his body as he thrust himself hard
between her thighs. She was the enemy.

"Nay!" She cried out, trembling. She swallowed hard.
"Nay, please, Alaric!" A whisper then, of fear, of supplica-
tion. "Alaric . . ."

Something in her tone, in the plea he had dragged
from her, brought him at last to sanity. They had known
each other so very long—even if they had been enemies
all that time. As a child she had known he would never
hurt her. She had even dared to tempt him time and time
again. He had always admired her courage; she had respected his strength. It had cost her to beg him, he knew.
And she had lost her father today, he reminded himself.
Her world was gone.

The violence did not leave him, but he was master of himself once more. As suddenly as his brutal assault had begun, it was over.

He did not feel remorse—for in truth, she deserved what punishment he could mete out. But he felt ashamed of his own loss of control. He had known that he could not stop the invaders from ravaging England, but he had sworn he would not be a part of it. He would never kill except in battle, never plunder, never harm a Saxon maid, never rape. But he had come so very close. In just seconds he would have breached these portals of her chastity. He was ashamed.

Fallon lay still beneath him, breathing shallowly, her heart pounding. Her eyes were wide open, but showed no sign of tears. She stared up at the top of the tent, biting her lower lip.

When at last her eyes met his, they sizzled like a summer sky. She spoke again, and there was a husky timbre to her voice. "How could you . . . give me . . . to anyone?"

For a brief moment he thought with absolute fascination that Falstaff had been right. She was beautiful beyond imagination, and worth any price a man might pay. With a wrenching realization he knew that he had given her to another because he knew she could too easily touch him. God, if any man had learned not to be a fool for a woman, it was he. Years and years ago he learned the folly of love.

He did not love Fallon. They were wary, respectful enemies at the very best, and that was all they had ever been. Nay, he did not love her, but he cared, and he knew the intoxicating excitement of being near her, of tasting her lips, caressing the sweet fullness of her breasts, and pressing his mouth to the beauty of her flesh.

England lay before the Normans. And Fallon was dangerous. If she caused trouble, and if William succeeded in being crowned king, he would order her execution. And here he was, William's right hand, contemplating mercy.

He felt her tremble beneath him; he felt the silken heat of her body. He knew that with a single movement, a simple thrust, he would take something away from her forever. Why did he pause? He asked himself angrily. She had tried to kill Falstaff, his best and most loyal friend.

But she had acted in self-defense, Alaric realized it was that simple. He could not hate her for it.

He longed to soften, to soothe her. It was a laughable impulse, for he was her enemy, and she would scarce accept gentle words from him.

A sound like a sob escaped her, and she struggled against him—but her writhing only served to bring her naked flesh closer to his. Then she closed her eyes and remained still, as if to avoid goading him into the simple thrust of movement she must surely have been expecting.

Soothe her . . .

There would be no soothing for her. Saxon England was damned, and Alaric knew it. More villages would burn, men would die, children would go homeless. Fields would be trampled and ravaged, and hunger would be the common man's lot.

Saxon maids would fall to Norman warriors, and Fallon, Harold's daughter, would lose her life if she did not come to heel.

Alaric's body shook with burning tension. Keen awareness charred him, yet he was in control again. Surely she thought he was taunting her—teasing until he chose to come in for the kill. That was for the best. He had to be cruel to bring her to submission—else William would.

He rose from her carelessly and adjusted his hose and tunic with a casual lack of interest. He ignored the bleak pain that paled her beautiful features, the way she grasped for the bedcover.

"So, my lady," he murmured, bending to retrieve the dagger she had used against Falstaff and attempted to use

against him, "now we have no further problem, no point
of discord. You would murder Falstaff, believing he
should not touch you, as you were a princess of England."

Alaric walked back to the bed, leaned over her, and
offered her a tight and mocking grin. "But now you know
that at any time you may become nothing more than the
whore of the Norman bastard's bastard henchman. You
are mine, Fallon, to do with as I will. Give yourself no
more airs of grandeur. Harold Godwinson is dead; the
Normans will rule England now."

Blue fire soared into her eyes; they were liquid with
tears, and aflame with hatred. She moved swiftly to strike
out at him, but he was ready. He caught her hand and
held it tightly until she cried out. Her hair swept over her
face, and she lowered her eyes.

And then Alaric made his mistake. For no matter what
had happened that night, no matter what violence had
raged, he could not change the things that had been, and
pity surged within him. "Fallon," he murmured, and he
sank back down beside her, "I am sorry about your father; he was a brave man."

The tears spilled over onto her cheeks, and she sobbed
in terrible silence. She did not want Alaric's sympathy. He
knew this, but she was too wretched to push him away,
and he wrapped his arms around her shoulders and held
her. The candles flickered against the night as he held her,
saying nothing. He lay back against the pillows and used
the pad of his thumb to smooth the tears from her cheeks.
At a loss against the depths of her misery, he did what
came naturally to him, and he whispered senseless words,
kissing her forehead, kissing her eyelids, stroking her
sleek, raven-black hair.

He kissed her lips.

And as a ragged sob escaped Fallon, her lips parted
beneath his. Everything within him seemed to burst and
explode in glittering white-hot desire. Her kiss answered

his, softly, hungrily. In her he could feel the tempest rising swiftly, too, as it had done when he wrapped his arms about her that first time in Normandy. Desire had grown, flowered; it blossomed between them now undeniably, as sweet as summer flowers, as heady, as exquisite. She trembled beneath his touch and seemed to fuse with him. The very air about them seemed to crackle with lightning, as if a wild summer storm thundered near. She sobbed softly, and her arms were suddenly around his neck. He teased her lips with the tip of his tongue, and showered little kisses about her mouth before claiming it again, sliding his tongue deep within it, drawing hers forth to play as the fever of desire gripped him ever tighter.

He had wanted her for so very long. He had denied himself too often. He could not think of the battle, of the war. He could not recall Falstaff or Harold or anything of the past—nor did he care if there was such a thing as a future. The sweet and feminine scent of her filled him, and the heady sensation of her kiss nearly drove him to madness.

He caressed her with the greatest tenderness, but with a total, perhaps still ruthless, determination to seduce. He kissed the length of her throat, stroked the curve of her breast, stripping away the fabric that clothed her until she was beautifully bared to his touch. Where his hand had lingered, soon did his lips, and he encompassed the budding rose crest of her nipple with the ardor of his mouth, giving no quarter when he heard the sharp intake of her breath and felt her hands fall to his shoulders. He could not give way. He would have her now, and have her knowing that she came to him, tenderly initiated, nay . . . hungry.

He was barely aware that he whispered still. His mouth returned to hers with a heady demand while his touch played along her legs. He drew the white gown high up over her hips, and eased his weight upon her. A sound escaped her, a whimper, but he gave it no thought, for as he drank from her lips, she did not turn or twist, but seemed drugged and sweetly stunned, a captive of his caress rather than his strength. Her eyes were closed and her face was pale, and the waning golden candlelight made her exotically beautiful. She did not fight him. But had she struggled, the result would have been the same: the white light burned inside him, so hungry, so hot, that he knew her time had come.

He kissed her as he stroked her thigh, kissed her still as he blindly fumbled with his clothing. Kissed her still when the burning shaft of his desire touched her intimately.

Now his kiss caught her cry as he moved carefully into her, breaking past the barrier of innocence, and claimed her as his own. The fire within him urged him to swift passion, yet he capped that desire, for he was determined to bring her with him and to leave no doubt in her mind that they had risen together.

She twisted then, trying to escape his lips, trying to escape the invasion of his body. She cried out and pummeled his chest. He caught her hands and forced them down; then he laced his fingers with hers. Their eyes met as she struggled; tears stung hers. "Alaric . . . you hurt me."

"Nay, it will hurt no more," he promised her, and he moved down to take her mouth once again. She tried to twist away from him; he laid claim to her lips anyway and kissed her until she grew breathless, and silent in protest.

Then he moved again, and at last gave free rein to the raw, blinding need that had brought him here. She sheathed him like a glove, hot and liquid, and as passion led him to ever sweeter heights, he felt her surge against him, and suddenly he was aware that she moved, too, that she arched and writhed beneath him and met his every thrust. Her nails dug into him, and he smiled at their touch, rising above her to see her eyes. They were closed, but her lips were wet and slightly parted. Her eyes opened then and beheld him staring down upon her and she cried out as if in horror, but he laughed and swept her into his embrace again, thrusting ever more swiftly as he kissed her again, kissed her lips and her throat and her breasts, one and then the other, and each with greater tenderness.

She cried out, and surged with strength against him. Alaric held himself taut, savoring her pleasure. Then he thrust against her for his own release and held tight again, shuddering as the waves of release swept him, and the seed of satisfaction seeped from his hardened form, and into the very depths of her.

Then she swore. More furiously than he had ever heard her swear before. She slammed her fists against his chest, and in defense, he caught them again. He let her struggle until she exhausted herself, and while she fought him, he railed against himself in silence. He had been a fool. He had known better than to go near her. He had been haunted with desire for her ever since she grew up, ever since he kissed her the first time when she slipped into his room in Rouen and found herself caught in his grasp . . .

But he needed to be cold, to display neither sympathy nor tenderness, for he could offer her naught that could soothe her spirit. He had not meant this, but he could not resist her. She could not know how easily she touched him, for she would dare almost anything, and she must have been aware that the world had changed. That William would ruthlessly silence her, or any member of her family, if he felt it necessary.

Her words broke off in a dry sob, and he pushed himself above her. He forced a brutal smile to his lips. "We've both known that was coming, haven't we, Fallon?"

She stared at him incredulously, and he saw that tears were forming in her eyes again, though she blinked them back. Then hatred filled their sky-blue depths, and she threw herself desperately against his weight, her nails raking his face. He bit his lip and caught her fingers, and stared down into her eyes with all the distance he could muster.

"Thank you, milady, for a most entertaining evening."

"Bastard!" she hissed, and a single tear trickled down her cheek.

He touched it and whispered, "You did not fight me, Fallon."

She shook her head while her eyes continued to glitter in misted confusion. "I hate you, Alaric."

"You came to me willingly. You parted your lips to my kiss and put your arms around me."

"I hate you!" she repeated in a whisper.

"Tell yourself what you will, Fallon. I am a Norman, and I have brutalized you. The country will be raped, so please yourself and assure your heart that you have been raped as well. But by me, not by Falstaff. I am not madly entranced by you, Fallon. I am wary of your temper and your lethal tricks. God knows, I have nearly perished by a few of them." He paused, because he wanted nothing more than to kiss her again, to ease away the pain he had created. He was certain her suffering was the greater because of the very beauty she had discovered within it. What bitter irony, to know fulfillment in the hands of the enemy.

He released her hands, daring her to strike again. He rose from her and straightened his clothing, and smiled a grim, tight-lipped smile. "Fallon, remember—by English law you are mine. My property. My slave."

"I am no criminal to be sentenced or sold."

"Ah, but, my lady, you are. You have attempted and perhaps accomplished murder. Falstaff's services are a great loss to me. More valuable than yours, charming though they be."

She would try to strike him again in pure rage, he knew. He was ready for her, and he smiled with ruthless enjoyment. She cried out, humiliated, and his eyes met hers while he handed her a sheet with which to cover herself.

"Behave, slave," he taunted.

"Son of a jackass!" she spat at him.

"By English law, your crime is murder. Your punishment is slavery. And I, milady, am your master. You have always told me that you cannot be broken, but I swear it now, Fallon, you will bend or break."

She raised her chin—that movement he knew so well. "You have not broken me, Alaric. You never will. And I will never bend before your Norman bastard duke!"

He clenched his teeth, but maintained his smile. "Then the battle is truly only just commenced, is it not?" he whispered, seizing her shoulders and drawing her close to him. Then he released her abruptly and turned to stride out of the tent. Loudly, so that she could hear him, he ordered the guards to chain her if she made a single move toward escape.

He paused then, gasping for breath. There was a nip in the air. Fall was coming, and the icy winter's cold would soon follow.

God help him, what had happened? Was he, in truth, far worse than Falstaff? Was she a witch to have woven such a spell around him that he could not command his own will when she touched his life? Even now that he had finally had her, he was not quit of the fascination but ever more bound by it.

He paused by a tree to regain the strength that seemed to have been sapped from him.

And inwardly, he was sorry. She had fought him, and he had been the victor. He felt that, perhaps, from the very beginning, this night with all its fear, its rage, its violence, had been their fate. He had used force against her; she had forced him to betray his code of honor. Yet maybe it had all been destined, from the very beginning, to happen as it did.

Destined, yes, from the time they were born.

PART ONE

The Bastards

Chapter One

Normandy, March 1027

The girl was dancing when he first saw her. Dancing on the dirt road in her bare feet, the skirts of her chemise and bleaunt pulled high above her browned and shapely ankles. She swirled around, and Robert, count of Hiemois, caught sight of her eyes.

He didn't note their color at first; he saw only that they sparkled with incredible life and vitality. She was very young and her skin was soft and pure; she was beautiful. Her hair was a dark cape that whirled around her as she spun in the road with various partners; it was a feast day, he remembered. There was gaiety all around them, musicians and peddlers thronged the streets, and many of the young people danced.

But none of them danced as she did. None was so young, so lovely, so alive. None had breasts that strained against the simple fabric of her dress, none moved with such sinuous grace. Robert had been riding; he pulled in on his reins. Henri of Mortain, his good friend and adviser, pulled up alongside him. They had been discussing Robert's never-ending feud with his brother, Richard, duke of Normandy. Henri did not realize that he had lost the count's attention.

Henri considered it his sacred duty to see to Robert's welfare. As a young man, Henri had gone into the service of the old duke. He had always been companion to the duke's younger son, Robert, and he loved his charge. The elder son, Richard, had inherited the duchy, but Henri was convinced that Robert was the finer man. Robert was still less than twenty years old on this fine spring day, but already he was an inspiring figure, full of passion, with handsome features and a well-muscled body. Still, he did not always put the passion to good use; Robert often disagreed with his brother and brooded over having been born the younger child.

"It is as it should be, Robert," Henri said now. "Richard, as the elder, is duke; you must accept that."

"Yes, yes," Robert said absently, and Henri frowned, aware that his charge was no longer listening.

Henri saw where Robert's eyes were trained, and he smiled.

"Who is she?" Robert breathed.

"I will find out for you, my lord." Henri carefully urged his mount into the crowd and began to make discreet inquiries.

Robert watched the girl dip and bow; she seemed to float above the ground. She laughed, showing fine white teeth. She was perfect, and watching her as she moved, he felt the fires of his body kindle and burn.

He had to have her.

Henri returned to his side. "She is Herleve, the daughter of Fulbert, a tanner here in Falaise."

"She is beautiful," Robert said.

Henri, glad to see the young man interested in something other than usurping his elder brother's position, spoke softly. "You are the count here. You shall have her."

Robert looked at Henri, startled. Then he laughed. "That simple, is it?"

"She would be honored by your interest, I am certain," Henri said.

"Would she be? I wonder," Robert murmured.

He urged his horse forward through the crowd. Men and women fell away, most of them bowing to him. He was their count; he was the law. He was young and strong and powerful in his own right, and he was a son descended from the long line of Rollo the Viking, who had been granted these lands over a century ago in the time of Charles the Simple. Now Robert was theirs; he was handsome and young, and they loved him well.

Forward, forward, he moved, until everyone fell back. Only she remained. She had not seen him, and so she continued to dance. A piper played, and she laughed and she swirled and her hair flew out around her in glorious disarray.

And at last Robert stopped. He reined in his mount just feet from the girl, and when she swirled toward him at last, she saw him there, a majestic man upon a majestic horse. He was clad in silk and ermine, and she stared at him in stunned silence.

It was as if a beautiful god had come down from the heavens. She could neither move nor speak; she could only stare at him in awe.

Robert nudged his horse forward until he stood alongside her. He reached down and grasped her hand, smiling at her, feeling the pulse in her wrist, watching the rapid rise and fall of her breasts as she returned his stare. She was so very young and perfect. A rush of wind seemed to sweep through his mind and his heart and then fan the fire that burned in his loins.

"Will you come with me?" he asked.

He did not tell her where he would take her, nor did it seem to matter to her. She set her eyes upon his and nodded slowly. She was frightened, he knew, and yet excited, too. He could see that she knew his intention well from his very touch, and she would not deny him.

Nay, she would not deny him. She wanted him . . .

With a soft cry, he swept her up before him. People looked on, but he gave them no heed. He dug his heels into his horse, and the great animal began to race, taking them from the town.

And for Herleve, it was like a sweet dream. She had just begun to know herself, to know the honeyed sensations that could fill her with longing. She was a tanner's daughter, a practical girl, but she had already been given to wonder what it would be like to be with a man, and she had wondered who it would be—Michel, the blacksmith's son? Ralph, the innkeeper's boy? Or perhaps even Guy de Monet, the old soldier's handsome whelp.

Never in any of her imaginings had she thought that Robert, comte d'Hiemois, might sweep her away. Never, ever, in her fondest dreams.

Robert rode with her high into the surrounding forest. They came upon a hunter's cottage, and Robert called out. An old man appeared, and Robert tossed coins to him and spoke to him quickly. The old man nodded and smiled, and he called to his wife, and that old crone came forward, too, to greet the count.

They went into the cottage again, and then they reappeared and left the place. Robert dismounted and reached out his arms to Herleve, then carried her into the little cottage.

Inside, in the muted light of day, he stared down into her face and stroked her cheek. "You know why we've come?"

She nodded, and he bent his head to kiss her. She wondered what was sin and what was ecstasy and what was heaven. He would never marry her, she knew. And so it was sin, but for this sin, she would gladly pay. His scent filled her, and she felt a trembling begin within her.

She could feel his muscles, like hot steel; his lips were so commanding she seemed to lose all thought and reason and grow dizzy as the honey swept through her.

He raised his lips from hers and looked into her eyes. She touched his cheek, and she marveled again at his striking beauty. "Be tender, my lord," she whispered softly.

"I will be ever gentle."

It was a promise he meant to keep, yet the fire was consuming him. His fingers shook as he ripped off her clothing and cast his own about in disarray. He bore her down heavily to a poor pallet made of furs and straw, yet cloth of gold might have cloaked her, for she was stunning. Her breasts were full and large; they spilled from his hands like ripe fruit, and they filled his mouth as sweetly. Her body was quickly warm and wet, and though his promise of tenderness was laid waste by the fever of his passion, she never cried out; she never protested the heat of his kisses or the urgency of his hands.

Or even the burning thrust of his body into hers.

Herleve quickly forgot her pain as his excitement swept into her and became a part of her. She had sensed these things in herself, and now she gloried in the lusty, magical wonder he brought home to her.

In the end, she did cry out, clinging to him, damp and shaken and amazed. And he laughed, well pleased with her. Darkness was falling, and he had no urge to go home, no urge to be anywhere but with her. They lay naked on the pallet and he played with her fingers, and she told him about her father, and Robert was certain that Henri would go to him and compensate him for his daughter's loss of innocence. She was a bright girl with a quick smile, and though she was not the lady a man of his position might marry, he was heartily glad of her. As they talked and laughed he thought of the ways in which he could repay her and her father, Fulbert.

As night fell, he made love to her again, and then again, and he reveled in the bounty of her body and in the lustiness of her sweet young soul. When they slept, it was with contentment.

Exhausted, Herleve had thought that she would sleep soundly, like a babe. She did not, though. She could not forget the excitement, and so she stared at the roof of the poor cottage for hours and hours. She wanted to hug to herself her knowledge of him, she wanted to see with her mind each glorious moment again and again. When she finally slept, she thought that she would dream of him still, this fine lover of hers.

Instead she entered into a strange nightmare realm. A great black form fell over her, and when it was gone, she was naked and alone and trembling. Nor could she move. And deep inside her, where her lover had spilled his seed, she felt growth. She began to realize that from her a tree grew. It was a great, massive tree with branches that quickly became dense and thick, reaching out, stretching as far as the eye could see.

The branches stretched over land and then reached across the water, and they seemed to cover the earth.

She began to scream.

Robert awoke, and he held her and stilled her trembling. Then he listened to her dream with tender amusement. "I've left you no trees," he promised her with laughter, and he rubbed her belly intimately. "A wee babe, a son or a daughter, but something of flesh and blood, the spill of a man's seed, and nothing so unlikely as a tree."

He made her laugh, too. And he made her grow breathless again, and once more, in their hunter's cottage, they made love.

It was true, Herleve quickly discovered, that his seed grew within her. She often thought of her dream, and sometimes she was afraid, and she would tell her mother.

Her mother was impatient with her fears, for already the family was feeling the boon of Count Robert's good graces. Herleve's brothers had been given minor positions in Robert's court; her father's business flourished. Robert himself was eager for the birth of the child. When Robert was near, he was eager. But he and his brother were constantly in a state of near civil war.

On August 6, 1027, Duke Richard of Normandy suddenly died. Herleve saw very little of her lover then, but the country was quick to accuse him of fratricide. Although the dead duke had left behind a legitimate son, that child had been promised to the church. Robert became the duke of Normandy.

In the late fall, Herleve bore her child, a son. She groaned and sweated her way through labor, and she told her mother about her dream, for she did, indeed, feel as if a large tree were tearing her apart.

Her mother comforted her, and in time, her boy was born. They called him William the Bastard.

"Look, Mark. It is William the Bastard."

The Bastard. Now seven years old, William had been called the Bastard for as long as he could remember. He was at his mother's house, listlessly tending his stepfather's sheep, when he looked up to see Hugh of Cresny and his constant companion, ten-year-old Mark, coming near to tease him again. Bastard. His father might be the duke of Normandy, but William was a bastard, and boys like Hugh and Mark teased him at their whim.

He threw out more feed, keeping a cautious eye on the two of them. Mark stepped forward. "She was a whore, you know."

"Eh, Mark, he's too little to understand," Hugh called. "He don't know what a whore is!"

Yes, he did. William dropped the bowl of feed and

went speeding across the dirt. He lowered his head and butted it furiously against Hugh's belly. The ten-year-old set up a howl and grasped at William's hair, pulling clumps of it from his head. William didn't let out a sound. He put up his fists and began systematically to pummel his opponent's jaw. Hugh screamed and Mark came running. William struck out solidly to give Mark a fine black eye. But by then the two older boys were fighting together. Hugh tripped William, and Mark sat down hard on him. William gritted his teeth against the pain while Hugh kicked his ribs. He wouldn't cry. No matter what, he wouldn't cry. For as long as he could remember, they had called him "bastard," and for as long as he could remember, he had fought.

"William! William! What is going on here?" Herluin, the boy's stepfather, had come out, and he was pulling the older boys away. They were both silent in Herluin's presence. Receiving no answers, Herluin sent the older boys on their way. William lowered his head and waited for a sound thrashing himself—Herluin did not approve of fighting—but no chastisement was forthcoming, and at last he raised his head to find Herluin watching him peculiarly. "Clean up, William," he said. "Your father is awaiting you at court."

William would never forget that day as long as he lived. His mother did not come with him; she cried and kissed him good-bye, standing with his half brothers Odo and Robert in the courtyard while Herluin helped him to mount his horse. When William and Herluin arrived at court, they were challenged by the guards. Herluin gave his name, and William's, and they were ushered into a small hall, where they were told to wait.

His father's reign had been a bloody one, William knew. The civil war he had waged against his brother years before had caused dissent from the moment Robert became duke. He still battled to hold together the threads of his duchy.

"William! Come!" One of his father's guards, in colorful livery, appeared. He looked questioningly to Herluin, and Herluin nodded. William followed the man into a great hall.

His father was there. William wanted to cry out and rush to his father's arms. But Robert of Normandy shook his head almost imperceptibly, and William looked around to notice the other men in the room. They were the powerful men of Normandy—counts and archbishops, knights and warriors. Looking up at them, William felt very small.

His great-uncle, the archbishop of Rouen, stepped forward. He stretched out one hand and placed it on William's head. "My lords, your vows, please!" Robert of Normandy demanded.

And then, to William's surprise, all the great men went down on their knees before him. They swore to honor him as Robert's heir.

Later, alone with his father, sitting on his lap, William was able to ask Robert what it meant.

"I am leaving Normandy, William," Robert told him. "I am going on a great pilgrimage to Jerusalem."

"You should not be going!" William protested. "Father, I know that you have enemies—"

"You know too much for a child, son. And I've already been told that I should not leave but I have to go."

"But why, Father?"

Robert set William down and went to look out the window. "I am going to atone for my sins, which are many. I will not be gone so long. But I had to have from those men their oath, just in case something should happen to me. I had to make them swear that they would honor you as my heir."

"I am a bastard," William said.

"You are my son, and that is enough," Robert declared. Then he picked William up again and held him close. "Maybe the oath will not be enough, son, but I have made them swear their loyalty anyway. Maybe your bastardy can make you strong. You are such a little boy now. One day you may understand."

"I do understand," William said solemnly.

Robert smiled and ruffled his son's hair. "You will travel to the king, to Henry, in France. You will pay homage to him as my heir, and then he will be honorbound to assist you, if need be, for you will be his liegeman. I do all of these things only as safeguards. I will come home."

But Robert of Normandy did not come home. He was stricken with a mortal sickness while coming through Asia Minor. Early in the year 1035, he died.

Seven-year-old William was once again startled when rich and powerful men came to him and fell down on their knees and hailed him. He was still "the bastard," but he was now the bastard duke of Normandy.

The honor that fell to him that day often meant little in the stark years that followed Robert's death. As long as William's great-uncle, the archbishop of Rouen, lived, the duchy and his household were held together. When Robert, archbishop of Rouen, died in 1037, however, the duchy was split by dissension again. Count Alan of Brittany, William's chief tutor, was murdered. Osbern, his steward, was also murdered after a scuffle in William's own bedchamber. Walter, William's uncle on his mother's side, took to sleeping with him so as to guard him, and on more than one dark night they escaped together to some peasant's lodgings to save the young ruler from assassination. Some members of William's family died while others vied for power. Revenge and bloodshed ran rampant. It was nearly impossible for justice to be meted out by the ducal administration, and private wars raged so horribly that, in time, the church attempted to restore public order by instituting the Truce of God, an ecumenical dictum that outlawed warfare on certain days.

William had paid homage to King Henry of France, and Henry had made William a knight. As the anarchy continued in the duchy, Henry stepped in to serve as William's protector. He made no attempt to supplant his young vassal, but he strengthened a number of his own holdings.

By 1047, there was active revolt against William. But by now William, at twenty, was old enough to fight back himself. While he tarried in Valognes, William was warned that there was a plot afoot: he was to be captured there and murdered by Grimoald of Plessis. William escaped and rode hard, racing for the estuary of the Vire.

Pausing there to wait for low tide, William was startled to hear the approach of horsemen. Assuming they were after him, he took shelter behind the trees.

He was wary at first when a boy came into view, a noble lad, so it seemed, dressed in a long tunic over a suit of chain mail. His horse, too, was fine, a war charger many times larger than the boy.

But as the horse neared the river, William realized that the youth was large for his age, well muscled, and obviously trained in the arts of warfare. The youth rode to the river and stopped, then he turned his horse, obviously alarmed, as two horsemen bore down on him as if to attack him. Two of them in heavy armor, were swinging massive battle-axes.

William watched as the boy leaped down from his horse with a nimbleness that was surprising, considering the weight of the mail he wore. He watched the boy's face and saw the determination there, the pure will. The boy was striking. His features were well defined and noble, and yet already they were marked by toughness. Life had made him hard in very few years.

Life had taught him to fight.

The boy drew his sword from his scabbard and stood back, balancing the sword, to wait.

The horses bore down on him, great hooves thrashing over the terrain. The first horse neared him, and the rider swung a battle-ax at the boy, who easily avoided the blow, raised his sword, and unhorsed the knight. The man was quickly upon him though, his sword swinging mightily.

It was a fierce battle, and the youth waged it valiantly. William stood apart from it at first; the boy did not seem to need his help. He hadn't the weight or the strength of the grown man, but he had speed and coordination.

But now the second horseman raced toward the youth. Outraged, William realized that the men were intent upon cold-blooded murder. With a furious howl, he leapt from his hiding place and started forward.

The boy stared at him for one startled moment before he realized that this man was his salvation. He joined his own battle once again.

William lunged forward in a savage temper to engage the horseman. It was over quickly; William had learned to fight well because fighting meant survival. He caught the horseman in the throat with the tip of his sword, and the man went down in a pool of blood. William withdrew his sword from his fallen enemy and turned in time to see the youth take his stronger and older opponent; his foe went down, caught squarely in the heart by the youth's sword.

The boy was panting heavily. Sweat poured down his brow. He stared at William, gasping for breath. Then he bowed low, but with great pride rather than humility.

"Good sir! I am ever at your service. My life is a debt that I owe to you. May I know your name, that in the future the interests I serve may be your own."

William arched a brow, and then he laughed. "That's a fine speech, lad."

"It is no speech, sir, but God's own truth. My word is my vow."

"Boy," William told him, "I am your duke. I am William of Normandy."

The boy looked startled and then frightened. He fell to his knees. "Sire, I did not know—"

"Get up off your knees, lad, and tell me what a mere youth is doing here, being assaulted by such men?"

"A youth?" The boy queried bitterly. "A bastard, sire—" He broke off, swallowing so that his Adam's apple wiggled, and stared at William guiltily.

Again William had to laugh. "A bastard subject for a bastard duke. Go on, boy. You've still not explained yourself."

"I am the son of Jacques, comte d'Anlou. Nay!" Tears started to glaze the boy's eyes, and he shook his head furiously to clear them. "Nay, I am the comte d'Anlou, for my father lies dead this day, and these men were sworn to protect and defend me. They lied, for they did not like the fact that my mother was a shepherdess. This one here"—he toed one of the fallen bodies—"was my cousin, Garth. He wanted the title and the lands himself."

William nodded slowly. "It is a bitter battle, son."

The boy watched William with respect. "Aye. It is. But, sire, why are you here alone and unprotected?"

There was a growing suspicion in the lad's eyes; he was probably wondering if William could really be the duke of Normandy. William clapped an arm around his shoulders and laughed.

"Lad, I am at perilous odds this day. Guy of Burgundy,

Nigel, Viscomte de Cotentin, and good Rannulf of the Bessin have determined to kill me. I am running, too."

"Running? Where?"

"To the king. To our liege lord, Henry of France. I will ask him to fight my enemies with me."

The lad nodded. Then he did a curious thing; falling to his knees at William's feet, he took his hand.

"I will come with you. I will serve you."

William stepped back. "Nay! You are but a lad."

"A lad without a home, until I can win it back."

"There will be fierce fighting."

The boy raised his chin. "You have seen me fight, sire. I can best many a man."

"I believe, perhaps, that you can."

"I will be ever loyal—more so than most men. As you said, sir—a bastard subject to a bastard duke."

William paused just a moment longer. Then he pulled the boy to his feet. "What is your name? Your Christian name?"

"Alaric, Duke William."

"Alaric, then. And how old are you, boy?"

"Fifteen."

"You've the size for it, but you're lying."

"I am twelve, sir."

"Twelve? Mother of God, I'm thinking of bringing a mere babe into battle with me!"

"I am no babe!" the boy said angrily. He added shrewdly, "You're not much more than a lad yourself. You've barely twenty years behind you."

"Why, you insolent pup!" William chastised him, but he was smiling still. "Perhaps you're not so much of a babe, nor even a boy," William agreed soberly. "They have never let you be so." He shrugged and started back toward the trees.

"Where are you going?" the boy called out.

"The tide is down. It is time to cross the river. If you're

coming with me, come. But I'm telling you now, son, you may tend my horse or my weapons, but you will not ride into battle with me!"

Together, they rode to the king of France. As overlord of Normandy, Henry chose to consider the rebellion a war against his vassal and therefore against himself. Together he and William led a French army into Normandy, advancing toward Caen by way of Mezidon.

In Mezidon they were met by some men William had raised from Upper Normandy. They moved over the marshy plain of the Val d'Auge, passed Argentin, and camped at the side of the Laisin. Then the army moved on to Val-es-Dunes.

Alaric had promised to be nothing more than squire to William, but it was to be a fierce and bloody struggle, and despite his promise, Alaric could not stay out of it.

Alaric's land bordered Brittany, and he owed homage to the French king. But when William saved his life, Alaric had known that he would follow the Bastard until his dying day. They were two of a kind, perhaps, destined to meet. And now, seeing William ride out onto the field like an avenging angel, Alaric felt an ever greater loyalty, and he followed William into battle.

He was young, but he had been fighting all of his life. He was strong, and he owed William of Normandy his life, come what may.

There had seemed to be so many of the rebels at first. But they began to fall back before the furious host of the king and William. The rebels were panicking, and in wretched disorder, they raced for escape to the river Orne. Rannulf was the first to lose heart; Nigel of Cotentin fought long and arduously, but in the end, even he was forced into retreat, and the power of William's western enemies was broken.

Great cheers went up on the field; but no one cheered louder than Alaric.

William, after paying homage to the king, clasped Alaric's shoulder. "Alaric, comte d'Anlou, you were not to have been here on the battlefield!"

"I did not mean—"

"You did!" William said severely. But then a broad smile broke out across his features and he waved a hand, encompassing Alaric and the battlefield. He spoke not to Alaric but to the loyal Norman knights who now ranged around him.

"Take heed, men! Have you seen this pup of a boy? God help us when he grows; we'll all be in trouble."

"Aye, and he's a good fighter, that's for sure!" A huge man, of about twenty years, dismounted and came forward. He carried a Viking battle-ax, and Alaric wondered if he was some kin of the duke's, descended, too, from the famous Rollo who had come first from Norway and established the family line. "But," the big man continued, sizing Alaric up with a grin, "he's impetuous, Your Grace. Do you think he'll live so long as to grow?"

"Falstaff, I wonder about that myself. He is an impetuous lad. You may keep an eye on him for me. And for God's sake, keep him out of battle for the next few years!"

"But, sir!" Alaric protested. "I have proven myself to you; you have seen that I can manage—"

"No twelve-year-old boy should manage the art of killing painlessly," William said. "Come. I've a longing for home. We'll ride."

Alaric rode along behind the duke in silence. As the sun set, William turned to him. "Perhaps you'll see one more battle, since, through no fault of your own, you've been bred to it. In the near future, we'll send an army into Anlou. We'll prove ourselves worthy bastards, eh, my friend?"

"Aye, Your Grace!" Alaric swore. "Aye, Your Grace!"

Chapter Two

On the night Fallon was born a nightingale sang in the darkened sky. Sipping on good English ale, Harold listened to the song and mused with some humor that whatever pain or strife befell men and women, the land remained the same; birds would sing and earthworms would till, and majestic deer would roam the forests.

He winced as Edith let out another cry, louder this time. God, let her be well, let all go well, he prayed silently. He was twenty-three, a young man, but this child would be his third, and though his "Danish marriage" to Edith Svanneshals was not blessed by the church, it was as proper and respected in society as she was loved and honored by Harold.

Harold sighed softly. He could not take Edith legally to wife in church because of his position, because of the family name his father had fought so hard and long to bring to prosperity. Somewhere in his future, he might deem it necessary to marry in the church for political reasons. Edith understood this, and she never sought to burden his conscience with her own desires. Harold loved her all the more for it, yet now, as she gave birth to his third child, he felt her pain keenly.

"Earl Harold!"

He turned from the open window of his home in the

small peninsula village of Bosham. Mercy, one of Edith's women, stood there, a weary smile stretching across her pretty young features. Harold raised a brow in question.

"A girl this time, Earl Harold, a wee girl, and more beautiful than any babe you'll ever see!"

"Oh?" Harold questioned, grinning. He was dearly attached to the little boys Edith had given him, but he had yet to see a "beautiful" newborn. "My lady Edith is well?"

"Awake and well, and anxious to see you, sire," Mercy said.

Harold nodded and, tossing his mantle over his shoulders, followed the woman. When he entered Edith's bedchamber, he waved a hand in dismissal and the other women who had helped with the birth hurried away. Edith lay upon new sheets, with furs drawn near to her chin to stave off the cold. She was pale, but never more beautiful herself, Harold thought, with her long golden-red hair spilling over the pillows like a golden pool. Harold moved quickly toward her, dropping to one knee and taking her hand.

"A girl, my lord," Edith murmured. "Are you disappointed?"

"I've two fine sons already," he reminded her with a rueful grin. "And, God willing, we shall have many more, my love. Show me my daughter. Mercy claims she is especially beautiful. Has she no wrinkles upon her wee face?"

Edith laughed and pushed back the bedcover. The babe lay beside her, cleaned and swaddled. Harold lifted the infant tenderly and carefully in his large hands, moving aside the linen to study the little face. It was true, he marveled. She was not yet an hour old, and she was beautiful. Her cheeks were bright, and her mouth was like a little rosebud. Her eyes, when they opened full were a deep, deep blue, like a bottomless ocean. And her hair was rich and full, and blacker than any raven's wing.

"She is glorious," Harold said. He held his daughter tight against his chest and bent down to kiss Edith. The baby let out a howl, and he returned her to her mother. He shook his head. "Where did she get that hair?"

Edith chuckled, smoothing the tendrils from the baby's forehead. "From the Godwins, I dare say. But her eyes! Harold, they are as Nordic as the North Sea. Inherited from your mother, I believe."

"They could change," Harold reminded her.

"They will not," Edith told him with conviction.

"You are very, very sure." Harold smiled, then reached into the leather pouch he wore at his waist and produced a beautiful gold brooch, which he presented to Edith after kissing her hand.

"Harold, it is beautiful."

"It cannot touch the radiance of the mother or the child."

"Harold . . ." Edith sat up and studied the workmanship on the brooch, her love brilliant in her eyes when she looked back up at Harold. "Thank you, my lord."

"Thank you, my lady."

She smiled and lay back, and even as he sat there holding her hand, she drifted to sleep.

Morning was coming. Dawn would break soon. Harold took his daughter in his arms and carried her to the window, to the first rays of light, and let the swaddling fall away from her. She stared up at him, wiggled like a little worm, let out one cry, then stuck a chubby little fist into her mouth. Harold laughed softly, delighted.

His infant daughter was, indeed, a precious beauty.

Fallon was not yet a year old when she was first introduced to the court of Edward the Confessor, and to the king himself.

Edward loved the child. Just as Edward had always

been fond of Tostig, Harold's brother, he seemed to find a special emotion for Fallon.

She was an exception. Her smile was radiant, and she never lost her glorious coloring. Her hair remained a gleaming, rich blue-black, her eyes were like cobalt, deep and fascinating, and she was sweetly loving. She liked to sit on Edward's lap and play with his beard, and Edward would roar with laughter. Within a year of her birth she walked, and walked well, and she had even begun to use words. Eager to learn, she followed her brothers around and mimicked her elders in both English and the Norman French spoken by many of the king's retainers.

Things might have gone along very well, except that the king was visited then by a certain Norman friend, Count Eustace of Boulogne. On his way home from England, Eustace stopped at Dover and, with his group of armed and armored men, demanded accommodations. One Englishman, who refused to accommodate the armed foreigners, was attacked. In turn he killed the Norman. A melee followed in which many Englishmen and foreigners alike were killed.

In London, upon hearing the news, Edward was furious to learn that his friends had been attacked in his kingdom. It was Godwin's duty to punish the town of Dover, since it lay within his earldom. But Godwin believed that Englishmen had a right to justice and that, by English law, they had been set upon first. He refused to punish Dover. The king was so enraged that he again accused Godwin of conspiracy in the death of his brother years and years before. Harold tried to be a peaceful negotiator between Edward and his father, Godwin, but both men were beyond compromise, and the quarrel was terrible.

Edith retired to the countryside with her children; Harold rode with his father and his brothers in an army to accost the king. It nearly came to civil war as the king's army met Godwin's across the river Thames. But men of the witan came forward, and the other earls refused to fight for either army, declaring that they would not fight their countrymen.

In the end, it was decided that Dover should not be punished, but Edward banished Godwin and his sons from England.

Edith did not accompany Harold into exile because he told her he would return soon. But Harold was startled when he received a message from the king. Edward wanted the girl, Fallon, left with him.

"Well, he'll not have her!" Harold exclaimed furiously, alone with his wife and father. "God's blood! He sends us away and thinks to keep my daughter."

"Send her to him," Godwin commanded softly.

"What? Father, you are mad!"

"Nay, I am not. Send her to him. He loves her dearly; he dotes upon her. He has sent his own wife into a nunnery for being your sister, Harold, but he asks for the child. She is our link. Send her to him. Her mother can remain near. The king is angry with you, but he will care for Fallon well."

"She is not yet four years old!" Harold protested.

"She is a child, yes, but she is your daughter and my granddaughter, Harold. She is precocious and fiercely loyal to us. She will be our eyes and ears at court when we cannot be there."

Harold looked at Edith, who bit her lip and lowered her head. She had the boys to worry about, three of them now, and though she loved Fallon dearly, she wasn't going to fight Godwin. The idea of leaving Fallon with the king made sense to her.

"Edith?" Harold demanded.

"She will be spoiled by the king," Edith said simply.

Harold sank back into a hearth chair and sighed. He lifted a hand in surrender. "Send her, then, to the king.

And, Father, I pray that you are right, that we return quickly.''

Godwin shrugged, and dark clouds swept his face. "We will return. Edward the Ingrate! He does not know that I run his country for him and his foreign friends. We will come back, son, in glory. I promise you.''

The Godwins and the Saxon guard left England. Alone in the king's household, Fallon passed more than a year, and there she celebrated her fifth birthday. She was lost and lonely and frightened, and not even the beautiful gifts bestowed upon her could make her forget that she had been taken away from her father and her mother. No gifts could make her forget that there had been terrible strife around her and that she was a prisoner as well as a guest.

She loved her uncle Edward, but that couldn't compensate for her loneliness and her bitterness. Fallon knew that her beloved father and her grandfather and her uncles had been sent away. She knew that there had been a terrible fight, and that it had all been because of the French-speaking people, the Normans.

She could speak their language, though. She had been taught both English and Norman French, for Edward had thought it important to know both languages. The Normans were their neighbors across the water, he said, and the Normans were their friends.

Fallon knew that the Normans were not *her* friends, nor were they her father's friends, or her grandfather Godwin's friends. They had taken her away from her family, and her father had bade her be good until he could come for her.

She would be good, but she would not forget that she was Godwin's granddaughter. She would never befriend a Norman. Nay, she would not even consent to look on monstrous people who had caused her family to be divided!

It would be difficult for Fallon to keep this resolve.

While Godwin and his sons were away, there was a constant influx of Norman visitors to the king.

And the most important of these was William, the bastard duke of Normandy.

Chapter Three

Alaric would never forget the first time he saw Fallon. Nor, in later years, would he cease to wonder at the amusement and the anger she had caused him to feel.

Edward the Confessor was at his palace in Worcester at that time, and it was there that William and his party came to see the English king. William was well aware that Godwin and his sons were out of the country, having been sent into exile by King Edward.

Alaric had seen the spark in the duke's eye, and he knew that William was already dreaming of the English throne. His claim to it was through Emma, Edward's mother. It was a weak claim, but William was an ambitious man.

The Norman party was graciously welcomed to Edward's court, and William and Edward clasped each other like dear old friends. On their first night in Worcester, William and Alaric were served innumerable delicacies—eel and salmon and roe, pheasant and boar and venison. Wine and ale flowed freely, and the usually saintly Edward even called in some dancers, who proved graceful and quick and enchantingly erotic. Later, Alaric went to his bed in a large private chamber in the palace. His head was spinning with wine and with confusion. He'd spent months learning the English language, but he'd not used it once, for Edward was fluent in Norman French and, in his present frame of mind, he was determined to speak that language in his court.

In the morning, Alaric woke with a dreadful headache. He opened his eyes, aware that it was day. Birds were trilling, and the sun was shining in through the open shutters. He groaned and started to turn over.

It was then that he realized he was not alone.

He saw her head first, bowed by his bedside as she knelt there, performing some task over his boots. He frowned, wishing he could shake the dryness from his tongue and the cobwebs from his head. For several moments he knew only that a girl with lustrous raven hair was busily filling his boots to the brim with dirt.

"Stop that!" he commanded.

Startled, she looked up. Equally startled, he stared into her eyes. They were blue—deep, dark, bewitching blue—and fringed with long black lashes. Her cheeks were flushed, her lips, red as wine, were pursed.

She was a child—a very beautiful little girl. She looked at him quickly, then finished filling his boots with dirt from her leather pail. "I told you to stop!" he snapped at her. He reached for her, but she stood quickly and darted away. Forgetting himself, Alaric sprung from the bed and tried to catch her. Then, realizing he was naked, he grasped the sheets and wrapped it around himself.

His head had begun to spin wretchedly, but he reached for her again. She eluded him by ducking beneath his arm. He lunged for her, tripped over the sheet, and fell heavily to the floor.

"Who are you?" he demanded, climbing carefully to his feet. She didn't answer him, but retreated across the room. There she stood staring at him with those enormous blue eyes. A slight smile played on her lips. She couldn't have been more than seven or eight years old, Alaric thought, but already, she was garbed like a fine lady. Her little bleaunt was fashionably slashed at the sides, displaying the fine fabric of her chemise beneath. Her gown was trimmed in mink, and she wore a girdle crafted in gold mesh. Who was she? Alaric wondered fleetingly. Edward had no children. It was a standard joke to wonder if the English king even possessed the royal equipment necessary to create children.

So who was this child, dressed so nobly, pouring dirt into his boots?

"Answer me! Who are you?"

She still said nothing. He thought perhaps she didn't understand his language, so he repeated the question in careful English. She sneered at him then, and he did not appreciate this child finding his halting use of the English language worthy of her mockery.

"Answer me, now!"

Still she remained silent. But when he would have spoken again, she made a sudden dash across the room, trying to slip past him and escape through the door.

This time Alaric caught her and dragged her back. She twisted her head quickly and bit his wrist. Alaric let out a howl of pain and fury as he released her. She kicked at his leg, and he caught her again. This time he dragged her to the bed so that he could sit without having to fear the indignity of losing his sheet.

"Let me go, Norman bastard!"

She spoke in English, but he understood her, and he was stunned by the use of such a word by a child. For a moment he took it as a personal affront, but then he realized that she was simply parroting what she had heard her elders say.

He caught her chin and raised it to make her meet his eyes. "What did you say?" His eyes narrowed sharply.

"Norman bastard!" she hissed.

"My lady, a child does not say such things," he warned her. "Now, you have come here and willfully harmed my belongings. Although I am a guest, you have hurled an insult at me. You will apologize, *mademoiselle*, or else you will rue this day."

She did not appear frightened in the least. Indeed, she stared straight into his eyes and laughed. "*Messire*, I call you Norman because you are a Norman, and I call you bastard because you are a bastard."

It was the wrong side of too much. She was more precocious than any child had a right to be. And she had apparently been spoiled to the teeth by some doting guardian. Alaric still didn't know who she was; he only knew that the taunt had riled him. His head felt as if drums were being played within it, he could still feel her teeth on his wrist, and his shin ached where she had kicked him.

"Little lady, take it back!"

She remained undaunted. She tossed back that mane of long hair and eyed him regally. "Norman bastard!" she said, and then she spat in his eye.

That was it. Still holding her wrists, he flung her over his lap. He didn't wonder who she might be; he didn't care in the least. He brought the palm of his hand down on her buttocks with a will. He could afford to put some strength into his act; she was well protected by thick layers of clothing.

She didn't cry out, but she struggled like a little wildcat. Alaric grimly held on to her wrists with one hand and spanked her with the other. He knew he might have to pay a high price to some English noble, but he didn't care; this insufferable brat would not get away with her rude behavior.

When her struggles got her nowhere; she went as still as death. She did not burst into tears, nor did she make any sound at all. After ten good swats, Alaric let her fall to the floor.

She was up immediately, spinning around. There were

tears in her eyes, and her chin, though it trembled, was held high. She stamped a foot in fury. "Do you know who I am?"

Alaric folded his arms over his chest and smiled pleasantly. "I believe I asked you several times. You refused to answer me."

"I," she told him imperiously, "am Harold's daughter."

"Who is Harold?"

"Godwin's son! Harold is my father, and you will be sorry for what you have done to me!"

He burst into laughter. The sound of it seemed to enrage her. She stamped her foot again, then pointed a finger at him. "William, bastard duke of Normandy, you will be sorry!"

Alaric arched a brow. "I beg your pardon. I am not Duke William."

She was startled. "You're not Duke William?"

"No." He offered her a grim, tight smile. "I am a Norman bastard, *mademoiselle,* but still, an apology is in order."

"An apology?" She stiffened her spine, incredulous. Watching her, Alaric could see that his anger was fading, and he was simply amused now. She was truly a little beauty, feisty and determined. He felt sorry for Harold, Godwin's son. This girl of his would surely run him ragged. Were he Harold, Alaric determined, he would marry her off to some strong and ruthless knight as soon as she was old enough.

She spoke serenely and with great superiority. "When hell freezes over, sir—that is when you will receive an apology from me! And I do promise, sir, that you will pay dearly for the injustice done to me this day!"

She spun around and left the room, managing to slam the heavy wooden door. Alaric winced, feeling the slamming of that door as if it had actually smashed against his head. He lay back down, pressing his thumbs and forefingers against his temples. He longed to sleep away the pain, but Harold's raven-haired daughter was scarce gone before there was a pounding on his door. "Alaric! Up with you, my friend, now!" The door was flung open and William entered, resplendent in a scarlet mantle. "The king is ready to go hunting; we are to join him. What, man, you're just now awakening?"

Alaric groaned and opened one eye. William, for all their wine and ale the night before, was refreshed and sharp. Alaric sat up and swung his feet to the floor, pressing his head between his palms once again. "I have not just awakened. I received a visitor this morning." He put his hand out. "One about so high—and as mean as a viper."

William laughed. "Well, then, I believe you have made the acquaintance of Fallon, lady of the house of Godwin."

"The same," Alaric muttered. He arched a brow at William. "You've met her?"

"Oh, yes. She accosted me in the hall. She meant to fill *my* boots, not yours, you know. But she isn't one bit sorry. It was not such a nasty prank, she says, because we Normans do not know how to behave, nor do we respect the law. We are barbaric and crude. If we had not behaved like savages, Count Eustace would not have fought with the English at Dover and her family would not be in disgrace."

Alaric grunted. "If the family is in disgrace, what is the little darling doing here?"

William chuckled, clapping him on the back. "Why, Alaric, can a fine knight such as yourself have had difficulty with a slip of a girl? She is Edward's pet, it seems, and is here at his command, as is Godwin's youngest son, Wulfnoth. I believe I shall take one of them back with me to Normandy."

"Please, God, make it Wulfnoth, and not that child!"

William laughed, slapped him hard on the shoulder, and headed for the door. "We shall see. Dress and come to the courtyard quickly. You know Edward's ways—he will have to invoke heaven's blessings for an hour ere we start to hunt, so hurry."

"William—wait!" Alaric called after him. William paused, and Alaric stood, holding the sheet around him and squaring his shoulders. "I should warn you—she drove me to distraction and I spanked her. If she runs to Edward with tales of my brutality, I want you to be prepared to hear of it."

William arched a brow and mused for a moment. "I don't think our little friend will run to Edward with any tales. She seems to like to handle things her own way. Besides, Edward might reprimand her for being rude to a guest, and Fallon may not care to be punished twice for the same infraction. Dress—time flies by, and I would be about my business." With a grin, William left the room.

Alaric dropped the sheet and put on his chausses, pulling the knit leggings over his feet and calves and thighs, and tying the garment, which combined hose and tight pants, at his waist. He slipped into a clean chemise and belted a short leather bleaunt over that. He fastened his mantle with a golden brooch displaying the arms of Anlou, a flying hawk above a great cat. His mantle was made of thick crimson wool lined with silk and was trimmed with rich fur. William had taught him long ago never to deny his birth but to wear his position proudly. He would be seen as the man that he made of himself.

He hurried belowstairs. The horses and hawks and falcons and their handlers were already assembled, and Edward had already begun his plea for God's blessings on the hunt.

Within an hour they had brought down many birds. Edward had his falcons and hawks hooded and sent back to the palace. He was for deer now and a boar, if they could bring one down.

They rode—Edward, William, and Alaric—three abreast into the forest. Their retainers stayed behind. They had been comparing Normandy to England, with William being particularly gracious. He sympathized with Edward when the king complained about Godwin's power.

But then the king admitted with a sigh that Godwin had always stood by his side, and Godwin held the power to rule England, to levy taxes with the agreement of the people, to mete out justice.

"These people are proud," Edward said. "They believe in their law, you understand. Even the poorest slave can find pride in his position. He seeks to belong to the strongest thane. The cottagers are proud that they are not slaves, and the villeins are proud that they are above the cottagers. The thanes are proud of the earl or the bishop from whom they hold their land, and the proudest men of all are those who hold their land direct from the king—from me. They are pleased to gather at their hundreds—their local meeting—and they will form a committee for any situation. They still celebrate their pagan holidays, but they are fervently Christian. I was appalled by this trouble with Eustace in Dover, you must understand. Yet Godwin would not punish the town, for by law the people were entitled to protection of their property. Do you understand this, William?"

"Aye, aye!" William said impatiently.

Alaric shot him a quick glance. No, William did not understand at all. In Normandy, William was the power. Those who thought to deny that power were dealt with swiftly and ruthlessly. As William had once told him, he had been born fighting, and he had learned that quick and heavy discipline was often the kindest measure in the long run. But William did not really understand what was being said here. The English were different—far different—from the Normans. Alaric had learned that well as he listened to the accounts of how the ruling committee, the witan, had dealt with the threat of civil war between Edward's and Harold's men. The anointed king was held sacred—that much had been proved, but he was not above the law. One of the English servants in the hall had explained to Alaric that the king was, perhaps, accountable to the law even more than other men. After all, he was king—the example for other men to live by.

"God has made me king," Edward murmured, reining in his horse. "But He has not seen it within His wisdom to grant me children."

"He is wise, Edward," William murmured. "He has made you a saintly man. Perhaps we cannot be all things."

Edward stroked his beard. His face seemed very long and somber, and Alaric discovered himself pitying the English king. Life had made him somewhat bitter, strange—even saintly. If only he could enjoy life as he enjoyed the hunt.

"I have left no heirs for England."

"I would be your heir, cousin!" William exclaimed.

Edward smiled. "William of Normandy! In my lifetime, my cousin, my friend, my good ally! And in my death—"

"Not for years and years!" William interrupted.

Edward laughed. "You are a passionate young man, William. Aye, why not, at my death—perhaps you will be king."

"Your promise, sire!" William said, his voice deep and low and catching in his throat.

Edward cried out as the hounds suddenly rushed past him. "There! The hunt goes by us!" He sent his heels into his mount and went racing after the hounds. William glanced at Alaric with exasperation, then urged his mount forward.

It was a wild boar the dogs had scented. Following their baying, Alaric swerved through a copse to the glade beyond. The dogs had cornered the boar, a mean-looking fellow with curving tusks and a sneering regard. The king burst into the clearing. At the sight of the quarry, Edward's horse reared, and the king was thrown to the ground. The boar snorted and charged the stunned and fallen man.

Alaric dared not take time to defend the king with bow and arrow; he leapt from his mount and threw himself upon the charging animal. He sucked in air as the animal tossed him aside and dragged him across the ground. For one moment, Alaric's eyes met the boar's; they gleamed with a maddened fury—they gleamed with death. The boar wanted nothing more than to twist his tusks into flesh and blood. He had the strength. If Alaric let go, the boar would trample and gore him. He gritted his teeth. No matter how the animal shook him, he dared not let go. Straining, he held tight. Seconds raced by, and seconds could mean his life. He shifted his hold carefully to one hand, freeing the other. Then he took his knife from its sheath and rammed it into the animal's soft underbelly.

The boar roared with fury and shook himself. Alaric was certain he'd be thrown against the trees and trampled to death. Then, squealing, the boar slowed. Alaric quickly drew his knife up to the animal's throat, ending its life and its pain with all speed.

The beast fell dead upon him. Panting, Alaric lay there. Then he rolled, and the boar fell from him. He had just stood up and was ruefully looking at his blood-soaked mantle when William burst out of the underbrush.

"Alaric!" The duke fell to his knees, seeing the blood.

"Sire!" Alaric laughed. "It is the boar that bleeds, not I."

"You are unharmed?"

"My pride, sire, is ruffled."

William sat back on his haunches, studying Alaric. "You saved the king's life, you know."

Alaric shrugged and brushed the dirt and leaves from his clothing. "I am in ill repair," he muttered.

William stood, a smile playing upon his lips. "Edward will thank you, I am certain, with any number of gifts—a new mantle among them, I daresay. Now, as to whether I should thank you or not, I do not know. I might have become a king myself. As it is, I am afraid I shall have to wait for years and years."

Alaric stared at William. There was a bright sparkle in his eyes, and Alaric was glad to see that William was not serious. He was ambitious, but not murderous.

"I am proud that you are my man, young Count Alaric. With each year that passes, you prove your worth more." He laid a hand upon Alaric's shoulder, studied his eyes, then clapped him hard. "When I am king, you will be an earl. I swear it, friend."

There was a thrashing in the bush. Two men in the king's livery appeared before them. *"Messires!* The king is anxious."

William led Alaric forward. "He needn't be. Count Alaric is fine, but the boar has suffered mightily."

They plodded on through the brush to the glade where Edward, ashen and pale, sat on a fallen log. He stood when he saw Alaric and, hurrying to him, set his hands on his shoulders. "Lad, you've saved my life. This night my kingdom is yours."

"Sire, I merely battled the boar. I crave no reward."

"None but a new mantle, eh?" Edward queried, fingering Alaric's blood-soaked clothing. "We shall see to that."

Alaric glanced at William, who grinned and shrugged. Alaric looked at the king. "And perhaps a bath, sire."

"That is a simple enough request," the king said. He

looked at his retainers. "Onward—we return to the palace."

An hour later Alaric leaned back, eyes closed, in a giant wooden tub. He sighed softly as one of the kitchen boys poured another bucketful of hot water into his steaming bath, and he leaned back, grinning, thinking that this was, indeed, the way life should be lived. He was, he mused, a nobleman himself, and if he'd ever had time to remain on his land, he might have ordered whatever luxuries he chose. Riding with William was hard; luxury came seldom. Perhaps that was why he could cherish this beneficence the more. He was a hero this day, and he would enjoy it.

Suddenly, a scorching pain shot across his belly. He sprang up with a curse of pure rage.

"Boy—" he began thunderously, but he broke off quickly as a cascade of indignant fury swept through him. This was no kitchen lad who stood before him—he had been attacked once again by the five-year-old curse.

The girl sensed his anger, and it seemed to him that perhaps she had not meant to cause him pain, for she stepped away quickly.

"They said you wanted water," she said.

"Water—not a scalding!"

"What good is cold water for a bath?"

"What are you doing in here?"

"Bringing you water!" She insisted.

The stinging on his belly was easing. Keeping a wary eye on his young torturer, Alaric sat back in his bath again. "I cannot believe, *mademoiselle*, that you are so eager to serve me that you would assume a kitchen boy's work."

She was silent for a moment. He closed his eyes briefly and tried to swallow the pain.

"They say that you saved the king's life," said the girl.

"Do they?"

She didn't answer. He opened his eyes. She was some distance from him, and, curiously, she looked as if she might be ready to cry. He almost felt sorry for her—this pretty little thing with her long ebony hair and her enormous blue eyes and rose-petal cheeks. Harold would be in for some real torment one day, Alaric thought. He would have suitors vying for her right and left.

And, he thought with a twinge of malice, with any luck, her father would choose for her a fat and aging knight who belched in bed.

"I wish the boar had eaten you!" she said to him suddenly.

He yawned, pretending that she was nothing more than a mild annoyance—which she was, of course. "Boars do not eat people, little girl," he replied loftily.

"Well, then, I wish he had gored you! And trampled you. And sat upon your head!"

He opened one eye and cast it sternly upon her. "You are being rude in the chamber of a guest. You are interrupting my bath. If you do not leave, I will spank you again."

"You will not touch me again, Alaric of Anlou," she retorted. "I heard them speaking today, my Uncle Edward and your bastard duke. They said that you were barely more than a boy yourself."

"Really?" he said politely.

"That's what they said," she taunted.

"I am many years your elder, little princess. And I am much, much stronger than you."

"Muscle cannot always make up for cleverness."

"Touché, my sweet. Where did you hear that?"

"It is what my father says, and he is a very clever man."

"I am sure he is. Now, if you will be so good as to depart my chamber . . ."

She didn't move. He grasped the sides of the tub and

stared at her firmly. *"Mademoiselle*, if you do not leave my chamber now, I will tell—"

"If you tell the king, he will do nothing," she interrupted him demurely. "He dotes upon me."

"I would not think of telling the king. I can only promise you that I will find your father, wherever he is, and tell him of your behavior toward a guest in your home, and in your country."

She was silent at last, staring at him. Then she raised her chin—a characteristic stance, it seemed. "Who wants to be in a room with a Norman bastard anyway?"

To his vast relief, she turned and left.

Alaric relaxed in the bath once more. He drained the tankard of ale that had been brought to him, then rose and dressed for dinner.

He was seated next to the king. Edward was pleased with the arrangement—throughout the meal, he clapped Alaric's shoulder. To Alaric's right that night sat Wulfnoth, Harold's youngest brother, the only male member of the house of Godwin remaining in England. The king had sent for him that day.

Wulfnoth was slim and quiet—a pleasant enough lad, near Alaric's own age. Alaric discovered that Wulfnoth would be returning to Normandy with them, as a "guest." Wulfnoth knew, as did everyone else, that he was really a hostage in William's court.

Alaric discovered that he liked this soft-spoken and intelligent man. He told Wulfnoth what he could of hawking at William's court, and they discussed differences in the laws of the two countries.

Toward the middle of the meal, the king suddenly frowned. "Where is Fallon?" he demanded.

Wulfnoth shrugged, not wishing to face Alaric. "You know our niece, sire. She does not wish to dine in the hall today."

"Then where is Elsbeth?" the king demanded. "She has no control over Fallon; the child runs free."

"She runs free," Wulfnoth told Alaric with amusement, "because none of us seems capable of handling her."

I could well handle her, Alaric thought, but he said nothing.

Edward summoned a servant and ordered that Fallon be found and brought to the hall. "She is Harold's daughter," the king explained to William and Alaric. "You must meet her. She is our pride and joy; we take great pleasure in her." He sipped his wine and added, more to himself than to his guests, "Godwin is no scholar, and he surely is no man of religion, but he has seen to it that his children and their children have received the best education. Harold is a man of rare talents; he speaks many languages— English, French, Danish, Norse, Flemish, and Latin. He knows the Scriptures as he knows the law." He smiled suddenly, paying attention to his guests once again. " 'Tis a pity my wife is not here." He cleared his throat. She was not there, they all knew, because in his anger with Godwin, he had banished his own wife—Godwin's sister—to a nunnery.

William winked at Alaric, who grinned in return. Edward was known for his rages, which were always followed by a plea for forgiveness from those he had offended. His wife would be back at his side soon enough.

"Ah, there she is!" the king cried. "Fallon, my pet, come and meet your uncle's cousin William and his friend, Count Alaric."

She was even more elegantly garbed than she had been earlier, and for her years, she had a very regal grace. She was dressed in royal blue from head to toe, with white ermine at her cuffs and collar and the fine-fashioned gold girdle at her waist. She wore a crown of fresh flowers— roses to match her lips and her cheeks.

She came and stood before Edward very sweetly, her lashes lowered, her hands folded before her. She fell into a curtsy before him, then kissed his bearded cheek.

"Good evening, Uncle," she said, then slipped on past him to offer the same greeting to Wulfnoth, who smiled.

"Fallon, greet our guests, please," the king commanded.

Very sweetly, she curtsied before the two men. Her eyes did not meet Alaric's, but if she feared any report against her by him, she showed no sign. He watched her in silence.

"Fallon, why are you not sitting down to dinner with us?" Edward asked her.

"Why, sire, I thought you would wish me to dine in the nursery so that you and your guests could enjoy more mature conversation," she said smoothly.

"Well, then, child, you shall sing and play your lute for us later," he told her, and turned his attention to William.

Alaric slowly grinned, watching Fallon. "Is that the true reason you did not come?" he asked her.

She cast him a furious gaze, and her hand moved nervously toward her bottom. "I could not sit!" she snapped, and as he burst into laughter, she hurried away.

Later she did indeed entertain them as she had been ordered. She played beautifully, and her voice was lovely and melodic. It was hard to imagine her in a fit of temper.

The next day, William and his party took their leave of Edward. The duke had what he had come for—Edward's promise that, in time, the English throne would be his. Wulfnoth, too, was ready to ride with them.

Before they left, Edward kissed Alaric on both cheeks and thanked him for saving his life. Alaric assured the king that whatever he had done had been the greatest pleasure.

Fallon was ordered to stand at the king's side and

bestow good wishes upon their guests as they departed. But she complied icily. "Godspeed," she said tersely.

"And God be with you," Alaric said, bowing over her hand with a good and tolerant humor, "until we meet again."

She smiled and whispered sweetly, "When we meet again, Count Alaric, may the English boar have the good sense to devour the bastard Norman!"

He laughed. "Keep wishing, little princess. This Norman bastard has a very tough hide."

"Ah, but my father and grandfather will be back, Norman. And they will gore you, because you and your duke threaten England!"

She did not look at him again, but stood proudly beside Edward. Alaric paused in surprise, because she was right, and she did not know it. William did threaten England—the England that she knew, at any rate.

Chapter Four

"Godwin, earl of Wessex, has returned from exile!"

Duke William and his party had been gone from England for nearly a year when this cry rang through the palace and was echoed by soldiers and servants alike, with excitement by some, with trepidation by others.

With so much going on, Fallon found herself ignored. Edward's guards and messengers carefully avoided her, the cooks and servants whispered about a new threat of war, and only Elsbeth, Fallon's maid, paid her any heed at all.

"They say he has come to the Isle of Wight," Elsbeth told her, nodding grimly, as if she had expected this. "They are greeting him as a hero, as well they should. Bah! What is this place without the earl to join us? It is a den of Norman thieves, all grasping for their little part of England!"

"Grandfather has returned!" Fallon joined in. "And father will be with him!"

Elsbeth crossed herself. "Aye, child, your father is with him. And he will be a great hero, too."

Fallon didn't care terribly who was or wasn't a hero; she just wanted to go home. She wanted her father to toss her into the air, and she wanted to curl up beside her mother in her parents' big bed. She wanted to play with her brothers again, and most of all, she wanted Harold himself again. No one was like her father. No one could be so grave one minute and laugh so easily the next. No one listened to problems as her father did. And no one but her father allowed her to train with her brothers at arms.

Harold never minded that Fallon was but a young girl. He would always smile and say, "Aye! My lass has a way with a sword; she may learn with the boys." And when her mother protested, he would sometimes grow grim again. "Edith, it has been a long, long time since the Vikings raided our country," he would say. "We are a peaceful nation of farmers and fishermen now. But who knows?" He would shrug and wink at Fallon, and she would know that her mother was afraid of some terrible danger coming to her, so perhaps it would be all right, after all, for her to learn to defend herself.

But Edward, the king, wouldn't hear of such a thing. He insisted that Fallon study music and languages, and read the holy Scriptures. She did love dear Edward, though. Fallon was perhaps the one person—other than her father and grandfather—who did not fear Edward's cruel and vindictive rages. When angered, the king would nearly foam at the mouth. Then, when it was all over, he would spend endless hours on his knees asking God's forgiveness for his show of temper. Fallon believed that God did forgive him—after all, anyone as penitent—and pathetic—as Edward surely deserved God's forgiveness.

But now Fallon was in a trembling ecstasy over her family's return. The days that followed were torture for her. Edward sent ships to meet Godwin. They did not find him—he found them.

Godwin followed the king's fleet right up the river Thames. He had gathered more ships and more men, and he had taken down his sails and passed right under the arches of London Bridge. The king's fleet waited on the north bank, between London and Thorney Island.

Godwin drew his ships to the south bank, the border of his earldom.

Fallon was in the hallway when the first messenger from her grandfather arrived at the palace. The place was abuzz. What would Godwin say? What would he demand?

Fallon escaped Elsbeth to creep to the walls of Edward's privy chamber and peek through the open doorway.

The messenger knelt before the king. "Godwin and Harold swear their loyalty to Edward, his most beloved and sacred majesty!"

Edward's eyes narrowed. He fidgeted nervously. "Go back to Godwin," he said. "Tell him he is to remain in exile."

Fallon bit her lips as tears sprang to her eyes. No! Her father was back; she wanted him, she wanted to go home. At that moment, she hated Edward. Her grandfather had come home, and he, too, had pledged his loyalty! and Edward was being stubborn and cruel.

But one small girl's heartache couldn't change the will of the king. The messenger was sent away.

When Elsbeth found Fallon, the girl was in tears. "I am going to run away!" Fallon determined. "I am going to my father!"

"Child, child!" Elsbeth remonstrated, trying to hold her. Elsbeth was only a teenager herself, a girl from the Fens who loved her place at court. "You mustn't think of anything so dangerous. You wait and see; things will come right." Elsbeth was heartily afraid her charge would escape her again and attempt to leave the palace. And there was danger on the river; there were sailors of all manner there, rough and ragged foreigners, and even what sometimes seemed like the scum of the English race.

Elsbeth had little faith in humanity. She knew there were men who would hold the lovely Fallon for ransom;

there were men depraved enough to take a beautiful child for their own entertainment. She was not about to let such a thing happen.

"Elsbeth, I must go!" Fallon insisted.

"Nay, you must not. Come, we'll go to our chambers."

Fallon lowered her head and suddenly agreed. She went to her room with Elsbeth, feeling the tension, the pall that seemed to hang over the court.

Fallon waited until supper was brought to their room, and she was careful to keep Elsbeth's cup filled with ale.

When finally Elsbeth fell asleep in her chair before the fire, Fallon made her way from the room.

It was easy to slink along the palace halls; it was even easy to slip outside, for the guards were accustomed to seeing her, and they smiled at her now with greater fondness, for they knew the heartache she must be suffering.

They were easy to elude, but as she left the palace behind her and came upon the shops of fishermen and shipbuilders and blacksmiths, she grew uneasy. People stared at her so strangely! Old hags with blackened teeth watched her, as did heavy bald men with no teeth at all. She quickened her pace and nervously slipped around a corner. If she could only reach Edward's fleet! She could call out to one of the captains, and under a flag of truce he could take her to her father.

The night was hastening. When Fallon turned a corner into an alley, a dark figure suddenly sprang up in front of her. She screamed and stepped back, only to find herself accosted by a second man who plucked her up so that her feet dangled uselessly in the air.

"What 'ave we 'ere, eh, Reggie? What 'ave we 'ere?" he demanded coarsely. Fallon bit her lip and stared at him in distaste. His hair was black and greasy. He was missing one front tooth, and his breath was foul.

"Let me down, you oaf!" Fallon demanded, and she managed to deliver a good, solid kick. The man swore unintelligibly and dropped her, but his companion was there, laughing heartily, and ready to catch Fallon.

"The king will have your head!" she promised, and the second man, Reggie, sobered quickly. "Eh, Elwald, look at the girl's clothes; she *is* kin to the king."

"Then she might well be worth a shiny coin!" Elwald said, coming toward her again. He touched her hair and smiled his ugly, leering smile. "She is a pretty pet, is she not? They whisper that the king, er, likes boys, but maybe it is little girls, eh? I would enjoy a little girl like this myself." His eyes gleamed as he looked at his friend.

Fallon didn't know what they were talking about, but she knew they reeked of evil. Her heart sank, and belatedly she wished she had listened to Elsbeth. What were they going to do with her?

The men started to argue. Reggie had the good sense to be concerned for his head; he didn't want Elwald touching her, not in that way. Elwald said she could always be found at the bottom of the Thames; Reggie wanted the money.

Fallon listened as their voices grew louder. They were so involved with one another that they paid little heed to her. She began to back away from the pair, and when she had a little distance, she turned and ran.

"Eh!" Reggie screamed. "She's near gone!"

Their feet pounded in the dark alley behind her. She could smell the sea, she was so close. And she was a good little runner, she knew, but she was nearly out of breath, and they were much, much bigger than she. Soon they were upon her, and the stink of Elwald's breath descended around her like a miasma as his hand closed around the nape of her neck.

"Little witch!" he swore.

She screamed, loud and long and desperately. Elwald clamped a hand over her mouth and she bit him. "What, ho! I'll kill the witch right now and be done with it! I'll break her pretty little neck, by the saints, I will!" He raised a hand as if to crack it against her face.

Suddenly a whistle pierced the air, and Fallon watched as her captor went rigid. She realized that the whistling sound had been made by the arrow whose shaft now protruded from Elwald's chest. A bloody stain had begun to seep across his shirt.

Elwald loosed his grasp on her and fell slowly to the ground. Fallon was just barely aware of the sound of horses' hooves bearing down on them. Reggie was lunging toward her, a long-bladed curving knife clamped between his teeth. He tried to grab her arm and run.

"Nay!" Fallon screamed, as she kicked and fought. She could hear the hoofbeats, louder and harder against the ground.

"Leave the girl or pay with your life!"

Reggie froze at the harsh command. Fallon looked up to discover a mounted knight. She knew the voice; it was familiar, yet she could not place it at first. All she knew was that he was truly an imposing figure, like a giant astride the heavy horse. He wore a gold and black tunic over a coat of mail, and through the open visor of his helmet she saw his eyes flash with fight and fury. He held the point of his enormous sword at Reggie's throat.

"Let go of the girl," the knight said quietly.

Reggie seemed to growl. "Damned foreigner!" he muttered. He let out another sound as he pulled his hand back to throw his knife.

It never left his hand. The knight made the smoothest, swiftest of movements, and Reggie gave off a gurgling sound. Fallon fell to the ground while Reggie clutched his throat. Blood poured from the wound in a crimson stream.

The knight dismounted and reached for Fallon. She inched away from him, dimly aware that she had been rescued, but still frightened.

"Take my hand, you little fool!" he commanded roughly.

She gasped, her eyes widening. "Why 'tis you! Count Alaric, the bastard of Anlou!"

He grasped her hand with impatience, then lifted her high and nearly threw her across his horse's back. For the first time, tears stung her eyes, she felt so humiliated. Two men were dead; they had been slain for her sake. They had intended to hurt her, she knew.

"Aye, 'tis Alaric, *mademoiselle*," he murmured before leaping up behind her. "Sent to find you by your most worried guardian."

"Edward?" she asked. She tried to turn around. She knew that her stern rescuer, beneath his chain mail and steel, was not just any Norman—he was the Norman who had humiliated her! Punished her! She had not been able to sit down comfortably for days.

"Aye, the king—who is in a sad state as it is—was forced to take time out from important affairs to worry about a wayward child."

Fallon was sorry; she knew she had been wrong. But she tossed her head defiantly. "My father is here," she said. "If you think you can beat me again now that he—"

"If your father has any good sense, *he'll* beat you this time, Fallon. But make no mistake, milady—if you give me any trouble now, I'll be most happy to tan your hide again."

Fallon rode in silence, and once again she felt tears rising to her eyes. She had behaved foolishly, and this hated Norman had been the witness. Now, in the end, her efforts were to no avail. He would take her back to Edward.

"What are you doing here, *messire bâtard?*" She answered sweetly.

He emitted an oath of impatience. "Isn't that like the pot calling the kettle black, little girl? I am here with gifts for King Edward from Duke William, and I have saved your life. You should be grateful that I came upon you in time," he muttered.

She turned in the saddle, looking up as he guided the great horse through the crowded alleys. "What?" she demanded sharply.

His mind was already on other things. She sensed his frown as he stared down at her. "I have come with gifts from William for—"

"Nay, nay!" She cried impatiently. "You said, 'Isn't that like the pot calling the kettle black?'"

"Well, you are so determined to call me names, princess. Surely you are aware that you are a bastard, too!"

"I am not!" Fallon insisted furiously. "My parents have a Danish marriage."

"In England, perhaps, but in Normandy, milady, we'd call you a bastard. So cease your taunts."

"This isn't Normandy!" Fallon insisted. "This is England. We haven't your loutish manners here, nor—"

"Fallon, please, shut up. I am weary, and I'm not your doting uncle. Tonight I came to your rescue; I killed men for you."

"I was managing well enough by myself."

"Aye, many men would be sorry they had tangled with you. But, Fallon—" He broke off, hesitating.

She didn't know exactly what he meant to say, but she felt a scurry of unease sweep along her spine—a hint of something ugly and evil she had sensed before, in the alley. Alaric had saved her from more than she knew. For one moment she let down her guard and stared up at him, her lips trembling. "He really meant to hurt me. To—kill me."

His arms tightened for a moment. "You must never underestimate men, Fallon. Aye, they meant to hurt you."

Scared and exhausted, she leaned against his vast and

broad and very powerful chest. She shivered and closed her eyes, and when she opened them, she realized that they were not going back to the palace.

"Milord—"

"I am taking you to your father, Fallon," he informed her.

"Thank you!" she whispered fervently. "Thank you, sir, so very much."

"Don't thank me. I am bringing you here, for Edward said that it was best. I am following the king's desires, and not yours."

"Because you are a Norman lackey!" Fallon said, detesting his cool dismissal of her.

Beneath the visor of his helmet, his eyes fell upon her. She shivered and squirmed uncomfortably.

"Be glad, *mademoiselle*," he warned her softly, "that you are no parcel of mine to guard or guide, for I am certain that many a meal of bread and water and many a sound thrashing would do you well."

"Well, sir Norman bastard," Fallon said sweetly, "be sure that I shall never be in any way beneath your jurisdiction! Never!"

"Shush!" he commanded her sharply, and she realized that they had come to the riverbank. Alaric dismounted and began talking hurriedly to the king's soldiers, saying he needed a boat and a flag of truce. He stepped forward, and his voice went so low that Fallon could not hear him. But when he came back, he swung up behind her with no explanation. He led his well-trained horse down a wooden dock, where he was directed to ride onto a barge. Fallon clung to the saddle as the horse's hooves beat over the wood. Behind her, Alaric was completely at ease.

He did not dismount on the barge, nor did he indicate that she might. He was silent as the cool river breeze brushed by them and the oarsmen hurried them across the river. In moments Fallon felt her heart take flight, for she could see her grandfather on the deck of a boat with its sails fully reefed. He waved to them and indicated the dock and the shore. The oarsmen rowed them around, and Fallon clung tight again as the great animal flew through the air, came down on the dock, and trotted ashore.

"Grandfather!" Fallon called joyously.

Godwin held out his arms to her as Alaric lifted her down. Her grandfather hugged her tightly. He looked at the horseman who had brought her, cocking his grizzled head for an explanation. "You are Count Alaric, William's man?"

Alaric nodded, threw his leg over his horse's back, and slid to the ground with silent agility.

Godwin smiled. "Normans are running from England, young sir," he said softly.

Alaric tossed his mantle over his shoulder and smiled. "I am aware, my lord earl, that the witan has again interfered in this quarrel between you and the king, demanding negotiation. I believe your property has been returned to you and you are reinstated in your command—and, yea, I know that some of my countrymen are running, but I do not run, sir."

Godwin smiled slowly, then set Fallon on the ground. He put his hands on his hips, threw back his head, and laughed. "So you do not run, my French friend."

"Norman," Alaric corrected.

"Aye, Norman." Godwin reached forward and clapped him on the shoulder. "So you do not run, and you have brought me my wayward granddaughter. You are welcome here, Count Alaric."

"Thank you, sir."

At that moment, Fallon saw her father. He was coming from the riverbank. Like Alaric, he was dressed in mail and a long tunic. He wore no helmet, and his hair was thick and free, a flame of burning red Saxon glory. He rushed toward them and swept Fallon off her feet and into his arms, where he held her tightly. Fallon clung to him. "Princess," he whispered to her. She squeezed him and kissed his cheek, and he balanced her weight on his hip as he stared at the man who had brought her to him. "What has happened here?" he asked his father.

"This Norman has returned Fallon unto us. This is Alaric, count of Anlou. We have heard of you here, son," he said, turning to Alaric. "The balladeers think highly of your prowess with arms."

Alaric shrugged. "The poets romanticize everything, I fear."

"I thank you for my daughter," Harold said, still watching the Norman gravely. "How did she come to be in your protection?"

Alaric hesitated. He knew Fallon didn't want him to tell the story of the attack in the alley; she knew her father would not like it.

"I wanted to be with you, Father," she said, clinging to him.

"May I have the whole story, sir?" Harold asked of Alaric.

Still Alaric hesitated.

Godwin prodded him. "Come, sir! Speak up, and the truth, we beg you."

Fallon cast Alaric an evil glare, but he was not watching her. He shrugged once again. "It would seem the young lady was eager to be with you. She escaped her woman and departed the palace near the time of my arrival. The king was distressed and sent me to look for her. He said that if I found her, I should bring her to you."

"And, pray, sir, where did you find her?" Harold asked anxiously.

"In the hands of cutthroats, I'm afraid," Alaric admitted. Fallon felt her father's arms tighten around her, but then he set her firmly on the ground and glowered down at her. "You were told, I am certain, not to leave the palace."

"Father! I had to be with you."

"And so you put yourself and this foreign knight into grave danger. Fallon, you will be punished. Severely."

She wouldn't cry; she vowed to herself that she would not cry—not with Alaric still standing there, looking on with smug satisfaction. She stiffened her shoulders, but then her father said she could go to her mother. Fallon hadn't known that Edith was with them, but Harold turned her sternly by the shoulders, and there was Edith, waving to her with tears in her eyes. Fallon raced toward her, so happy to see her mother that she did not look back.

Fallon was not punished for her foolhardiness. There was too much going on. The wise men of the witan created a peace between Edward and Godwin. Godwin and Harold were to have their earldoms returned—and it was true that Edward's Norman and French friends were fleeing England by the score. Tomorrow Godwin would make a speech, declaring his loyalty to the king.

Although the Normans as a race were most heartily detested in England, Alaric spent the evening dining at the house Godwin had taken on the bank of the river. There was a good deal of drinking and merrymaking, and Godwin and Harold both questioned the younger man on William's ways and battle tactics.

Fallon had been sent to bed, but she was wide awake, so she slipped to the top of the stairs to listen to the conversation. Long after her mother, grandfather, and uncles had left the dining room, Fallon stayed and listened as Alaric sat with her father, talking and drinking ale.

Alaric complained that Englishmen ate and drank to excess; Harold claimed that it was better than making a living of warfare.

"You tell me you are so lawful and enlightened, yet you make men slaves," Alaric said.

"A man is sold into slavery to pay his debts after he has committed robbery. And be damned, man, when a fellow is too daft or too weak to fend for himself, he is better off as the slave of a man who will keep and defend him."

Alaric shrugged and grinned and drank more ale, and Harold laughed. Then they discussed some fine point of the law. Harold stood at last, and Fallon saw that her father wobbled slightly. "I'd best see to Edith, and my bed," he murmured. "Tomorrow will be a long day." He paused. "Sir, I thank you again for my daughter. I fear she was in grave danger."

Alaric spoke hesitatingly. "That she was, Harold. But perhaps the men would have sold her back to you."

"And perhaps they would have abused and broken her," Harold said shrewdly. "She is an exceptionally beautiful child; we are proud of all our children, but sometimes we marvel over Fallon. I fear for her most often, though, for she is much like my father; nothing stops her and nothing daunts her, and I am afraid that she has Godwin's tremendous pride as well. But she is my dearest treasure, Norman knight; I am extremely in your debt."

As Alaric demurred, a bumping noise was heard. Fallon, so intent on listening to their conversation, had tumbled down the steps. She landed hard at her father's feet.

"Fallon!" he cried, hauling her to her feet.

Now she was in serious trouble, and she knew it. Hoping to transfer Harold's wrath from herself to Alaric, she looked entreatingly at her father. "Don't be so nice to him, Father!" she insisted. "He said I was a bastard!"

Harold looked sharply at his guest. Alaric gazed at her with no sign of alarm and apologized smoothly. "The lady has a penchant for reminding me of my status; I am sorry, but she had stung me with the label one time too many. I lost my temper and returned the compliment."

Her father cast her a questioning look, and Fallon wanted to crawl beneath the floor. "Father, he is a Norman!" she cried. "And Grandfather said—"

"You were eavesdropping when you heard what your grandfather said, young lady," Harold told her angrily. "Go to bed. I will deal with you in the morning."

She gave Alaric one more glance, hating him. Here was her long-awaited reunion with her father—and thanks to the Norman bastard, the occasion had turned bitter. She drew herself up to her full height and swung around. As she left the room, her father—to her mortification—apologized for her again.

"Marry her off quickly," Alaric advised, laughing. "Sir, were I her father, I'd have her betrothed now, and to some sturdy fellow at that!"

Harold answered slowly with a sigh, "I've had hundreds of marriage offers for her already," he said quietly, "from as far away as Spain, and even from the Byzantine Empire. She's barely a child, though."

"Aye, just a child."

Fallon did not like being dismissed so. In the morning she was heartily glad to see the hated Norman go.

Chapter Five

A year after Godwin's return to England his family gathered at Winchester. It was the second day of Easter, and they had celebrated the holy day with the king and then sat down to dinner. Fallon was with her mother and Elsbeth at the end of the table, but she was very proud to see her father and her grandfather seated on either side of Edward. It had been a joyous Easter and a loving occasion, and it seemed that there had never been discord between Godwin and King Edward.

Many delicacies were laid before them; the king's servants had worked long and hard to create such special treats. Boars and deer were roasting on a spit in the center of the room, over the fire that also served to warm the diners. Musicians played softly at one end of the hall.

Fallon coaxed a bit of meat into her little brother's mouth and stared with some fascination around her. Even Edward, with his long face, looked beautiful that night in his bleaunt of purple trimmed in gold. Her father was garbed in red, and Godwin wore cobalt blue. Her aunt, the king's wife, was there, young and very beautiful, but Fallon thought that none of them outshone her father, for he was very handsome, and still very young, having just celebrated his thirtieth birthday. He was tall and strong and charming, and Fallon thought that he was surely the grandest man who had ever lived. She loved him with all her heart.

Elsbeth had reminded Fallon that she had been disobedient all year, and so, even as she watched her father, she lowered her head to utter another prayer, asking God's forgiveness for her waywardness. Her father had warned her that her pride was a terrible sin and that nothing came to anyone, serf or slave or king, except through God's bounty. She quickly apologized for having been so trying to King Edward, but as far as the Normans went, well, surely God understood that she couldn't welcome the wretched creatures into England. Then she thanked her Creator, for it had been a beautiful year; the weather had been good, the harvests had been bountiful, and the flowers had never seemed as beautiful as they were this spring.

Just as she finished her prayer, Fallon was distracted by her grandfather. Godwin laughed amiably and reached out to help a servant who had nearly tripped over the dais. The man stumbled, then caught himself. "Ah, and one brother helps the other, does he not?" Godwin teased the fellow, offering him a steadying arm.

"Aye, as my brother might have helped me," the king interjected, "had he lived."

Fallon saw her grandfather stiffen. She knew that he had been accused of having something to do with the death of Edward's brother years ago. But he had been cleared; his peers had found him innocent.

Fallon didn't know if the king meant to upset her grandfather, but she knew that Godwin was upset. She wasn't even sure that Edward meant anything at all by the statement; perhaps he was just lamenting the loss of his brother.

"I—" Godwin began, but then his voice caught strangely. His face began to redden, and suddenly he fell over upon the king's footstool.

Fallon heard her mother cry out, and suddenly confusion reigned. Her father was up, bending over her grandfather; his brothers were ranged around him. The king seemed to be beside himself, and his servants were rushing everywhere. Godwin was carried into the king's own chamber, and Edward sent for his most trusted physicians.

Fallon was not allowed into the room. Elsbeth took her back to the nursery with her brothers.

"Grandfather is very, very sick," Galen, the oldest, said.

Tam, the baby, began to cry. Aelfyn, a year younger than Galen, squared his shoulders. "People are already whispering. They are saying Grandfather choked because he was guilty of murder."

"He was innocent!" Fallon cried passionately. "Grandfather is innocent. Edward did not mean anything by his remark!" But Fallon was scared. Had Edward believed for all these years that Godwin had been involved in his brother's death? Would he now take his revenge on the family?

"We needn't be afraid," Aelfyn said, awkwardly settling an arm about her shoulders.

"Don't be ridiculous. I am not afraid. I will never be afraid," Fallon said. She picked up Tam and hugged him close to her. "It's all right, Tam. Everything is all right. Grandfather will get well."

But she was not convinced, nor were the boys. Perhaps an inner instinct warned them that nothing could be the same again, that their gruff and powerful grandfather would never pinch their cheeks and set them upon his knee or even raise his voice and rail against them again.

As it happened, Godwin never even spoke again. On Thursday he died.

* * *

In the months that followed his father's death, Harold became the most important man in the land, after the king. With Godwin gone, Edward clung to Harold. One night, as Fallon eavesdropped outside her parents' room, Harold laughed with Edith, telling her that the king could scarce make a move without him. "I think," Harold mused, "that I am a bit easier for the king to stomach than Father was. I haven't his temper."

"Nay," Edith assured him tenderly, "you are quiet and thoughtful. You listen to people, and you do your very best to undo all the disasters that the king creates with his wild promises. You are patient with him, and kind and understanding to everyone. You are a very great earl."

"Umm," her father murmured skeptically. He kissed his wife absently, then began to pace the room. "I've discussed the succession with the king. We are going to discreetly send messengers to search the Continent for other possible survivors of the royal line."

"Surely no direct heirs can still be alive!" Edith protested.

"Ah, but they can. Think of it, my love. There were seventeen children between Edmund and Knut and their three wives. Perhaps someone does survive. Anyway, we shall search." He paused. "Edward cannot live forever, I am afraid. And where else can we look? We shall have a Danish king again, I fear, unless we find an heir. And the men of the witan want no part of a foreigner, so they claim."

"Why can't you be king?" Fallon asked, stepping quickly into the room.

Harold laughed, then scooped up his daughter and set her on his lap. "You are most certainly a princess, sweet, but I am no king. I am now the premier noble in the land, and we shall be content with that. I learned from my father how to guide a king, how to govern, how to protect the law. But we are not royal, princess—merely noble. So

I must *help* kings, but not *be* king. It gives me great pleasure to help rule. Do you understand?"

Fallon wasn't sure she understood, but she was glad to
see him smiling, and so she nodded studiously.

Alaric had met Morwenna of Arques just before his trip
to the English court on the duke's behalf. The meeting
had come about through a strange set of circumstances.
The count of Arques had gone into open revolt against
William, duke of Normandy, who heard of this revolt
while he was in Rouen and was furious to learn of the
man's perfidy. He was even more angry to learn that his
former ally, the king of France, would fight at the side of
the count of Arques.

In a wild rage William set forth with his half brothers,
Odo and Robert; Alaric and Falstaff; and another twenty
knights and their squires. Outside the castle fortress of the
count of Arques, they quickly engaged in heavy warfare.
Alaric was like a demon that day; he rode straight into the
fray and fought bitterly, his sword his only weapon. Men
fell and fled before him, and in no time the first battle was
over, with all the opponents dead or disappeared behind
the walls of the fortress. Yet even as the duke and his men
drew together in victory, Alaric and William looked at
each other and knew that they would have to lay siege to
the fortress of Arques.

As the duke's men paused before the fortress, Morwenna looked down upon the soldiers. She watched
Alaric with interest, thinking him the most exciting man
she had ever seen.

The daughter of a Welsh princess, and a cousin of the
king of France, Morwenna was both wealthy and beautiful. Her hair was a glowing auburn and her eyes were a
bewitching emerald. Men loved her on sight, and she
enjoyed their adoration. She lived with her uncle, the

count of Arques, and she did fairly much as she chose. So far she had chosen not to marry.

But that was before she saw Alaric fighting like a demon from hell.

"Who is he? Who is that man?" she asked her maidservant, as they looked down on the battle from an arrow slit high above the ground.

The maid looked out and saw the shield with the hawk and the cat. "It is Count Alaric, my lady. You must give him no heed."

Morwenna was puzzled. "Because he is the enemy?" she asked.

"Because he is a bastard."

Morwenna smiled and leaned against the stone wall, feeling the thunder of her heart. "He is young," she murmured.

"He is a bastard," her maid said crossly.

Morwenna laughed. "My cousin Matilda married a bastard—the great bastard duke whom my uncle's men fight this very day."

Her maid sniffed and wagged a finger at Morwenna. "Methinks, milady, that you are too fond of broad shoulders and strong arms. He is the enemy, and you know him not. You had best forget him."

Morwenna recognized that she could do little else for the time being. Reluctantly she turned away from the window. It was true; she did not know him. But she could not ignore the heat that swept through her body, nor could she cease wondering what it would be like to feel his lips and body hard against her own.

Beyond the fortress walls, King Henry of France was investing Walter Gifford with the task of preparing the castle for a long siege. Alaric rode with William to intercept the reinforcements Henry had ordered his men to bring to the fortress.

The two sides met in a heated battle, the duke's men

ambushing the king's men near Saint-Aubin. Count Engeurrand, who had been in rebellion against William for many years, was slain in the battle.

The siege continued, and soon the fortress was starved into submission. The terms of surrender were surprisingly lenient. The count of Arques was sent into exile, but William granted mercy to the people.

Morwenna was ashamed that she could feel so little compassion for her uncle, but he had always been a cold man, and he had shown her little tenderness. She did not flee with the family, and when the victorious party of the duke entered the castle for a meal that night, she made her appearance before them.

A hush fell over the room when she appeared, standing alone in a gown of sheer white and gold. Then, in the silence, the minstrels started to play, and Morwenna began to dance. Her movements were lithe and sinuous. Each step she took was an exercise in grace, and her every curve and swirl and turn was sweetly sensual. Surely Salome had not danced with greater appeal when she sought the head of John the Baptist.

And Morwenna sought no heads. Merely the love of one particular man.

That one man did notice her—he felt his blood rise hot and heavy. Alaric could see that she was no peasant girl, no whore, to be taken without thought. He knew that if he was to have her, he would need to wed her.

"She is wealthy, too," William whispered. "Her father left her fine lands near the Vexin, and they say that her coffers are filled with Eastern gold. Her lands border a fine stream that runs into the river Seine. Not to mention that she is a rare beauty."

William grinned, watching Alaric, who was watching Morwenna. She reminded him of someone. Her movements, her grace, her beautiful eyes, and the perfection of her features all seemed familiar. It puzzled him for a moment, and then he realized with a start that he was thinking of Harold's little daughter. He was thinking of a child. He laughed at himself, dismissing the notion, and concentrated again on the sensuous beauty before him.

Morwenna noticed his eyes on her; she was careful to watch for them and then lower her own. He was even more arresting now, so near, than he had been from a distance. His eyes were one moment a soft, haunting dove gray, the next as hard and cool as steel. His features were fine; even the slender battle scar on his cheek could not mar his handsome and rugged appeal. His dark hair was cropped short, and she longed to reach out and touch it.

To her consternation, he did not seem to be completely beguiled. True, he watched and smiled, and at one point raised his glass to her. But too often he turned his attention to his duke.

The musicians ceased to play; she fell into a beautiful curtsy before the duke, and when he applauded her, she spoke to him sweetly. "I crave your mercy, Duke William."

William laughed. "Morwenna, get up. I have no grudge against you." She rose, flushing, and then she realized that Alaric was watching her, a twist of wry amusement on his lips. William must have felt the tension there, too, for he turned to Alaric. "I don't believe you and Morwenna have met," he said. "She is Matilda's second cousin, the niece of the lately departed count. Morwenna, I give you Alaric, comte d'Anlou."

Alaric rose and bowed deeply before her. She saw that he still smiled with what appeared to be amusement, and it infuriated her. He was not awestruck, as he should have been, though surely he must have appreciated her dance!

"Morwenna . . ." he murmured, and that was all. She bowed stiffly and fled the hall, anxious to reach her own quarters high above. She did not go to her room, but paused upon the stairway, breathless. A slight sound behind her alerted her, and she swung around. He was there, still smiling, leaning most nonchalantly against the stone wall of the stepwell.

"It was a very graceful dance. Dare I hope it was meant to tease and seduce one man in particular?"

"You dare too much, bastard," she retorted.

"Ah," he murmured and, still amused, came forward to pull her into his arms. Her heart slammed against her chest. His hot lips touched hers, and they burned and consumed hers until she feared she would faint with ecstasy. She pressed herself against him, aware of the hot liquid that coursed through her. She, Morwenna of Arques, who had kept so many brave knights leaping like lapdogs on the strings of her slightest whim.

As he raised his lips from hers, she could hardly stand. With wide eyes she clung to him and stared up at him, desperately struggling for some sense of pride. "I am Morwenna of Arques. Kin to the king of France, daughter of a princess. I should not wed a bastard."

"Then bed one," he countered. She cried out softly, but when she lifted her eyes, she saw the tenderness in his look, and she raised her face to his, hungry for his kiss. She knew then that she would let no obstacle, bastardy or other, keep her from wedding Alaric.

In the end, it was he who drew away from her. He caressed her cheek and said softly, "I will speak with William. I must hie to London soon with a message for the English king, but when I return, my love, I will take thee to wife."

"Oh . . . Alaric!" She leaned against him and told him of the first time she had seen him. How she had fallen in love, watching him from the arrow slit. She told him humbly that she feared she had not thoroughly attracted him, but he laughingly assured her that she had.

With another kiss, he left her to speak with William. The duke's party soon took their leave, and she was

pleased to learn after their departure that she and Alaric
would be married at Rouen as soon as he returned.

Their wedding took place shortly after his return from
England. The occasion was splendid. The duke and his
duchess stood as witness, and beautifully dressed nobility
filled the church. The feast that followed was rich, and the
musicians had never played so sweetly. Wine flowed
freely, and despite the warfare that had plagued the
duchy, there was an air of peace that day.

The night was even sweeter.

Morwenna smelled flowers on the night breeze. Windows opened to the gardens at Rouen, and the moon rose
high in the dark sky. Morwenna's women brushed her
hair to a high gloss and dressed her in soft silk.

When her husband came to her, he said not a word.
She trembled when he entered the chamber and stared at
her. Then the burgeoning warmth filled her as he walked
toward her. He kissed her and slipped her gown from her,
and she nearly cried out, for his touch was so sweet
against her flesh. He laid her upon the bed, and as she
stared at him, uncertain, he began to stroke her. She soon
lost all sense of reason. She did not realize that she began
to move, to writhe, to await some promised fulfillment of
the flesh.

By the time he divested himself of his fine wedding
garments, she was near to tears, reaching out for him. In
the moonlight she saw him, aroused and powerful, and
her heart took flight again. His kisses seared her lips, her
body, and if there was a moment's pain, she knew it not,
for his passion was both strong and gentle, and all too
quickly it swept her away.

Nor did he tire. When morning came at last and he
held her tight, she marveled over what had passed, savoring the repletion that filled her. She felt drunk with the
potency of love, and she kissed his hand, then rubbed her

cheek against it. "We will be happy forever and ever," she whispered fervently.

She could not know then that the very force of her love was doomed to destroy it.

The battle had been won, yet the campaign continued. Several counts of the region were up in arms against William, and the king of France was eager to side with them against his one-time protégé, William of Normandy. A double coalition invaded Normandy. Henry of France entered Nantes with one of the counts; two others, the counts of Clermont and Ponthieu, entered eastern Normandy. A French force moved into Mortemer and gave itself over to unrestrained pillage and rape.

Alaric was with the Norman force that accosted the French there, using the weapon of savage surprise to great efficiency. The French who were not slain dispersed, and the victory was so complete that the king of France himself, who had prepared to meet William in battle across the river, departed for home.

It was a fine victory, but Alaric could find small pleasure in it. Death and woe were the aftermath of battle. Even as he traversed the streets on his great battle steed, Alaric felt sickened. He passed the bodies of millers and blacksmiths who had tried to defend their families with picks and hoes against the heavy lances and swords of the invading French army.

And he stepped over the bodies of women and girls who had been raped and slain, or simply left to survive or die, as chance would have it.

Alaric gritted his teeth at the sight of the horrible waste of life and limb. He looked around, thinking sadly that no higher purpose could justify such suffering. He vowed silently that he would never be a part of an invasion like this one. He was a warrior. He would duel with men in battle, but he would never be part of senseless pillaging or rape.

He turned his mount about to find his men and return to William's side. But as he rode down the street, he was suddenly shaken by an anguished scream. He urged his horse forward, and cantered upon a strange scene. Around a fire in the street, survivors of the carnage had gathered for warmth. Across from the fire was a young girl, filthy and in rags. Once she must have been very lovely, with tawny hair and eyes and the entrancing beauty of youth. Now her face was a mask of terror. It did not take long for Alaric to realize that she was being taunted by a group of townsmen. She clung to the wall, facing her tormentors.

He rode hard into the scene, scattering the men before him. He stared upon them with cold fury. The girl collapsed in a flood of tears. Alaric dismounted, went to her, and helped her to her feet. "What in God's name goes on here?" he demanded sharply. Still holding the girl, Alaric caught one of the townsmen by the scruff of the neck. "What goes on here?" he demanded again.

"She was with the Frenchies," the man mumbled. "She should not mind the touch of her own."

"By God's grace, man, I should slay you here!" Alaric looked at the girl. Her eyes had gone glassy, as if very little life remained in them.

"My lord, perhaps you should avail yourself, too," the townsman said. "There were so many Frenchmen . . . twenty, at least."

Alaric swung on the man in a fury. "May God forgive you, for William will not!" He lifted the girl into his saddle and swung up behind her.

He did not know how to reassure the poor girl. He tried to tell her that no one would hurt her anymore. He covered her with his mantle to keep her warm and asked her questions. He learned that her name was Lenora, that her family had been killed in the invasion, and that she was fifteen years old.

When he reached his men, he turned her over to Falstaff. He wanted her taken to his home, where his wife awaited him. Morwenna, he was certain, would care for her tenderly until he returned.

Tales of Alaric's rescue of the girl reached Morwenna before Lenora did, but the tales had changed from truth to fiction. Morwenna, on hearing them, was consumed with pain and jealousy, certain that Alaric had sent Lenora to her because he was enamored of the girl. Lenora's listless attitude did not help to allay Morwenna's suspicions.

Outwardly, Morwenna tried to be calm, to display her usual generosity and kindness, but she quickly turned the girl over to the blacksmith's son, a huge brute of a man, to be his wife. It was a cruel thing to do to a mere child who had already been so brutally used, but by then Morwenna was insane with jealousy.

At that time Perth, one of her kinsmen, arrived from across the Channel. He was a handsome young swain whose eyes sparkled the moment he saw her. In the days that followed, compliments tripped off his tongue, and he began to fall helplessly in love with Morwenna. He had never seen a woman so beautiful.

Perth wished to respect his absent host, but he was smitten. On his second week in Alaric's home, Perth came upon Morwenna in a fit of tears. "My lady!" He fell to his knees beside her and tried desperately to determine the source of her anguish.

"Oh, Perth!" She had supped with him, ridden with him, danced with him, sung for him. Now she naturally fell into his arms, sobbing. "She's killed herself. The little slut—she has killed herself!"

Perth did not understand how Lenora's death could be Morwenna's fault. Distressed for her, he began to kiss her, and Morwenna, sick at heart, accepted his touch. Alaric had been gone so long—he was always on campaigns with William. He had fallen in love with Lenora, and now Lenora was dead. Morwenna had been deceived and used, and now she had sinned. And all because Alaric had chosen to be unfaithful to her.

Morwenna permitted Perth to kiss her and touch her. And when he swore his undying devotion, she consented to allow him to visit her chamber.

By morning's light, she was remorseful. The taste of vengeance was sour in her mouth, and she was appalled to be lying naked in her husband's bed beside another man.

She did not know what noise she heard or what movement she sensed, but something drew her eyes to the doorway. There stood Alaric.

Morwenna shrieked. His eyes had never been so cold, nor his face so hard. She jumped from the bed, remembering her nakedness too late. With no help for it, she ran to him and threw herself at his feet. "Mercy! My lord, mercy!"

He didn't speak, but threw her from him with a fury. He drew his sword, bloodstained already from his campaign with William. Dazed, Morwenna sank against the wall as Alaric approached the bed and wrenched the covers from it.

Perth, who was awake and frozen with terror, stared at him and began to beg for his life.

"Silence!" commanded Alaric. "Stand like a man and defend yourself!" He tossed clothing to Perth and crossed the room in heavy strides to toss him a sword. Still, his first blow knocked the sword from the man's hand, and Perth trembled before him, begging for his life. Morwenna began to weep and babble. Alaric silenced her with a gesture. He had learned about Lenora's death, and he could not understand it. He had loved Morwenna—or had thought he loved her. Yet behind his back she had dealt cruelly with a guest he had asked her to care for.

And she had slept with another man.

He swallowed sharply, looking down into her tear-filled eyes. He had to leave the room; he had to be away from them both or he would shed blood.

"Stop!" he said. "Quit your weeping, Morwenna, and I shall spare both your miserable lives—" he began.

But it wasn't to be. The foolish Perth had raised his sword behind Alaric's back. Alaric caught the shadow of a movement and spun. He parried the blow and his sword continued to fall, slitting Perth from gullet to groin.

"Fool!" Alaric cried out, bending over him. "Fool, to die for a night with a maid!"

He did not know he intended the words until he spoke them. Then he turned slowly and looked at Morwenna, who was convulsed in a pool of tears. He should touch her, he knew. He should touch her and try to understand her. She was his wife.

"Alaric!" she cried at last, but when she raised her eyes to his, something brought about another spate of tears. She lowered her beautiful head, and he reached out a hand to touch a lock of her hair. "Forgive me!" she begged him. She looked at him again. "I was so jealous; I could not bear that you had loved that girl!"

He listened to her, confused, then realized what she was saying. He shook his head. "Morwenna, I never touched Lenora."

"Forgive me."

"I will try," he promised her. She was so beautiful; he wanted to forgive her, but something within him had died. He would never trust a woman again—not Morwenna, not any woman. "Morwenna, I will try to forgive you," he said again, "but I cannot stay here longer now, for I would gladly throttle you."

He left her and returned to William's side, quiet and

deadly. He told no one exactly what had happened, but balladeers sang of his duel with Perth. Alaric gritted his teeth each time he heard the songs; once, William had to restrain him from lighting into the hapless minstrel who sang the tune.

One night William sent Alaric a Saracen slave girl who had been taken in a raid. The night worked some kind of magic. Her touch had soothed Alaric. Her whispers were gentle. When he awoke in the morning, he thanked William, but he did not keep the girl for himself. He returned home.

Morwenna trembled before him when he entered the hall. He stretched out his arms to her and she rushed for him, and she cried while he softly forgave her.

Shortly after his reunion with Morwenna, Alaric was called back for a new offensive in the west. Months passed before he was able to leave William's side, but finally he was summoned home. The best physicians in the duchy, he was told, had already been sent to care for the ailing Lady Morwenna.

Alaric rode hard and desperately. When he arrived, he found the servants grouped together in the hall, some of them crying softly. Alaric pushed past them and raced up the stairs.

Morwenna lay in their bed. Her hair was spread out in skeins of gold against the white sheets, framing a face that was pale and ashen, already cadaverous. Alaric fell to his knees and gripped her hands. A physician stood quietly at the foot of the bed.

"What is it? What ails her?" Alaric demanded.

The physician motioned him to come to the foot of the bed. Alaric swore at him, but the man raised a hand in sorrow, and Alaric swallowed back further words.

"Count Alaric, I have done everything possible—"

"What ails her?" Alaric interrupted. Again the physician hesitated. "Damn you, speak to me!"

The doctor inhaled and said softly, "She was with child, Count, she—she tried to abort the baby."

"God in heaven!" Alaric whispered in horror. The man had to be lying. Alaric wanted to choke him, to make him say it was not true. "You must save her," he insisted.

"I—I cannot. I can only let her die in ease."

Alaric swore. He knelt by Morwenna's bedside again, stroking her hair and cheek. Finally she opened her eyes. She stared at him and smiled and touched his cheek. "Forgive me, Alaric," she whispered. "I did not know if I would bear a bastard."

"Nay, the child would not have been a bastard! You are my wife, Morwenna." He wanted to shake her; he wanted to love her. He wanted her to forget her foolish fears. His cheeks were damp with tears. "I would have welcomed the babe, whether or not I had sired him. Oh, God, Morwenna! You knew I had forgiven you."

"I never forgave myself," she whispered, "but I did not mean to leave you, love!"

They were her last words. She closed her eyes and sighed, and it was her last breath. She was as beautiful in death as she had been in life.

Morwenna's body lay in state in the old family chapel. Alaric never left her side. In brooding silence, he sat guard over her, until it was time for the priest to turn her earthly remains over to God. She was buried in the family vault, beside Alaric's father.

Two weeks after her death, Alaric rode out again. William tried to give him solace. "You are so young; you were both so very young," William told him. "In time you will love again, and you will take a wife again."

"Nay, never," Alaric vowed softly. "Love makes fools of men and vixens of women. And marriage, bah! What is it but an empty promise. Nay, William, I care not if I sire bastards from here to the ends of the earth; but I'll not marry, and I'll never love again."

William said nothing more. He knew that time alone could heal his friend; for now Alaric must brood. William would keep his young friend occupied; that would be the best comfort he could offer.

In 1058 Harold Godwinson took his family home, to Bosham for one year. Fallon loved their massive stone and wood home, where they celebrated all the holidays, both pagan and Christian. The summer was warm and fragrant and lazy. Cows lowed in the pastures, and Harold's serfs and villeins alike seemed pleased with their lot. Fallon swam in the brook and rode and raced and played with her brothers and the villeins' children. Con, the blacksmith, made her a beautiful small steel sword, one she could wield easily, and she worked with her brothers' Italian sword master in the yard. Bosham was a fine village, typical of the England Fallon knew and loved. Her father was not just thane here; he was the earl, too, and his people loved him.

There were about two hundred people in Bosham: twenty of them slaves or serfs that her father had taken in battle or bought to redeem some crime; one hundred cottagers or cotters, and eighty or so villeins or geburs. The elders would sometimes travel to the next town for the hundreds meeting, and a lad from Bosham might court a girl from a nearby village, but the commoners did not travel far. Fallon enjoyed her father's tenants, for when she played with the children, she was always allowed to take charge, and she enjoyed keeping her friends, the lads included, in awe of her.

Her father often had to travel to the north, for the Scots were ever grumbling and making raids into England. Her uncle, Tostig, was earl in Yorkshire now, and her father was pressed to give him and the king aid. Actually, though Harold was the king's right-hand man, among Godwin's children, it was Tostig whom Edward favored. Harold knew this and accepted it with no complaint.

If anyone awed Fallon, it was her father. He accepted whatever happened, and he worked quietly around it. He loved and served England, but Fallon suspected that he was happiest when he was home on his own land with his family. He often came home tired and weary, but his evident joy in being among them lit up Fallon's world.

It was on Saint Catherine's day, the year of her family's reunion, that Fallon first saw Alaric again. She was holding court with the village children and attempting to teach Geoff, a cotter's son, how to wield an oak branch like a lance. Some of the other village children had gathered behind them. It was a beautiful, cool, and lazy afternoon, and they were all laughing with glee, teasing Geoff when he could not follow Fallon's lead.

Geoff good-naturedly dropped the oak staff and said, "Fallon, I haven't your sword master. I cannot learn to fight."

"But you must learn, Geoff!"

"Why?" he asked innocently. "Whom shall I fight? The Scots are at war in the north, and the Welsh give trouble now and then, but here there is peace. The Danes have not raided in fifty years."

She frowned, because that was true. Bosham was a sleepy, lazy place. But a sudden spark of genius came to her. "The Normans, Geoff! What if the Normans come?"

"Why would they come?"

"To fight us, of course." She placed her hands on her hips and asked him, "Geoff, have you ever seen a Norman?"

He shook his head uncertainly.

"Have you?" Fallon asked the other youths and lasses. They all shook their heads.

"Well, let me warn you! They were here often in my grandfather's day. They came to bewitch King Edward.

They wanted him to give them England, but Father and Grandfather would not let that happen. We must beware! The Normans are fierce and frightening. They are not like normal men." Fallon paused, looking at the wondering faces of her spellbound audience. She had to go on. "They are devils, cast out from the pit of hell. They have tails and cloven feet, and when they talk, you can see that their tongues are forked."

Fallon stopped speaking, suddenly aware that she had lost her audience. The children were all staring over her head, and their mouths had fallen open with awe.

A tingling of unease swept along Fallon's spine. Turning, she nearly cried out.

A knight on a pure black charger had come upon them. The horse was sleek and beautiful and immense; the man was much the same. His dark head was bared under the late afternoon sun, and his clean-shaven face was a rugged frame for the icy steel of his eyes. He was dressed in a garnet-colored, gold-trimmed bleaunt over chain mail, and his helmet sat before him on his saddle. Even from where he sat on the great horse, his own height and size were evident, as was the nobility of his bearing. He stared down at Fallon with steely amusement. It was her long-hated enemy, Count Alaric. Fallon gasped in surprise and a certain amount of fear—she would never forget the humiliation of the spanking he had given her.

"That is a lively tale, *mam'selle,*" he said simply, bowing to her from the saddle. "My, my. I did not realize that I had sprouted horns." He made a slight movement, and his great horse stepped around the children. Behind Alaric rode a group of men leading packhorses. The men followed Alaric, carefully skirting around the children and inclining their heads to Harold's daughter.

"Lor' love us!" exclaimed the baker's daughter. "Who was that? Seemed like some god!" She crossed herself hurriedly, realizing her blasphemy.

Fallon wrinkled her nose with distaste. "That was no god!" she said impatiently. "That was a Norman!"

"Why, I saw no tail on him—nor horns!" Geoff exclaimed.

"Oh, well," Fallon murmured, "not *all* of them have tails." She turned and hurried across the fields. Her enemy had come to her home. She had to find out why.

Chapter Six

By the time Fallon reached the house, the Norman horses were stabled, and the new arrivals were within the hall. She was about to enter when suddenly a hand was clamped over her mouth and she was pulled into the shadows.

"Fallon, 'tis me!"

She recognized her brother Galen's voice. Nearly three years her senior, and almost sixteen now, he seldom bothered with her these days. He was growing up. Twice now he had ridden with their father. He tended to feel the superiority of his age, and he loved to taunt Fallon with it. His hand dropped from her mouth, and she saw that he was staring beyond her to the doorway. He shushed her before she could speak. "He rides into a foreign land, yet he does not post a guard," Galen said. "He knows that no harm could come to him when he rides here in peace." Her brother stared at her then. "Father sent word to Normandy, you know."

Dismayed, Fallon stared at her brother. She had not known.

"Father wants Duke William to release his brother, Wulfnoth," Galen went on.

Fallon remembered her handsome young uncle well from her days in Edward's court. "Normans!" Fallon spat. She could not remember that time without feeling the old pain of abandonment, nor had she ever been able to forget that the crude behavior of a Norman knight had caused the quarrel between Edward and Godwin to begin with.

"You had best not take that attitude, Fallon. Father has said that we are to be nice to this Norman, and it is all your fault."

"What?" Fallon lashed out.

"You are still such a child, Fallon," Galen said with that edge of superiority that so irked her. "He saved you when the dock scum would have had their way with you and slit your throat. If you had not run away from the palace—"

"Don't you dare tell me that, Galen!" she said, biting her lower lip. It did gall her to remember that she had been rescued by the despised young Norman knight.

"You don't know what might have happened to you if Alaric hadn't rescued you," Galen snorted disgustedly.

"Aye, Galen, I do!" she retorted. She had some idea, at any rate. Maids whispered and men teased, and she had heard much in the course of her young life.

"It is your fault that he is in our house—that father thinks of him as a friend."

"My fault!" Fallon protested. "I have battled him most bitterly!"

"I'll bet you're afraid of him," Galen taunted.

"I am not! I am afraid of no man!"

Galen smiled. "You're afraid of Father. And so am I," he admitted. Fallon smiled at him. They were all in awe of their father, though they weren't sure why. They all hated to earn his disapproval, because they loved him so much and because it seemed to hurt him so much when they behaved badly.

Fallon raised her chin. "All right, then, I am afraid of no Norman. And no Saxon either—except Father."

"Prove it!" Galen said.

"How?"

Galen shrugged. He stared at his sister with wide blue eyes very much like her own. "I don't know. Do something to him. Fill his boots with sand."

Fallon shook her head. "I've already done that."

"What?" Galen demanded with new respect.

"Never mind, it was a long time ago. But he might remember."

"See. You are afraid."

"I'm not!" Fallon was aware that Galen was urging her into trouble, but she had never been able to resist a dare. She smiled sweetly at her brother. "We shall see who is, and who is not, afraid of the Norman bastard."

She swept past her brother and entered the hall, where she found the Normans comfortably sprawled out about the hearth. Only one man remained standing: Alaric of Anlou. He stared at Fallon as she entered the room, and his darkly handsome features gave away none of his thoughts. For a moment, she trembled. Galen was right; she was afraid of him. There was a new tension in his face. He was still young, but a ruthlessness that Fallon could not quite fathom had been born within him. To play with his temper before had been merely to flirt with excitement. Now it seemed like deadly folly.

"Fallon!" her mother called.

Edith, beautiful in a yellow gown with her hair piled high and topped by a ring of daisies, came hurrying toward her. With her back to their guests, she whispered, "Fallon, your gown is muddy and there are twigs in your hair—and we've guests! You will greet them, then take yourself to your chamber to wash and dress for our meal!" She brought her daughter before the men.

"Milords, our daughter Fallon. Fallon, please welcome Count Alaric and his knights, Falstaff, Beauclare, and Romney."

Fallon curtsied to each of the men in turn, her cheeks burning as she faced Alaric at last. Harold sat in the midst of the men, watching her with a slight frown. He considered her too old to appear before guests in such disarray. His frown would surely deepen if he knew she had told the village children that Normans had horns and cloven feet.

Alaric bowed slightly and with a tinge of irony in his voice reminded her father that he'd had the pleasure of meeting Fallon before.

"Of course," Harold murmured. He lifted his hand, and Edith quickly steered Fallon toward the stairway.

Elsbeth waited on the upper landing to usher Fallon to her bath. While Elsbeth prated on about Fallon's unladylike behavior, Fallon concentrated on her brother's dare. When she was thoroughly scrubbed, she dressed in a chemise of soft pink silk, and Elsbeth helped her slip a bleaunt of royal blue over it. "You've grown so tall," Elsbeth told her with disdain. "If you'd only act like your father's daughter . . ."

Then she stood back and clapped her hands. "You are so lovely, sweeting," she murmured, and kissed her. "It is hard to stay angry with you. Here, put on your new girdle, slip into your hose and shoes, and let me tend to your hair."

Fallon was pleased when Elsbeth plaited her long black locks and coiled them into a crown studded with daisies. When she was dressed, she could not help smiling; she felt very grown up, and even pretty.

"Go on down, now," Elsbeth urged her. "Show your father how proud he can be!"

Fallon gave her a quick kiss and ran to the stairs. Then she slowed her gait, her heart beating. Ladies did not run; they walked.

She straightened her shoulders and carefully descended the stairs, step by graceful step. All talk in the hall suddenly stopped; when she reached the landing, Fallon realized that even her father was staring at her.

She paused at the foot of the stairs, uncertain. "Father?" she murmured.

Harold leapt to his feet and hurried to his daughter.

Alaric straightened, stunned by the change in Fallon. An hour ago she had been a girl, a child. Strikingly pretty, but a child nonetheless. Now she was . . . a lady. Tall and lithe, with budding breasts, she was lovely with her startling coloring and her delicate features. He lowered his head, smiling to himself. He remembered how he had always thought that Harold would need to worry seriously about her one day.

That day was coming quickly. She stood on the portals of womanhood now, and she was already enchanting. Alaric bit back a smile as he saw the smitten faces of his men. He wanted to warn them to be careful. She was very young—and dangerous, too, he thought silently, for though her eyes were warm when they beheld Harold, they burned with a blue fire of hatred when they fell upon himself and his party.

Fallon was cordial throughout the meal. It was an informal night, and Galen, Aelfyn, Fallon, and even Tam had been allowed to sit at the table with the adults. They spoke French at the table, and Alaric found himself smiling and lowering his head often to hide his amusement, for it was obviously painful for young Fallon to use the language.

When the meal ended, the children were allowed to leave the table. Edith retired with the children, and Alaric's men went to the cottage where they would be quartered; only Alaric was staying beneath Harold's roof.

When the two men were alone at last, Alaric looked unhappily at his host. "I'm sorry, sir, but William refuses to release Wulfnoth. Your brother fares very well; he is a guest, you know, and not a prisoner."

"I know," Harold said wearily, "that 'guest' is a polite word for 'prisoner.' "

Alaric sighed. He liked both Harold and Wulfnoth, and he was sorry that he couldn't persuade William to change his mind.

"I see your brother often," Alaric said softly, handing Harold some letters Wulfnoth had sent.

Harold nodded. He took the letters and looked them over. "Perhaps in the future . . ." he murmured.

"Aye, perhaps in the future." Alaric hesitated. "Harold, I believe that William will hold Wulfnoth until Edward's promise is fulfilled, and he has become king of England."

"What?" Harold said sharply.

Alaric realized that this was the first the English earl had heard of the king's promise. "The king promised the throne to William," he said.

Harold shook his head. "I am sorry; I mean no disrespect to your duke. But the king is not free to make such a promise. Surely you are aware that the witan must decide on a new king. And William's claim is very weak." He leaned forward, "Alaric, when my father died, we set forth to search for legal heirs. We found an heir—the grandson of Edmund Ironside. When Edmund's son was a lad, King Knut turned him over to the Swedish king, with orders that he be slain. But apparently the Swedish king did not relish the task. He gave the boy to the king of Hungary, and he grew up there. We brought him back to England. Unfortunately, he died on his home shore after the journey, but he left three children. His son Edgar Atheling, is just a boy, but Edward plans to bring him up as his own. He resides in London now as the king's ward." Harold paused, lifting his hands helplessly. "Alaric, if the boy were not here, I believe the Scandinavian kings might have a greater claim to the throne."

Alaric nodded unhappily. "Aye, Harold, I understand

your witan and your laws. But I also understand William. A promise is sacred to him. He has fought for his power. He takes what is his." He grimaced. "Ah, well. Harold, I will try to reason with him again where Wulfnoth is concerned. And I will ask you to believe that he does not suffer. If he is a prisoner, he is at least regarded as a guest. On that I give you my word, which I consider sacred."

Harold nodded. The two men clasped hands across the table, then Harold raised his tankard of ale, and Alaric raised his, too. "Thank you," Harold said quietly.

"I am afraid I have been of little service to you," Alaric said. "But I am glad to be here, and I thank you for your hospitality."

"You are always welcome in my house."

"Well, I've land here myself, you know." Alaric grinned. "Edward made me a thane."

"Aye, I know, for your land lies in my earldom. It is good land."

"Unfortunately, I seldom see it."

"One of your sons will inherit it," Harold murmured. Then he paused unhappily. "I did not mean to speak so thoughtlessly. We have heard of the death of your wife. I offer my deepest condolences."

Alaric lowered his head and nodded. "Thank you."

"You are a very young man. You will marry again, surely, and have many fine sons."

"No, I think not," Alaric said politely. He rose. "It was a long day. I will retire, if I may."

"Of course." They started up the stairway. Harold left him in his doorway, and Alaric found that his things had been neatly arranged for him. He was weary, and he thought of nothing but sleep. He found his bed and sank into it, then raised himself instantly, smothering a startled cry.

His bed was wet, soaked clean through. Along with the coolness of the night, it chilled him like a blanket of ice.

He gritted his teeth, and his torturer's name came quickly to his mind: *Fallon.* Who else but that sweet young beauty presented to them at dinner? Who else but the wayward vixen?

He was almost angry enough to cry out his displeasure and bring Harold running. Someone needed to bring a switch down upon the girl with a heavy hand. Too many people doted upon the lass.

He did not call out, however, but dressed silently and belted his hauberk about him, sliding his sword inside it. He went down the stairs and quietly eased himself out to spend the night in the cottage with his knights.

In the morning Harold himself appeared at the cottage door in a rare temper. Alaric had barely risen, but when he saw the earl there, he quickly reached for his vestments. "Harold, I was about to return to the main house; I did not know that I arose so late—"

"Nay, Alaric, give no voice to me! I come with the heartiest apologies. My wife came by your room this morning and found the evil done. The children were dragged from their beds and Fallon was quick to admit to the deed when I promised to punish them all. She is chastened, my friend, I do assure you. She will come to you to offer her apology. She will make atonement."

"Harold, it is not necessary—"

"It is," the English earl stated simply. "Sir, please, if you and your men will come, we will break our fast together."

Falstaff at last had a chance to demand of Alaric what had happened to send Harold from the manor to their more humble abode. Alaric mumbled that it was but a childish prank. "A cold and sodden bed, no more," he said, grimacing.

Roger Beauclare, a bare youth of eighteen and newly knighted by the duke, started to laugh. Falstaff's lip twitched; then Jean Romney began to laugh, too. "By the minx who called us demons, no doubt!" he mused.

"Aye, no doubt," Alaric agreed as his own lip twitched, and then he laughed. It was the first time since Morwenna's death that he had been able to do so.

They strode together, good companions, to the manor house. Edith greeted them, and at the table they were served. Harold's young sons were visible that morning, but not his wayward daughter.

Later Alaric repaired to his chamber above and was about to summon a page to shave him. He was startled to find Fallon standing in the center of the room waiting for him.

"Milady," he greeted her with a wary nod.

She lowered her eyes instantly, then raised them to meet his. "I have come to apologize, milord."

"Oh. Have you?" He leaned back against the wall, crossing his arms over his chest. He watched her for a long moment. She did not lower her eyes again. Her chin remained high, and her deep blue eyes met his with little humility. Alaric offered her a cold stare. "You are not sorry in the least, are you?"

She hesitated; she had been commanded to apologize, and so she must. In spite of all her sins, she found lying difficult. "Sir," she said softly, "you are a Norman. The root and cause of all evil within England."

"*All* evil?" he asked her skeptically.

She shrugged and lowered her eyes again at last. "Normans have near caused civil war in this country time and time again. They seem to grasp for England, to stretch their fingers like frightening skeletal bones for this land."

"Do they?" Alaric murmured uneasily. She could know nothing of William's quest for the English throne, yet she seemed to sense that a threat might indeed come their way.

She turned from him suddenly and walked to the still-shuttered window. She cast it open, then murmured, her back toward him, "I am sorry, Count Alaric, at your recent bereavement. Mother said that I am exceptionally cruel, for I sought to wound you when you were so recently made a widower. I am sorry about your wife."

A strangled sound escaped him. When Fallon turned, his features were taut and grim, and his bronzed skin was pale.

"Sir—"

He interrupted her, speaking harshly. "Your sincerity is duly noted, Fallon. You may leave."

"I—I may not," she murmured uneasily. In his anger, he seemed dangerous indeed. She had not been afraid to meet her punishment before, yet now, suddenly, she trembled. He had changed, she realized again. He was a man who would be ruthless if crossed. She had been a fool to taunt him, even to meet Galen's dare.

"You may go; I have said so."

"Nay, I—" She paused, flushing. "I have been ordered to serve you."

"What?"

"Father ordered that I shall serve you this day." She hesitated, then seemed to know that she must speak. "I am to offer you either a willow switch or myself in your service. The choice is yours."

This caused him to laugh. "Now, this, milady, I do find amusing. I am amazed that, even at Harold's command, you would bare your back to me or lower yourself to serving such a demon!" She said nothing, but stared at the floor. He could well imagine that her temper was soaring, and he was glad of the chance to goad her. "Sit, then, milady, and I will think on what service you can render me."

"I'd rather not," she replied. "I am most fond of standing."

He laughed again, for it seemed that Harold had indeed taken a switch to his daughter this time. Harold was proud, and he would not see a guest dishonored in his house.

"Ah . . . you cannot sit, I see."

"It is no matter," she said coolly. "My father's hand is a gentle one. By the morrow I'll not remember his angry touch."

"Umm. Well, trust in me, then, little girl. If ever I take a switch against you, it will not be with a gentle hand. And you will not forget it for days to come."

She swallowed; he saw that she breathed a slight sigh of relief. But still she spoke proudly. "I will remind you, sir, that I am a child no more. And I have never forgotten your less than gentle hand, Norman," she spat out, losing control of her temper.

He chuckled softly, "Fallon, you are still a child, for only children play at such pranks. And, girl, I did you no ill then. But it seems to me that you do not bend. Have you not heard? A willow that does not bend to the wind will break? Will you be broken, then, Fallon?"

'It seems to me, sir, that the man or woman who bends is but a coward. Nay, I do not bend. Nor can I be broken, I do assure you. Take the switch; I care not. I do not break."

"So you say, yet you stand before me."

"Aye, Norman, for I love my father. No violence on his part could bring me here. I have come only because I have hurt him, and in that love I bear him I am willing to seek amends. Even——"

She broke off, biting her lip. Alaric thought rather bitterly of love, for he had seen little good come from it. Morwenna, through her love for him, had brought about the death of a young shattered girl and then had caused the death of her lover, herself, and her unborn child.

"Even what, Fallon?" he demanded wearily.

"Even—with you," she replied.

"Ahh. Such abject humility tears my heart, princess. Well, then, serve me. My horse is stabled below and would dearly love a good rubdown and curry. And when you've finished there, my helmet and sword and shield could use some spit and polish and elbow grease. And when you have finished there—"

Something of a growl sounded from her throat. "Norman! How long do you intend to stay?"

"Oh, I don't know," he said pleasantly. "With such service offered to me, I shall stay awhile, I think. Time enough for you to carry through with your chores." His bed had been changed, and clean sheets and warm furs lay upon it. He offered her a smile and dropped onto the bed on his back, lacing his fingers behind his head. She stared at him and his eyes narrowed. "Get to it, milady!"

In a fury, she spun about.

Alaric called a page and was shaved. Then he went to join Harold in the hall. The earl had promised to ride out with him to his own lands on the morrow.

Later, Alaric ventured out to the stables, keenly interested to see if his orders had been carried out by his unwilling Saxon servant. To his surprise, he found that his huge black stallion, Satan, had been brushed to a shiny gloss; his hooves had been cleaned and his mane neatly braided. Then, from outside the stable, he heard soft voices. He went to the doorway.

Young Fallon sat curled up on a pile of hay, lazily chewing on a piece of the stuff. Her fine ebony hair was free and her cobalt eyes were alight with good humor. Her breasts pressed against the tight fabric of her chemise and bleaunt, and she appeared far older than her years, bewitching as any young siren.

She laughed, and Alaric saw that she sat with young Roger Beauclare.

Roger was busily polishing Alaric's shield. As he

worked, he sang a bawdy love song and Fallon laughed gaily.

Alaric watched for several moments, and his temper mounted. Women, it seemed, were vixens at a young and tender age. She had entranced young Roger, who watched her like a puppy dog; she smiled with pure bliss, like a cat well pleased with herself, for she had not served Alaric in the least.

Alaric stepped forward into the sunlight. Fallon gasped and sat straight and young Roger Beauclare tried to hide the shield behind his back. Alaric smiled pleasantly. "What have we here, young friend? Why, 'tis my own shield, I do declare. What is this, then?"

Neither of them spoke. They gazed at each other in guilty panic. Then Roger stuttered and tried to explain.

"My lord, I thought to give the lady a hand, for she faltered beneath the weight."

"Ahh," Alaric murmured, staring at Fallon. "And did the weight of the brush keep you from grooming the stallion?"

Roger choked back a reply. Fallon arched her throat and said softly, "Anything of yours, Count Alaric, is a heavy burden to me."

"That is what punishment is all about, is it not? But then, you would not know, milady, for I imagine you are easily able to cajole others to perform your tasks."

"Milord," Roger tried once again. "I only sought to help—"

"If you wish to help her, Roger, then give her no assistance at all. She has two choices. One is to serve me."

"And the other?"

"She knows the other well." He stared at Fallon, and he spoke to her softly, yet the threat in his voice was unmistakable.

Her eyes met his in a terrible clash of wills; she was a

strong little vixen, but he'd be damned if he'd be bested by a child.

At last Fallon's gaze wavered, and she stood to take the shield and rag from Roger. She did stagger beneath the weight of the shield, but she ignored Alaric and smiled ravishingly at young Roger. "Pray, sir, do continue to sing. I enjoy the company."

Roger glanced at Alaric uneasily. She smiled sweetly to her foe. "Count Alaric, you said that I must serve. You said nothing about doing so in my own company, did you?"

"Nay, I did not. But let me not discover that Roger has done any more of your work for you."

It was not a threat, Fallon knew, but an assurance. When her eyes met his, he knew she understood that.

Alaric left the two of them and returned to the manor. Edith suggested that he might enjoy a hot bath in his chamber; she would send the servants with water.

Alaric thanked her, admiring Harold's gentle Edith. She reminded him much of Matilda, William's wife, who had the same sweet gentleness tempered by dignity and pride. Alaric imagined in them both a touch of temper, too, fiery and sweet.

In his chamber he was glad to relax in the steaming tub. Musk had been added to the water, and its scent curled around him pleasantly with the steam. He closed his eyes and sank deeper. The water helped to soothe him, for he was bothered both by William's refusal to release Wulfnoth and by Harold's report that Edgar Atheling was being groomed as Edward's heir.

He was so lost in his thoughts that he did not hear the door open and close. He became aware that someone had joined him in the chamber when something fell into the tub and steaming water splashed over his face. He opened his eyes to find Fallon standing several feet away from him, her eyes still swirling blue pools of icy anger.

"Soap, milord Alaric."

"What are you doing here?" he asked her curtly.

She bobbed a curtsy. "Why, I've come to serve you, sir. I brought your sword and scabbard and shield. What you've asked of me is done. But alas! Your bath water grows cold!"

He remembered all too clearly her gentle administration of hot water in the past. "Fallon, nay—"

But she had already snatched up the kettle.

"Fallon, I warn you—"

In his nakedness, he could not rise. Mercilessly, Fallon poured the water into the tub, stinging his waist and thighs—and more delicate areas. He let out a bellow, and when she tried to run, he caught her arm and pulled her across the tub. Her eyes widened with fear as she saw the fury in his look.

She struggled from his hold, all too eager to escape him now. In panic she twisted and struggled, yet he barely seemed to notice her movement, which frightened her further. "I will leave—"

'Aye, leave, milady witch. But listen to this first. Whatever nastiness you dole out in the future, you will receive in equal measure. You are a child no more; I will no longer give you that advantage! Should you scald my water, I swear, you will scald along with me in it. And if ever I am again offered a switch to lay upon your back, I will take that opportunity to heart. Do you understand me?"

"Aye!" she cried out, her cobalt eyes full open, her cheeks flushed, and her hair a river of midnight beauty as it spilled down her back. A child, nay, he thought. A little siren who had boldly seduced his own man to do her will.

"Get out!" he commanded her, releasing her at last.

She pulled back. But she could not leave, it seemed, without the last word.

"Adieu, monsieur—bâtard!"

The next day, Alaric viewed his lands and met his vassals in Harold's company. He and his men stayed a night there, and then rode out for Normandy. He did not see Fallon again during his time in England. The next time he saw her, it was to be on Norman soil. And then, there would be no doubt that she was no longer a little girl. Harold's beautiful child had grown into an even more beautiful woman. And she and her father were doomed to be prisoners in the Norman court.

Chapter Seven

"Father!"

Harold, hurrying from the small house he had taken with his family on the Isle of Wight, turned to see his daughter racing toward him through the summer flowers. He paused, and she caught up with him, breathlessly taking his arm. "Father, where are you going?"

"Fishing," he replied.

"With hounds?"

He grimaced, for his dogs were baying about his feet in loud confusion. "Well, fishing and hunting. I had thought to set sail, fish, and turn westward into the forest with the hounds."

"May I come?" she asked him.

It was in his mind to refuse her. He was setting out because he needed time alone to think; Edith understood this, but Fallon could not. He sighed. He knew that she was worried, that she wondered where his heart lay. Two years ago, Harold had waged war against King Gruffydd of Wales on Edward's behalf. The king's own people had slain him, and Harold had been left to return Gruffydd's young widow, the English sister of the northern Earl Morkere, to her family.

Stories had quickly arisen, perhaps naturally, for it had read as something of a romance. He had rescued the

damsel in distress, and the balladeers sang that he had
married her on his return to Wales.

The stories were untrue. But Fallon had been upset,
and he worried for her. She knew that his position might
force him someday to take a church-blessed wife for political purposes.

In the last six years, he had seldom been at home, but
at times he had been able to bring his family to London,
and at other times he had been able to travel southward
to Bosham. Fallon, of all his children, seemed to love him
dearly and miss him most sorely.

"Please, Father, may I come with you?"

He knew he should refuse her; he had told Edith he
needed time to be alone. He thought perhaps that he had
loved Edith so fully for so many years because she always
understood him. Being the right-hand man of King Edward was no easy task.

Looking at his daughter, he hoped that Edith would
understand once again. He wanted Fallon with him.
When he gazed at her as she stood there amid the summer flowers, his heart swelled and he realized with a pang
that she was an adult now. She neared her eighteenth
birthday.

Taller than her mother, Fallon was blessed, or cursed,
with an even more feminine figure. She was slim and
graceful, with high, full breasts and sweetly curved hips
that hinted of a sensuality Harold did not want to accept
in his daughter. That she remained an innocent lass he
knew; she had been too strictly brought up with thoughts
of church and duty to be anything other. But the time was
quickly coming when he would need to choose a husband
for her. He had already seen her with one of the young
swains at court, a handsome young soldier of Danish
descent called Delon, and he knew she was infatuated, if
not in love. Although innocent, she was aware of her
sensuality and of the power it gave her.

Her ebony hair cloaked her shoulders, highlighting the radiant flash of her eyes. Her lips were parted slightly as she eagerly awaited his answer, and her cheeks were a soft red with the warmth of the summer sun. He paused only a moment longer. "Aye, daughter, come with me. It will be a special time for us. Well"—and he winked—"for you and for me and for James of Huntington, master of my hounds, and Justin Sewell, captain of our ship, and his sailors. Run, tell your mother that you accompany me. Then hie along, for I am eager to be off for some sport."

Fallon gave a glad cry and obeyed him.

Edith nodded with sweet composure when she learned that her daughter would sail with Harold, but when she followed Fallon to the door to wave her on her way, she paused to stare at the summer sky. "I do not like this weather," she murmured.

"Mother! It is beautiful. The sun shines like gold."

"But feel the wind . . ." Edith murmured. Then she smiled. "Maybe I am imagining things. Godspeed. Bring us back fine food to smoke for winter." She kissed her again, and Fallon hurried out to find her father.

The morning was beautiful as they set sail. The sun rose high above them, and Harold and Fallon and James of Huntington brought in a fine catch. Fallon laughed as her father struggled with an exceptionally feisty fish. When it was landed among them, he called for wine; the captain's mate brought them a full skin and two chalices from which to drink.

Harold talked to Fallon then. He spoke about Edward's tempers, about the many things he had to do to appease the enemies that the king provoked. Fallon listened to him, and she was glad to be with him. Then he leaned forward and gripped her hands and held them between his own. "I love you," he told her. "I love your mother with all my heart, as I do your brothers. You understand this?"

She nodded, swallowing, aware of what was coming.

"Fallon, you still must understand that a time may come when I must enter into another union. I will never do so because I do not love you or your mother, but for expediency only. I never mean to hurt you."

"But it does hurt, Father," she told him softly, then seeing the pain imprinted on his handsome features, she kissed him quickly. "But I do understand," she said. She wanted to assure him, even if she had to bend the truth. "Please do not fret on my account. I do understand. I—I just cherish our time together."

"And it is growing short enough, is it not?"

"What do you mean?"

"I could have married you to a number of young nobles, from Seville to Oslo these past several years. Soon enough you'll become a bride."

"Father! You'd not send me to a foreign country!"

"Well, now, it depends," he teased her. "You need a man with a stout heart, lass, and perhaps a heavy hand."

"Father!"

"Your behavior has improved with age," he told her amiably. "But, my dear, I still say, heaven help the man who loves you!"

"Father, I protest!" she said softly, touching his cheek. "You have taught me well of love, and where I love, there I am eternally faithful. When I pledge my troth, it will be forever."

"Even if I choose your mate?"

"You will not," she told him with smiling assurance. "I know that you will not, for you have refused all offers so far, and I can only assume that you do so in the firm belief that I shall love where I may."

"Hmph!" Harold grunted. "Don't be so confident, lass. Mayhap I'll send you to a Norman lord to see to the welfare of your uncle, who has been languishing these many years amongst them."

"Nay!" She cried. "Don't even tease so, I implore you. Send me to Spain, if you will, to Italy, to Byzantium. But I pray you, Father, do not send me to those barbarians."

She had barely said the words when a flash of lightning lit up the sky and a fierce clap of thunder shook the boat. Harold jumped to his feet in dismay; of a sudden, the sky blackened and the wind buffeted them about like flotsam.

"Mother of God," he murmured, and he crossed himself hastily. "I should ne'er have brought you, Fallon."

"Father!" Fallon quickly assured him that she wasn't afraid of the storm, even as her heart thundered. What had they said? What had they done? It was as if God had grown angry and turned a beautiful summer day into the pit of hell.

As if the sky had opened above them, rain began to fall in great torrents. "Fallon, get below!" Harold ordered his daughter.

"Perhaps I can help!" she cried.

Harold did not have a chance to dispute her again, for James was shouting, trying to calm the hounds, and at the helm, Captain Justin Sewell fought hard to steady the boat. There was little point to his effort. The rain slashed down and the wind howled ferociously, and they were tossed between the blackened sky and a swirling sea that was alive with foaming whitecaps. Harold shouted to Justin, and Justin shouted in return. Fallon clung to the mast and fought alongside the sailors to trim the sails.

It seemed that the storm raged forever. Fallon made endless vows to God, praying fervently to Catherine, her favorite saint, to see them through. Finally the sky grew light again and the wind began to lessen. Her father and Justin studied charts to see where the storm had taken them.

Fallon bit her lower lip. The storm had pushed them south. The land that she could see was not English soil, but some part of the countries of France.

Normandy, she thought.

And then, when all seemed calm, a mighty wave swept over them. Fallon screamed; something boomed and cracked, and their small ship pitched precariously. Fallon heard her father call her name, saw him reach for her. She shouted to him in reply, but then another wave rode over them, and water filled her mouth as she was thrown into the whitecaps.

A broken timber floated past her. She caught it, dimly aware that the murderous waves were carrying her toward the shore. Then she closed her eyes and knew no more.

Finally her senses returned. She was aware of a ferocious ache in her head as she opened her eyes. The sky above her was blue and calm. The sun was high. She lifted an arm over her eyes to shade them from the sun, and saw a simple man in shepherd's garb standing over her.

"Mon Dieu!" he swore, then added, "An angel has been brought to us from the sea."

"Fallon!"

She heard her father's voice, and with a glad cry, sat up and reached out to him. He hugged her, kissed her cheeks, and hugged her again.

The shepherd offered her his smelly cloak against the chill, and she thanked him heartily. He continued to stare at her as if she were an angel.

Even as Harold searched the shore for other survivors, men appeared on horseback, in full armor. Fallon stared at them in dismay. "Have we come to Normandy?" she whispered.

"Nay, Ponthieu," said one politely, drawing his mount before her.

"I am Harold, earl of Wessex," her father said.

"Aye, sir, well may you be an English earl, but for now, sir, you are the guest of Count Guy of Ponthieu."

Her father cast her a desperate look, and Fallon realized that these men did not think her an angel. She was
a "guest"—a prisoner.

The knight dismounted and took her arm to help her
up. She shook off his touch and told him coldly that she
would mount on her own.

They rode to the castle of Beaurain. There Fallon was
pushed into a bedchamber, and the door was barred; her
father, she was told, was being taken to the dungeons.

William was at Rouen when the news came to him that
Count Guy was holding Harold Godwinson.

The messenger who stood before the duke spoke fleetingly, with a bit of awe. "Harold was shipwrecked on the
beach. The captain was saved, and his master of the
hounds, and even the dogs. And they say that Harold has
a woman with him, ebony-haired and exotic. The shepherd who first stumbled upon them swore that the sea had
spewed up an angel."

"An angel?" They were at supper in William's hall,
and the duke turned a curious eye to Alaric. "Who is this
angel?"

"I would warrant it is Harold's daughter," Alaric said.

"Poor dear!" Matilda protested, thinking of her own
growing family. "And she is in the hands of those
knights . . ."

William patted her hand absently. "Don't fret, my love.
If I know the wily count of Ponthieu, he will be interested
in financial gain, not in the lass." William slammed a fist
against the table and laughed in good humor. "Harold,
here! What a fine state of affairs. Go back, my man," he
told the messenger, "and remind Guy that he is my vassal.
I want Harold and his company turned over to me immediately. We will ride to Eu in the morning. Guy can meet

me there with his guests. Guy will be recompensed, but I want Harold as soon as possible. Am I understood?"

The messenger bowed low and voiced his understanding.

Alaric rose and said, "William, perhaps I should ride with this man and see that no harm comes to Harold and his daughter."

William cocked his head curiously. "No harm will be done them, of that I am certain. I will need you with me on the morrow. You forget," William added testily, "that while you know Harold well, I have never met the man. I will need you at my side."

Alaric nodded, bowing to the wisdom of the duke's words. But when it came time to retire, he found that he could not sleep. He could not fathom why he was so anxious to reach the Englishman he had not seen in so many years.

In the morning, they rode to Eu with a great assemblage, for William was determined to appear before Harold in all splendor. Guy arrived as scheduled and offered up his prisoners. And while William hurried forward to embrace Harold like a long-lost relative, those around him who knew the duke well were aware that Harold but exchanged one jailer for another.

Still, it was a grand reception, and when Harold and William were well and duly met, Harold brought forth his daughter.

"Ahh, the angel!" William murmured.

She had changed, Alaric saw quickly. Even astride the borrowed mount, she looked tall. Her bedraggled gown hung about her like sacking, and still her shape was entrancing beneath it. Her face was indeed an angel's, rose and cream, and magically fine and delicate. Her vixen's eyes were so deep a blue they rivaled the sky and the sea. Her hair hung free behind her in long flowing waves like a cascade of raven-colored silk. She came forward, and

William smiled pleasantly, remembering the child he had met that long-ago day in Edward's court. "Milady Fallon! I left a little girl in England; in Normandy I greet a woman grown splendid and fair. Tell me, my dear, do you remember me?"

"Aye, that I do," she said sweetly, and when she smiled, even Alaric caught his breath. She had indeed grown uncommonly beautiful, like a sorceress sent to test the fortitude of men. "How could I forget the great duke of Normandy?" she added.

William took her hand and bowed over it. As the duke lowered his head, Alaric met her eyes, and he saw startled recognition in them. He also realized that she thought William anything but the "great duke of Normandy." He smiled in mocking acknowledgment of her thoughts.

"Alaric!"

Harold greeted him with true warmth. William urged his mount aside so that Harold and Alaric might meet. Then he raised his hand and said that they would briefly rest, then head for the capital at Rouen. "But first," he said wryly, "let our guests dismount from these nags of Guy's and be given decent Norman horseflesh!"

Laughter went up among his men, and even Harold smiled. The mounts they rode, Fallon had discovered, were fine ponies that William had paid for, along with their release into his hands. "Harold," William murmured, as a large bay steed was brought forward. Fallon's father thanked William and mounted on the fine stallion. "Alaric, see to the lady."

She wanted to cry out in protest. But it was a small thing, she realized, and William might have requested any one of his men to assist her. To protest would be absurd, and so she held silent.

Alaric dismounted and bowed to her. "Milady . . ." he murmured, reaching up for her with obvious impatience. His touch made her want to cry out, but she stared

straight into the bottomless gray of his eyes. She felt his
hands, like molten steel, against her; large and powerful,
they spanned her waist, touching her with a curious blaze.
His eyes held hers, and she felt the sizzle of lightning as
she came against him. He did not set her down; he swept
her from the pony to a bay mare, and as he did so, their
eyes held and the dizzying heat swept through her.

The contact lasted just seconds. Yet after he left her to
remount his own steed, she could still feel his touch; she
knew where his hands had touched her, for his heat
lingered. She felt the iron hardness of his chest and the
sinews of his arms.

"We ride!" William commanded.

They came to a manor belonging to the duke and held
by an old knight, Sir Riley of Coutances. The mighty
horses' hooves clattered over a courtyard of brick as the
party assembled there. There was a scurry as William's
men vied to reach Fallon and help her down from the bay
mare.

Alaric, Fallon noted, watched from a distance, that
cool, mocking smile still curling his lips.

They rested and feasted upon boar and pheasant and
eel and dark red wine. William reviled Guy of Ponthieu
for having treated an earl of England as if he were a
pirate. Harold thanked William for coming to their rescue, and William, it seemed, could not resist a self-
satisfied smile before replying that it was, indeed, his
pleasure—he had long awaited a meeting with the greatest of English earls.

William wished to spend the night in Rouen, and so
they started off soon after their meal. Fallon smiled
sweetly as one of William's men helped her mount, and
then she looked about. She was startled to discover the
gray-eyed Alaric staring at her from atop his great black
stallion several feet away. He smiled slowly, and she
flushed and turned from him.

She urged her mount forward, anxious to escape Alaric's gaze. There was little need, in truth, for he rode beside her father. Harold, to her annoyance, spoke to him like a good friend. Fallon kept her head lowered and listened to their conversation; they spoke French, since Duke William knew little English. He complimented her father on his fluent use of the French tongue, and Harold reminded William that he had been taught the language from infancy. Languages had come to him easily, he told the duke, and he had been glad of this, for his fluency had helped him on his pilgrimage to Rome.

"Alas," said William, "I've had no such chance to travel. Perhaps during your stay you will enlighten me on many things. We are sadly lacking in knowledge here. We learn to fight, to court, and to swear homage to the church, but little else. I envy you your learning."

That much was not mockery, Fallon decided, yet she hoped her father knew better than to trust the Norman duke.

"Duke William, I believe we are both men of circumstance of upbringing. King Edward is a man fond of the arts and artists, of science, language, poetry, and music."

William laughed. "But it is not so easy, ever attending to the whims and rages of the king!"

Harold—who, in the privacy of his home, often complained about the Confessor's ridiculous tempers—would not malign the king in this company. Fallon didn't hear his reply, however, for a voice she knew well interrupted her thoughts.

"So, milady, you have stumbled into my country. I wonder, should I bid you welcome? Or should I fear for my life and sanity?"

She felt his gray eyes upon her, giving nothing away. Fallon turned from his gaze to watch the road. "My Lord, you jest. You do not fear me. Indeed, I am most surprised that you recall we've met."

"I bear a scar on my hand, milady, made by the teeth of a vicious little girl who did not care for my nationality. And I am ever grateful that my scalded flesh has healed. You are most difficult to forget, milady. Again, I beg to know—should I run for cover, milady?"

She tossed her hair back and turned to stare at him once again. "Now you taunt me, sir, for the tricks played by a child. You may indeed rest assured that I've lost interest in icing down your bedding or scalding you in your tub."

"I am, milady, vastly relieved."

"You mock me, sir."

"Nay, I do not," he told her gravely. "I came to see if we are now at peace or if you still consider me your enemy."

"Now, milord, you betray your conceit. I have not thought of you at all."

"Ah, that is well and good, milady."

"Oh?" She glanced at him mildly and tried to ignore the force of his gaze. She felt that she was at a painful disadvantage now, for she was well aware of him as a male—acutely aware of his hands, strong and bronzed on the reins, and of his thighs, muscled beneath tight hose, nearly touching her own as they rode side by side.

"Aye," he told her, his bold gaze never wavering from her. She shivered. "Good for you, milady. I wished to warn you that I am in no mood for mean, hateful tricks."

"*Warn* me?" she retorted, shocked that he would speak so with both her father and the duke nearby. "Don't you mean *threaten* me, sir?"

"If I ever make a threat to you, milady, take heed, for it will not be an idle one. If I make a promise, I do not forget it. For now, milady, I only warn you." He inclined his head toward her, then urged his mount forward.

Fallon seethed. She longed to take him by his Norman

hair and slam his Norman pate against a Norman buttress.

But of course she had to remain docile. She and her father were not at home. They were in Normandy as "guests" of Duke William.

Alaric did not speak to her again as they rode. She heard him conversing smoothly with her father and William, comparing the laws and ways of the two countries. When they paused in a small village for water, it was the other knights who hurried to her assistance, and even when they came at last to William's fine home in Rouen, Alaric kept a cool distance, mocking her with his eyes when the other men battled for the honor of assisting her. She ignored him and bestowed radiant smiles on the other knights, thanking them sweetly in their own language.

Chapter Eight

Fallon wanted to despise all things Norman, but she had found that she was keenly interested in everything around her. It was summer, and the land—where it had not been devastated by constant war—was radiant and beautiful. Castles dotted the hills and the valleys, vast structures, made primarily of stone, built to withstand siege and warfare. One young knight explained to her that they lived by the Truce of God, which forbade warfare on certain days of the week. "If we did not have this," the knight explained, "we should not eat, for when our steeds race across the fields and our swords clash in battle, little is left behind."

And now they were in Rouen, and Fallon was amazed by the architecture of the city, the variety of churches and abbeys and residences and shops. The city was almost as large as London, but very different in appearance, for the English built mostly with wood whereas the Normans were fond of brick and stone. William's castle in Rouen was fascinating, at once beautiful and immensely strange. These barbarians, Fallon concluded, built well.

But as time passed she ceased to think of the Normans as barbarians. As she stood with her father and William in the castle courtyard, shivering slightly from the night chill, a soft and feminine voice came to her.

"This must be Fallon, Harold's daughter." Matilda, William's duchess, a petite and pretty woman with flashing eyes came to her and took her hands, surveying her with a warm, sweet smile.

This woman, Fallon decided, would be impossible to dislike, and she smiled back tentatively.

"Why William, it is just as I feared; Guy gave no care to our English guests at all!"

"Nay, my sweet, I fear he did not."

"Sir Harold, my man will show you to your chamber; I am sure you must be weary. We are ever so lucky that the storm did not take you to the bottom of the sea! I will take Fallon myself and see that she is given a hot bath and clothing and sent to bed upon clean, fresh linen!"

"We thank you, Lady Matilda," Harold said, "For your warm hospitality."

"It is our pleasure. I have heard from Alaric of the warmth you have always extended to him on my husband's behalf."

Fallon knew that Alaric watched her, and she felt her flesh burn, wondering if he had ever mentioned to this woman her own particular brand of hospitality. She determined that he had not, for the duchess set an arm about her waist and steered her toward the great hall of the castle.

"You must call me Matilda, Fallon. And if you need anything at all, you must come to me." Her hair was a soft brown and her eyes were a flashing hazel, and she seemed far too diminutive and fragile for the hardened warrior she had married. But Matilda had a curious strength about her, and Fallon liked and trusted her instantly.

Fallon did not see much of the hall that night. She was led up a curving flight of stone stairs and brought to a double door, which Matilda promptly opened. A steaming bath awaited her before the hearth and the huge bed, which seemed to dwarf the room, was strewn with clothing, cool summer linens and silks, chemises and bleaunts and girdles and hose and even an assortment of soft leather shoes.

"You are overly kind," Fallon told her sincerely.

"Nay," Matilda demurred. "I've six children and another on the way. I'm quite capable of looking out for one more. And I knew what it is like to be cast upon a foreign shore," she added softly. Then she helped Fallon out of her muddy gown and into the tub. Fallon was embarrassed at having the duchess herself serve as her maid, but Matilda was a practical woman—and a curious one, Fallon realized.

Fallon could not believe that the small and lovely duchess could have borne six children, and Matilda was glad of the compliment. She was so sweet and gentle that, in the end, Fallon had little difficulty in climbing into the tub and relaxing while Matilda washed her hair, laughing at its thickness.

Time passed pleasantly. Matilda spoke about her children and coaxed Fallon to talk about her mother and her family. In time, a servant came to the door with broth and hot milk. As Matilda talked with the woman, Fallon chose a long, soft white chemise from the things laid out on the bed. She put it on, climbed into bed, and closed her eyes. She thought about the wretched night she had spent locked, cold and shivering, in a dirty chamber in the castle of the count of Ponthieu. This was almost like coming home. The bed was soft and warm. She slept as sweetly as a babe.

The next morning Fallon learned that her father had gone with Duke William and Alaric to do battle against Conan of Brittany. Matilda explained the cause of the fight to Fallon—the duke was riding to assist Riwallon of Dol, and to fortify his stronghold at Saint-James-de-Beuvron on the border.

Fallon could not believe that William would ask her

father to ride with him into battle. Matilda tried to calm her, and yet she remained upset, and the days grew long at the Norman court. Fallon was sure that the duke felt no goodwill toward her father, and she was afraid for him. Perhaps even Alaric, despite his claims of friendship all these years, would turn traitor on some foreign battlefield. Fallon knew that she was not a guest here, nor was her father; as kind and gentle as the duchess was to her, she was a prisoner just as her father was.

Fallon's one pleasure was the time she spent in the nurseries trying to teach the younger children English. Occasionally she was allowed to see her uncle Wulfnoth. He was, she discovered, not abused in any way, and he was resigned to his life. He was not a prisoner in a dungeon. His status was that of hostage, and he was treated with the respect due a man of his family and position.

In due course, word came that William and his party were returning. The duke had been victorious, and the messengers claimed that Harold of England had proved himself a valiant warrior. His Norman companions took great pride in his valor, and Duke William had knighted him in the Norman fashion upon the field.

Fallon was greatly relieved, but her happiness was not to last. For on the night that her father and William returned, things would begin to bode ill for them.

She felt glad now, however, as she stood upon the steps and listened to the trumpets and the clatter of the horses' hooves as the men returned from battle. One of the gowns Matilda had given her was a soft tawny gold, with a braided girdle for her waist and a chemise in summer yellow to wear beneath. Her hair fell against it in bewitching contrast, and the night wind lifted tendrils to sweep about her face as she eagerly sought her father's face.

He came in beside the duke. She noticed with annoyance and a flutter of her heart that Alaric rode on William's other side. When Harold dismounted, she hurried to him with a cup of welcoming wine and a warm embrace.

"Fallon!" He held her to him, then stepped back.

"Father!" Tears glazed her eyes as she looked at him; he had gone to battle without even kissing her good-bye.

His eyes told her the story then; he knew that she would have protested, and so he had gone without telling her. She smiled. He was back, well and unharmed. She would not harp over what was done.

"Come," Harold said. "Let us toast our victory this night."

Fallon glanced past her father at Alaric, who had dismounted from his midnight-black steed. His eyes fell upon her, and for once they did not mock. She felt heat rise to her cheeks, and she had to clench her hands at her sides to keep her fingers from trembling. She turned from him quickly and slipped her arms about her father again.

The musicians were already playing when they entered the hall. Men and ladies milled about, taking their seats according to their degree of importance in the court. The highest nobles sat to the right and left of the duke and duchess, with the lower knights finding their seats along the ells of the tables. That night Harold was seated to the duke's left, and Fallon found herself wedged between her father and Alaric, with whom she shared a single silver chalice, as was often the way at the duke's table. Fallon, though thirsty, could not bring herself to touch the cup. The count amused himself by conversing with the lady to his other side, but Fallon ached with a painful awareness of him. Too often she felt his knee brush her own. She was aware of his heavily muscled arm, too near. She knew his scent and the timbre of his voice, the sound of his laughter, and even the sweeping caress of his eyes when they fell upon her. She tried to give her wholehearted attention to her father, but he was engaged in conversation with William.

She started at the sound of Alaric's voice whispering close to her cheek. *"Mademoiselle,* though I may wear demon horns and sprout a devil's tail now and again, I do swear I bear no poison upon my lips to taint the wine."

He raised the cup to her. She felt the blood drain from her face, and she drank too swiftly. "Thank you," she sputtered. "I am not thirsty."

"And I am not a demon," he murmured, looking into the empty chalice with amusement.

Embarrassed, Fallon realized that she had emptied the cup. Her action had been rude, and she felt Alaric's eyes upon her again. Then he lifted his hand, and a servant came quickly to refill the chalice. He picked it up and smiled at her. "Nay, Fallon, it is I who should be wary of tricks. Yet see—I do not fear to drink from the place where your lips have gone before. Indeed, I am honored."

His eyes remained upon hers as his lips closed over the rim of the cup where hers had been. She watched him, aware that she grew dizzy and curiously warm. He set the cup down and turned away again.

There was entertainment that night. Jugglers and fools and dancing bears, and a beautiful great cat brought through Spain from Africa, which leapt over burning boughs. Then the floor was cleared, and there was dancing. Fallon swirled in her father's arms and in her uncle's. Then she demurely consented to be escorted by numerous knights. She had no way of knowing that she was the envy of many of the ladies; she needed to dance that night, to smile and flirt and play, though she did, in her heart, consider all the Normans barbaric.

She saw Alaric but once. He was holding the arm of a buxom redhead, who whispered to him and leaned insinuatingly near. Fallon ignored them both, sipped more wine, and danced merrily.

The duke had remained quite sober, Fallon realized,

and appeared serious in spite of the merriment. As the hour grew late, Fallon heard him ask Harold to join him in his private apartment. Trying to shake the dizziness from her mind, Fallon hurried after them down the hall. She was instinctively aware that something very important was about to happen.

The duke entered his outer chamber where a long table stood before a hearth with a banked fire. He did not close the door. Fallon, hidden behind an arch, looked in. There were various men in the room, including William's half brothers Odo and Robert, and the archbishop. Fallon, peeking through the doorway, saw them circle about, and her fingers flew to her throat as she thought of some secret rite.

"I'll have your promise, Harold," William was saying softly. "You must swear that when Edward dies, you will be my voice at the witan. You will stand fast for my claim to the throne."

In the wavering candlelight, her father tried to explain. "William, I have not the power—"

"Nay—Edward promised me the throne. Harold, I ask only that you promise to be my voice and to secure the promise for me. Perhaps now, while Edward lives, you and I shall begin to build a force in Dover." The duke smiled eagerly. He looked almost like a boy, and his voice rang with passionate sincerity. "Harold, you and I together! Think what we can do for England!"

No! Fallon cried inwardly. England would never submit to the chains of Norman rule! Yet she wondered if her father was not about to agree with the duke. He and William were of an age—young, powerful men. Harold had dealt with the excesses and idiocies of King Edward for a long time. Perhaps he believed that William would be a better ruler.

She saw that William held something in his hands beneath the table.

"Give me this sacred promise, Harold. Swear it."

Harold tried again to explain the workings of the witen-agemot; William wanted only his promise. In the end, Harold sighed, kissed the Bible William held before him, and quietly gave his oath to support William in his bid for the kingdom of England.

Stunned, Fallon began to wander down the hall. It could not be! Surely her father knew that the nobles of England wanted no part of foreigners. That was why they had scoured the Continent for survivors of the royal house all those years ago. Edgar Atheling was still a youth but in another few years, the people would gladly embrace him as king. Surely, her father had given his word only to secure their freedom. He must have known that until he gave his promise, William would never let them leave Normandy.

A loud sound behind her startled her. Fallon, aware that the men had left the duke's quarters and were filing into the hall, looked for an archway to hide in, but there was none. The voices in the hallway grew louder. Seeing a door ahead, she opened it quietly and slipped through it, hastily closing it behind her. Breathing shallowly, she turned, praying that the room would be empty.

She had entered some important noble's bedchamber, she decided quickly, for it was equipped with a desk and chairs as well as a large bed, several trunks, and shelves for armor.

A slight sound alarmed her, and she turned toward the hearth. A large wooden tub sat before it—occupied. In the tub, a man relaxed, his dark hair resting against the rim, a wet cloth over his face.

"Nigel, is that you? Fetch the kettle, will you, boy? I need more water in my bath."

Fallon froze, recognizing the voice. Then she cursed herself in silence. Of all the men to come upon, it had to be this one!

"Nigel, have you gone daft man? Answer me."

Fallon deepened her voice and let out a grunt.

"Hurry, boy," said Alaric, his face still covered with the cloth. If Fallon just poured the water into the tub, he might not look at her. But if he caught her in his room . . .

She didn't want to think about it. Biting her lip, she circled the tub.

"Come, Nigel, I'd rather not keep a lady waiting."

The buxom redhead, no doubt, Fallon thought waspishly. She shrugged. He was a barbarian; he liked bovine women.

Fallon nervously grasped the kettle, eyeing him to see that he kept his eyes closed, and the cloth atop his face. She came over with the water and stood tremulously over him. Naked, the man gave her even greater alarm. The water lay slick against his muscular arms, and the dark hair was matted on his chest. His knees were drawn up. She trembled, suddenly nervous beyond measure.

"Nigel—" he said impatiently, removing the cloth and turning around. Fallon dropped the kettle and attempted to run, but a heavy hand clamped down on her arm and she was drawn into the tub atop Alaric.

"You again!"

The water soaked her clothing, molding it to her body as she lay in his lap and stared into his furious eyes. She felt the strength of his arms, the scent of musk, the hardness of his thighs beneath her, the breadth of his chest.

Fallon struggled against him, shoving against his chest, finding it slick and inflexible. "Let me up!" she cried, and tried to strike his face. He grimly caught her wrist and twisted it. "You sodden bastard Norman rat!" she swore with vehemence, twisting in desperation.

"Cease!" he commanded her, but she struggled on. He swore in a full variety of languages as her clothing became ever more wet, sticking like a glove to her body and her soft form was crushed ever closer to his hard one.

Soft silk lay flush against her breasts, outlining their shape and form and ripe fullness as if she were naked. She twisted again and gasped as the tight-muscled heat of his chest touched her. Color rushed to her damp cheeks, and to her horror, she felt her nipples harden against that aching brush with masculinity. She went deadly still and stared at him.

"I always said you needed a good thrashing," he said hoarsely. But his eyes were steadfastly upon hers, hard with fascination. She could not move, for she felt compelled to return that stare. She had never been more acutely aware of each fiber of her body.

In those moments he forgot she was Harold's daughter. He forgot he had known her as a child. He did not even remember her name.

He knew only that he had never seen, touched, known, or felt a woman so seductive, so beautiful. Ebony hair trailed over his fingers, her eyes were eternally blue as they gazed into his, and her lips were parted, as if a sound would escape them. None did. He lowered his head and caught those lips with his own. The taste was sweeter than honey, more potent than any wine, and as a fierce roaring sounded in his head, he parted her mouth with the consuming thrust of his tongue, drinking ever more deeply. He touched her cheek, and his hand roamed free, curving over her breast and enjoying the firm ripe weight and seductive form of it, rubbing his thumb over a nipple grown pebble-hard and sensuously sweet. Still the heat rumbled within him, and still the kiss went on. He no longer held her wrists. He felt her hand against his chest, as if she would push him away. Then her fingers went limp, and a soft sound came from her throat. She might have twisted her head, but he held her too firmly. She could not fight him. She didn't have the power.

It was the first time she had ever felt such fire. It rose within her, filling her limbs and swirling in her belly; it seemed to cast her into a nether world. She forgot that he had not the right to kiss her; she forgot that he was the enemy; she knew only that drops of honey burst inside of her and swirled. He engulfed her. The coercive power of his lips against hers, the feel of his naked flesh touching her, holding her, the stroke of his thumb against her breast . . .

It came to her then that she lay, drenched and shameless, upon a naked man, in his bath. The sweet fire that swept through her was her greatest humiliation, for it was surely not possible to despise a man so and yet burn at his touch.

She was Harold's daughter.

His mouth suddenly rose from hers. His hand, with no apology, lay against her breast. He stared down at her intently, and his fury seemed all the greater. Her lips, swollen from his kiss, trembled. "Bastard!" she said on a strangled sob.

He smiled without amusement, holding her still, though she sought to struggle against him. "Be warned, Harold's daughter," he told her.

"I despise you, Norman bastard!" She wanted to scream, to rave, but her voice came out in a trembling, broken whisper.

Suddenly his smile deepened and he drew his finger down the line of her cheek. "Perhaps, Harold's daughter, this will teach you that though you may tease boys and bend them to your will, you ought never to taunt a man, for you will receive what a man has to give. Milady, I give you this chance to leave."

She felt suddenly, through the soaking cloth that covered her, a shaft of masculine hardness. She had indeed taunted him. While he smiled at her in deadly warning, she gasped, feeling that probe against her flesh. Her breath caught in her throat and her eyes widened at the size and power of it. Panic seized her and she thrashed against him, mumbling incoherent words. His arms came about her firmly, and he rose, naked, still holding her. She stared, crushed against him, and mute for once.

"Milady," he mocked, "what is this game? Time and time again as the years have passed, I have begged you leave me to my bath in peace. Now it appears that you are at last anxious to run."

"I'll scream!" she whispered at last, swallowing.

Her words brought forth a husky peal of laughter. "Again, *mademoiselle*, it would be my right to do the screaming. But, as you will. With me, I promise, you'll not hide behind your father, for I am always honest with him, and he with me."

He stepped from the tub, still holding her in his arms. Then he let her slide slowly down the length of him, studying her eyes as he did so. A crooked smile curled his lip once more. "Milady, I do believe you might have been mine for the taking."

She drew back a hand to strike him. Too quick for her, he captured her wrists and held them behind her back. Again she was aware of his arousal, and it sent both terror and fire raging through her. "Fallon, behave."

She simply could not. She kicked his shin, swearing in the five languages she knew. "Conceited barbarian slime!" She told him at last. "I would rather have a true demon ten times over, a toothless old beggar, or a crippled thief! Let me go!"

To her amazement, he did. He released her so swiftly that she nearly fell. Then she caught herself and, dripping, stumbled toward the door.

"Fallon!" he called.

Unthinking, she turned, and gasped at what she saw. He stood there, coldly furious, staring at her. He was the perfect warrior, nearly godlike in pride and form, a bronzed and muscled male body, sleek and glistening from the bath, and fully threatening in its power.

"Fallon, you are not a child any longer. So take the gravest heed, and I beg of you, avoid me in the future."

She suggested that he should sleep in pig manure, then slammed her way out into hall, forgetting that she was coming from a man's room with her clothing completely drenched.

Luckily the hour was late, and despite her rage and lack of discretion, she was able to reach the solitude of her chamber without encountering anyone else.

Once there, she numbly stripped away her sodden clothing and pulled on the soft white sleeping gown. She crawled into bed and, despite the summer warmth, pulled the covers about her and shivered. She couldn't even think about her father's vow and England's dilemma; she could only touch her mouth and tremble, remembering Alaric's kiss.

Chapter Nine

Fallon had no chance to speak with her father in private the next morning. William had decided that they would spend the day hunting to provide food for a great feast, a farewell banquet for the earl of Wessex.

She was glad to be leaving, but in truth, in certain ways, she had enjoyed William's court. An intriguing variety of men and women flavored William's home. The Spanish dancers had told her about the Moors, and the Infidels from Africa, and the peace that a mighty warrior named El Cid had created among the Spaniards of both religions. A Venetian glassblower had told her about the trade that flourished along the shores of the Mediterranean Sea, and among Matilda's servants was a beautiful dark-skinned woman who came from Egypt in the north of Africa and who entertained Fallon with fascinating tales of giant Pyramids that rose to the sky, built to house the mortal remains of great men of the past. Fallon would sorely miss many of the people here, including the duchess and her children.

In the great hall, men and women were preparing to leave for the hunt. Fallon saw her father by the mantel, where he talked with William and Matilda. She joined him, and murmured her thanks when the duchess offered her a pair of hawking gloves. Two of the duke's children—young Robert, thirteen, and Adela, a pretty girl of ten—would be joining them. Fallon looked about the hall, and noticed that Alaric was seated at the high table, his gloves lying casually across his knee, laughing with the redhead who had drawn his favor the night before. He turned to Fallon almost as if he had sensed her presence across the room. Despite herself, she flushed furiously, and he bowed deeply to her before offering his hand to the redhead.

Curiosity caught hold of Fallon's heart. She sought out her uncle Wulfnoth and asked him who the redhead was. He told her that the lady was Mary of Tara, of one of the Irish royal houses. "Out for a mate, I daresay," Wulfnoth told her with a wink. Then he sighed. "Well, she will find good sport with Alaric, one might well imagine. But ne'er a mate."

"Why?" Fallon demanded sweetly. Wulfnoth thought her charming; apparently Alaric did, too. Wulfnoth declared she had wealth—why would a man hesitate to make her his wife?

"Alaric has said he'll not marry again," Wulfnoth told her, watching his niece with frank curiosity. "He has been a friend to me in this place, and I've come to know he means what he says. There's been a fair amount of court gossip about the two of them, naturally, and Mary is convinced of her own charm. Many wagers have been laid upon the outcome of this flirtation . . . but now, my sweet, perhaps you will explain to me your interest in the count and his love." Wulfnoth arched a brow. "Have you an interest in Alaric? If so, guard your heart well, my lovely. He is a fine enough fellow to call friend, but those eyes can be as gray and forbidding as a winter sky, and I'll warrant his heart is as cold."

"Nay!" Fallon said hurriedly. "I spoke with curiosity, and no more, Uncle. I despise the man."

Wulfnoth smiled and pursed his lips. Suddenly there

arose a wave of good-humored laughter from where her father and the duke hovered together. Adela was blushing very prettily as she stood by her mother's side, between her father and Harold, who were smiling at the pretty child.

" 'Tis done, then," Duke William said, his voice ringing about the hall. "Adela finds you to be such a fine and gentle knight, my friend. From this day forward, I shall consider my daughter betrothed to the great earl of Wessex, Harold Godwinson."

Fallon gasped in horror. Surely this was some crude jest, for her father had just passed his fortieth birthday, and the girl was but ten. Fallon swallowed down a sudden nausea and reminded herself that it was probably nothing but pretty play. Her father had complimented the little girl, and in turn, William's daughter and William himself had complimented her father. It was a jest, nothing more.

It was all a mockery, she thought. They were not guests, but prisoners. The count of Ponthieu had been a more honest man, placing walls around them. William was more subtle.

Fallon was suddenly anxious to be quit of the hall. She heard little more of what was said, and drew to one side of the room. When the horn was blown to gather them for the hunt, she gladly accepted the assistance of a stable boy. When they left the palace behind them and entered the forest, she was quick to look for an escape route; she did not wish to see her father or Duke William, and for some short period of time, she craved to see no Normans at all. She lagged behind the others and then, in a shrouded copse, turned her mount and headed in a westerly direction while the hunt veered south.

The forest was dense and dark, with narrow trails beneath the trees. Overhead, branches wedded branches. A low ground fog rose, and upon occasion, Fallon could hear the soft cry of a bird. Other than that, the wood was still, and as the mist swirled and whispered about her horse's hooves, this part of Normandy, at least, seemed like a magical land, a haven of peace.

She heard a loud snap, and she instantly regretted having left the hunt. How far had she come? She was alone in a land of savage and barbarous people. William dealt swift justice, but no manner of ruler could rid a land of poachers and thieves.

The wind was beginning to whip mightily; if she screamed, no one would hear. She had nothing with which to defend herself except a small dagger that Matilda had given her to wear in a soft hide sheath at her girdle.

Her horse grew restless, shying backwards, its nostrils flaring, ears pricking. The animal reared and whinnied. Then Fallon heard a sudden shout, and a man leapt at her from the trees.

He fell atop her, carrying them both to the ground. The horse reared again, but even as Fallon rolled with her attacker, another man appeared and caught the fine animal. Fallon stared up into her attacker's face, a face with narrow lips grimly taut, dark eyes, clean-shaven cheeks, and a long scar. She stared at him one moment while fear took root inside her. Then she screamed and began to struggle in earnest. Straddling her, the man bared his teeth and leered menacingly. "Beauty and fire, eh, vixen? Struggle, then, me lovely, and the more I'll enjoy the day!"

She had not spent years in the constant company of her brothers and their masters for naught. This man was no knight, just a petty thief who sought to prey upon a lone woman. Fallon reached for the dagger, fighting down the fear that gripped her. She had never taken arms against a man to hurt and kill, and she was terrified that she would not be able to strike him. Yet if she did not . . .

"Pretty, pretty thing!" he murmured. He leaned close

and breathed in the perfume of her hair. "A lady, imagine. And, lady, the things I shall teach you—"

"Hurry! 'Twill be my turn next!" the second man said.

The hushed threat brought Fallon to life. She kneed her attacker with all her strength, and as his features went white with pain, she plunged the dagger into his side. He let out a tremendous howl and twisted away from her. "The bitch! She's pierced me! Slain me! Leave the horse—finish the girl."

Fallon seized the hilt of the dagger just as the second man caught hold of her ankle. She kicked out in growing panic and menaced him with the dagger. He let go of her ankle briefly and began to rise.

Free! Fallon stumbled to her feet, panting and gasping. She raced into the woods, praying that he would not come after her. The wind was rising in an ever greater fury, and she could barely see the path through the trees.

A sudden shout pierced the forest. Fallon turned, but already the trees blocked her view of the scene she had left behind. The roiling sky seemed to be falling on her, bringing the thick gray mist about her feet, blinding her.

Stumbling, she kept running, aware that someone was pursuing her through the forest.

She felt that her lungs would burst, that her legs would give way beneath her, and yet she ran on. Despite the wind she could now clearly hear the thrashing, loud and distinct, through the foliage and bracken. She could hear her heart, hammering out a frantic beat. She could hear her breath, great rasping gasps for air.

Hard behind her she heard his breath, and the thunder of his heart. Then he was upon her, sweeping an arm about her waist to hurl her to the ground. Her hair tangled about her and she couldn't move or see. He caught her weight atop him as they hit the ground, softening the blow for her, grunting as he took it himself. Then he rolled over, pinning her beneath him. And still she could see nothing, feel nothing, except for the beat of her heart. She screamed out in agony and in anguish, "No! No! *No!*" She had come too far to give up now. She struggled fiercely, pitching herself from side to side, flailing, and at last she was able to raise her dagger against him. "By God's own blood!" A voice swore, and though she aimed sure and true, her wrist was caught in a vise that caused her to scream again, releasing the dagger.

"Fallon!"

She heard her name, but didn't understand. Shivering and panting, she tried to strike out again, but her wrists were caught and her name was softly repeated, "Fallon!"

This time she knew the voice. She went dead still beneath him, and he began to smooth the tangled hair from her face. At length she could look up and see him—Count Alaric, straddling her now as the thief had done, but gently smoothing her hair with the one hand while he secured her wrists with the other.

She went limp. "My God!" she gasped, close to tears.

"My life," he muttered with a curiously gentle smile. "You are talented with this blade, lady. I did not think you would use it against me."

"I did not!" she claimed indignantly, and she struggled to sit up, but she was effectively pinned to the ground. She recalled their encounter of the night before, and the wind that tore about them was suddenly hot and living. It swept into her limbs. She remembered too well his fine and powerful body, which could easily force hers to submission.

"You nearly killed me with that blade," he said.

"And a pity I did not!" she choked out, anxious to be free of his disturbing touch. "Pray, sir, I did not know—"

"I called your name."

"I did not hear. I was sorely afraid—"

"There is nothing to fear any longer," he said darkly. He stood up at last and reached down to her. She trembled as he took her hand, understanding that both of her attackers were dead, that Alaric had killed the second man. When she met his eyes, there was something new in them, some fierce anger.

"What in the Lord's name did you think you were doing, girl?"

She stiffened, trying to smooth back her own hair, searching for some dignity. "Doing? Why, sir, I but set out for a ride—"

"Alone, in a dark forest?"

"I wished to be alone!"

He said nothing, but reached out a hand to her, and she noted the strength of it and the bronzed color and powerful length of his fingers. Again something swept through her as he touched her—something of the raging wind and the dark tempest.

"Come," he told her. "Your father is beside himself with worry, and I blame him not, milady, for you attract every manner of man, from thief and knave to besotted nobleman."

She wanted to protest, to assure him that such events were no fault of her own. But the sky chose that moment to release its fury, and it seemed that the heavens had opened. Rain poured down on them in a sudden fierce cascade.

Alaric tightened his hold on her. "Milady, move!"

She had little choice but to follow as he dragged her along. She was blinded in truth now, for a tempest raged, and she could barely make out his broad back before her. She stumbled over a tree root and fell. He helped her to her feet, then lifted her in his arms. "Nay!" she cried. "Set me down!"

"I'll not be drowned by your whim!" he growled impatiently.

She could protest no more, and he strode boldly through the cacophony of wind and rain. Nay, she had little choice but to cling to him. He wore no armor today, but was robed in finery, and she felt the hard warmth of him as she was crushed to his chest. Again a tempest rose within her as she remembered his hold of the night before, the pressure of his lips against hers.

Once they reached the clearing, he whistled. Suddenly Fallon was certain that she was a captive, in the torrential downpour, in the arms of a lunatic Norman. His great black stallion heard the signal, though, and came forward. Alaric set her in the saddle and mounted behind her.

He knew the forest well, and in a matter of minutes, they came to an abandoned cottage. Alaric deposited her before the door, muttering that he would see to his horse and join her. He stared down at her from his great height atop the stallion, and she found herself nodding mutely.

She slipped inside. The place was small and bare, but it was clean, and it kept the rain well away. Outside, the rain beat a rhythm on the roof and shutters, and the wind was an endless moan. She cast off her mantle and groped her way toward the hearth to see if there was firewood.

The door burst open with a shriek of the wind and Fallon turned. Alaric stood there, framed in the doorway, his mantle sailing about his shoulders. A streak of lightning lit up the blackened sky, and he was suddenly a silhouette of power and strength. He set his saddle on the floor, then turned and forced the door closed, and darkness descended upon them.

He came to the hearth and knelt beside Fallon; quickly he found logs and kindling. Within a matter of moments, a tiny flame appeared, and soon a blaze began to take hold. He warmed his hands before it. Fallon began to shiver. She felt his keen gray eyes upon her.

"Take off your wet gown as well," he commanded.

She stared at him; he had indeed gone mad in the forest. But he chuckled softly and murmured, "You've a chemise beneath it. Both garments will dry more quickly if you strip down to one."

"I am fine, thank you," she told him stiffly. But she still shivered, and she sensed that her lips were nearly as blue as her eyes.

He let out an oath and impatiently stripped a blanket of fur from the small cot in the corner. She started to thank him, but he hauled her to her feet. "Try to use what sense the Lord gave you, milady!" he told her crossly, and before she could move her numb fingers, he had stripped off her girdle, seized the hem of her gown, and peeled the garment off over her head. She choked and swore, but even as she struggled, he wrapped the blanket around her. "That should do you better, I think."

She stared at the fire while he moved about, hanging up their mantles and her bleaunt to dry. As the fire lapped high and she watched him furtively while he removed his own short tunic and chemise, stripping down to his chausses and boots. The firelight turned the rippling muscles on his chest to gold, and she swallowed and looked into the flames again in confusion. She hated no man as she did this one, she assured herself. No man other than Harold had ever raised a hand against her, except this one. No man had ever spoken to her so crudely or so curtly.

And no man had touched her . . . as he had last night, bringing forth all the fiery hatred within her, yet touching off something else of fire, something that burned through her as if lightning seared her very being. Her pride could not bear him to touch her; her heart could never forget that he was a Norman, savage bastard who mocked her.

Still, her senses betrayed her, and hate him as she would, when he came close, she felt the sizzling, rough and potent on the air. She feared him as she feared the lightning striking the earth.

The rain continued to pour down on the cottage.

Alaric opened the shutters only to be doused again. He swore and turned to look at the girl.

He felt as if the water that cloaked him had turned to steam, and he thanked God for the sturdy material of his chausses, for she was a wonder to behold. The furs had fallen from her shoulders, and she had stretched her hands before her, seeking warmth. The soft gauze of her chemise had dried quickly, and it stood apart from her body now. Against the firelight, her soft form was outlined as clearly as if she sat before him naked. Raw hunger swept savagely into his soul as he stared at her; he recalled both the anger and the longing she had evoked in him not twenty-four hours ago. Her breasts were high, the nipples full and hard and rosy, as ripe as summer's first fruit, as sweetly tempting. He had held that sweet weight in his hands, and now he itched to touch her again, and he wished fervently that he had given no heed to her welfare, but had kept her well clad. He knew of no woman so perfectly chiseled and formed by her maker as to arouse the ardor of a man.

He had never thought that the mere touch of a maid could so bewitch him, as it had when he touched her. His fingers had seemed to sizzle from that contact, and holding her last night, he had nearly lost control. He smiled at himself, briefly, ruefully. He knew the lass. He knew her pride, and he knew her claws; she was glorious, beautiful trouble. He did not fear for his heart, for it had been shattered and it could never be repaired. He did fear for his soul and good sense, for there was a quality about Fallon that laid hold of his fantasy and his dreams. A man could easily die for wanting her.

He opened the shutters again in a sudden fury and let in the cold rain. Then he slammed the shutters closed again and swore. If only he had not touched her last night . . .

She stared at him as the shutters slammed. Nervously,

she pulled the blanket about her shoulders. "What is this place?" she asked him.

"A hunting lodge," he told her irritably. "And we'd not be stranded here in the storm if you had not run off like a wayward child."

That charge brought her to her feet. Fine, he thought. He had never felt more tense and ready for battle.

"I did nothing of the kind!"

"You have always been a spoiled brat, Fallon." He smiled at her with exaggerated politeness. "Always."

"And you have always been a barbaric bastard!"

"And you, milady, deal in the seduction of soft-bearded boys. You hate me because I have never fallen for your false smile or soft-spoken lies."

"Lies!" Fists clenched at her sides, she faced him. "You speak nothing but lies!" Tears stung her eyes, and he was suddenly sorry for this petty battle he had begun. "You and your kind are the masters of deceit and lies! How dare you, Alaric!" Her voice trembled with emotion. "How dare you!"

It came to him then as a whisper, and in that moment he saw not the pride that was her strength, but the vulnerability within her, and the tender ardor of youth.

"Lies!" she spat again. "Your good courageous Duke William spent last evening coercing promises from my father—"

"Has it ever occurred to you, Fallon, that your father might find it easier to serve William than to undo all the calamities caused by Edward? Harold and William are of an age; they are both warriors. William is fierce; your father is wise. Together they could create a strong and just rule. And Edward promised the crown to William years ago."

"Edward would promise the crown to his pet hound if the whim struck him!" Fallon snapped.

Still they faced each other across the room, and still

Alaric felt as if he were afire. He did not know if he cared for her or despised her; if she was a shrew or a tender maid. He only knew that he desired her mightily. The wind raging around the cottage shrilled out a warning.

"William seeks to make fools of all," Fallon continued bitterly, her eyes falling from his, "speaking of a betrothal between my father and a child!"

Alaric reached into his saddle-bag for a skin of wine. "Ah, so that's the problem!" he declared at last. "A hint of marriage for Harold makes you realize that you are as much a bastard as I am or the duke himself. There is nothing wrong with your father's actions, by your own laws. It is your pride that is wounded."

She hurled herself across the room at him like a whirlwind, her nails raking across his naked chest before he realized her intent.

"Fallon!" In a roar he thundered out her name, dropping the skin of wine, seeking to subdue her. She had the strength of ten ordinary women, and in her blind anger, she was as ferocious as a cat. He swore as he evaded her nails, caught her shoulders, tossed her on the bed, and threw a leg over hers. She lay beneath him panting, her eyes still flashing her venom. "Hold, Fallon," he warned her. "You cannot best me."

She tried to rise, and her chemise fell from her shoulder, baring much of the swell of her breast. "You best yourself, you braying jack—" she began, but then she realized her circumstances. His knee lay against her bare leg; he was atop her again, his face so near she felt the warmth of his breath, their bodies fused in the heat of struggle.

He was silent, too. Whatever realization had come to her, he had known tenfold. He stared at her, his eyes as dark and tempest-laden as the sky. All of him was taut, like living, breathing steel.

He released her wrists, but she stayed motionless, staring into his eyes. Sweet warmth infused her, and she could not move. Nay, she could not move when he kissed her again, his mouth near brutal when it descended upon hers, boldly sweeping into her being. She tried to twist her head, but his fingers were entangled in her hair and held her still. She felt his leg moving against her naked flesh, and the heat inside her seemed to spark and flare anew. Then she gasped, parting her lips more fully to his, as she felt his hand on her breast, caressing the naked flesh, his palm rough and almost painfully exciting against the softness of virgin flesh and the dusky rose peak. Sensations surged through her, rocking her again and again. She lay there stunned, sweet honey seeping over her. Nor could she move when his lips strayed from hers in ragged passion to fall against the arch of her throat and downward, his mouth now encircling her breast, his tongue sweeping against it, bringing a startled, anguished cry to her lips.

Then, as suddenly as he had touched her, he released her. He nearly shoved her from him, covering her shoulder with the fallen chemise. His passion had become anger again, sweeping around both in massive burning waves.

She bolted to her feet, shaking. She found her bleaunt and donned it swiftly, swearing as she did so, yet she barely knew what words she spoke herself, or if she railed against him in English or in French.

"I should have stabbed you," Fallon told him, her voice soft and honeyed once again, "and I should have taken careful aim!"

He laughed. Fallon grabbed a rusty old tankard and threw it his way. Alaric ducked, and then some new emotion played havoc with his senses, and the bitterness fell away from him like a cloak. He came to her and even as she watched him warily, he lifted her hand to his lips.

"Let's call a truce, milady. I believe the rain slackens. We must ride back."

His gray eyes, warm and filled with humor, looked into hers. "Aye, a truce," she whispered, "for now!"

And it remained so, for he returned her to her father, and very soon, she returned home.

Chapter Ten

Autumn had come with exceptional beauty in 1065, Fallon reflected as she watched the laborers on Thorney Island working to complete the king's new abbey, known as the West Minster, that it might be distinguished from Saint Paul's. Dazzling sunshine fell over her where she lay upon her mantle on the soft grass, and she had seldom felt so sweetly at peace. The king was in the west on his annual hunting trip; her uncle Tostig was with him. Her father worked here.

"It will be a beautiful piece of work, will it not?"

Fallon turned to smile at Delon, who lay beside her. He was a handsome man, with rich red-gold hair and a thick beard to match. His eyes were blue and gentle, and they sparkled as they watched her now.

Fallon stretched and nodded, closing her eyes. Delon leaned over her and pressed a light kiss against her lips. Her eyes opened and she gazed at him affectionately, lifting a hand to smooth his beard.

"Take heed, sir; my father sits in yon chamber," she said, inclining her head toward the palace.

He smiled and caught her hand, pressing his lips tenderly against her palm, then surveying her once again. "And a bower of beech and chestnut surround us here, and your father has discreetly turned his head time and again that I might kiss you. In fact, love, I think your father wonders at my patience, since he procrastinates in granting me your hand, and you do nothing to press my suit—loving me one day, spurning me the next."

"I never spurned you!" Fallon protested, laughing at his dramatics. "And I love you daily," she added, her laughter fading. He kissed her, not so lightly this time, and she slipped her arms around his neck and pressed her lips to his. She did love Delon. He was descended from the Danish kings and old English aristocrats; he was handsome, young, and eager; he loved her with a great tenderness. He accepted her pride and her ways and her temper, all with a gentleness that endeared him to her greatly. He was thane of a multitude of shires, he had traveled and read extensively, and best of all, to Fallon's mind, he was English. Her father approved of him, she knew. But as Harold hesitated, so did she. She cared for Delon greatly; no man was kinder or easier to please, and she enjoyed his company greatly. She cared for him; aye, she even loved him, treasured him dearly . . .

It was just that she wanted more. She didn't understand her feelings herself; they confused and dismayed her, for he was so very fine a man. But when he kissed her, she did not feel as if the sun had opened up inside her, as if she were ablaze within.

As she had felt in the arms of the Norman knight.

Fallon broke away from Delon, rolling to her side in sudden shame and horror, feeling her cheeks burn. She smelled the rich, verdant earth and felt the autumn breeze caress her, and still she shuddered, pressing her cheeks tight with her palms. Dismay filled her, and she wondered what manner of woman she could be to spurn a gentle lover's kiss and recall the touch of a sworn enemy.

"Fallon?" Delon murmured, concerned. "Have I hurt you, love?" His fingers, long and slender, touched her hair. She spun back to him, sweeping her arms around him and pressing her mouth to his in a wild embrace. She ran her palms recklessly over his chest and pressed as close to him as she could, holding fast as she kissed him. Still no passion arose, yet she swore to herself in that moment that she would marry him, and that the hunger would come, and if it did not, she would nonetheless cherish him all the days of their lives.

She took her lips from his, rubbing her cheek against his beard, then lying back against his arm. A new blue fire touched his eyes as he gazed upon her with something of awe, and he groaned softly and pulled her against him. "Fallon . . ." he whispered her name again, then touched her cheek. "God has cursed me to love you!" He told her. "I marvel at the purity of your beauty. I lie awake in endless torture while I await your word."

"You—you have my word, Delon," Fallon promised him.

"What?"

"You have my word!"

"You'll marry me?"

"Aye."

"When?"

Fallon laughed. "As soon as possible. As soon as father says we may."

Delon rose, caught her arms, and pulled her to her feet. He laughed and lifted her high into the air, then spun with her in joyous circles. She fell against his chest as he lowered her to the ground and stared down at her with tenderness and adoration. "Most cursed of men, most blessed of men; Fallon, no man should know such happiness as I feel this day."

A shudder ripped through Fallon, and a fierce chill tore along her spine, a feeling of foreboding.

"Fallon! You're shivering."

"Nay, nay!" She forced herself to smile radiantly, to lay her head against his chest again and feel the beat of his heart. She gave herself a mental shake and vowed to banish any ridiculous thoughts of evil to come. What evil could there be? England was at peace, and the country prospered. Her countrymen admired her father for his even temperament and his justice, and Harold ruled the English well. There was nothing to fear.

"Fallon—" Delon began again, but broke off suddenly. A host of horsemen had just come from a barge and now descended upon the king's residence with grim speed.

"What has happened?" Fallon cried.

Delon caught her hand and pulled her along. "Come, love, we must find out!"

They ran across the garden and marsh to the palace and were breathless when they came upon Harold, seated behind his desk while the king's messengers spoke. Harold appeared ill, and Fallon gave no thought to propriety but came around to his side and fell to her knees by his chair. Absently he took her hand and patted it. His brooding eyes fell upon hers, and he tried to smile, then returned his attention to the king's messenger.

"My brother Tostig is still with King Edward?"

"Aye, Earl Harold. The king and your brother ride to return here now, but King Edward would have you seek out these rebels immediately and negotiate a settlement."

Harold sighed bitterly, and it seemed that he spoke more to himself than to anyone else there present. "And what if the rebels' claims are true? What if Tostig *has* defiled their churches, stolen and plundered from them, and governed them ill?"

"Rebels have invaded his capital of York," the messenger said. "They have killed Tostig's retainers and stolen from his armory, and they threaten to ride south. They demand that the king remove Tostig and set Morkere, the brother of the earl of Mercia, in his place. King Edward demands that you ride north now and bring this to a settlement."

Harold nodded. "Aye, I will ride north now." His eyes fell upon Delon, who commanded a force of guards for him. He nodded a command, and Delon threw a miserable glance at Fallon before turning about to attend to his duty.

Harold rose and spoke to the messenger. "You may tell the king when he arrives that I have gone to meet with the rebels and that I will do all in my power to bring about a peaceful settlement."

The chill that already seized her swept across Fallon's spine once again. It seemed as if an ill wind had been set in motion and that no hand could stop it. Her father and Delon rode out that day.

There was to be no settlement. The thanes gave Harold evidence that his brother Tostig had taxed them unjustly, twisted the law, and murdered his enemies. They would not have him back, and they demanded that King Edward give them a new earl, Morkere, or else they would ride south to wage war against the king himself.

It was a horrible time for her father, Fallon knew. Tostig claimed that Harold had stirred up the trouble himself out of jealousy. Harold wearily denied the charges, but the king ranted and raved. Edward tried to summon his army, but the men refused to assemble. Meanwhile, the rebels in the north marched south to Oxford.

Fallon spent many hours at her father's side while her father grieved. It hurt him terribly to see his brother so despised, for their father had tried to teach them family loyalty.

But Harold's father had also taught him to respect English law and Englishmen. The English had been ruled by consent; they would fight against autocracy now.

Fallon did her best to soothe her father. She tried to

love her uncle and reason with the king, who still softened in her presence.

Harold prayed, and discovered in his own soul that he had to support the people against his brother. And in the end, King Edward had to relent, and give the people of Northumbria the earl they demanded, young Morkere. Tostig, exiled by Edward, swore to be Harold's enemy.

As November passed and December came, the great sadness that had encompassed them all at Tostig's exile abated somewhat. Fallon and Delon decided to speak with her father on Christmas Day.

Winter came, bleak and hostile, to Thorney Island. Edward took joy in the near completion of the abbey, which had been his life's work. Year after year, he had supervised its building.

As Christmas neared, the sky remained gray, the marshes brown, and the air cold. The palace grew crowded, near bursting at the seams, for eight of England's archbishops had arrived with their retinues for the consecration of the new abbey. High officials and thanes and the other earls arrived for the convening of the witan, which always met at Christmas wherever the king chose to be.

Christmas Day arrived. Fallon's mother and brothers remained in the south, at Bosham, since Harold had sent word about the crowded conditions on Thorney Island. Before mass began, Harold came to Fallon. His gift to her was an enormous emerald brooch for her mantle; her gift to him was a new crimson mantle of soft wool lined with mink. They embraced, and Harold touched her cheek and smiled. "Whatever befalls me," he told her, "I have been blessed. Your mother has loved me selflessly all these years, and she has given me you and your brothers."

Fallon hugged him fiercely. She thought guiltily of all

the mischief she had caused over the years. "I love you, Father," she replied.

He laughed and stood back, surveying her in her Christmas finery with an assessive eye. "Young Delon has said that the two of you will speak with me this evening."

She lowered her eyes. "Aye, Father."

"Is it what you want?"

"You approve of him?" she asked anxiously. "Do you, Father? Do you find him to be a just and fitting man?"

He laughed, and assured her that he found many fine qualities in Delon. "I admit, Fallon, that I've thought of marriages of greater advantage, yet I am too besotted by you to send you away, but would have you by my side. There is but one other I would have thought of for you," Harold said, and for a moment his eyes seemed to be far away. "One even stronger than you. My only fear is that you will overpower gentle Delon at every turn."

"Father—"

"Nay, give it no mind. He is kind and courteous, and his courage and honor are not to be questioned. He will speak tonight, but I will ask you both one thing. You have known each other long and well, but still I ask you to wait one more year. At Christmas next, you will wed. Agreed?"

She nodded and kissed him again. A year seemed fine to her; Delon might not find great pleasure in the idea, but he loved her, and he would wait.

Despite the brooding weather, it was a joyful day. There were so very many people about. Edward was well, reigning over mass and the banquet to follow in all his regalia. It was a day of sweet and gentle spirit, and when the feasting was over, Delon and Fallon came before Harold, and when he had given them his blessing to wed, they knelt before the king, who also gave his blessing.

But by the next morning everything had changed. Edward had been taken ill and was unable to attend the consecration of the church that had been his life's work. At first there was hope that the king would recover. But as the days slipped by that hope waned. Finally Edward's physicians came forward to tell the most powerful men of the kingdom in hushed tones that the king was dying.

A pall fell over that drear winter season. At times, Fallon sat with the king; her aunt, his wife, hovered ever near him. The witan met, and they argued in confusion over who would be king.

Harold spent his time between the king's bedside and conferences with the rulers of the land. For hours they spoke in earnest tones. Edgar Atheling had been summoned, since he was heir to the throne, but he was still just a boy; the country needed someone stronger. Edward had not spoken, and so they didn't know his will. The Scandinavian kings had some claim to the throne, but they were foreigners. There were the Godwins, Harold himself and the exiled Tostig. And there was William of Normandy—a foreigner, and a foreigner more hated by some than the Scandinavians.

Fallon and her father sat silently at Edward's side on the last day of 1065. The king's wife sat at his feet; Robert FitzWimark—half Norman, half Breton, a good friend to the king—sat at his other side with his wife. Harold asked his sister if there had been any change, and the queen answered with a softly whispered no.

Harold turned to leave, and Fallon rose to follow him. He leaned wearily against the wall outside the sickroom and took her hands. "I have tried," he told her. "As I said, I believe Edward made some promise to William of Normandy years ago. I have stated William's case as clearly and as loyally as I might, but Englishmen reject him with a fury. If only the king would speak!"

Fallon tenderly squeezed his hands. "Father, you were coerced into giving the Norman a promise! He would have held us prisoner still, as he holds your brother Wulf-noth. Father, you owe that man no loyalty!"

"Mayhap the king will speak," Harold murmured. "How much easier it will be to choose if he could but speak his will!"

The king did not speak. In the first few days of January, he tossed in delirium, but his mind remained deep in sleep. On the fourth day he was restless, and it was decided that he must be roused.

Fallon was behind her aunt when Edward was at last brought to consciousness. At first he seemed weak and lost, but then he smiled and his voice grew strong. He looked at the assembled earls and thanes and priests and loved ones, and he spoke in a strong voice. "I have dreamt, my friends. Dreamt of two fine monks I knew long ago in Normandy and who have lain dead these many years. We walked together, these monks and I."

The king's face was marked by a ghastly gray pallor. The men looked at one another; they wanted him to name an heir, but he spoke of dreams. Yet none could interrupt him. Fallon felt an uneasy chill; they were all caught in an eerie tableau, inside a castle cloaked in winter's mist.

"For our wickedness, God has cursed our country," Edward went on. "A year and a day from my death, demons and devils will come to the land. They will purge it with fire, and there will be fear and terror and lamenting. Our good Lord will cease to haunt this land with fire and the sword and bloodshed only when a green tree, split asunder, will join together of its own accord and bear fruit and leaves and new life."

The archbishop of Canterbury murmured that the king was raving. No one else whispered a word, for the king was known for his gift of prophecy.

"Do not mourn for me!" the king's voice boomed out again, and Fallon suddenly felt tears spring to her eyes, for despite all his strange ways and tempers and beliefs, Edward had always been kind to her. "Pray for my soul; I go to God. The king who died for us will not allow me to die forever; I go into eternal life."

The queen let out a sob and reached for Edward, who took her hand. "May God reward you for your gentle service. Always you have been a devoted helpmate to me." Then Edward took Harold's hand and placed the queen's hand in it.

"I charge you to look after the queen," he told Harold. "Deprive her of none of the honors I have bestowed upon her. I commend this woman and my kingdom into your keeping. Honor her as my queen and as your sister. Summon the foreigners of my court; have them swear a new oath of fealty, or see them safely to their borders, according to their choice. See that my earthly remains are placed in the new church with all the proper rites, and do not hide the fact of my death, but spread the news quickly to all men, so that they may pray for me, a sinner."

Edward smiled weakly and fell back against the pillows, deep in a coma again.

Silence reigned in the room, and all men looked to Harold. Then the priest moved forward and gave the last rites to the king.

Fallon wondered desperately what it had all meant. Had Edward meant to name her father heir when he urged him to care for the country? Or had he meant only that Harold should continue in faithful service to the Crown?

Fallon didn't know. Numbly, she remained at the king's side, holding her aunt's hand. Men slowly left the chamber, and Fallon knew that all of Thorney Island would soon ring with the king's words—words spoken to her father, words warning that England was about to be cursed.

Fallon began to shiver. A mantle was placed about her

shoulders, and she looked up to see her father standing behind her.

"The king is dead," a priest announced. The queen began to sob anew. Harold and Fallon left the king's chamber together.

They had barely reached the hall before Wulfstan of Worcester barred Harold's way. "Earl Harold, we must convene the witenagemot."

Fallon watched as her father was led away. The hall was deserted, and she leaned against the cold stone wall. She didn't know how long she stood there, but soon she heard shouts, and she knew that the witan had named her father king.

She didn't see him again until he came to her bedchamber late that night. She heard the tap on her door and, knowing that it was Harold, she flew to the door to bid him enter. He came in and hugged her fiercely.

"Edward will be buried in his abbey in the morning." He hesitated. "And I will be anointed king in the afternoon."

She stood back, seeking from his eyes or his tone to know if he was glad or dismayed. She could not tell.

"What think you?" he asked her carefully.

She shook her head. "No man, Father, is more capable of a just and careful rule. You will be challenged from near and far. But if you are pleased, then I am joyous; and if you are sad, I pray I may be a strength to help you."

He hugged her again, then stepped away from her. "I had never thought to be king, but, Fallon, by God, the witan has chosen me, and in the witan lie the law and the power of England. I cannot refuse to rule. I am neither proud nor humble, but I, too, believe no other man is more capable of ruling this country." He gazed at Fallon, and she saw in his eyes that he was glad of the faith given him by his peers. She cried out and ran to him, and he swung her about in his arms.

"It is late," he murmured, setting her on her feet. "And in the morning, we must pray for Edward, as was his wish. Good night." He kissed her forehead and left her.

Later, in her chamber, Fallon lay awake and thought about Edward's dying words, and she began to shiver again. What had the king meant when he talked of his dream? She remembered the strength of Edward's voice when he spoke of the two Norman monks—and when he prophesied that England would be cursed, that fire would rage over the land.

The next morning, Fallon sat in the new abbey beside her aunt and comforted her during the requiem mass. And in the afternoon, she attended the ancient ceremony in which her father was anointed king. It was sacred, and it was solemn. When the archbishop asked the people if they accepted Harold as their king, they shouted their approval: *"Vivat!"* Then Harold swore an oath to his people—a promise of peace, justice, and mercy.

Delon stood next to Fallon and squeezed her hand as the archbishop anointed her father's head, shoulders, and hands with oil. Prayers continued—that Harold would defend the people and the church, and ever battle the Infidel. He was invested with the symbols of power—the ring of unity, the sword of protection, the crown of glory and justice, and the scepter of virtue. The benediction was given, and voices rose in song. And when it was over, Harold was king, bound to his people, as his people were to him.

Later, over a subdued meal, Fallon was able to speak to her father alone.

"Father, it is done. You are king of England!" she kissed him, and noticed that his smile was weak. "What is wrong? Are you ill?" She asked him anxiously.

"Nay, nay." He shook his head. He sighed and lowered his voice. "Nay, I am king, and I am glad; I'll never deny it. But while I stood in the church today, I remembered that I gave an oath to stand for William, and now that oath plagues me."

"But, Father, you *did* stand for him! The witan rejected him!"

He shook his head. "William, I am afraid, will not understand our law."

"You were coerced into pledging your loyalty to him," Fallon said bitterly. "You kept your word."

Harold sighed. "Aye, that is the comfort I keep in my heart. A man's oath is sacred, and I have kept my word, whether William can see that or not. Still . . ."

"Still?"

"There is grave danger ahead. Now that I wear this crown, I must fight to keep it.

Cold fear coursed through her, and she lowered her head, biting her lip so that her father would not see her shiver. Fire would sweep through the land, Edward had said . . . but those were the ravings of a dying man, she assured herself.

Yet she sensed already that her father's prediction would come true—he would have to fight to maintain his rule; he might have to fight for his very life.

Fallon crossed herself quickly. "God be with us!" She murmured, and her father softly echoed her words.

Not far from Rouen, Alaric was testing the strength of his bow. Nearby, William was stringing his own bow. Snow covered the ground, but the party prepared to hunt in good spirits.

A scurry of sound came from the road. Alaric turned and saw that a messenger hurried toward them. William stepped forward, and the messenger dismounted swiftly and fell to his knees before the duke. His voice was soft and muted, but his words carried.

"King Edward is dead. Earl Harold is crowned king, anointed the very day of the funeral."

"What?" William's voice was thick with disbelief. He flung his bow aside and leapt atop his steed to race across the snow toward his palace.

Alaric hurriedly stopped the messenger. Edward's death was not unexpected; they had heard of his illness weeks ago. But Alaric knew that William had expected to be invited to England when Edward died. Nothing in his mind had readied him for the shocking news of Harold's coronation.

Much was at stake here. William had made no secret of his belief that he would be king of England. Not only was his dream hereby crushed, but his pride was shattered, too. And his pride was great.

"Tell me again, boy," Alaric commanded the messenger. "Edward died, and Harold was made king?"

"Aye, anointed at the new West Minster, even as the flooring dried over the old king's burial spot near the altar. Aldred, archbishop of York, performed the ceremony."

"And the witan?"

"They say Harold was the witan's choice ere Edward spoke, and that Edward gave them some final word, if not the clear determination they so craved."

"You know this is true?"

"Word came by an English ship, Count Alaric."

"Thank you, boy." Alaric gave the lad a coin, then quickly mounted and rode after William. He found him in the hall of the palace, his head pressed against a pillar, his face white, his eyes cold and bleak. William FitzOsbern, a trusted man, stood before him; Alaric threw FitzOsbern a glance of inquiry.

"I have advised His Grace," FitzOsbern said, "that there is no use trying to hide the news; they speak of it already all over the city. There is no time to regret what has happened; the duke must act."

Alaric nodded to FitzOsbern.

William suddenly swore. "The crown was promised to me! And Harold swore his fealty!"

Alaric shrugged, risking William's temper with his honesty. "Harold was a prisoner here—"

"A guest."

"A prisoner, William, when he swore that oath. And his country is not a private domain, like Normandy. He had no power to swear he would make you king. Not even Edward had that total power."

"England was to have been mine!" William snapped, his eyes narrowing. "What would you do, Alaric? Defend that usurper? Make me the laughingstock of Europe?"

"William, I have been your friend for eighteen years," Alaric said tightly, "and I have never deceived you with false flattery or lies."

William stared at him; he looked as if he might explode. He crushed his temples between his palms. "I will immediately send a protest to Harold."

Alaric hesitated. "Send a protest if you like. But it will do little good. Harold has been anointed king; he will fight to keep his crown."

William's jaw twisted. "I mean to be king of England." He gazed at Alaric sharply. "You know the English, my friend, and you know English law. You're even a bloody English thane, appointed by Edward. What must I do?"

Alaric shook his head unhappily and stared through the window slit to the beautiful clear sky. "Harold is no fool," he said. "For all practical purposes, he has ruled England for the last ten years. He is English, and the people want an English monarch. He keeps the peace as well as he wages war; his subjects will accept him, and the witan has already chosen him."

Alaric hesitated, gazing at William, feeling that the

white beauty of the winter day was a cruel irony. Bloodshed would soon be their lot. "If you want England,
William," he said, "you will have to take it by bloody
force."

William nodded grimly; he had been expecting that
answer. "Call together my most powerful supporters—
my brothers, the counts of Eu and Mortain and Avran-
ches. FitzOsbern, too, has advised me to act, and so we
begin now. If Harold wants war, it is war that he will
receive." He paused, watching Alaric. He placed his
hands on his friend's shoulders. "I know you are with me;
I know you will raise troops and command them in my
service. If we are fated to conquer, then we will conquer
together. I will gather my forces and write my formal
protest to Harold immediately." He paused, inhaling
deeply. "But, Alaric, I wish you to go to England at once
to carry my warning to Harold and to seek his surrender."

Alaric held still, fully aware that Harold would not
surrender. Then he sighed. "Aye, William, if you wish it,
I will go."

It was a fool's errand, Alaric thought wearily, but he
would be glad to see Harold one last time as a friend
before meeting him on a battlefield made crimson by
rivers of blood.

As he turned to leave, his heartbeat quickened. He
would see Harold again, aye. And he would see Harold's
daughter, proud Fallon, who haunted his dreams and
teased his senses even as he tarried with other, gentler
women.

Fallon . . .

PART TWO

The Warriors

Chapter Eleven

"Never betray weakness, never leave open a place of vulnerability!" Fabioni, the sword master, warned Fallon.

She nodded beneath the visor of her helmet. The tip of her tutor's broadsword swept before her, and she gracefully danced back, meeting the steel of his sword with her own.

"Bravo!" Fabioni applauded. He was a small man with dark curly hair and bright eyes. "You have the speed of the cat, my lady, and the eye of the eagle." He bowed to her with great ceremony. "A few minutes' rest, and we will begin again."

Fallon nodded again, discovering that she had little breath left with which to speak. She sank down on a bench in the garden where they practiced and watched Fabioni fall upon a bench himself. She had seen him best many a stronger and heavier man with his agility, and because of that, she respected him highly. Harold had tried to dissuade her from continuing these lessons, but she had steadfastly reminded him that she needed to be adept at defending herself.

Despite the fact that both the northern earls, Edwin and Morkere, had been in London and joined in the witenagemot in proclaiming Harold king, the thanes of the north country felt that they had not been properly consulted on the matter. Harold had immediately ridden to York, not with a show of arms, but with his daughter, the saintly Bishop Wulstan, and a number of his other followers. King Edward had never traveled to York, and the people had been therefore doubly pleased by this visit by Harold. There had been talk that Harold might even marry the sister of Edwin and Morkere, and such an arrangement might well come to pass, Fallon knew, because her father needed an alliance with the northern earls. But Harold's party had long ago returned home and as yet there had been no wedding. Fallon now waited with her father on Thorney Island for the Easter mass and the meeting of the witan that was to follow.

England was decidedly behind Harold, she knew. But the country was surrounded by hostile forces. A protest from William of Normandy had arrived not two weeks after her father's coronation. Svein Ulfson of Denmark— her father's cousin and a great-nephew of King Knut— could well decide to claim the English crown. And Harald Hardrada, the berserker king of Norway, was ever ready to seek warfare. Fallon knew that her father worried about his brother Tostig, too. It was rumored that he had appeared in various courts, seeking assistance to wage battle to earn back his earldom. "Sometimes," Harold had murmured to Fallon, "I fear that Tostig has lost his senses. He does not think or reason; he seeks only revenge."

For Harold, Tostig presented perhaps the greatest dilemma of all. He could not reinstate his brother, for the northern thanes would not accept him. Gytha, Godwin's widow, remained in London, where she bemoaned the fate of two of her sons—Tostig in exile, and Wulfnoth a prisoner in Normandy.

From the beginning, Harold had planned for warfare. His housecarls were the mainstay of the army, the true fighting men, the warriors of England. They had fought in Wales with his father, and they were nearly as fierce as their Viking ancestors, adept with double-headed axes and the great maces they often carried into battle. They were just a part of the army, though, and sadly, the fryd—the thanes of England and their men—owed the king only so much service a year, and they had not seen warfare in fifty years.

A tall blond figure came around a yew tree, and Fallon leapt to her feet with pleasure. "Delon!" Fallon called to her betrothed. She had barely seen him since her father became king. He had been sent to scour the countryside, to warn the people that danger lurked at their doorsteps, and to summon the fryd, the fighting force drawn from the people and called upon for the defense of the land.

He walked to meet her, arching a brow at her apparel. She was decked in the leather armor most popular with the English. Her broadsword, especially fashioned for her, was far lighter than most, and easy for her to wield.

"What's this?" Delon teased her. "You would best us all, and put us to shame?"

Fallon kissed him lightly, then stood back, her eyes alight in a challenge as she slid her visor up. "You would make fun of me, sir?" She brought the tip of her sword against his short tunic. "Arm yourself, milord!"

He bowed, accepting the challenge. "Milady!" With a smile, Delon turned to Fabioni. "Your sword, sir!"

Thus armed, Delon thought to make quick play of it. Fallon laughed with pleasure as steel clashed against steel and her betrothed quickly learned the folly of his words. Never betray weakness; never show vulnerability! Fabioni's words stayed with Fallon as she deftly moved among the daisies and asters and roses. Delon flashed her a smile as she parried one of his thrusts, then laughed sweetly as she saw sweat beading on his brow.

"Beg mercy?" she taunted him, her smile softening the words.

"Nay, not yet," he assured her. "Would you have me be the laughingstock of your father's entire army?"

She smiled again, because his eyes were the color of the spring sky and she had really missed him. "There's none here but Fabioni and myself, milord. And we'll not tell if you cry for mercy!" She panted slightly, and her words came between each thrust and parry. Delon was strong, and he was practiced in his craft. Eventually, she knew, that strength would tell against her. Fabioni had warned her from the beginning that a woman or a small man could best a warrior only by speed and cunning.

"I cannot cry defeat—" Delon began, but she saw him pause, and she took a deadly advantage of that pause, stepping in and catching his blade with her own, so that it doubled against his wrist and went flying. He stared at his sword, and then at her, in disbelief.

"I shall have to demand a rematch," he told her.

"Aye, sir! I shall have to take you on again, and any other foolish man who doubts the prowess of the king's daughter."

"Hmmph!" Delon said, eyeing her in consternation. Fallon laughed, caught his hands, and kissed him again. "I am exhausted," he said, "from living in the saddle these months."

"Oh, aye!" Fallon told him, her eyes wide and innocent. "Surely that is the only reason I could catch you off guard."

"Now you mock your betrothed."

She smiled, for she was proud of herself, and excitement raced through her. "Delon, could I doubt your true power? I have taken unfair advantage!"

"That's better," he said, but he grinned, too, and hugged her against his chest. She touched his bearded face. "Delon! Truly, I'm glad to see you."

His eyes fell upon her face and he stroked her hair. "And I missed you as a blind man misses the sight of the earth and sky." Reluctantly he released her. "I must see your father immediately. Will you await me at dinner?"

She nodded. He kissed the tip of her nose and parted from her reluctantly. Fallon turned to dismiss Fabioni. He raised his sword and saluted her, ending the lesson. Fallon reflected with a broad smile that she was really very good with her sword.

Suddenly, from behind her, a deep masculine voice rang out in a mocking challenge. "The king's daughter battles against green lads, just as she seeks to seduce them. *Mademoiselle,* dare you take your blade against a man full grown?"

Fallon spun about, shivers cascading along her spine. It could not be him!

Alaric stood before her, his blood-red mantle tossed over his shoulder, his feet spread wide, the tip of his sword touching the earth before him. The breeze lifted his mantle and the lock of dark hair that played over his forehead. Steel-gray eyes sent her a vibrant dare, and she knew she had to meet his challenge.

"What is this?" she demanded scoffingly. "A fool Norman upon Saxon soil? Why, I have never doubted your recklessness or that of your bastard duke, but surely you have not come to take the country for him by yourself, *monsieur!*"

"Would you defend it yourself, *mademoiselle?*" He circled her warily.

Fallon noticed how silently he moved and took care to follow his every motion. "Aye," she murmured softly, raising her eyes to his as he paused just a few feet from her. "If it comes to it, milord, I'll gladly defend my king and country on my own against all and any who seek to assault them."

He arched a taunting brow as she raised her sword in readiness. "I've come in peace," he murmured.

"No Norman has ever come here in peace," she retorted.

He smiled, and raised his weapon. His very confidence caused her to quiver, but she silently swore that she would not fail. She had bested Delon, had she not? But Delon was a young man of twenty, while Alaric had now passed at least thirty summers, and grown harder and more assured in his Norman craft of war with every one of them.

Steel clashed, and she felt the reverberation of the blow down the length of her arm. She drew back and parried when he thrust lower. Again she parried, as his blade rose near her throat.

She was backing away from him, she realized. He gave no pause and no mercy. Ruthlessly his blows fell, again and again, and so quickly that she could not imagine how he raised his heavy blade with such speed.

"Will you surrender, *mademoiselle?*" A taunting smile played on his lips.

"Nay, never. 'Twould do us all a great ill were the Saxon king's daughter to yield to a Norman. Never, sir!"

"Oh?" The query was soft, and she jerked back with a cry, amazed, as his blade cut cleanly and swiftly through her leather armor, slicing open the chemise she wore beneath without leaving a scratch on her flesh.

Fallon gasped and instinctively clutched at the gaping edges of her chemise. She swore then and lunged at him too quickly. Their swords locked, and she came face to face against him and felt the warmth of his breath fanning her cheek when he spoke.

"Anger is deadly, milady. You should not lose your temper."

"You should play fair."

"In battle, Fallon, men fight to kill. What is fair in that?"

She pushed away from him, one hand clasped to her

breast, the other gripping her sword. To meet his next
thrust, she was forced to relinquish her hold on her torn
clothing. She met his thrust, but was embarrassed to
realize that he was enjoying the view she now offered him.
And still he was ruthless. He raised his sword again; she
parried. Again, and again, and again.

She was breathless, and she knew she could not fight
much longer. She bit her lip, then gazed past his shoulder,
her eyes fixed on empty space. "Father, no!" she called
out, feigning alarm. "He does not seek to harm me; it is
but play—"

As she had hoped, Alaric swung to counter what blow
might come his way. He quickly realized that no one was
there, but by then, Fallon was able to dart to one side and
bring her sword against his throat.

Pained, wary, he beheld her. She smiled sweetly.

"*Mademoiselle,* you spoke of fair play?"

"There is no fair play in battle, *monsieur!*" she reminded
him, innocently sweeping her lashes over her eyes and
beholding him again. "Was that not the lesson you just
taught me?"

He nodded, then winced as her sword pricked his flesh.
His eyes narrowed upon her; then he spun abruptly,
avoiding her blade and bringing his own up with such a
ferocious blow that hers was torn from her hands and flew
in an arch to the ground.

Fallon swore and lunged to retrieve it. Ere she could
reach the blade, he pounced on her and together they
went rolling across the soft, verdant earth. Fallon grasped
for her sword, but he braced himself over her. Her sword
lay just inches away, but even as she strove desperately to
reach it, he hovered comfortably above her, his weight on
his elbows, the sinewed strength of his legs preventing her
from movement.

She looked at him in annoyance and encountered his
leisurely grin. Swearing roundly, she attempted to twist

away from him. When she gazed at him again, she saw that he smiled no more. His features were harsh, nearly savage as he stared down at her. He rose, catching her hands even when she attempted to evade them, and tugged her to her feet. "Go inside," he commanded her crossly. "Dress yourself."

Startled, she glanced down. Her chemise was further rent, her breasts all but bared. Color seeped into her cheeks as she recalled their last meeting. She remembered his touch. She remembered his rough, calloused palm and the strength of his hands and the heat that had ravaged her blood and her limbs . . .

"Oh!" She cried out, stepping back from him. She raised a hand to strike him, and bit her lip as her palm found its mark. He could have stopped her, she thought; fear took root in her heart as she stared at the merciless slate of his eyes.

Instead, he bowed low to her. "A pleasure, as always, Princess," he murmured.

He turned and left her, striding quickly away. Fallon watched him, and lowered her head, praying fervently that the wretched fever he awoke in her would subside. She hated him so much that she trembled with it. She longed to best him as she longed for little else in life.

"Norman bastard!" she muttered. He had no right to be here, so calm and so assured. His duke longed for bloodshed and war.

She trembled even as she speculated about his purpose in her father's court. And later that evening, after she had bathed and dressed for supper, she discovered that the fever had not left her. She prayed wretchedly that God would pick him up in a tempest and hurl him back across the Channel.

God, unfortunately, chose instead to deposit Alaric at her side for the evening meal. Delon was far down the table, but Fallon could feel his eyes upon her. Alaric and

Harold spoke to each other in tones of sadness. They understood each other; they weighed their words, and they were cordial, but they could not change their circumstances.

"Alaric," Harold said, breaking off a piece of bread. "You know that I did not seize the crown. Edward spoke, the witan voted, and I was named king. I did not seek to overthrow any man. But I am king by English law, and by English law I will remain so."

Fallon glanced at Alaric. His head was bowed; he had known what he would hear. "William has asked if you intend to keep your promise to wed his daughter."

Fallon gasped aloud. Her father frowned at her severely, and Alaric turned to her, his brow arched at the interruption. Fallon stiffened and reached for the chalice that stood between them. His fingers closed around it at the same time. They stared at each other as Harold unhappily answered Alaric.

"You know, and William knows, that the marriage talk was just play, a meaningless compliment to a pretty and well-mannered child. Still, as an earl, I would gladly have married into William's house. But an English king can take no foreign queen without the consent of the witan. Nor can I keep old promises concerning my children. My life is no longer my own."

Stunned, Fallon stared at her father. He looked at her briefly, then lowered his eyes. Alaric's gaze remained on Fallon. He stared at her for a long moment before turning back to Harold. "Aye, Harold, I know your position full well. And I understand William, too."

"And you will serve him," Harold said.

"Aye."

Fallon grasped the chalice and drank down the ale. She looked unhappily across the hall again and saw Delon, his eyes full upon her, hurt and confused.

"Alas!" Alaric said. "The maid does have a heart. Tell

me—the young blond lad with the pretty whiskers you so soundly bested at arms—is this a lover lost?"

"Lost?"

"The stakes have changed, milady. They may call you a princess, but they will make you a pawn."

"You are mistaken," she said coolly. "I will not be a pawn."

"Ah, the lady will never bend." He raised the cup to her. "So you will have your way. But what of that young man who pines for you? How I pity him, milady!"

"Oh?"

"I pity any man who loves you, Fallon." He beckoned a servant to refill the chalice, then sipped and offered the cup to her. Her fingers trembled, and she feared to touch the chalice lest he notice. He took her hand, curled her fingers about it, and pressed the rim to her lips. "Aye, Fallon," he said softly. "I pity the fool who loves you, for you are a flame that burns too brightly, and an ice that chills the heart, a wildness in sore need of taming. That gentle lad is not for you. What you need, milady, is a man, not a boy. A man who cannot be deceived by your wiles."

She leaned back and gave him a curious smile. "And you consider yourself such a man?"

He did not answer right away, but his gaze raked her body in a bold manner that stole her breath away.

"Perhaps," he answered casually at long last. He stroked a finger down her cheek. "Were I so inclined. But as I've told you, I'm not of a mind to marry again."

A flame that burned too brightly? She wished she could sear his flesh like the blaze that rose with scorching flame in the center of the hall. "I would never—"

"I know. You would rather wed a thousand demons, or some such thing."

"And you, sir, show your distaste in the most curious ways."

He laughed, and for a moment, against the firelight

that filled the hall, she was keenly aware of his handsome features. "Fallon, I have never denied your beauty. To desire you is easy. To care for you would be folly."

He leaned so close that his whisper fell against her cheek. She shook her head, reaching for the chalice again, but he held it tightly. "Sir, I eagerly await your departure from this land, for Normandy or for hell!"

"And which is your preference?"

"I find them one and the same, *monsieur*," she said, and letting go of the chalice, she stood. Harold stared at her curiously. She dropped him a quick curtsy and, making no excuse, ran from the hall.

The next night a strange light was seen in the sky. As evening fell on Easter Sunday, she heard a commotion near the entrance to the church and, curious, hurried toward it. Alaric was there, listening to a priest as he pointed to the sky. There were whispers and murmurings, and Fallon became aware that the people saw the light as an omen of doom.

"It's in the Book of Revelation!" a woman screamed, falling to her knees. "Armageddon falls upon us! Our sainted king Edward has spoken, and fire and brimstone will fall upon us. Surely Godwin killed Alfred, and now his son sits upon the throne. God will punish us all for the wicked ways of our nobility."

"What nonsense!" Fallon cried out heatedly. She strode forward, not knowing what she would say, for the light in the sky frightened her, too. She had been there when King Edward had spoken, and she felt herself shivering now. Dear God, was there such a thing as destiny? Surely all of England could not be made to pay for one sin of the nobility? God could not be so callous.

"It is some action of the stars and the planets, nothing more!" Fallon cried. She spun about, lifting her skirts above the mud that filled the streets. She crossed to Father Damien who stood talking with Alaric.

Father Damien sometimes frightened Fallon more than any mystical words or blazes in the sky. He was a priest, aye; one who truly eschewed worldly ways. He was ascetic in all his habits and gentle in his manner. He was from Fens, a part of England where the old ways had died slowly, where Viking raiders had taken pagan wives. He answered to Christ, yet found no ill in the joyous celebration of the ancient holidays. He seemed ageless, with his dark hair and dark eyes. He had traveled all over the Continent and was knowledgeable in many things.

"Father Damien?" she murmured, hoping that he would speak.

He stayed silent a long time, and she could hear the beating of her own heart while the world seemed to hold still around them. Alaric's eyes were upon her, and he watched her with a certain respect for the courage with which she had spoken against the crowd.

"It is but a comet," Father Damien said slowly. "A special type of star with a tail. Men spoke of them when I was in Italy; they have been seen before, crossing the southern seas."

Fallon breathed a sigh of relief. The crowd before the cathedral dispersed. Fallon turned to follow Father Damien back into the church. Breathless, she caught up with him. "Father!"

He paused, turning to her. She hesitated, suddenly finding that she didn't know what to say.

"Father . . . thank you."

He bowed to her. His dark eyes surveyed her with an intensity that made her nervous. "There is such a thing as a comet," he said evasively.

"What do you mean?" she said sharply. "Father, you are a man of God! Surely you cannot believe in omens and curses, and—"

He shook his head. Fallon saw that he was looking beyond her. She turned to see that Alaric had come into the church behind her.

" 'Only when a green tree, split asunder, will join together of its own accord,' " Father Damien murmured.

Fallon spun back to him. He was staring at Alaric.

"What nonsense is this?" Alaric said.

The priest shook his head. "There are things older than time, Count Alaric," he murmured. "We are not meant to understand God's ways."

Fallon had the curious feeling that he was seeing something, some future, which neither she nor Alaric could begin to comprehend. Fallon was more frightened than she had ever been.

Father Damien kept looking at Alaric. Then he bowed again, determined to pass on into the nave. "Count Alaric, we will meet again."

"Now that, Father, is nonsense," Alaric said softly. "We both know I will not return. We both know—"

"That war will raze the land," Father Damien finished. Alaric looked at Fallon. "Count, I repeat, we will meet again."

Staring at Alaric, Fallon was dimly aware of the priest's footsteps echoing and fading as he departed. She went back outside. A new crowd was gathering to watch the light that rent the darkened sky.

"Doom!" someone screamed.

"Judgment Day is at hand!"

"Doom comes with the Normans, who will attack us for their own gain!" Fallon called out. She jumped up on a hay wagon in the road and spoke with passion. "There is no curse on England! God has given you a good king, a king who listens to all men, a king who judges men with a warm heart and an open mind. A king who loves the land and has served it these many years!"

Voices rose in agreement. Thus heartened, Fallon con-

tinued. "There is no curse on this land! The only curse we
might encounter is the scourge of war that others would
make upon us! The curse lies across the Channel, where
a savage bastard duke prepares to march against us. Good
people, it is foreign princes, not your duly anointed king,
who will bring us pain!"

"Normans!"

"Aye, the wretched Normans!"

Fallon realized then that Alaric had followed her; that
he stood before her now with a darkening face and eyes
that bored into hers with furious reproach. She swallowed, suddenly aware that the crowd was now ranging
round him. A missile flew past his head—a pebble tossed
by some goodwife. The crowd began to swarm.

"No!" she whispered. The crowd would kill him. There
were at least fifty men and women milling before the
church doors. They would swarm against him, they
would crush him, they would kill him. And she had in-
cited them to it.

"Nay, nay!" she cried, but her voice could no longer be
heard, for the people were shouting out their hatred of
the Normans. She tried desperately to press her way
through the crowd.

"Hold!"

Even above the din, Alaric's baritone voice could be
heard. He suddenly leapt onto a cart, holding the vicious
blade of his broadsword before him. "Peace be with you,
good folk. I am a guest of your anointed king. You may
well kill me, but ere I fall, I will take a goodly number of
you with me. Would you spill your blood so foolishly?"

There were grumblings in the crowd. Several men who
held sticks dropped them. The grumblings became mut-
terings, and one by one, the people began to turn away.

And then they were alone in the darkening night, with
the comet streaking across the ebony sky above them.

Fallon felt the pure and lethal fury in his eyes; it scalded her soul.

"Fallon, do you seek my death so passionately that you would watch the blood run here before this church? It will run soon enough, milady."

"Aye! Aye!" She cried, shaken. "You will come against us! 'Tis a pity they did not slay you. One less Norman knight for us to battle later!"

He stared at her for a long moment. Then he bowed, a twisted, ironic smile curling his lip. "Pray, Fallon. Pray for England. And if you've any sense, pray for yourself. If you ever fall to me, *mademoiselle*, I promise that you will pay dearly."

He turned, and strode quickly toward the palace. Fallon watched his broad shoulders fade into the darkness, and she looked up at the sky again.

No matter what she said or did, the people would see the comet as an omen. She cried out softly to the night, for her father might well see it as an omen, too.

"No, God, please no!" she murmured softly. But there was no answer in the night, and as a chill descended upon her, she hugged her arms about her shoulders and ran back to the palace.

She hurried to her father's private chambers. Pausing in the antechamber, she saw that Harold was not alone.

Alaric was with him. They spoke in quiet words, and then both men rose. They embraced like old friends.

Fallon swallowed and flattened herself against the tapestries in the antechamber. Alaric walked past her, and Fallon knew that in the morning he would be gone.

He and Harold had met for the last time as friends. If they ever came face to face again, it would be at sword's length, and they would fight each other to the death.

Chapter Twelve

The comet was visible in the night sky for seven days; it had barely disappeared before word came that a hostile fleet had been seen off the southern coast.

It was not, however, William's army.

A very tall, white-blond Dane rode with the messenger who came to Harold. He was introduced to Fallon as her cousin Eric Ulfson, a prince of the royal house of Denmark. He had come to her father with the news that her uncle Tostig had traveled throughout Normandy, Flanders, Norway, Denmark, and Sweden, seeking to build an army to march against his brother. It was Tostig's fleet that now threatened the southern coast. The fryd was in confusion, for the men had been told to watch for a Norman fleet. They were now amassing food for Tostig, not in support, but rather as a bribe, that he might disappear.

Harold prepared to ride to meet his brother, and Fallon soon found herself more and more in the company of her Danish cousin. He was a striking man, very handsome in his pale Nordic way, and a heavily muscled warrior. But his eyes, pale and devouring, were always upon her. She didn't like Eric. Curiously, she found herself comparing him not to Delon but to Alaric. Why? she wondered. Eric was her ally, and Alaric was her enemy. But they were both veterans of countless battles, and both, she knew, desired her.

But there was something different about the two, even in the way they looked at her. Something warm caused her heart to flutter and beat too hard when Alaric gazed upon her; even hating him, she trembled to his touch. But something cold stirred within Fallon when Eric's eyes fell upon her.

"Eric is more like Harald Hardrada than the Danish king," her uncle Leofwine said once. "He plays the Viking still; he has been on countless raids on the Baltic Sea and into Russia. They say he fights like a berserker, and that nothing is sacred to him."

"But Father welcomes him here," Fallon said.

Leofwine shrugged. "It is good to have allies in days such as these. The Danish king is content with his own kingdom, while Harald Hardrada in Norway is still to be feared. Be courteous to our Danish cousin, Fallon."

She was courteous, though Eric's presence chilled her. One night, as he sat by her side, he kissed her hand, and she felt naked as his eyes surveyed her. "Fallon, I would that we were enemies, as of old. I would sail in here and take you away with me."

Fallon took her hand from his as politely as she could. "But we do not live in days of old," she told him. "We are kin of sorts, and you have come as our friend."

"Ah, and perhaps one day I will be called upon as your ally. I will fight any battle for you; I will defeat any enemy."

Fallon forced a smile to her lips and tried not to shiver. "Thank you, milord, but I hope such a time does not come."

"Nevertheless, lady, remember that I am your servant." His pale eyes told a frightening story. He would kill with gusto and pleasure. Perhaps that was the difference, she thought, between Eric and Alaric. Count Alaric, she thought, would kill with little relish. He was a knight and would do so only in defense of his liege. Eric would kill for the joy of it alone.

She looked across the hall and saw Delon, and their eyes met in misery. Harold had been keeping them apart, and they were both afraid that the king did, indeed, intend to use his daughter for a pawn. But perhaps it was just the tension of the times. Harold had not known a single moment's rest since he had taken the crown. He was not a man to break a promise, and Fallon knew how heavily it weighed upon her father that he had broken his vow to William of Normandy. The comet had disturbed him for that reason, and he had spent many long nights on his knees, seeking answers to his dilemmas.

Fallon was glad when Eric Ulfson rode with her father to meet her uncle Tostig's threat.

As it turned out, there was not to be a confrontation between the two brothers then; Tostig's army, on hearing that Harold was coming, began to desert. Tostig sailed north, seeking refuge with the Scottish king. From the coast, Eric Ulfson sailed for Denmark.

Harold now prepared to ride south, to his base of operations on the Isle of Wight, and Fallon would accompany her father. They could both go home, for Fallon thought her mother would be able to ease the worry from her father's brow. It was summer, and the land was lush and beautiful, and the king could enjoy some well-earned rest while they awaited the Norman host from across the sea.

Alaric stood with William and his half brothers, Robert and Odo, studying the chart of coastal England. Their faces were grim, for they would be at the mercy of the winds, and William was going to attempt something that had never been done before. Vikings had crossed the seas to raid and plunder, but William sought to cross the Channel to make war; he was taking with him thousands of horses and a curious mixture of men. He had spent the winter and early spring convincing his own magnates that his quest was justified, but all of Normandy was just the size of one English earldom. He had to leave a certain amount of his army behind in Normandy, lest trouble arise there in his absence. To acquire the army that he needed he made promises, and as they stood there that day, Alaric was painfully aware that there could be no turning back. It was a risky venture; though William spoke with confidence, they were at the mercy of the fickle wind. And when they landed, they would be a small host in a large and hostile country. Also, Harold knew they were coming. As soon as they landed, they would be met.

William gestured across the map, indicating the south-eastern coast of England. They discussed the wind and the places where they could attempt to land, each man putting in his opinion. William chose an area he knew well from the Norman monastery there. Their voices were all quiet and subdued, for there could be no guarantees. Many of William's greatest magnates were still calling it a fool's quest.

There was a rap on the door, and FitzOsbern entered at William's bidding. He stared at the duke, and a slow smile spread across his features.

"We've been given the papal blessing!" FitzOsbern said. The duke gazed quickly at Alaric, who had suggested, along with Bishop Lenfrenc, that their cause might become a holy war rather than a war of conquest. If the pope could be convinced that English religious practices were lax, then he would give the duke his blessing. Now they had it.

Still smiling broadly, FitzOsbern came into the room. "The pope has sent his banner, and he has sent a ring with holy relics for you to wear. Harold stands in excommunication!"

William nodded.

FitzOsbern continued excitedly. "Already barons and knights flock in from all over Europe to ride at your side!"

William ordered that a keg of wine be brought out so that they all might drink to this small victory, and after much celebrating, Robert and Odo and FitzOsbern departed to their beds. William and Alaric laughed over old battles and drank more wine.

Then William gazed at Alaric, and lifted his chalice. "You do not approve of this battle." He shook his head, staring into space. "Alaric, they tell a tale that on the night I was conceived, my mother woke from a curious dream. A tree grew within her, and it spread its branches from Europe across the sea." His voice grew husky with excitement. "By God, Alaric, do you not see this as fate?"

Alaric paused, thinking of the comet that had trailed across the sky. It had been seen in many countries, and the general consensus, related by travelers and churchmen, seemed to be that the light in the sky had something to do with the English problem. Did God work in such ways, he wondered? Was there such a thing as fate?

He turned to William. "William, I know nothing of fate. Were I the last man left standing at your side, I would fight for you still with no thought of surrender. If I am saddened, it is because I admire Harold, and I admire the English."

"I had *meant* to rule them justly," William murmured.

"But now," Alaric said, "assuming this lunacy upon which we embark brings forth fruit, you will be king of a country full of sullen people who hate you, and us. You will have to ravage the land. What other finance will you have for your venture? Your Norman knights will seek land and riches; the mercenaries who travel with us will destroy everything they touch. I am sorry only because I know what must be."

William stared at his cup. "I admire Harold, too," he murmured. "But the die is cast." He lifted his cup to Alaric. "Who knows, my friend? We may perish in the attempt to cross that cantankerous sea!" He swallowed down a long draft of wine. Alaric watched him, and they touched their chalices together. They laughed, but their laughter was painful. William was right. The die was cast.

"See that little boat house yonder?" Harold, lying on a blanket of thick green grass beneath an endless blue sky, pointed to a little shack on the dock at Bosham, Chichester Harbor. Fallon chewed on a stem of grass and shielded her eyes against the sun as she nodded.

"Once," Harold said, "when we were very young, Svein and Tostig and I accidentally dumped a huge catch of fish back into the sea. We were frightened of your grandfather's temper, and so we hid in that little shack for hours."

Fallon smiled to think of her father as a small boy, hiding in a small building. "What happened then?" she asked him.

"Your grandfather caught us, and we were all well switched, I do assure you." He paused for a moment, then smiled again. "When your grandfather was in exile, he determined to return here despite Edward's anger. We sailed here from Flanders, and when we came to Pevensey Harbor, and onward, and everywhere, the people cheered Godwin and his sons. Ah, Fallon, I love it here, as nowhere in England."

"It is very beautiful here," she agreed. A movement behind her distracted her, and she turned to see her mother, smiling and barefoot with her skirts hiked high, carrying a basket with loaves of bread and cheese. Edith was still so lovely, Fallon thought. She looked like a girl today, with her soft blond locks and bare brown ankles.

Fallon stood. In the distance, she could hear a clash of steel. Her brothers, her uncles, and certain of her father's closest retainers, including Delon, practiced at arms. The sound disturbed the peace of the summer's day.

"Fallon!" her mother cried as Fallon started to walk away. "I've brought some food."

"I'll come back, Mother," Fallon promised. She gave them a wave and started toward the water, determined that her parents should have some time alone. She came to the little boat house her father had pointed out to her and she sat on the dock there, stripped away her shoes and stockings, and dangled her toes in the cold water. She rested her head on her knees, and sighed softly. Summer was waning, and the men of the fryd growing restless. The men owed the king only two months' service, and they had given more than that already. Many came from villages far inland, and they had heard nothing of their families. Winter would come, and there was work to be done at home. Southern England was being stripped. The king had forbidden his men to plunder, but even as he paid for provisions, they were having to send farther and farther north for food to feed the vast horde.

Soft laughter rippled across the field of grass and summer daisies, and Fallon turned to see her parents. They lay together now, stretched out on the grass, and it was her mother's laughter which had come to her.

For a moment a pain gripped her heart, and Fallon thought that that was what she wanted. A love like that, so sweet, so pure, that it defied all understanding. If they were not one before the world, they were still united by their hearts, and perhaps that was all that mattered. Edith had never cared that Harold had not made her his wife. "Nay . . ." Fallon murmured aloud. She would never stand for such a relationship herself. Her mother was gentle, but not proud, and Fallon had little control over her own pride. "Nay, I would never live as Mother has!" She heard the melody of her mother's laughter again and wondered what it would be like to love so deeply and so well that the world did not matter at all.

Fallon frowned suddenly. She felt the pounding of horses' hooves against the dock and earth before she heard it. She glanced across the field and saw that her father had heard the horses, too. He was standing, and her mother was rising behind him. Riders in her father's colors burst out of the forest and came to a stop before Harold.

Fallon stared at the scene for a moment, then rose. Forgetting her shoes and stockings, she started to run across the green grass, beneath the radiant blue sky. Breathless, she stopped behind her mother, and as she gasped for breath, the bird-song seemed louder than the words of the messenger.

"Father, what is it?" Fallon demanded as he turned at last, his face haggard and his eyes haunted. "Have the Normans come at last?"

"Nay, nay! We agreed that we should hold the ships until the Nativity of Saint Mary. Tomorrow. I will lead the housecarls back to London tomorrow, and the chartered ships will return to the Cinque Ports. We believe that the duke will wait until spring to attack."

He kissed Edith. "So we have today," he told her.

The next morning Harold's men came riding up to the door of the house. Harold mounted his horse. Fallon came running out and hurried to him. "Father, your sons stay here to guard the coast, and Mother stays, too. I will go with you."

Harold had meant to argue, but he smiled and shrugged instead, for he knew it was very difficult to win a battle with her. "Come then, Fallon."

Delon dismounted quickly and helped her mount her dappled mare.

Ever since the comet had shot across the sky, Fallon had been afraid. She simply had to stay with her father, in case there was some small way in which she could defend him. She loved him, and could not bear to lose him.

At the mouth of the •river Dives, Alaric stood on the dock staring at the ship that would take him across the Channel. He wet a finger and lifted it high. Still there was no breeze.

He looked around the harbor, which was crowded with William's ships. They were of Viking design, hastily built, and ranging in size from thirty to seventy-two feet; all had dragons' heads at their prows.

The air was completely still. A murmur went up among the more than ten thousand men gathered here. They felt that God was against them, since no breeze would come from the south to carry them across the Channel. Falstaff, quieting the horses, turned to Alaric, who shrugged. William came toward him.

"Not even a breeze," William muttered in disgust. "And I've ten thousand men sitting idle on my own land, men who will ravage it at the slightest instigation. God help us! But it takes all my power just to control these men!"

"The wind has come from the north," Alaric said. "And there has been no breeze at all. Surely, William, it must change soon. After all, aren't we speaking of fate, here?"

"I hope it is not my fate to be mired in the muck of this river!" William swore.

Then Alaric felt it; a soft breeze that touched his cheek in the heat of the day. "William . . ."

Cries went up all around them. The wind was coming from the south at last. As soon as the tide changed, the fleet could travel out the mouth of the river and set sail for England.

On the thirteenth of September, a terrible storm broke out. As Harold and his men rode, word reached them that many of his ships, returning to London, had been lost. He accepted the news with sorrow and hastened the journey.

Two days later they passed through the Sussex forest and across London Bridge. Fallon was proud to see that the city turned out to welcome her father home.

But two days later a messenger rode in to say that Harald Hardrada and Tostig had just attacked in the north; they had burned the city of Scarborough.

The wind shifted to the west; Duke William's ships were blown off course, and in an effort to survive, they sought any harbor. Ships, horses, and men were lost, and many of the survivors deserted. Alaric listened as William was advised to give up his quest. William demanded his advice.

Alaric smiled. "William, what matters any advice? You are determined on this course."

"I want your opinion!"

"Well, we have always known that this is a fool's quest, my liege." Alaric saw the duke's famous temper rising and he swept an arm out to indicate the ships that surrounded them. They were the fifty ships that Alaric himself had pledged to the duke from his own resources. He had nearly five hundred loyal men in his command. Of his personal force, the storm had cost Alaric two ships, twenty men, and as many horses. "William, I am, as always, with you."

"If I quit now, I will lose all respect."

"You know that you will not quit."

The duke nodded. There was a great assemblage of men, and he stepped out among them and fell to his knees. "God's grace be with us!" he called out. "I will not falter in my cause!"

Cheers began to go up. The storm had been a disaster; everything could have failed. But William had sworn that, by right, England was his. He had to prove it.

Fallon lay awake, restless and uncertain. She heard a cry in the night, and she rose, frightened. She wrapped a blanket of furs around her shoulders and ran out into the hall. She heard a second cry. It came from the king's quarters.

She stared reproachfully at the guard as she neared the door to her father's chambers. The guard shook his head. "Milady, he sleeps poorly. The pain in his leg bothers him this night."

"Get the physician."

"The physician has been here. The king ordered him back to his own bed."

Fallon nodded and went to her father's side. A bowl of water and a cloth lay there; she pressed the cloth against his forehead. He awakened, started, then smiled at her.

"I must ride in the morning," he said.

"You cannot; you are ill."

"I am the king, and I will ride."

"You are a stubborn old man."

"Old! I am not old. I am in my prime." He smiled slowly again, tenderly touching her cheek. "You are a stubborn minx, much like the old man, eh?"

"Oh, Father! I love you so much!"

"And I love you, my beauty. What happiness you have brought to me, my girl."

"Don't!" She pressed a finger against his lips, fearful that he would speak of some omen. He shook his head and assured her that all was well. She was not sure that it was so, for it was nearly dawn, and Harold had barely slept.

Her father finally dozed. There was a soft rapping, and Fallon flew to the door. A monk waited there with the guard and Father Damien. Fallon swallowed fiercely.

"This is Elfin," Father Damien told her. "He must see the king."

"Why?" Her throat was dry, and she was wretchedly nervous.

Father Damien smiled with gentle understanding. "All is well, Fallon. Let him enter."

Harold was awake again, sitting up. Elfin hurried in and told her father he was from the abbey at Waltham, which Harold himself had endowed.

"I dreamt of good King Edward. He came to me and said I must tell you that you will go to battle and you will prevail. And you will no longer be in pain."

"Thank you for coming to me, Elfin," Harold said.

Fallon saw her father's slight smile and knew that he was skeptical. But after he had ushered the monk and the priest out, he turned to her, incredulous.

"Fallon, my leg pains me no longer."

"Truly?"

"Truly." He smiled. "See? I am not so old, my child. I am truly in my prime. And I will be victorious."

Fallon nodded, and accepted his good-bye kiss. He did not know that she would be riding with him. She had told Delon that she felt she had to be near her father and that one way or the other, come Vikings or Normans, she would ride with Harold. Delon had brought her leather armor and a helmet and visor and even chausses and a short tunic. She would tuck her hair up beneath the helmet, and none would recognize her except Delon and his friends. "Your father will personally slay me for this," Delon told her.

She swept her lashes sweetly over her cheeks. "I will take care, Delon. I promise, if it comes to battle, I will take cover, and my father will not discover me. Oh, love! Thank you so for helping me!" She kissed him, and he forgot his fears and doubts.

They left London on the twentieth of September. In a military feat that men would long remember, Harold marched his army north nearly two hundred miles in three and half days, traveling day and night. Fallon was exhausted, but her heart sang, too, for all through the long ride, in town after town, the fryd had come out and men had rallied to her father's side.

In Tadcaster, ten miles south of York, they learned about the defeat the English had suffered at the hands of Tostig and Harald Hardrada. The men of York and Northumbria, led by the English earls, Morkere and Edwin, had clashed with the Vikings at Fulton. A vicious, bloody battle had ensued, and the Vikings bragged around their campfires that the rivers were dammed with the bodies of defeated Saxons. Harald Hardrada and Tostig had not taken their army into the city of York, for they planned to set up their headquarters there, and they did not want that worthy prize destroyed.

Not a man had welcomed Tostig back to his old earldom. And according to the wounded soldier who breathlessly relayed his message to the king, Tostig had promised the crown of England to Harald Hardrada.

"Your uncle has surely gone mad!" Delon whispered to Fallon. She nodded, noticing the sorrow that lined her father's face. It was the greatest horror for him to do battle against his own brother.

"Tostig means to take hostages tomorrow at Stamford Bridge, you say?" Harold demanded. When the man nodded his anxious agreement, the king commanded that they would silently slip into York, and prepare to meet the invaders in the morning. The men who would have been hostages were to march at Harold's side.

Fallon did not sleep that night. She lay beside Delon in the tent she shared with him and his closest friends, who were sworn to secrecy about her identity. They had joked that night, but they were all nervous about the battle to come. No man of sense met a Viking battle-ax without respect.

Morning came. The army amassed at Stamford Bridge and waited as Tostig and the Vikings approached from the village of Riccall, where they had camped. Fallon waited breathless as her father, disguised, went forward to offer peace to Tostig, if he would desert his Viking enterprise. He refused.

It was later said that Tostig recognized his brother, but gave Harald Hardrada no sign that it was the king himself. This was Tostig's last honorable act: He did not betray his brother, nor did he betray the Viking with whom he had cast his fortune.

Horrible, blood-curdling cries filled the air. Delon whirled on Fallon. "Now! Get back! It begins!"

Horses and soldiers pressed forward, and the cries rose like a massive tidal wave. The Viking horde was upon them. Battle, hand to hand and vicious, ensued on the York side of the bridge. Fallon's horse reared and she was thrown to the ground. She rolled to one side, barely escaping the hooves of other horses. She sat up just as a double-headed ax cleaved the skull of an English thane.

It was her first sight of bloodshed, her first taste of war. In panic she realized that her father was at the fore, that her uncles Leofwine and Gyrth were with him, that Delon and all his handsome young friends were meeting the deadly clash of steel.

Fallon heard a cry from the river, and she crept over to the source. A young man lay there with his thigh ripped and torn. She tore strips from her mantle and quickly bound the wound. Someone leaped at her, and a Viking with the eyes of a berserker was upon her, drawing a blade from a sheath at his ankle. He raised it above her, but ere the knife could fall, the Viking went rigid. The young man whose thigh she had bound had skewered the enemy through with his broadsword.

He turned to Fallon, and died.

"Mother of God!" Fallon murmured. But she did not panic. She went among the men, giving water where she could, tying up wounds. As the day dragged on, she came upon one of her father's surgeons, and together they tended the wounded. As morning turned to afternoon, she was numbed and inured to the horror of it; she worked with single-minded desperation to save what lives she could.

"Fallon!" She had long since cast away her helmet and visor. Most of the men merely stared at her, dazed, as if she were an angel of mercy. But this was her uncle, Leofwine, looking up at her, and his disapproval was vast.

"Uncle!" She ignored the reproach in his eyes and bathed his forehead. She worked in a fury to remove his armor, tunic, and chemise, and discovered a slash across his rib cage. She felt his eyes upon her as she carefully tended the wound. When she looked at him again, she saw that his lip was caught in a wry grin. "Girl, your father will have your hide."

"Shush, Uncle." She paused then, and tears stung her eyes. "My father—"

"Harold was well when I left him. He crossed the bridge. I believe the battle is breaking. Harald Hardrada rushed forward like a true berserker and was slain with an arrow in the throat." He swallowed, pained. "And my brother Tostig took up Hardrada's standard, the Land-Ravager, but now the standard has fallen, and they say that he has died, too. The Vikings are retreating for their ships." He closed his eyes. Fallon wiped her uncle's brow again and felt fresh tears form in her eyes. What madness had caused this?

Dusk began to fall, and Fallon discovered that it was true—the enemy was in full retreat. But the river ran red with blood, and bodies were heaped atop one another, tangled together in death, Vikings and Englishmen.

"Fallon!"

She spun about. This time it was her father, and she did not fear his anger, for she was so glad to see him alive. With a hoarse cry, she ran to him as he dismounted and flung her arms around him. He held her for but a moment, then pushed her from him. "Fallon! What foolishness is this? You could have been slain! Delon! That young fool—"

"Nay, Father! It was my idea, and no one else is to blame. I could not let you ride alone!"

"You're a woman—"

"And your daughter. If I were a son, I would be expected to stand beside you."

"But you are not my son, Fallon. And something happens to a man when he must shed blood. It rests upon his heart, and it eats into him there. But a man is stronger—"

"Father, you know I am adept at arms."

"Adept, yes, but a woman. Fallon—at any time, I could lose everything. Don't let me fear that I should lose you, too."

"Father, I did not risk my life. I stayed behind, and I was helpful—ask your surgeon. Perhaps I even saved lives."

He smiled at her. "Perhaps." Then he frowned again and demanded to know where she had been sleeping. When she told him, he was furious all over again, even though she assured him that every man in his army had been gallant. "No matter. Delon and I will certainly have words. And tonight, daughter, you will sleep in a guarded chamber in York that adjoins your father's!"

She bowed to his command. She didn't see Delon that night, nor could she eat when the English feasted, for the taste of blood seemed to be all about her.

In the morning, she was at her father's side when the remaining power of the Vikings surrendered to him.

Harold had always despised slaughter. He freely pardoned Harald Hardrada's sons and kin when they swore never to come to England again. He took no reprisals, but bade them leave.

Listening to him, Fallon smiled against the tears that rose in her eyes, and offered up a silent prayer, thanking God for his life.

Looking about her, Fallon was startled to see a familiar figure. Father Damien had traveled with them, and she had not known it. He was watching the king with an expression of abject misery; Fallon feared that he knew of some secret ill that had befallen her father.

Suddenly Father Damien looked her way, as if he had sensed her eyes on him. He stared at her a long moment, then nudged his horse and moved away. Fallon tried to follow, but he disappeared into the ranks of the army, and she could see him no more.

For nearly a week the army remained at York. Fallon and Delon were not allowed to speak to each other but Fallon did not think that her father's temper would remain so fixed for long. She sought to earn his forgiveness by a pretense of meek and mild obedience, and she tended to the wounded as she had during the battle. Working with the surgeon, she learned a great deal about mosses and herbs, how to cauterize wounds, and how to sew them cleanly and neatly, and even how to set a broken bone. She knew that her father watched her working, and that she had earned his grudging approval.

One afternoon she came upon a lad with a serious gash

in his temple. She bathed away the blood and applied the mud poultice that the surgeon had prepared. As she bound the wound, the youth opened his eyes; they were soft blue, like a spring flower. He whispered to her, and she realized that he spoke in his native language—Norwegian.

She bit into her lip as his eyes closed. She could not bear to see anyone suffer—neither an Englishman nor an enemy. The boy was flesh and blood, just like her own brothers.

A shadow fell upon her. She looked up to see Father Damien watching her.

"You've a healing touch," he told her.

She smiled weakly. "Will he live?"

"Aye, and he'll become an Englishman. He'll never travel homeward again."

"You speak as if you know."

Father Damien shrugged and turned away from her. She could not see his face. He said, "Your father plans a feast this night. Be with him. See that he is happy."

Father Damien walked away. Fallon stared after him nervously.

It was true. Her father did plan a feast that night, and they dined in the hall at York. The young earls Morkere and Edwin were there, and at her father's insistence, Fallon danced with them. She laughed and chatted and was careful to see that Harold's cup was full, and that the night was fine for him.

Then suddenly the musicians ceased to play. A pall fell over the room. Fallon, on the arm of the young Earl Morkere, felt a chill seize her spine, and she trembled.

Through the dancers in the center of the hall walked a man, worn and weary, dusty from the road, and travel-stained. He pushed through them all and fell before her father.

"Water!" She heard herself call out. Then she pushed

away from the young earl and ran to the fallen man. A servant supplied her with a skin of water, and she pressed it to his lips, then smoothed some of the water over his cheeks. His eyes opened, and they were wild as they stared about.

"Peace, man, what is it?" Harold asked gently, crouching down beside her. The man's eyes fell upon his king, and he moistened his lips to speak.

"The Normans have come. William the Bastard has landed at Pevensey Harbor."

Chapter Thirteen

Even as they prepared to ride south, another messenger arrived from the coast. Exhausted and worn from riding, he sat at a table in the palace in York, telling Harold what he had seen and heard. Fallon, sitting to a meal she could not begin to taste, felt a deep sense of dread rising within her. She had feared the Normans all her life, and now it seemed that her fears had been well founded.

The man who came to them, Derue, had served in the fryd, he told the king, but was from Pevensey himself, and so, when the fryd had dispersed to go home, he had remained on the coast. He had been among the first to see the Norman fleet out on the sea.

"They landed, and there was no one to fight them," he said. "They came straight in, and no beast was safe, for they took unto themselves all the fine manors, and they slew cattle, sheep, and pigs. They had brought their own lumber, and they hastily set up a fort. The duke is a confident man; they say he awoke in the morning aboard his own vessel with no sight of the other ships and sat there cool as ice and ordered food. His ships were behind him, and they soon appeared. He stumbled upon the English soil when he left the *Mora*. Some whispered this fall to be an evil omen, but the duke was not distressed.

As he fell he said that he had not taken England single-handedly but with both his hands.

"Pevensey did not serve his purpose. He split the army, and they moved, inland and by the sea, to Hastings. There, at the Norman abbey, he has made his headquarters; he has built another fort. And everything is laid waste by his men."

Fallon looked nervously at her father. He was listening to the man gravely. "We must reach London," Harold said, "as quickly as possible."

Fallon was at his side as they traced their steps south. Harold had not forgiven her and Delon for the deception they had played on him. Fallon missed Delon; she missed his quiet acceptance of all that befell him and his gentle love. She missed his ability to make her believe that all would be right, no matter what threatened.

When they neared London, Harold ordered the soldiers to go on ahead; he intended to stop at the abbey at Waltham, where the monk Elfin lived. With a weary smile, he told Fallon that she should go on to the palace at Thorney Island. She shook her head, and he shrugged, knowing that she would come with him.

Fallon followed her father into the church. While he went to a forward pew to pray, she knelt in the rear. She tried to pray, but fear numbed her. She stared straight ahead at the Holy Rood, a stone crucifix encased in silver. It had been found buried on a hill, and although no one knew who had buried it, miracles were attributed to it. Her father had long ago had the abbey built as a special place for the Holy Rood.

She wanted a miracle now: She wanted her father, haggard and exhausted though he was, to expel William from the land. Fallon lowered her head and prayed. As she knelt there, she found new assurance. William was a Norman, a foreign invader. The English people were fiercely loyal to her father—let the Normans say what they would. William might have had an army, but Harold had a country behind him. The English would not falter, and they would not fall. The invader would be expelled.

She did not realize that dusk had fallen until the monks began to move about the abbey and light the candles. Then her father rose from his knees. As Fallon did likewise, there was a sudden shout.

"It has moved! It is a miracle! My God, the king has come, and there has been a miracle!"

Fallon didn't know what had happened. The monks began to rush around, and there was loud arguing. Fallon hurried up to her father, who seemed as much at a loss as she.

One of the monks came before her father. "You bowed to the crucifix, King Harold. It has bowed in return, I swear it!"

"The king's prayers are answered!" someone cried. "He will be victorious!"

"I pray that may be true," Harold said. He turned with Fallon on his arm, and she trembled to see a dark-clad figure in the middle of the aisle.

" 'Tis only Father Damien," Harold told her. But her heart quickened despite the words, and she saw that he appeared very grave.

When they were again outside, Fallon turned to Father Damien. "All claim a miracle!" she told him. "Yet you look sad, as if the earth had opened beneath us."

He bowed to her, and his dark eyes seemed to hold all the mysteries of heaven and hell. "A miracle, surely, Princess."

"You show scant faith in my father."

"I believe that he is beloved of God, milady, and that he is a very great man. May I help you to your horse?"

Annoyed by his mysterious gaze, Fallon shook her head. She'd ridden as a warrior for nearly a fortnight; she needed no help to mount her horse.

Night was upon them, but they rode on to London. Her uncle Gyrth was at the palace, anxious to meet them in the great hall with news. "King Edward's old Norman friend, Robert FitzWimark, warned Duke William in no uncertain terms that you had just come from a triumphant battle against Viking raiders. He has told the duke that you are strong, that he must guard his defenses well."

Fallon removed her gauntlets and went to stand before the fire.

"I shall prepare a message," Harold said. "I shall send a monk from Waltham, and I shall ask William to leave us in peace."

Despite the blaze burning in the grate, Fallon shivered. William, she knew, would never leave them in peace. She closed her eyes and leaned against the wall.

Alaric, she knew, was back in England, at William's side. He would lead hundreds of men against her father. She remembered his cold, slate-gray eyes and the way he had so easily bested her in their mock battle. Even the Saxon housecarls spoke of him as one of the greatest warriors in Christendom. And he was back.

Then a flash of curious heat flooded through her. Her fingers moved to her lips, remembering the touch of his mouth against her own and the way he had looked at her in the square before the church, when her passion had nearly driven the crowd to violence. He had threatened her that night, warned her . . .

He was only one man, she reminded herself. He would probably die on English soil. But still the warmth seeped through her, to be followed by new shivers, and she did not know what she felt for him. Surely she despised him and all that he stood for. How was it, then, that when he touched her, she felt a keen and blazing fire, unlike any other heat she knew?

She lowered her head in shame, telling herself that she

loved Delon, that when they were wed, she would be a good and loyal wife. She would think of no other man.

Something caught her attention and she stared across the hall. Father Damien was standing there, watching her. He walked over to her and stretched out his hands toward the warmth. Firelight played upon his handsome and haunting features.

"Why were you staring at me so?" Fallon demanded.

His eyes met hers and he watched her for a moment. "You were thinking of the knight who met the crowd on the night of the comet, were you not?"

She gasped. "How did you know? If you are a seer, Father, I wish that you would foretell the battle that must come, and tell my father how to fight it."

"I am not a seer. Sometimes I see, but . . ." He shrugged and looked toward the fire. "I saw a tree, a beautiful tree that withered as if it would die, but then it grew together, and became green again."

"The Confessor's vision," Fallon murmured.

He shrugged. "I am from the Fens, milady. Many of my people have only recently given up Druid sacrifices for Christian ways. There is much in life that cannot be answered, and so I do not seek answers. We live with mystery and bow down before it." He straightened and smiled at her. "Excuse me, Princess. I believe I will retire."

He walked away from her, then paused and turned back. "He is here among us."

"I beg your pardon, Father?" Fallon frowned.

"Count Alaric is here on English soil."

She smiled. "Father, no ancient art is needed to divine such a fact! If Duke William is here, then so is Alaric."

She felt his dark eyes across the room as he nodded to her. Then he said softly, "He will live. He will survive the battle. And so will you."

"I will not be fighting."

"As you say, milady." He bowed and left her. Fallon heard her father droning out a message to the monk, who was to repeat it word for word to William. She walked up behind his chair and kissed the top of his head. He absently patted her hand and, exhausted, she retired for the night.

She woke up just before dawn in a cold sweat, trembling with fear. She'd dreamed that she lay upon the earth and that a gigantic horse had thundered across the land, nearly trampling her beneath its hooves. But the hoofbeats had ceased, and when she had dared to open her eyes, she had done so only to meet the cold gray eyes of Alaric d'Anlou.

She rose and splashed water over her face. Then she squared her shoulders and assured herself that she would never see him again. The Normans were destined to be beaten and to run, tails between their legs, back across the Channel.

Two days later, the monk returned from his errand. Fallon sat tensely in her father's hall and listened. The monk had given William Harold's message: that William had come uninvited. Harold bade the Normans return home before he was forced to recall his pact of friendship with William.

William had sent back a message of his own, restating his grievances. Fallon barely held her temper. William now not only accused her grandfather of having murdered Edward's brother some thirty years before, but he also accused her father—who had been but twelve years old at the time! William insisted that the crown was his by right—and that he was ready to lay his claim before the law of England or Normandy.

"Why, that is nonsense!" Fallon claimed. "Norman law

counts for nothing here, and the English have already spoken their choice!"

The monk bowed to her and said, "The duke has also offered to meet in single combat."

Harold rubbed his fingers over his forehead. "A noble gesture, but worthless, too. If I fall, the English will still accept no foreign king. And if he falls, God knows, his men would continue to savage the countryside."

Fallon knelt by her father's side. "Father, you battled the Norsemen well, and you were victorious. You are a proven warrior and a good king. Don't go to battle against William. Not now. Let some other man lead."

The monk cleared his throat. Harold looked at him. The man was very pale, and he lowered his head miserably. "King Harold, there is something else that you should know. The duke carries with him the papal banner. He wears a ring that contains holy relics. The Norman monks claim . . ."

Harold was standing. "They claim what?" he demanded.

"They claim the pope has excommunicated you. The same fate awaits all men who fight for you."

"What?" Harold roared out the word. Then he sank back to his chair and laughed, but his laughter was bitter and pained.

"Father, damn them for the lying rodents that they are!" Fallon exclaimed passionately. "Were we ever given leave to defend ourselves before the pope? This banner that William carries he gained by some false and treacherous means. Father, it means nothing!" She stared into Harold's pale and anguished features.

The king rose again and paced the room in a fury, then spun upon the monk. "Tell William that I leave the matter in God's hands!"

The monk nodded, bowed deeply, and was gone.

Gyrth, sitting silently at the table, slammed down his

tankard and stood before his brother. "Harold, man, listen to me! Fallon showed good sense. You are the only king we have; you must not ride into battle with William. Let me lead the battle. If I am lost, England is not. While I lead an army toward Hastings, you can call up a greater host of men from across the country."

"I will meet William in battle."

"Harold, it is foolishness not to heed me—"

"I will meet William in battle, and God will judge us, as he is now my witness!"

Fallon had never seen her father so adamant, so unreasonable.

She and her uncle exchanged a long look, and Gyrth shook his head unhappily, then left the room. Fallon, aware that her father noticed neither of them, raced after her uncle.

Gyrth turned, hearing her footsteps. She paused before him, and he lifted her chin. "Fallon, we have been a proud breed, but you are the radiant flower among us. So lovely, and so passionate. I thank God that you are on our side!"

"Don't tease me, Uncle, not now!" she entreated him. "I am so very afraid! Father—"

"Fallon, can't you see?" Gyrth interrupted her. "Harold has determined that this is a private war between him and William, with God as their judge. He sees no campaign, but a single battle. Him or William."

"Your advice was sound," Fallon said.

"I will stay beside him."

"We must help him!"

"Offer him your deepest love, Fallon. He is a good man, and a God-fearing man, and William's possession of the pope's banner now weighs heavily upon him. So pray, Fallon, for England." He kissed her forehead. "We shall ride tomorrow, I am certain. God keep you, Fallon."

Her uncle left her and hurried down the hall. Fallon inhaled a shaky breath.

There was no choice in the matter for Fallon. She must don her armor and mail once again and ride with the army. She could not let her father go to battle alone, not when his soul was so heavy. She had to be near him.

"God forgive me for deceiving him again!" she whispered desperately. She had proved at Stamford Bridge that she could be useful, that she could perhaps make a difference for some poor injured soldier. And at Stamford Bridge she had also learned to tolerate the terrible smell of blood, and to swallow down her nausea at the sight of the maimed and the dying. She could be of help, she knew.

Come what may, Fallon would ride to battle.

Fallon had hoped to rely upon Delon again. But when he saw her mounting a battle steed, he was furious. He told her that she would surely get him cast into a dungeon this time, if not drawn and quartered or hanged.

"Delon, already the march has begun. Shush, or you will have my father back here upon us! If he catches me, I'll tell him I'm anxious to reach Bosham, and Mother."

Delon sighed wearily and Fallon smiled. She softened as she stared down at him, for he was no longer angry, but pained. He gave into her so often, sometimes at grave risk to himself. Commanders shouted as they brought the foot soldiers to order, and there was great commotion as a horse reared and nearly trampled the men gathering to mount. Fallon reached for Delon's hand and wound her fingers around his. "I promise, Delon, I'll not endanger our union again." Her voice grew desperate. "Delon, please! Father is distressed by this papal business. He rushes to meet the Norman bastard when others could wage this battle. I must be there."

He nodded at her. "You will turn off for Bosham?"

She smiled, and did not answer him.

It was not so long a march to Hastings as it had been to York. Late at night on October 13, they arrived at Caldbec Hill, where they were to meet more men.

Fallon had not turned off for Bosham.

The army gathered for the night along the ridge above the Santlache Valley, which her father had chosen as his defensive position. Fallon turned to find Father Damien watching her.

She moistened her lips nervously, then turned back to loosen the girth on her saddle. "I am staying here, Father. There is nothing you can do about it. Tell my father, if you like. I'll not leave."

The priest came forward and helped her with the saddle.

"I knew you were here," he told her. He hefted the saddle to the ground, and she murmured a thank-you. He saluted her and walked away, murmuring a blessing. There would be much call for his services this night, she thought. Thousands of men had gathered to fight.

Delon came up behind her, slipped his arms around her waist, and pulled her tight against him. He lowered his cheek against the softness of her hair. "I feel chills in my bones, my love. As if the planets and stars might collide, as if the end of the earth might be imminent."

Fallon trembled, then turned to look toward the town of Hastings. Somewhere nearby the Normans waited to engage in battle. The valley would run red with blood, and one man would be a victor.

Let it be Father! she prayed.

"We should rest," Delon said.

But he was in command of many men, and he had to see to their provisions. Fallon leaned against a tree and looked up at the moon. She shivered as she saw the curious haze that surrounded it. The mist was red, the color of fresh-drawn blood.

The sounds behind her seemed to fade; she had to find her father. She started to wind her way through the men gathering at their campfires. She walked carefully at first, and then she began to run. She ran and ran, and the light from a hundred small fires burned against her cheeks. She saw her father's tent and burst inside it.

Harold was there with Leofwine, and Gyrth and Galen, her eldest brother. They were studying a sand model of the ridge and valley, but when she entered, they all looked up, surprised.

"Galen," Harold said. "Take her back to Delon; the young man will worry."

Galen offered her a wry smile, but as he started forward to obey Harold, the king rose. "One moment."

He slipped an arm about her shoulders and led her from the tent. He stared up at the night sky, then he kissed her forehead, and rested his chin upon it. "If anything goes wrong, tell your mother that I loved her, that she was the happiness of my life."

"Stop it, Father!"

He looked very young and very handsome that night, every inch a king. "Men say such things before any battle, Fallon. I promise you, before Harald Hardrada sailed and before William of Normandy set off for our island, both men saw to it that their will was known to others. Don't gaze at me so, daughter. I say merely if . . ." He paused, then looked at her again, smiling. "If anything goes wrong, cast yourself upon the duke's mercy. Go to Alaric—"

"Nay!" she cried out. "Never!"

"Fallon—"

"If anything were to go wrong, Father, I would flee. I would find Mother and Aelfyn and Tam, and we would flee to the north. Please, Father, don't—"

"Alaric is an honorable man. If you surrender to him and swear an oath of loyalty, he will see to your welfare."

She lowered her head, horrified by his talk. It was madness! Even if they lost the battle tomorrow, Harold could assemble his men again farther inland and await support from the north. He should not be speaking so. "Father, please be careful tomorrow."

"I intend to. And you, my beauty, go to Count Alaric should you need refuge. Tell him I bade you to seek his mercy. You are precious to me, Fallon."

She thought, with new fear rising inside her, that if he was hurt or slain by a Norman, she would care for nothing, except, perhaps, revenge. She would never surrender, as long as she lived.

"Fallon . . . ?"

She would not lie to him, but neither would she give him further cause to worry. She smiled radiantly and threw her arms around him and kissed him on both cheeks. "Sleep, Father. You are weary and worn." She stroked his cheek. "Delon is trustworthy, I promise you. We have waited this long, and we will wait until you choose to bless our union. Take care, Father!"

She was near to tears again. She kissed him quickly, and turned to hurry back among the men.

She dared not think that it might be the last time that she would ever see him.

The men had barely formed ranks before the Norman attack began. "Mother of God!" came a cry as arrows rained down upon them.

Delon began shouting orders to his men. Fallon, catching her breath and backing away from the professional advance of the housecarls, saw her father's standards—the Dragon of Wessex and the Fighting Man—being raised. As far as she could see, men were arrayed along the ridge. Commands were shouted, shields were raised, and the arrows found little space for damage.

Then she heard the thunder against the earth—the pounding of hundreds of horses' hooves, beating out a rhythm. A horn sounded, and she could see the bulk of the Norman army as it marched forward. Foot soldiers with slings and arrows and javelins were followed by the horsemen. The sound of the hooves was a rampaging pulse across the land.

A man screamed and fell at her feet. A bloodcurdling cry began, and a housecarl moved forward, swinging his battle-ax, a savage desire for vengeance upon his features.

Fallon had sworn to stay away from the battle, but she could not. The man at her feet moaned, and she fell to her knees, eyeing the arrow that pierced his shoulder. She bit into her lip, placed her hand against his chest, and used all her strength against the weapon. The man screamed again as she pulled the arrow free.

She tore the soft bleaunt she wore beneath her leather armor and hastily bound the wound. With tremendous effort and a burst of desperate strength, she dragged the man down the hill and propped him up against a tree. He opened his eyes briefly, then passed out.

How horrible it was! Perhaps just a mile away the world was silent. There, soft and beautiful fall colors filled the land—oranges and browns, and a few radiant reds. The breeze that kissed the land was cool, and it was harvest season; the earth was ripe and giving and beautiful.

But not here.

The rumor went out that the duke was dead, and an ancient, pagan cry—even older than the Viking ways—went up among the Englishmen. A Norman withdrawal began, and the hill was flooded with the furious roar of victory and triumph. Men began to tear down the ridge after their retreating attackers.

Fallon stood and, with bloody hands, shielded her eyes from the sun. She walked in despair as a Norman horseman put a halt to his force's retreat. Heavily armed knights bore down on foot soldiers, slicing and hacking as they went. Screams rent the air. This was no retreat; the line of Englishmen along the ridge faltered.

An injured man fell back against Fallon, and his weight toppled them both to the ground. His forehead was streaked with blood, and his eyes were pain-filled. " 'Tis over," he said hoarsely. "Leofwine—"

"My uncle! Is he injured, is he hurt?"

"Gyrth is slain."

"Oh, God!" Fallon gasped.

"Leofwine, too, is down," the man went on. "In the valley, toward the forest. They tried to run, but the Normans cut them down. They must retreat and band together again."

Gyrth was dead. Loyal, handsome Gyrth. She wanted to cry out at the pain. The cries and the screams and the clash of steel went on and on; warnings were shouted as arrows rained upon them in a sudden volley.

"Leofwine! You say the ridge . . . ?"

The man opened his mouth, but no word came from it. His eyes closed, and she knew that he was dead.

Fallon hurried to the north side of the ridge, where they had camped. Trembling, she pulled her helmet and visor over her face, then drew out her specially made sword. She did not intend to do battle, but she had to help her kin. Gyrth was dead, and perhaps even now Leofwine lay dying. She couldn't pause to cry; she dared not mourn or even think. She had helped other men; God help her, she had to save her own blood.

She grabbed a Saxon shield from a fallen man and, faltering slightly under its weight, started down the ridge.

A Norman swung his ax at her, but she ducked beneath his weapon, her breath catching in her throat. She did not stop to fight him, but hurried on. She slipped and slid over the mud and mire created by the mixture of earth and blood. When a sword was raised against her, she parried the blow and ran. Finally she came to the valley beneath the ridge, and the forest beyond it.

"Leofwine!" She entered the forest screaming her uncle's name. There was no answer. A man, tearing past her, grabbed her arm.

"Run! Deep into the forest! We have been shattered; all is lost! We must escape and must regroup. We must reach London and find reinforcements!"

"Nay, sir, wait! Leofwine, the king's brother—"

He waved an arm at her and left her.

Fallon hurried onward. She stumbled upon a wounded youth, a young boy with nothing but a slingshot for a weapon. She fell down beside him and tried to bind the gash in his belly. "We must get you out of here!" she told him. She glanced up and saw that men were still escaping.

"Blessed angel!" the boy addressed her. His eyes were glazed with pain.

"Nay, blessed child!" she murmured. "You fought for my father, lad, and you gave your all. Now hold."

She rose and caught the arm of the next man who sought to flee. "Wait, sir, I beg you, I need help."

The man stared at her as if she were crazy. She shook his arm. "I've an injured boy here. Help him!"

The man swallowed and regained his courage. "I'll take this one, but you must hurry. There's Normans coming and coming—Frenchies and other damned foreign mercenaries, and the Norman knights."

Fallon gazed around and saw that it was true. Norman knights were riding down the ridge in force now. Fallon leapt to retrieve her sword and stolen shield, and slammed her visor down over her face.

She began to fight fiercely, hearing Fabioni's instructions in her mind: Never betray weakness, never betray weakness; shift and parry, shift and parry; never betray weakness.

Cunning was a weapon far greater than strength, and agility was a power with more reward than brawn alone. She was vaguely aware that Englishmen were escaping because she was able to keep several Normans occupied with swordplay. She injured some; she dared not wonder if she had killed any, or think what would come of her when she was finally exhausted and a furious Norman sword came in for the kill. If she could just break through the circle, she, too, could escape into the forest.

Then suddenly there was a new man among them. He paused, watching the struggle, and she dimly heard him shout to the others that he would take this one himself.

Then he rode toward her, and as he raised his sword, she tried to meet it with her own, but to no avail. His strength was astonishing; she let go of her sword, clenching her teeth against the pain in her arm as she fell to the ground with the power of his blow. She closed her eyes, awaiting death, as he circled her on his horse. Then he dismounted from his ebony steed and placed his bloody Norman sword against her throat.

"Surrender and live!"

She wanted to cry out in horror. For it was Alaric who had taken her, who thrust his weapon against the pulse of her life.

Of all the men in William's army, it was Alaric demanding that she yield. And she knew that she could never, never surrender.

He reached down to touch her, to wrench her visor and mask away.

"Nay! Leave me be!" she screamed.

She saw his eyes widen in fury, and she knew it did not

matter that he lifted her visor. She had already given herself away.

Brutal, ruthless hands touched her, stripped her of her last defense. He gazed down at her, his eyes as cold as ice.

They had met as warriors, and she had lost. He had come to conquer, and he had done so.

Chapter Fourteen

Fallon remembered little of what Alaric said to her, except that her father was dead. Taken away by guards, she sat numbly in a cold room in Hastings and waited, knowing not how long she waited or what she waited for.

Men paused outside the door, and she heard them talking. One of them described Harold's death. It was worse than Fallon could have dreamed.

"Aye, an arrow. Through the eye. Then four Norman knights moved in; some say William was among them. They tore the Saxon to shreds, sliced him to ribbons. They seek his body now."

"Oh, God!" she whispered. Her heartache was unbounded. A numbness came over her in the black void.

The door opened. A coarse, heavy woman stepped forward and sliced through Fallon's bonds with a knife, then dragged her to her feet.

"Allez!" She commanded. "You come."

Fallon didn't bother to tell the woman that she spoke French. She was too weary to fight, and she allowed herself to be dragged along. They left the fort and came to an outbuilding. Inside, a number of laundresses were scrubbing clothing in large tubs of water, and cooks were working over giant fires. Fallon wondered if she had been summoned to become a slave in the kitchen. If so, she was ready to work. Anything to forget that Harold of England lay dead, butchered that very day.

They stopped in front of a large tub of water from which steam rose. The heavyset woman commanded Fallon to get in. Had the Normans become entirely barbarian? Did they intend to boil her and consume her for their victory feast?

Then the woman produced a square of soap. Fallon shook her head, determined that if she was to be the victim of a rapist, he would have her at her very worst. The woman tugged on her sleeve.

"No! *Non! Comprendez?*" In French, Fallon called the woman a fat Norman whore and said she wouldn't move an inch to oblige her.

In the next few moments, Fallon became convinced that Duke William should have had his laundresses and whores wage all his battles, for she was instantly overwhelmed. Her tormentor whistled, and assistance came quickly. Fallon screamed as the women bore down upon her, knocking her to the ground and ripping her clothing from her shred by shred. She rocked, she kicked, she fought—but when they moved away, she was naked, without a thread remaining on her. The heavy woman caught her by the hair and dragged her to the tub. Fallon entered the bath head first.

Again she tried to struggle; the woman set her lips in grim purpose, and Fallon nearly drowned. In the end, bone weary, she went limp. The woman washed her hair and scrubbed her body, leaving her no modesty. When it was over, she was dragged from the tub and dried, and dressed in a soft white chemise of air-light silk and a gown of Flemish lace. Her hair was brushed endlessly, and perfume was touched to her throat and shoulders. Fallon sat motionless through it; nothing much seemed to matter. She stared at the cooking knives and thought of plunging one of them deep into her own heart.

No . . . She raised her chin slowly.

The enemy did not rule England yet. Harold was dead, but a hostile countryside lay before these Norman scum. She had to keep living, and she had to keep fighting, like Harold, who had never given up. He had beaten back the Viking invaders with courage and mercy, and had marched forward to another battle. Her father had never quit, and he had never surrendered. He had played the game out until the very end. She would escape to the north. She would join her brothers.

"Alez!" the heavyset woman commanded her again. Fallon stared at her, then rose. A warm mantle was thrown over her shoulders. She was led through the outbuilding, among the industrious cooks, most of whom were Normans, although there were some newly acquired Saxon servants. As they passed a worktable, Fallon deftly seized a small knife and swept it inside the folds of her gown.

She was walked out of the fort and through the field that stretched before it. Hundreds and hundreds of Norman tents were arrayed before her. A few men sat around campfires; most of them seemed to have retired for the night. Fallon kept her head low, wondering what awaited her.

The woman stopped suddenly, lifted a tent flap, and thrust her inside with a mighty shove, stripping the warm mantle from her as she did so. Fallon caught herself with her palms as she hit the ground, then inhaled sharply as she surveyed her domain.

A squat table stood before her. On it she could see wine, bread, cheese, and meat. She dragged her eyes from the food to see that a bed stood nearby—not a simple pallet, but a bed with a frame of wood and strung rope, a thick mattress, linen sheets, and fat pillows. Suddenly she was terrified. She inhaled sharply, wondering what had kept fear at bay for so very long.

She had been brought here as someone's prize. Sheer horror awaited her.

She began to shiver as she recalled the dreadful stories that had come in from the coast after the Normans landed. The soldiers had murmured that William meant to enrage her father by decimating the population of Wessex as he went. Homes had been razed, livestock slaughtered, men killed, and women brutally raped.

Fallon was so dizzy she feared that she would pass out. The Normans had seized the women of Wessex in the passion and rage of conquest; they had taken their victims in the streets, in the mud, in their homes, wherever they had been found.

This was different. No sudden passion had made her its victim. She had been bathed and pampered, and here lay food to please her and a bower that might well suit a bride.

Alaric?

No; this would not be his way. This definitely did not reflect his mixed feelings for her. He had touched her only because circumstance had thrown them together. He desired her, yes, but he also despised her.

Fear streaked through her as she realized that Alaric had given her to someone else as if she were a fine mare, a manor house, or a hunting hound! He had made a present of her, and some Norman warrior would soon come here to claim his reward for a battle well fought.

Weakness swamped her. Surely this was for the best, she told herself. Hadn't she wished that any other man had come upon her in the trees? Did she not hate Alaric above all Normans?

Aye, this was for the best. She trembled, remembering his touch, and knew that no other man had ever made her feel that way. Without him near her, she was still free. She could still fight, and she would conquer.

A movement behind her made her turn. She braced

herself against the ground and stared warily at the man who entered the tent.

She had seen this man with Alaric earlier. He was massive, with thick curly hair and a curly beard, and he offered her a shy smile. He told her good evening in English, then apologized for his poor use of the language. He came farther into the tent and poured wine into two brass goblets; his fingers shook as he did so. He offered a chalice to Fallon, and in fury she knocked it from his hand. He bit his lip, picked up the goblet, and poured more wine into it.

"Please, Princess. My name is Falstaff. I am your friend. I cherish you above all women." He spoke so softly and with such reverence that Fallon accepted the wine this time, but was careful never to take her eyes from his.

The wine was good. It helped to ease the agony in her heart and in her mind.

She felt his eyes consume her as he took in every detail of her figure beneath the white lace gown.

"I will marry you!" he said suddenly.

"Sir, I promise that I will never, never marry you."

He shook his head. "Please, milady, I don't wish to hurt you."

"If you love me," she whispered. "Let me go. Let me return to my own people."

"I cannot."

"Why not?"

He shrugged, and she was suddenly sorry that she could never love him, for he looked as sad as she felt at that moment. "William would skewer the man who released you," he said, raising his hands helplessly. "Milady, mercenaries roam England. Cruel men. Were you free, you would but become a shared prize among many."

"Not if I could reach my people!" Fallon pleaded desperately.

She felt panic rising within her when he sat beside her and touched her cheek. "Princess, love me, and I will die to defend you!" he swore.

She froze as he lowered his head and tried to kiss her. He placed his hand clumsily on her breast, and she jumped to her feet and ran. With a cry of distress he was after her.

There was little space for her to move, and he trapped her against the skin wall of the tent. She spun around to face him, curling her fingers around the little knife she had stolen from the kitchen. "Please! Please don't touch me!" she begged him.

"I have to," he told her, stepping forward.

She didn't want to kill him. She had never wanted to draw blood at all. Her father had been right. Killing was something that changed men and women alike. As much as she despised Normans, she did not want to kill them . . . but she would not submit to force.

"Come gently, fiery lass—" he began, and he reached for her.

She drew the little knife from the folds of the white gown and thrust it hard into his belly.

He stared at her in amazement, clutched his abdomen in both his hands, and cried out in pain.

Suddenly, guards burst into the tent. They stared at the fallen knight and looked at her as if she were a witch or a sorceress, "Christ above!" One of the men crossed himself. "I'll go for the count!" he said.

Alaric.

He despised her; he had not wanted her. He had given her away, and the friend upon whom he had bestowed her now lay in a pool of blood, dying.

But she couldn't move. She stayed there, huddled against the tent, terrified.

Suddenly Alaric burst into the tent, larger than life. He filled the space; he filled the very air with his aura of command. He had shed his mail, but his sword was still belted to his waist. He stared at her with shock and hatred, then fell to his knees beside his friend.

She was still dazed, still frightened, but she dimly heard him order the guards to take the man Falstaff to be tended to with the greatest care.

Then they were alone, and she thought she would suffocate. She tried to stand straight, but she trembled inside. She had to escape from him; she could not bear to be near him in this small place where his eyes were like steel and smoke and fire and his fury reached out to encompass her like a palpable thing.

"You murderous bitch!"

"I had no wish to kill him, or even harm him. He attacked me, and I fought back."

"He adored you! He was hopelessly enamored of you!"

"I was not enamored of him!"

"You might well have killed him!"

"He shouldn't have attacked me!"

"You were his property. I *gave* you to him!"

That easily, she thought. That horribly, that wretchedly. That morning she had been honored as the king's daughter; no man would have dared touch her.

And now she was property? Nay . . . never! Her fury rose, as did her hatred for Alaric. Vile, bloody Norman bastard.

She raised her chin and swore that her old enemy would never best her. He could give her to a thousand men, and she would despise them all. Eventually she would escape. And if she ever slew a man, it would be this one.

"I am the king's daughter, a princess of England. The daughter of Harold Godwinson. I am not *property*—"

She broke off when he began to swear at her in a rage and took a step towards her. He announced that she was no princess, but his slave. William had given her to Alaric—she was property.

Anger bubbled up inside her again. The day had been too long; too much had been lost. She swore back at him, and told him that she did not recognize the authority of a Norman bastard.

"English law recognizes the ownership of slaves—Princess! Whether criminals condemned in court or prisoners of war."

She was about to start crying again, and that she would not do before him, but she refused to show weakness. Time and time again she had assured him that she would not bend or break, and still, she was very near to falling to her knees before him and begging him to say that the events of the day had never been.

She could not do that. In his towering rage, she barely knew him. And she was trembling furiously herself. She longed to escape. Wildly, she exploded at him, calling him a barbarian. He responded, but she hardly heard him. She fought, barely knowing what she said. The violence rose like heat between them, and suddenly his strides, long and hard, brought them face to face. The fire of his fury seemed to leap from him, to encompass her. She promised that she would always fight him; he swore in a deadly quiet voice that he would gladly tear her limb from limb.

He was too close; she was suffocating. And she was afraid. She had never thought she could be so terribly afraid of Alaric. But the violence about him was tangible and alive. He moved even closer and his words fell against her like blows. Her fingers curled and she realized that she still held the little knife with which she had downed Falstaff. She didn't know whether it was courage or fear that made her raise it again; she only knew that she was desperate.

But he was not Falstaff; perhaps he had even anticipated some trick. He hit her hand forcefully, and the knife flew out of her grasp. The next thing she knew, his fingers were tearing into her hair and he lifted her and threw her upon the bed that Falstaff had made for lovers to share. "Saxon bitch! By God, you will be humbled!"

"No!"

He fell upon her. In wild panic she raged against him; even while fear filled her, she sought inside herself for some courage. He spoke quietly, but he actually threatened her with death.

"See to it, then!" she challenged him. "Slay me, but—"

"Bend!" he raged. "Bend, lady! Ask for mercy, beg for your life. Fallon, by God—"

She could not bring herself to claw at his eyes, and so she spat at him.

He went so rigid that fear seemed to flood her in an instant. His eyes, like steel, tore into her. She felt him with every fiber of her body; the arms that held her prisoner, the sinewed thighs that pressed against her legs.

Suddenly he laced his fingers with hers and held her arms above her head. His free hand was like a brand as he swiftly tore the top of her gown and pushed her skirt high over her waist. His hand touched her naked flesh, and she stifled a cry of distress and astonishment at the heat of it and at her awareness of the desire he so boldly sought to appease.

She was Harold's daughter, she reminded herself. Harold's proud daughter. Delon had given her tender, chaste kisses, but no man had ever done more—except this warrior.

And not even this was the same!

For in those curious moments in the past, he had never pursued her in brutal vengeance. She had known his kiss, and it had burned and consumed her, but he had never been ruthless. Now he looked at her not only with desire but with a burning hatred as well.

"Barbarian!" she whispered, her eyes wide, her tears barely in check. She found a stronger voice. "Barbarian bastard, gutter whelp of Normandy!"

His face was an angry mask, his jaw locked. He had never appeared harder, never more like steel and stone. She twisted against the strength of his arms, but they might as well have been walls that pulsed with life. His flesh was sizzling, and she trembled beneath the heat of his muscles. She swore still, staring into his features— ruggedly handsome features, now twisted with lust and rage.

He pushed away from her suddenly. Stunned, she gasped at her newfound freedom and glanced about for a means of escape. She attempted to rise from the bed; he caught her arm with one hand and tossed her back with a force that left her breathless.

And only then did she realize that he had left her only to doff his sword and scabbard. He wrenched his tunic and chemise over his head, and in the pale firelight, the rippling sinews and muscles of his chest and shoulders gleamed gold. She inhaled sharply, but before she could move, he was on top of her. Wearing only his chausses, he made her very much aware of his body in all its male power and heat.

"No!" She tried to scratch, she tried to kick. She had a certain wiry strength, she knew, and yet it was as nothing against him. He deflected her every blow and secured her wrists, then parted her thighs with his knee and slammed his weight hard against her. She had no power to escape him then. He lay hard against her. If she but moved, she would touch him more intimately.

"Beg quarter, Fallon!"

"Quarter! From you! I shall die first!"

He pinned her arms to the mattress and pressed his weight against her, his jaw in a tight, merciless lock.

"Bastard!" she hissed. He ignored her, and she began to fight again, desperately now, writhing and sobbing.

His eyes held no mercy. The steel in them had dissolved into combustible violence. He hated her. He touched her intimately, but with contempt, his hand raking over her savagely. She could feel his naked belly hard against her own.

Fear and misery won out over pride. Her voice faltered as she whispered, "Nay! Nay, please, Alaric. Alaric . . ."

He went deadly still. He did not release her, and she felt hot tears beneath her eyelids.

This was Alaric, she reminded herself numbly. The man she had sought so often to torment over the years. The man who had touched her with fire again and again, but always given in to her. The man who had been her father's friend, who had rescued her from others more than once.

She stared at him, and before she could stop them, the words were out. "How could you give me to someone else?"

Silently he hovered above her. She did not know if he heard her; his eyes were a gray enigma. She choked back a sob and tried to turn away from him, aware that she had brought herself into dangerous contact with him. She could feel him so thoroughly, so keenly! Heat raged through her limbs. His flesh was hard against hers, and it made a liquid fire burn inside her. He had to move; he had to pull away from her before she began to scream and cry in abject humility.

And then, miraculously, he did. Fallon quickly covered herself with the linen sheets, and Alaric silently donned his tunic.

"So, my lady," he said softly, after retrieving the knife she had stolen. "You tried to murder Falstaff because he dared to touch a princess of England!" He strode back to her, a sardonic smile on his lips. "But now you know that you are nothing more than the whore of the Norman bastard's bastard henchman. You are mine, Fallon, to do with as I will. Give yourself no more airs of grandeur. Harold Godwinson is dead; the Normans will rule England now."

She forgot the fear that had driven her to plead for mercy. She stared at him and saw a cool, disdainful enemy, and she hated him afresh. How could he speak the name of Harold Godwinson so dismissively? She rose to her knees, despising him, determined to strike him.

He caught her wrist in such a cruel hold that she cried out at the pain of it. He stared at her with cold brutality, and she gritted her teeth, lowering her head so that her hair might hide the emotion with which she might betray herself. Harold was dead; England was lost. The tears were spilling from her eyes and down her cheeks, and there was nothing she could do to stop them.

"Fallon!"

He eased his hold; he whispered her name. He sat down beside her and drew her against him. "I am sorry about your father; he was a brave man. I'm sorry . . . I'm sorry . . ."

She was lost, she was wretched, and she was stunned by the change in him. He had been so ruthless, but now his tone was soft, and he was suddenly the man she had known for so many years. His hands soothed her; his words were tender. He held her so gently, so comfortingly, that she hadn't the strength to push him away. He eased her down against the pillow, his eyes seeking hers as he leaned over her. His lips touched her cheeks and her forehead, kissing away her tears.

Then his lips touched hers, and she felt all her emotions collide and explode. She could not deny the blistering heat that swept into her with the sweet tenderness of his kiss. In those moments, he was friend, not foe, and no matter what might come or what had been, they shared

a simple truth in those moments as they grieved together
for Harold, the slain Saxon king. She felt his grief even as
she felt the raging fire that seared her limbs. Again and
again they had clashed; again and again the blaze had
been kindled.

In a hundred years, Fallon would never have yielded to
force. But this was something else.

She did not really know what course he had charted for
her; she knew only that when he kissed her something
within her welcomed him. Her lips parted to his, her arms
curled around his neck. And she trembled, alive with heat
and vibrance. There was no violence here; there was no
force but only gentle persuasion. His tender kisses fell
across her face, then he possessed her mouth again, and
he filled her as he seemed to drink from her. He whispered senseless words, and she was soothed. His arms
held her, and she was secure.

He smoothed back her hair, murmuring. With passion
and fire he seared her throat, and she could not have
stopped him when he cradled her breasts in his hands,
teased and stroked them like a lover, igniting a searing
new fire in her, sent the flames swirling into the very
center of her being. A wind raged around her, fanning the
sea of fire within. Alaric was the wind, and she could not
stop him. If she would whisper in any protest, his lips
would catch her words, and she would forget them again
in the tempest of his kiss.

He touched her with ever greater abandon. She felt the
hot caress of his rough palm against her thigh, stroking
her hip. She was dimly aware that she lay nearly naked
with him, that her gown was torn and twisted. His hand
slid up the length of her inner thigh, and he touched her
freely, but her gasp was lost to his hungry kiss, and even
as he touched her, he pressed his weight hard against her.
Panic seized her, but even as she realized how far they
had traveled, something hot and molten and nearly pain-

fully sweet sent a shudder rippling through her, and where he touched her the blaze went wild.

But then the feeling ebbed, to be replaced by a sharp and piercing pain. Brought back to harsh reality, Fallon tried to twist her lips away from his, to wrest herself from his hold, to escape the sudden sting of pain and humiliation.

He had called her a Norman whore this night, and now he had made her one.

She cried out in horror; she slammed her fists against his face and she fought the new tears that threatened to blind her. She could not dislodge him. The shaft of his body burned deep inside her, burned and invaded.

He caught her hands and held them, but even as she twisted to escape him, she felt his eyes on her, holding her still, making her breathless.

"Alaric . . . you hurt me!"

He shook his head. His features were starkly handsome, and his voice was soft when he spoke again, "Nay, it will hurt no more."

He took her mouth in a hungry kiss, then laced his fingers with hers and began to move against her in slow, steady, rhythmic thrusts, burying himself deeper and deeper inside her.

The painful sweetness began to seep into her body again. Her fingers fell limp. He ravaged her mouth, and he whispered words to her; he buried his face in her throat, and his lips seared her breasts. His teeth teased her nipples, and his tongue swept over her again and again, and he suckled heatedly, and all the while he moved.

She was not sure when or where the honeyed longing began. She moaned softly and arched against him, and splendor spilled through her. Their breath grew heated and came like thunder. The heat seemed to build, and she tossed as if in a wild tempest beneath him, awed by the sensations. He rose above her and she saw that his features were taut and hard and twisted in a mask of passion. He thrust his body harder and faster as he watched her. He placed his hand on her breast and felt her heart, and she closed her eyes as her body surged to meet his, ever seeking . . .

It came upon her like a dizzying magic. Like the comet streaking across the sky, like a sun bursting in a midnight sky. It was a honey that swamped her; it was the most shattering feeling she ever known.

And it had come from him.

He thrust against her one more time. His body arched, and it seemed that he flooded into her, sweeping and warm. For a moment they were locked together, motionless.

Then their eyes met, and reality came crashing down around her. Alaric was soaked with the heat that had claimed them, but he was still nearly decently clad, while her one garment was ripped and torn. He was still within her, she realized with horror. Surely he was amused by the ease with which he had had her. Surely he knew every sensation that had streaked through her.

He started to smile and she swore in a fury, pounding her fists with all her strength against his chest. He caught her hands, and he watched her with a fathomless expression while she twisted and fought, until she finally lay still, panting beneath him.

"We've both known that was coming, haven't we, Fallon?"

Any trace of a tender lover was gone; his words were cold and brutal, and they made her feel like a whore. She wrenched her hands free and tried to rake her nails across his cheek. He caught her fingers and held them fast, and offered her a distant smile.

"Thank you, milady, for a most entertaining evening."

"Bastard!" she hissed. A tear trickled down her cheek as she felt the callused pad of his thumb against her flesh.

He whispered to her once again, "You did not fight me, Fallon."

She gritted her teeth and stared at him. "I hate you, Alaric."

"You came to me willingly. You parted your lips to my kiss and put your arms around me."

"I hate you!"

He shrugged. "Tell yourself what you will, Fallon. I am a Norman, I have brutalized you, the country will be raped, so please yourself, and assure your heart that you have been raped as well. But I am not Falstaff, Fallon. I am not entranced. I am wary of your temper and your lethal talents. God knows, I have nearly perished by a few." He paused, watching her. Then he released her hands and stared at her still, and she knew that he was daring her to raise a hand against him again.

He rose from her at last. She wanted to scream out her relief to be free of him. She grasped the sheet instead, determined to cover herself.

He straightened his clothing, but his grim, taunting smile remained in place. "Fallon, remember—by English law you are mine. My property, my slave."

Her temper came alive and soared. "I am no criminal to be sentenced or sold—"

"Ah, but my lady, you are," he assured her. "You have attempted and perhaps accomplished murder. The loss of Falstaff's services is a great inconvenience to me. His services, you see, are far more valuable than yours, charming as yours may be."

Her temper was ever her bane. She had ignored his taunts before, but now she cried out and rose, desperate to strike him, to hurt him. But he was ready for her. He caught her hands and pulled her to him, crushing her bare breasts hard against his chest. Fallon cried out; she felt color flood her cheeks, and he smiled with ruthless humor at her embarrassment. He pressed a sheet into her hands. "Behave, slave," he said softly.

"Son of a jackass!"

"By English law, Fallon, your crime is murder. Your punishment is slavery. And I, milady, am your master. You have always told me that you cannot be broken, but I swear it now, lady—you will bend or break."

"You have not broken me, Alaric! You never will. And I will never bend to your Norman bastard duke!"

He smiled at her pleasantly. But she heard him grind his teeth, and enjoyed one moment of triumph. He dragged her hard against him once more. "Then the battle is only just engaged," he whispered.

It seemed that aeons passed, a lifetime in which the churning gray slate of his eyes held her captive as surely as the strength of his arms. Then he released her, and she fell back on the bed. He spun around, dismissing her, and strode from the tent.

Fallon looked down at the sheet and saw the evidence of her loss, and hot tears welled up in her eyes again. Her father was dead, England was lost—and she had surrendered her innocence and dignity.

She turned her face into the pillow as tears racked her. In less than a day she had lost everything that had been dear to her in life.

She sobbed herself into a merciful sleep.

PART THREE

The Conquerors

Chapter Fifteen

Alaric did not return to his quarters that evening. He asked where Falstaff had been taken, then hurried to see his old friend.

Falstaff slept; the physician told Alaric that they must wait and see. If there was no infection, and if the wound healed cleanly, Falstaff might well live. But one could never tell with such injuries. Many, many men lay wounded. They were still being carried back from the battlefield as the living went about the grim task of separating those who breathed from the dead, among whom they lay.

When he emerged from the physician's tent, Alaric saw that dawn was breaking. He had barely walked ten steps before he was stopped by a messenger.

The duke had spent the night upon the battlefield, the messenger informed him. He had sent men to find Edith Svanneshals and bring her to the battle site. The dead Saxons had been stripped of their mail and weapons and thrown naked on a heap. William needed Edith to find Harold's body among the slain. Alaric was to accompany her.

He held Edith to his side as they came to a ridge that scooped low to a valley. Bodies were piled there, frozen in the contortions of death. Many were naked, and many were dismembered.

Harold's body would be mutilated, too, Alaric thought.

Edith sagged against him. He feared that she would be sick. Alaric had fought many, many battles, but the bile still rose in his throat as he stared at the macabre scene.

"Edith," he whispered softly, "let me take you from this! I can talk with William; we'll find someone else for this cruel task."

"No!" She straightened, and though she retained a ghastly pallor, she smiled again. "I must know, Alaric. Already they whisper that he lives, that he has escaped the battle and will return. I must know. And if he is dead, then I crave the burial that your duke swears he will give him."

Alaric nodded, understanding. But the sea of Saxon bodies was daunting. A priest was passing among the corpses at some distance; with a start Alaric recognized the man as Damien, the curious clergyman who had spoken so strangely on the night the comet first appeared.

Father Damien walked among the dead, murmuring prayers and blessings. He raised his head, and his eyes met Alaric's. He nodded gravely, then lifted his hand and beckoned toward Edith. "I believe that we may have found him," Alaric said. He took Edith's arm and led her toward Father Damien.

"Do not look long, my lady," the priest warned her. But she was staring hard at the horribly mutilated corpse, which had been stripped naked. She didn't scream, but a sound more horrible than any Alaric had ever heard tore from her throat, and she fell to the ground. Tears spilled from her eyes, and she lay upon the body that had once been a man.

"Edith, Edith!" Alaric reached down to her. He brought her sobbing into his arms and signaled to two soldiers to retrieve the body. Silently and grimly, they wrapped the corpse in purple cloth and carried it from the pile.

Father Damien's eyes met Alaric's above Edith's blond head. "Count Alaric," he murmured, bowing; then he stepped past them, following the body of his king. Alaric saw the priest approach William's tent. A shiver touched him, for he knew that Damien would demand to be allowed to accompany Harold's body to the gravesite. He wondered if the priest was his friend or his foe.

Alaric turned his attention back to Edith. Her sobs were quieting, and she hung limp against him. "Gyrth, Leofwine, Harold—all dead," she murmured. "Tostig, too, and Wulfnoth a prisoner all these years." She started to sob again, and Alaric patted her back feebly, murmuring soothing words. She pushed away from him suddenly, and stared at him with her enormous blue eyes, eyes that reminded him achingly of her daughter. He would have to tell her that Fallon was here. The knowledge might hurt her, but it would be better than the heartache of wondering.

"All dead, all gone, so quickly!" she said. "Alaric, I don't know where Galen and Aelfyn are. Tam is safe at Bosham. But I don't know if my other boys are alive or dead. He has told me—William has told me—that he will spare me, and if the children do not oppose him, they, too, will be spared. But"—she paused, and tears welled in her eyes anew—"if they war against him, he will offer no mercy . . . Alaric, even Fallon is missing!"

"Hush, Edith. Fallon is here."

She stared at him, amazed. "She followed her father to the very battlefield?"

"She was fighting," Alaric told her.

Her eyes closed in pain. "She is alive? She is not injured?"

"She is alive and well," Alaric said.

"He will not let me see her," Edith muttered. "Of that I am certain."

Alaric did not dispute her because he was sure that she spoke the truth. William was capable of a certain chivalry toward Edith, but he had been cold and ruthless in his appraisal of Fallon. In time, if he felt that Fallon had been duly chastened, he would allow her to see her mother.

Edith's eyes met his again, pathetically seeking reassurance. "She loved her father so much. She was his most passionate admirer, and she has always been stronger in her heart, I think, than any of the boys. She will keep fighting. Please, please, Alaric. I know you are a Norman, and I know you are the duke's friend. But you were Harold's friend, too. He trusted you. Please, in his memory, keep her safe from the Norman curse that has fallen upon us now—"

"Edith," he interrupted her softly, his heart thudding painfully. "Edith, she is in my care. I left her just minutes ago. I am the Norman curse that has befallen her. Yet what happened between us was not what you would imagine, but something that in truth began years ago."

Her eyes searched his again. He felt a burning sensation, and he stared at her, feeling sad and remorseful.

Through her tears, Edith suddenly whispered, "I'm glad it was you."

"Edith—" he began uncomfortably.

She touched his lips and shook her head. "Alaric, do you think I care what things come to pass between a man and a woman when death stalks the land? Or that I do not know the dauntless warrior that dwells inside my own daughter? Nay, Alaric, in time, bitter memories fade. Alaric, please, I beg of you, do what you must, but keep her alive!"

He didn't know what to say. Edith stared at him passionately. Nay! He could not battle Fallon endlessly. Yet he did not love her, and he could not be bound by such a promise. She had her father's temper, courage, honor, and passion. Someday she and Alaric would square off as enemies.

Edith touched his cheek. "Alaric," she whispered, "I have lost so much. I beseech you, please . . ."

His hand covered hers. He brought her palm to his mouth and lightly kissed it, then smiled at her. "She is my prisoner, Edith. I will keep her so, I swear it."

She stared at him a moment longer, then sighed, content.

Alaric wondered dismally just what he had promised.

Morning came. Fallon awoke slowly, opening her eyes, becoming dimly aware of light. She closed them again, and grief streaked through her. Sleep was the only comfort. Light brought with it a truth that gentle dreams could erase.

It was over; the battle was over. Her father was dead, and the coast was being laid waste.

She turned upon the ironically beautiful bed where she had lost the final vestiges of her pride, and she watched the patterns of the sun play across the walls of the tent. She could hear voices. Men were talking about her father's death. No one seemed to know the identity of the four Normans who had swept down upon him. They whispered about the duke, and someone denied that he had been there. Perhaps Count Alaric had been the one who struck the finishing blow. Sometimes it seemed that he was immortal, they said, for he was always in the thick of battle, and yet he never fell. Nay, it seemed that he seldom bled.

Fallon clenched her eyes shut tightly. Please God! Alaric could not have taken her father's life so ignobly! Not when she had lain with him so . . .

She rolled from the bed then, loath to touch it in any

way. Footsteps passed the tent, and she spun around, but no one came to her. Had she been forgotten? Perhaps.

Fallon moved to the entrance to the tent. There were no guards there now. Only a few men moved about, dousing cooking fires, cleaning cooking utensils.

Fallon heard a whinnying and she looked to the right. A number of horses were tethered to a pole. They were bridled, but missing their saddles and their trappings. She caught her breath and looked carefully about. If she could reach the horses, she might have a chance of escape.

She was scarcely dressed, she reminded herself. She had nothing to wear but the white lace gown—now, she recalled bitterly, torn and dishevelled. But what did she care how she looked when she escaped them, if only she could?

She waited just a moment longer, watching the broad back of a Norman who was kicking dirt on a nearby fire. He could not see her, and in his movement, surely, he would not hear her.

She streaked out of the tent in silence, then raced wildly toward the Norman mounts. Her breath came quick and ragged, and pain shot from the soles of her bare feet through her calves to her thighs, but she kept running as hard as she could. The horses were before her; she nearly reached them.

Suddenly a muscular warrior appeared. Fallon stopped as the man stared at her—as startled as she was. Then a slow, appreciative smile spread over his features. *"Chérie!* Did you find your companion of the night less than gentle? Alas, do not judge us all so cruelly."

She swore in disgust, trying to swerve around him to reach the horses. Another man blocked her way; he was older and heavier, and his eyes caressed her barely clothed form with ill-concealed lust.

"She'll be mine, lad!" he told the younger man. "Rank has its privilege!" He bowed to Fallon and began to walk toward her. "Let me introduce myself, *mademoiselle,*" he said, reaching out beefy hands for her. "Viscomte Rolf de Lisieux, and ever at your service, sweet Saxon pet— *oomph!*" He doubled over, swearing as Fallon kicked him hard in the groin.

"She doesn't understand you, oaf!" The younger man, roared. He switched from French to laughably bad English, and too late Fallon realized that he had come up behind her. He swung her into his arms and kissed her. She bit his lip, drawing blood. He swore and pushed her furiously from him. "Bitch!" he roared.

By then quite an audience of men had arrived, and they roared with laughter at the scene. Momentarily free, Fallon ran desperately for the horses. Heavy arms wound around her waist as a third man grabbed her, held her tight, and dragged her back.

"She's mine!" The viscomte declared, but the younger man let out some sound and leapt forward, brandishing a knife. Amazed, Fallon watched the two. She felt the arms of the third man go lax as he laughed and egged on the battle.

"Let's see if age can best beauty!" the man shouted.

"Hold tight the prize!" the younger warrior said. He lunged at the vicomte, and the other moved back quickly. In seconds a fierce fight was engaged. Fallon waited, barely breathing. When her captor cheered in triumph for the younger warrior, she slipped from his hold and tore for the horses. Shouts and confusion reigned around her, and this time, as she ran, no one stopped her.

Suddenly a command rang out in loud, harsh French—a single word spoken in a thunderous rage: *"Halte!"* Even Fallon, about to swing herself up on one of the steeds, heard the sheer power in the voice and paused, turning.

Alaric walked among the men. His mantle was thrown back over his shoulder, and his hands were on his hips. A deep, chilling fire burned in his eyes as he surveyed the men with contempt. "You fight, fools, while the prize eludes you?"

Fallon gasped. She thought that he had not seen her, but his eyes came straight to hers, and a mocking curl touched his lip as he bowed to her. The vicomte called out that he deserved the girl—the rose in their midst. Alaric silenced him with a look. The younger warrior was panting heavily. Alaric walked on by him and shook his head. "Fools! it is amazing that the Saxons did not best us. Harold is dead, but the Saxon's cub ties you in knots."

She heard a sharp intake of breath and her body seemed to burn as all eyes turned to her. Alaric's voice rose, and men moved away to clear a path as he walked among them. "She laughs and eludes you as you fight over her, yet I warn you now—the girl is mine. Most men know it, and others will learn. Touch her and you deal with me. She would love to see Norman blood spilled, so be warned not to entertain her so!"

Fallon stiffened at the contempt that laced his voice even while he proclaimed her his. Then she realized that she, too, was the fool, for no one had touched her; yet she stood by the horse and cowered like a child.

Nay! she cried out inwardly. He would not so easily tame her. She spun in a clean and perfect pirouette and caught the reins of a soft gray steed. She leapt with graceful agility upon the creature's back and slammed her heels against its ribs. The horse reared, the men fell back.

Fallon looked toward the forest and hunched forward as the steed turned to gallop. Then two strong arms grabbed her around her waist and she was dragged from the horse, shrieking. Alaric held her high above him and she observed his eyes. Then he let her fall against him, and as she slid down the hard length of his body to her feet, her torn gown caught on his vestments, and her legs were bared against the hardness of his sides. He swept his mantle from his shoulders and wrapped her in it. Shouts went up again, and he smiled at her with glittering eyes. His fingers tore into her hair and he arched her throat back, and his lips fell against the pulse that beat there before they claimed her own.

She fought him, barely able to breathe. As the moments passed, the world seemed to blacken before her. He held her so cruelly that she could not draw air. His arms were locked hard around her, and she could not move her own. Her strength deserted her, and she began to fall.

He swept her into his arms. She was so dizzy that she could not fight him. Barely conscious, she hung limp in his arms, gasping for breath.

"Remember," he told the men softly. "She is mine. Tell any who would challenge me that William has made her mine. And I have never been known to relinquish property. Messires!" He turned sharply on his heel and walked away with her. Still dizzy, Fallon gazed up miserably at the hard planes and angles of his ruggedly handsome features. He did not look at her; he walked and stared straight ahead.

Then his eyes did fall her way briefly, and she quickly lowered her lashes, her heart thundering painfully. His timely appearance, she knew, had saved her from the ruthless attentions of the men.

Was this the man who had killed her father? Had he charged in while Harold staggered about, blind and wounded, and delivered the final blow?

Suddenly Fallon found herself lifted high and set upon Alaric's great black horse. In a moment of near delirium, she thought of grabbing the reins and taking flight, but his eyes were ruthlessly upon her and his warning was barely needed.

"Don't even think about it, milady. Satan is trained to my whistle, and will carry you nowhere except to the warmth of my bed."

He leapt up behind her. She felt his vibrant hardness against her back, and she lowered her head, willing herself desperately not to remember the night.

She realized with a sinking heart that he was taking her to the wooden fortress erected by the Normans at Hastings. There were armed guards everywhere here—at the outer gates, before the door, lining the ruins of the old Roman wall. They saluted Alaric sharply as he and Fallon rode into the courtyard. Several pages hurried forward to take charge of his steed as he dismounted and reached for her, setting her on her feet. "You'll be safer here." He murmured distractedly. "Come along."

She pulled back on his arm, unwilling to yield anything to him this morning.

He caught her elbow and dragged her to his side, his voice nearly a growl as he spoke. "Fallon, I've had no sleep in nearly two days. I am too exhausted to tangle with you. Believe it or not, Princess, I am interested only in your welfare. Now, come along—"

"I cannot!" she cried out passionately.

He was aware that the guards watched him. Most of them were loyal to William and Alaric, but men would talk, and he did not dare allow word to spread that Harold's daughter still fought with such spirit. Nor had he much patience left. His body was weary from the battle; his heart and soul were weary from his encounter with Edith and from the sad discovery of Harold's remains.

"Fallon— Oh, never mind!" he muttered darkly, and bending low, he threw her impatiently over his shoulder. He strode into the fortress that way, called a cheery good morning to some of the men, and did not pause until he came before a certain door. When they entered, he tossed her hard onto his bed, which stood beside the wall. Even as she fought to breathe, he wrenched his mantle from her shoulders and pitched her into another breathless roll as he did so. She caught back a scream, thinking that he meant to take her in a fury.

"Don't try to leave this room; I will not make the mistake of leaving you less than heavily guarded in the future. I have sworn to keep you safe, and so I will do my best to see that no harm comes your way."

He paused for a moment, and she stared at the wall, her heart beating wildly. Alaric had sworn to keep her safe? To whom had he given such a vow?

"I'll send someone to you soon enough with water and food." He turned and headed toward the door.

Tears filled her eyes, and she spun on him, drawing the remnants of the white gown over her breasts as she called out to him.

"Alaric!"

He paused and looked back. For all his height and arrogant air of supreme power, he appeared exhausted. He was the victor. What could tear at him so greatly today? she wondered bitterly.

"Hurry, Fallon. I've business to attend to."

Her lip trembled and her voice faltered and grew husky and weak. "They say that my father was injured. That an arrow struck his eye, and that he lay defenseless and blinded. And that four Norman knights moved in on him and—and hacked him to bits."

He was silent; he did not deny her words. She felt the terror welling within her, and despite herself, her next question broke as a sob. "Alaric, please God, tell me that you were not among them!"

He hesitated. For a moment she felt that he would come to her, that he longed to touch her, just as she desperately longed to be assured. If she had lain so with her father's murderer, she would never be able to forgive herself, to live with herself.

"I would do that to no man," he said softly at last. "Much less to a friend and a king."

She lowered her head; her eyes swam, and she would not have him see her cry. She heard the door close softly, and he was gone.

William ordered Harold buried in a most curious place, Alaric thought. He wondered again about them all. Were not they, the Normans, the civilized ones? Were not the Vikings the barbarians? But perhaps it was not so, for the duke ordered the Saxon king to be buried not in a graveyard, but high upon a ridge that overlooked the coast, as if he would forever protect it. He allowed Father Damien to perform the burial rites.

A wind blew fiercely; the sky was as gray as steel. Thunder rumbled and roiled, and the few knights who had been allowed to attend the burial service felt a curious chill. Did God dwell here? Alaric wondered.

"Let Harold, the Saxon king, lie here!" William cried out. "Let him guard in death and in eternity this coast, which he sought to protect. Let him ever protect it!"

Lightning flashed ragged against the sky. Alaric watched as Father Damien stepped forward. The service that followed was not strictly Christian. Viking custom slipped into the rite—as in the fires that burned by the tomb. And then the priest began to chant in the ancient tongue. And there upon the coast was Harold granted rest before the Christian god, the Viking god Woden, and the even older gods of the Druids. Alaric wondered, watching William, what this last passage between him and Harold signified.

When it was over, Alaric made the sign of the cross. William and his men began to move away. Alaric looked up to find Father Damien watching him. He refused to be daunted by the mysterious Saxon priest, and so he returned the stare. "What is it, Damien? Do you, like many of these people, expect us to grow horns and tails?"

Damien shook his head. He removed his gaze to stare out at the gray mist that promised to claim the coming night.

"Nay, Edward warned us long ago that the fires would come and that demons would sweep the land."

"His deathbed prophecy?"

"Aye," Damien said, watching Alaric.

"So you are not surprised by our victory?"

Damien smiled. "The victory, Count Alaric? Aye, the victory."

"Do you doubt that William will take England?"

Damien laughed, and Alaric realized that he was a young man, near his own age, and truly curious for a priest. "You doubt it more than I do, my lord. Only a fool would stand here now and think that all of England has fallen in a single battle. You are planning your route even now to London. William has just begun."

"William will conquer."

"William will be king," Damien said, and he said it with no doubt, leaving Alaric to believe that there could be none. But still he smiled. " 'Till a green tree, split asunder, will join together of its own accord,' " Damien muttered.

"What are you saying, man? Speak to me clearly, if you seek something. Do not come to me with riddles."

"That is when the land will heal, and I tell you now, my lord, already that growth has begun. But you see, I warn you, sir. Your demons will sweep the land; fire will rage, men will die, and women will lament. But in the end, it is the land that will conquer. This island and these people." He bowed low to Alaric. "My lord," he murmured, and Alaric found the words sincere, "I am ever your servant."

Alaric watched him move away, and a metallic taste filled his mouth. He was dead-weary. God, he was sick with it already, the plunder and the bloodshed and the death.

Night was falling. The stars were rising high. The rain began to threaten as the wind rose. Alaric turned from the hill and mounted Satan.

He joined William, Odo, and Robert for a meal, and he watched William's impassive face as they discussed what their next moves would be, what villages should be taken, what course might be needed that Dover—a fortified city—might be forced to surrender. Without being explicit, they all knew that William was waiting—for offers of submission from the rest of the country, for an offer of power from the witan.

It was nearly midnight when Alaric was able to leave the duke's presence. He thought about finding some other place of rest for the night, for he was far too exhausted to deal with Fallon. But he set his jaw, for this was to be their fate for the time, and he was weary enough to feel ruthless.

He went to his room in the fortress, where a fire burned low in the grate. A tray held the barely touched remains of an evening meal.

Fallon lay upon the bed, her hair an ebony cover over her features. But as he closed the door, she started, and swirled around, coming to her knees, then edging off the bed. She was wary, ready for battle.

He was not. He stepped into the room, barely glancing her way. He cast off his mantle and hung it up, then removed his scabbard and sword. Methodically, not glancing her way, he stripped. Without a word, he snuffed out the candle and lay down on the bed.

In the darkness he could hear her heartbeat. He could smell her feminine perfume; he could taste her wariness. He waited several minutes.

Then he heard her inching toward the door. She would

try to grab his sword first; then she would throw open the door and attempt to run.

He waited until he could almost see her reaching for his broadsword. Then he bolted naked from the bed and slammed his weight against her, carrying her to the floor with him, then straddling her.

"Leaving, my love?"

She spewed forth a furious oath. She surged against him, trying to escape his hold. The white gown was twisted so that the soft mound of her femininity touched the shaft of his desire. He swallowed, gritted his teeth, and remembered his exhaustion.

He stood quickly, pulling her up in the darkness. "Take the gown off," he commanded her.

She paused gasping. "Nay!" she cried out, holding what remained of the fabric tight against her. "Nay, Alaric—"

Heartlessly he caught the gown at her breasts and rent it. She tried desperately to retrieve the pieces, but he jerked them away from her and tossed them on the fire. He heard her inhale sharply as the soft silk quickly caught the flame. She fell to her knees, trying to cover her nakedness with her arms.

"Sorry, Princess," he said softly. "I don't wish to lose you to the night." He walked over to her and laid a hand on her ebony hair, then tugged on a curl. "Get in the bed. Against the wall."

"Nay!" she denied him with a desperate little sob. Her eyes slowly rose to him, both pleading and challenging. "Nay, I'll not fall prey to you again!"

He smiled, then lifted her and tossed her onto the bed. He spun around and found a soft braided belt among the short tunics and bleaunts in one of his trunks. When he returned, she was struggling to her knees. She lashed out at him, and he swore as her nails raked his chest. Then he caught her hands, and tied her wrists securely with the braided belt. "Bastard!" she seethed, choking. She was fighting tears, and he was joltingly aware of her beauty as she stared up at him. Fire and fury glistened in those tears, and her eyes were as clear as sapphires against the fragile beauty of her face. Her hair was a wanton ebony mane, and her body was achingly beautiful, the ripe fullness of her breasts pressed forward by her arms, the slim length of her torso and legs exposed to his awakening ardor. She trembled, and he permitted his eyes to sweep boldly over her form, thinking her waist no larger than the circle of his hands, the curve and flare of her hips more lush than the summer solstice, and the ebony triangle against her thighs a temptation few men could resist, along with the satiny smooth and shapely perfection of her legs. His eyes returned to hers, and he smiled, pulling the belt tight around her wrists and tying the other end to the post at the head of the bed.

She began to rail against him in earnest. "You bastard!"

Malicious mischief swept through him, and he straddled her again. He ran his hands along the silken beauty of her ribs, just grazing the soft mounds of her breasts. "Aye, my lady, I've tied you up to torture you, to do with you what I will, against your every desire. Aye, my lady! This is what I have been up to all day long—plunder and pillaging and rape. Why, I've raped so many fair Saxon damsels this day that I am exhausted. I can fight no more, and so must tie and bind my victim hand and foot!"

Her eyes grew wider and wider as she stared at him, and she wriggled fiercely beneath him. Don't lunge so, my beauty, he thought, or else I will forget exhaustion and remind you that you have desires of your own and that we played at fire and lust long ere this came about!

"Oaf!" she cried out. "Get off me!"

He leaned against her, and his whisper touched her cheek. "Lest I hurt you, Princess?" His fingers played about her breasts, the callused pad of his thumb flicking over the hard rosy peak of her nipple. Then he watched her wide eyes as he stroked his hand down the length of her, adjusting his weight to caress the indentation of her belly where it curved below her hip. "Poor lady, so abused! Even now you quiver."

"If I quiver, it is with hatred," she assured him. Her eyes were huge, and he nearly smiled, wondering if she believed his words and his threats. "I swear I'll—" She paused, and he arched a brow, waiting. "I swear I'll never yield to you—again."

He tossed back his head and laughed. "Fallon, I could bring you begging for my thrust within you this very moment, if I so chose."

She started to gainsay him, then seemed to realize the words were meant as a challenge. She clenched her jaw hard, and he thought she might very well fight him to the death that night. No terror rankled so deep, he knew, as the fear of her own surrender.

"Good night, Princess," he said softly, and he rolled away from her. He offered his back to her and stared at the fire, willing sleep to come. Conscious of her rigid body beside him, he did not sleep easily. In time, he felt her relax, and he knew that sleep had claimed her.

Weariness overrode him, but he slept fitfully. To his amazement, he dreamed. In his dream he awoke to discover that Fallon was no longer tied to the bed, but that they were tied together. They lay naked upon the bed, and Father Damien stood over them, his arms stretched out to the heavens.

"Where a green tree grows together, the land will heal." Then the priest stared right into his eyes and said, "The land will conquer. In time it will be England. This island will win. These people will win. The fruit of the tree will be English."

Father Damien vanished. Alaric, truly awake now, bolted up.

The fire was nearly out. He turned and saw that Fallon still slept, Tears had dried on her cheeks, and her breasts thrust full and firm toward the night. He smiled with something near tenderness, then remembered his dream. He scowled furiously, drew the covers over her seductive form, and lay back, seeking sleep.

He did not sleep again. He lay awake in agony, clenching his teeth as his ardor grew.

He could turn and play the Norman bastard in truth, he knew.

But no, somehow he had been challenged. And he would prove to her that the desperate, hungry heat between them was not of his making—but of theirs.

Had he not met every challenge in life? This was but one more.

Chapter Sixteen

Fallon awoke to a tapping against the door. She was free, she discovered; no ties bound her. And Alaric was gone.

She pulled the covers tightly about her shoulders and murmured an uneasy "Aye?"

The door opened. A lad of about sixteen—with obviously newly shorn hair and clean cheeks—came in, huffing and puffing as he shoved a big trunk. Once the trunk was inside the room, he sat upon it and offered her a radiant smile. "How do you do, my lady?" He said then.

The question seemed so ridiculous to her that she almost laughed. She didn't answer him, but a smile did tug at her lips and she returned his curious stare.

He stood, and swept her an outrageous bow. "I am Richard, my lady. Richard of Elwald. I serve Count Alaric of Anlou."

Fallon inclined her head to him, but she could not suppress a swell of bitterness within her heart. This Saxon lad served a Norman lord with evident ease. "Elwald?" she repeated softly. She had heard the name of the village before, and something stirred within her. "Richard of Elwald," she repeated. "Tell me, Richard, how has Elwald fared in all this?"

"Quite well, my lady," Richard assured her.

"Quite well?"

His smile faded and his charming dimples disappeared for a moment's unease. "No invading force would dare to touch the town, milady. Count Alaric has been our thane since Edward the Confessor gave him the land many years ago."

She lowered her eyes. Aye, that was it, she could recall it all now. She had been just a child, and Alaric had been a very young man himself when he had saved Edward's life during the boar hunt.

Alaric had been made thane of Elwald, and William had been promised the throne.

"Anyway, my lady, since you are a Saxon," Richard continued, brightening, "my lord Alaric thought perhaps that I should serve you."

"Oh. And where is your lord Alaric this morning?"

He looked down at his feet. "I believe he is with the duke, my lady."

"You believe he is out plundering, burning, pillaging, and destroying England," Fallon told him flatly.

"They are waiting," Richard told her defensively.

"Waiting for what?"

"They are waiting for offers of surrender. William wishes to see what the English will do."

She was curious herself, but curiosity brought heartache. Her brothers had never been given any official titles, but they would surely fight for their father's honor. Edgar the Atheling remained in England. The earls, Edwin and Morkere, had not taken part in the battle at Hastings, for they had not been able to travel south quickly enough to join her father.

"Has anyone surrendered?" she asked Richard anxiously.

He shook his head.

Fallon lay back and smiled at the first piece of good news she had heard. Perhaps there was still hope.

Richard cleared his throat. "The trunk holds your clothing. Your mother sent it last night."

"My mother?" She bolted up so quickly that she nearly forgot to pull the sheet with her. She grasped the linen as Richard flushed, and she felt the color rise to her own cheeks.

"Aye," Richard said quickly, busying himself with moving the trunk against the wall.

"My mother was here?" Anxiously Fallon wrapped the linen about herself and rose. "Please, answer me! Where is she now? Why hasn't she come to me?"

He bowed his head as he sat on the trunk again. "She came to find the king's body." Fallon gasped, and he stared up at her entreatingly. Richard did not like to deliver bad news. "William ordered that Harold be buried with honor. Father Damien said the service."

Fallon turned away from him and sank down on the bed. To her surprise, he came hurrying after her and knelt by her feet. She saw his bright green eyes through tears. "You mustn't repeat this, milady, but . . ."

"But what?" she whispered.

"Well, we who have met him know that Damien is not quite an ordinary priest."

"Aye—so?"

" 'Tis said that a storm broke out when the king was interred and that the Norman host hurried away. The sky grew gray and then black. When midnight came, Damien went back to the gravesite and lifted his arms to the heavens. 'Tis said that a boat, sailing the night sky, swooped down, and Father Damien set King Harold's earthly remains upon the boat. 'Twas King Arthur's boat, and with him sat Alfred and Ethelred and all our great kings gone before Harold! Father Damien whispered more words. King Harold's soul was taken into the company of the great kings, and his body was sailed upon the midnight air to Waltham Abbey, where it was carefully tended in his special place, the abbey he made so sacred."

Fallon stared at him incredulously. She did not in truth believe that a boat had sailed through the sky—but there was something in the times that made her uneasy. She could not forget Edward the Confessor's deathbed prophecy, nor could she forget the comet that had streaked across the sky. She thought about how the Holy Rood at Waltham had bowed when her father prayed.

Apparently rumor about the crucifix had spread swiftly, for Richard whispered softly, "A miracle came to King Harold, they say, because God was preparing a place in a higher kingdom where he could dwell. And trust me, Princess! The story I have told you is true!"

She smiled ruefully at him. He wanted to reassure her, she realized. She thought perhaps he wanted her to know that her father's body had been disinterred after its Norman burial and secreted back to his abbey at Waltham.

Harold would have liked that, Fallon thought. She reached out and touched the young man's hair. "Thank you, Richard."

He blushed profusely and stood. "Now, my lady, if you'll allow me, I'll bring you water and some food. Would you like some wine? Ah, wait, I believe that they are running out of wine. Some good English ale, that's what I will bring you!"

"Richard, wait! Where is my mother?"

He hesitated. "She went back to Bosham. William has ordered that she is to be left in peace."

"And I was not allowed to see her? Alaric, damn him—"

"Nay, my lady. 'Twas not Alaric, but William, who thought it best to keep you apart."

He saluted her and cheerfully left her. Fallon hurried over to the trunk. Reaching into it, she bit her lip. The gowns were her own, and though she had not seen her mother, Edith's loving touch seemed to be within the trunk. She had packed carefully—soft hose, silk chemises, leather shoes, and even her riding boots. She had included bleaunts edged in fur for the autumn cold, and she had also enclosed Fallon's best mantle, one of heavy wool, lined in softest white rabbit.

There was a knock upon the door again. Wrapping the sheet tightly about herself, Fallon went forward and answered it. Richard had returned with a large tray bearing water and food. In the corridor behind him, Fallon saw two well-armed guards in helmets and mail. Their swords were at their waists and they held lances.

"I do hope that I won't prove to be too much for you to handle!" Fallon muttered to the pair of them.

Richard smiled, and the guards bowed. "My lady, we are given to believe that you could prove too much for an army," one told her.

She smiled sweetly and slammed the door.

Richard carefully balanced the tray and set it down on the trunk. He had brought her a large leather tankard of ale, fresh bread, dried fish, and a half-dozen beautiful red apples. She thanked him absently, but he hovered nearby, and realizing that he waited still, she looked his way.

"Please don't try to escape again," the boy said.

She cocked her head warily. "I've no plans to escape at the moment, I'm afraid, but why the warning?"

"You will be dealt with harshly."

Had she been treated with kindness thus far? she wondered bitterly.

Richard watched her unhappily and continued. "The guards who watch this door are from the count's own lands. You became somewhat of a wonder when you brought great Falstaff down. The guards have been warned that you also brought men of our own armies to blows. And if you give them one stitch of trouble, the count said you should be tied to a stake, and that he'd take a whip to your back himself when he returned."

"Did he, now?" Fallon muttered darkly.

"Ah! But it pained him to say it, my lady!"

Fallon, biting into an apple, arched a brow to him skeptically.

Richard continued, "He said you were far too beautiful to mar, that you were the true treasure of the Saxons, that—"

She couldn't help herself; she burst out laughing. Richard saw the sparkle that touched her eyes, and he was glad.

"He said no such thing, and you know it!" Fallon accused the boy.

"You know him so well, my lady?" Richard queried softly.

"Aye, in a way, I know him well," she murmured softly. I've known him a long time, if naught else. She started to smile again but controlled the curl of her lip sternly. "I know him well enough to know that of all the things you have told me, the only one I believe is that he would take a whip to my back."

"He said you were beautiful," Richard repeated staunchly. Actually, Alaric had said that she was a beautiful witch, but no matter, he had the truth close enough. "And he said that he cared for you." Alaric had said that he was bound to the family of the late King Harold. That, too, was surely one and the same.

She stared at him, with her skeptical smile growing, and she laughed again. She offered him an apple. "Will you join me, then, my storytelling friend?" He watched her, and his breath caught. Her eyes were a soft and fathomless blue, and her hair was like midnight, wild and tangled and curling down her back and around her hips. She was more beautiful than any woman he had ever seen. She was the old king's daughter, and a Norman prisoner now—the count's mistress, though they seemed so bitterly opposed to each other. And still, she was better off here, Richard thought, than elsewhere in these parts. He had heard William order that the town of Romney be razed and that no mercy be shown to those who dwelt there. Alaric had counseled temperance, but to no avail.

Richard stood in awe of Count Alaric, who was a tower of strength, graceful as a cat, with gray eyes that commanded obedience. Richard knew his fate in life was to serve some man, and Alaric seemed to him one of the best.

Richard was fascinated with them both—his Norman lord and this Saxon lady, the king's beautiful, proud daughter.

Fallon continued to offer him the apple. He shook his head. "Thank you, milady, but I've work to do. I'll come back tonight."

Bowing, he left her. Fallon chewed the apple slowly, staring after him. She smiled slowly, thinking him a kind lad, and more—he was her only link with the outside world.

She washed quickly, suddenly in a panic that Alaric would return before she could dress. Then she reminded herself that he was probably out ravaging the countryside and would not return until evening.

When she had washed and dressed, she began to pace the room. From the one small window she could see the men who had remained to guard the fort. Some of the less severely wounded lay about, idly whittling, gaming, dicing, and drinking.

And she could see some of her own people within the Norman fort—old women selling fresh fish and baby eels, men working at harnesses and trappings. Fallon heard laughter and saw younger women, their eyes alight, teasing the soldiers. Pain sizzled in her chest. While the land even now buckled with terror, some of the people were eagerly playing by the new rules.

A shriek of laughter burst out as a young girl with

brown eyes and a wealth of chestnut hair fell into a Norman soldier's lap. His hand closed eagerly around her breast, and he pressed a coin inside her bodice. Still laughing, she kissed the man.

Fallon drew back into the room, her cheeks burning. She sat on the bed, then lay down dizzy, pressing her temples.

The girl was a whore. But was Fallon any better? She was a well-guarded captive, yes, but she was well fed, with a boy to serve her needs. She had fought one Norman, Falstaff, even though he had been kind to her.

But she had yielded everything to Alaric, and now he laughed at her. She wished that he had taken her by force, because it was difficult to live with the memories of everything that had happened once he had gently taken her into his arms. She paled and her breath grew quick as she contemplated the future. How could she fight him when she did not understand what it was that drew them together? She ought to despise him, but as she had told Richard—she did know him well.

She shivered and began again to pace the room. She needed strength. She needed to remember her father, her uncles, and her own broken pride; she had to believe that the fighting was not yet over, that the English would rally. With those thoughts in mind, she would be able to hold Alaric off.

The day passed slowly. Fallon was anxious and restless, awaiting Alaric. But he did not return. When night came, Richard brought her food and a small candle.

She paced again, and still Alaric did not come. At last she lay down to sleep, wondering why she could not rest. She did not want to endure a scene like the one that had taken place the night before!

There was a whole country out there to be ravaged and taken, she reminded herself. Norman whores had followed Norman men, and many practical-minded Saxon

lasses were apparently determined to charge for what the
men could have taken for free if they so chose. Alaric
could be with any one of them. He didn't want her; he
had given her to Falstaff. He had only come close to her
because his rage had been so great. He had made love to
her simply because something inside them both, long
brewing and seething, had exploded in a hot spring. She
bit her lip, for even in thinking of it, the warmth flooded
through her again.

And then last night . . .

Fully clothed, she curled against the wall and assured
herself over and over that Alaric really was among the
men who had hacked her father to pieces.

She did not sleep until morning.

Alaric did not ride into Romney, but stayed on a
nearby ridge. He had little control over the destruction of
the town, but he did see to it that those who surrendered
were not butchered. The rewards that William had promised his men were reaped in Romney. Anything of value
in the place was loaded upon carts, and then the town was
burned. French, Flemish, and German mercenaries were
given free rein, and from where Alaric sat, grim and
silent, his cool gray eyes scanning the scene, it was a brutal
and barbaric picture.

He thought with gratitude and relief of Falstaff. The
great bear of a man was surviving, and surviving well, so
the surgeons said. In time, they could almost promise, he
would be up and about again.

He was grateful for Falstaff, furious all over with Fallon.

It was almost easier to watch the destruction. He knew
that he had probably saved a few lives by his words to
William and his presence.

Robert of Mortain was to stay in Romney to see that

William received his due. When dusk began to fall, Alaric lifted his hand to the men who had followed him, and they started toward a manor in a small village called Haselford. Roger Beauclare, riding at his side, asked him, "We'll not ride back to Hastings tonight?"

Alaric shook his head. The thane of Haselford had fallen during the battle, he had learned. The thane had had no lady, and so the manor, a beautiful place built sturdily in stone, stood empty. The people here were subdued, having already heard the rumor of what had come before, and what was due to happen in Romney. Their serfs and cotters and villeins were grateful that Alaric spoke their language, and they had fallen into his service quite easily. He had left behind a number of his banners to be displayed so that any other Norman contingent coming through would know that he had already claimed the place.

"I've a feeling that we'll arrive to a sumptuous meal," Alaric said, "for the Saxons of Haselford are glad of our protection. And I am tired. I haven't slept more than five hours in the last two nights."

Roger laughed suddenly, and Alaric looked sharply at his young friend. Roger attempted to sober somewhat, but he was still grinning. "And back at Hastings you have a dilemma, too." Alaric was still staring at him somewhat savagely so Roger hastily continued. "I've heard tell that you ordered Fallon Godwin brought to your chamber at Hastings, and I understand that Lady Margaret is less than pleased with the situation."

Alaric shrugged. It was true—Margaret was not pleased. At first she'd been angry, and then she had cried, and then she'd demanded to know how he could prefer a filthy Saxon to her. But rumors about Fallon were already flying fast and quick, and there were few men who did not find the Saxon king's daughter a rare and stunning beauty.

Alaric was not good with explanations, nor did he feel that he needed any, for he did not make promises. Margaret demanded to know if he intended to keep the girl. He suggested as kindly as he could that Margaret was free to sail back across the Channel, since the decision to come had been her own.

Margaret had stared at him, then murmured softly and sweetly that she would wait.

He should go back to her, he thought. Ride back, order a bath, close his eyes in the steam, and lose himself to Margaret's soothing ministrations.

He could not, though, and he did not know why. Nor could he go back to his own room, for he was sorely, sorely exhausted, and he could not deal with Fallon's pride, tears, hatred, and fury this night. He would win their private battle, he vowed to himself. But tonight he sought peace.

"I'm afraid that Lady Margaret must be unhappy," Alaric said.

"Margaret knows what she does, and what she wants. If she is unhappy with my present arrangement, she is free to move on."

"Just what is your present arrangement?" Roger asked.

Alaric threw his friend a sharp gaze, then laughed. "I don't know myself."

Roger turned away from him to look up at the pale blue autumn sky. "Were she mine," he said softly, "I would wed her and spend the rest of my days begging her forgiveness."

"God be with us!" Alaric said. "How could I have forgotten! All those years ago at Bosham! She was ordered to serve me, and she persuaded you to perform her tasks!"

Roger grinned at Alaric ruefully. "Aye. The sound of her laughter was well worth the effort." He quickly went on, "I am your man, Alaric, and well you know it. But if you ever leave her, I will be there—with your permission, of course."

Alaric lowered his head, smiling. It was good to have men so loyal, and yet he wondered why he could not turn to his friend and say "Take her, have her, wed her, slay her; it is no difference to me." He told himself that the reason was his vow to Edith. Nor could he trust Fallon with his men while Falstaff still lay so close to death.

"Ah, Alaric!" Roger said suddenly. "Why, smell! The air is full of the aroma of roasting meat so well seasoned that I fear I'll faint ere we reach the house!"

Alaric chuckled. It was true. The scent coming from the village was wonderful. He urged Satan on, and the huge black horse leapt forward and raced toward the buildings. Roger followed suit.

At Haselford they dismounted. Alaric was not so foolish as to take risks, and so he ordered twenty men to remain on guard until midnight, when those who had feasted first would take over.

The steward's name was Hamlin; he served them ale while the round, rosy-cheeked cook and her three daughters set out platters of lamb and roasted fowl. Alaric surveyed the hall from his seat at the head of the long trestle table. The hall had been built with stone and brick and very little wood. The walls were covered with richly woven tapestries, and the staircase leading to the floor above was elaborately sculpted with guardian lions. Red carpeting cascaded over the stone stairs, and the upper arches were decorated with a vast display of arms—lances and pikes and swords.

"My lord?"

He turned. Hamlin was standing behind him, nervously folding his hands together. "Aye, my good man?" Alaric queried. He was middle-aged, with long wispy white hair and a full beard. Alaric suppressed a smile, for he was an ugly old man to have sired the three lushly pretty and buxom blondes who served his men. Perhaps their mother had been a beauty. Or perhaps, years ago, Hamlin had been a handsome young swain himself.

"Has the meal pleased you?"

Alaric lifted his goblet of ale. "Everything here has added to my complete pleasure."

The old man expelled a sigh of relief and crossed himself.

"Is something wrong?" Alaric asked.

The steward shook his head and swallowed, and his misty blue eyes fell on Alaric. "Sire, your banners saved us today when a knight would have set fire to the buildings. Nothing was taken, for we assured him that you would return. My daughters, are safe this night. We've beds to sleep in and food to eat. I do not know why we should be spared when our people have met with such catastrophe, but I thank God, and for myself and the others, I beg that you stay on here."

Alaric watched him, amazed that any Saxon could beg him for anything. Yet he realized that Hamlin—like the others who served them that night—had left this small place only to travel to other villages; they had never seen Harold. They had never seen William. Hamlin knew only that others suffered and that he had been spared.

He gazed around him again and thought that he would indeed lend his protection to this place. He would ask William for the deed to it—should William ever be crowned.

"You've my protection," Alaric said. "Does anyone here write?"

"Aye, sire, the priest. He's gone to say prayers over the dead."

"When he returns, have him give me an accounting of every man, woman, and child here. List our assets—what plows and oxen we have, what ponies, what sheep and ducks. I will need to know what trades and crafts the men practice, too."

Hamlin told Alaric that they had two smiths, two tanners, a miller, and many fine carpenters, metalworkers, and stonemasons. He was proud of how self-sufficient they were, and Alaric was deeply glad to hear it, for it seemed that the winter before them would be rough. The Normans were in a deep predicament, though William would do his best, and Alaric knew that he would travel with the duke. Of the eight thousand men who had come to England, three thousand had been lost. And now they had to press on into hostile country.

But this haven, he determined, would be his.

He watched his men drinking and eating, teasing the girls good-naturedly. Weary, he patted Roger on the back and started for the stairs. At the landing he found a narrow hallway and several doors. He tested them until he came to the master's suite. There he found a fine big bed, many trunks, and a number of shuttered east windows. He decided that the room would serve him well, and knowing that his men were still on guard, he lay down wearily. Just before he closed his eyes, he noted that the double doors to the suite were several inches thick. He smiled, and slept.

In the morning, Alaric explained a part of his situation to Hamlin. Then he chose a group of men to ride back to Hastings for Fallon, and another group to stay behind and guard the manor. A messenger had arrived from William. The officials at Dover, the one fortified city on the coast, had heard of the devastation at Romney and had already surrendered.

As Alaric reached the outskirts of Dover, however, he discovered that some of William's army had begun to burn the town of Dover in spite of the surrender. William was angry, yet there had been such a great number of perpetrators that he could do little to punish them. He planned to offer the city compensation instead.

It was a long and difficult day. Alaric had to deal with sullen invaders and weeping residents, and William was in one of his foulest tempers. When night fell, the two men decided to avoid the roads through the forest, lest they be ambushed.

London was just a day's ride away on a swift horse, but they planned to take their time reaching it.

"God's blood! Why do we hear nothing?" William swore.

Alaric shrugged, but he knew the English. "I'm willing to assume that they will declare Edgar the Atheling their new king. Perhaps the earls, Edwin and Morkere, are in London now. There will be some sort of a stand. It's important that we go slowly and take care."

"They have sent no army against us," William muttered.

"And if we are lucky, they will not," Alaric said, "for we are badly outnumbered now, with so many dead at Hastings."

William sat tiredly in a camp chair. They were losing more men every day, for many soldiers had to be left behind to build forts and castles and to hold the positions they had taken.

Worse still, in the last few days, many men had died of fever and disease. William's physicians had agreed that the English water had done it—they had run out of wine. The men were so sick that many might well die.

William slammed a fist against his charts. " 'Tis lucky our wine lasted as long as it did, else Harold would have had no one to battle at Hastings, and we'd have ended ere we started!" He clenched his teeth, and Alaric wondered if William himself was ill.

He said nothing, though, and Alaric did not question him. It was late, and so he and his men camped on the road outside Dover. So many men had taken sick that chaos reigned in the city, and Alaric had to make judgments for Saxon and Norman alike in William's name. In the end, he and his men were forced to stay far longer than he had intended, nearly a week. When some semblance of order had been restored to the fortified city, Alaric asked William's leave to return to the countryside. William gave his consent, telling Alaric that he would begin a very slow march to London, and that he would have Alaric and his men back at his side long before he reached the outskirts of the city. "Take a week, Alaric, and then come back to me," William advised him. "I will take London before the New Year!"

Before evening fell, they were ready to ride back to Haselford. He was curious that his men seemed as eager to ride as he, but then the manor was a strange and peaceful refuge where hatred had not yet found a purchase.

By night they came upon the manor. Dismounting in the courtyard, Alaric looked curiously up at the shuttered windows on the second floor of the manor. Warmth began to flood through him, and he felt the steady beating of his heart. Was she there?

"My lord!"

He turned around and held back a smile, for he was being greeted by the cheerful young Saxon, Richard, who had told him that he wanted to grow up to be a knight.

His heart began to beat harder.

"Lad," Alaric nodded, acknowledging the boy. "Is she here?"

"Aye, my lord."

"Did she come willing?"

The boy grinned cheerfully. "Without a speck of trouble, I swear it!"

Alaric well doubted that, but Fallon was there, and he would see for himself in what mood she had come.

"Take Satan," Alaric said, tossing the reins to Richard. The boy looked up at the massive horse, and began to stutter. "Sir? My lord, take him where?"

"You want to be a knight, lad. Work up to it!"

He smiled as his men laughed. Roger offered to give the boy instructions, and Alaric entered the manor.

A fire burned in the center of the great hall and meat was cooking. There was a scent of cloves and cinnamon, and he knew that the household had been preparing for his return. Night was falling, and in the midst of war, he felt curiously warm in this hall. His hall. His men served him with loyalty, and these Saxons showed an eager determination to please. His food would be good, and his bed would be soft.

Except, of course, he warned himself, for the thorn that awaited him there. He closed his eyes briefly while he felt the fire take flight inside him. He had been afraid to think or feel while he had been away, but when he had lain down at night, she had haunted his soul, his body. His desire for her did not find simple appeasement, but grew. He wondered at how it had grown over the years; some force greater than either of them had kindled the blaze between them.

Yet he was not sure he should have been so eager to return, for he would not touch her in anger again, and he would never let her know the extent of her power over him. Nor could he let her believe him anything less than ruthless and determined, for to show her a weakness could well prove fatal . . . to Fallon.

His eyes traveled up the stairs, and he determined that, though he had had no wine, he would quaff a goodly quantity of English ale ere he approached his thorn.

Chapter Seventeen

In the hall, Alaric called to Hamlin. "Ale, my good man, if you will, please!" He sat down at the table and propped his booted feet high upon it. Hamlin brought him a tankard of ale, and another for Roger Beauclare, who sat beside him.

Before Hamlin could leave, Alaric had a few questions for him. "When did our guest arrive?"

"Guest, my lord? Ah . . . the princess?"

She was no true princess, Alaric thought, but that was the way the English thought of her. He wondered if he had used good sense in bringing her here. Although the Saxons sought his protection, they outnumbered his men.

He nodded. "The princess," he acknowledged.

"She came last week," Hamlin said a little nervously.

By then, young Richard of Elwald had come into the hall, carrying Satan's bridle to clean before the hearth. Alaric threw him an amused look. "She came willingly—nay, eagerly?"

The tips of Richard's ears turned pink.

"Willingly, sire?" Hamlin murmured uneasily. Jeanne, his youngest daughter, who was carrying a tray of food for the returning Normans, stared at her father, her eyes innocently wide.

"She came like a wildcat, she did," Jeanne blurted.

"Biting, kicking, scratching, and causing the men no small discomfort."

Alaric kept his eyes on Richard. "I see," he said. "Well, then, has she eaten? Has she been attended to?"

"My lord," Hamlin said, "we've none of us gone near her."

"She were the king's daughter," Jeanne said softly.

Hamlin stuttered for a moment, then tried to explain. "I am glad of the stand we've taken with you, Count Alaric and I swear my fealty, for you have spared us everything. But—"

He broke off, looking down at his feet. Richard set down the bridle and rose to meet Alaric's gaze. "We Saxons are not trained to battle, my lord," Richard said. "We're not good at war. 'Tis difficult, you see, to meet her courage when we've all surrendered without a fight."

"Why, you ungrateful little scamp—" Roger began, rising angrily, but Alaric stayed him with a hand.

"Nay, Roger, Richard speaks what he feels, and what the others are thinking, and it is good for me to know." He swung his feet down and rose to look down at Richard. "So, tell me, how has your lady been? Have you tended to her needs?"

Richard's eyes fell from Alaric's. "She has scarce spoken to me since we came. I have left her food, but she has not eaten. Since we left Hastings, she has had little to say. She will not eat, and she drinks but little."

Alaric stared at Richard hard for a moment, then spoke softly. "Then I'd best tend to the princess myself, hadn't I?"

He picked up his tankard and drank down his ale. The room stayed silent while all eyes fell upon him. He slammed the tankard down, and the sound echoed frightfully against the stillness in the hall.

"Roger, you'll see to the guard?"

"Aye, Alaric!" Roger stood quickly and nervously.

Alaric strode toward the stairs, and they all remained in a silent tableau. Then Richard broke from them and raced after Alaric.

"My lord!"

Alaric paused, his hand upon the stone balustrade, and turned to Richard. "What is it?"

"My lord!" Richard repeated. He lowered his eyes and moistened his lips nervously, muttering something.

"What? Speak up, lad!"

"I said, begging your pardon, my lord, I said—I said, please, don't hurt her."

Startled, Alaric arched a brow. "So, Richard of Elwald, have I proven myself to be such a monster, then?"

"Nay, sire! That is not what—"

"Then, lad, mind your own work and leave me to mine."

Richard swallowed and nodded, and Alaric continued on up the stairs. He paused then, looking back at Richard.

"Lad!"

"Aye, my lord!" Richard hurried toward him.

"You are fond of Fallon, I believe."

"I . . ."

"Never mind. Now listen to me, and if you wish her well, pay me heed. In time, I will call to you. Whatever order I give you, say aye to me, but pay no heed to any command except those for food, drink, or bathwater. Do you understand?"

"My lord—"

"Do you understand?"

"Aye." Richard stared at him with a curious smile hovering upon his lips. "Aye, Lord Alaric!"

Alaric nodded, and continued to the room he had chosen. The door to the room was secured by a heavy wooden bolt. He slammed it back and heard the clangor echo through the stone archways in the upper passageways.

The door creaked inward, and he paused, wary, his hands on his hips as he watched her.

She sat on the window seat, her feet curled beneath her, gazing longingly out the window. The cool fall breeze blew softly in, touching her hair, lifting ebony tendrils from her forehead. She was wearing a soft blue chemise beneath a wool- and fur-trimmed bleaunt, and her hair waved and curled down her back in splendid contrast. She appeared so fragile as she turned to face him! The gentle firelight from the hearth cast its glow over her, and the elegance of her features was caught in golden color. At the sight of him, her cheeks burned red, her breasts rose and fell, and she breathed too quickly.

She said nothing and did not move. He came into the room and carefully closed the door behind him. He discarded his sword and scabbard, cast aside his tunic, and removed the armor he wore beneath. In his chausses and chemise, he took a chair before the fire, and watched the flames.

"So, *mademoiselle*," he said at last, "have you been comfortable?"

"Comfortable?" she repeated, frowning. "How can I be comfortable, Count Alaric? I have no wish to be here."

"Ah, yes, but where you choose to be, I'm afraid, might soon be a battlefield."

"What harm could I—"

She broke off as his eyes fell upon her, cold and hard. "I do not underestimate you, Fallon. Nor does the duke. You are more dangerous than any of your brothers. Your passion can arouse the Saxons. Even when people are acquiescent, your tongue can stir them to rebellion. So do not plague me with what cannot be. I cannot free you to stir up the countryside or to join with what forces we have still to battle. Now I ask again, are you comfortable? Is there something lacking, that you should so shun the hospitality of this place?"

She lifted her hands, staring at him with something of confusion. He rose, smiling, and she sank back against the window seat, watching him approach her. "What do you want from me?" she cried suddenly, rising and clenching her fists.

He turned and faced the hearth again, using the poker to heighten the blaze. Then he set the poker aside and turned back to her. He could not read her features; he did not know what anguish she felt. "You did not greet me, love," he taunted her.

"Greet you!"

Alaric lowered his eyes, knowing he could well depend upon her temper.

"I did not greet you!" She stepped forward and dipped a low, mocking curtsy before him. "Count Alaric! My lord! Welcome back to this seized property. Did all go your way? Have you plundered and raided and raped with no ill befalling you?"

Her syrupy tones angered him. He could not forget the sights he had seen at Romney. But he forced himself to bow to her. "Aye, my lady! I burned and raided and robbed and raped, and came through it all with no ill-fortune, thank you!" Startled, she stared at him. Aware of his sudden advantage, he stepped forward, seized her in his arms, and pulled her close. "Can you greet me in no sweeter way?"

She struggled against his hold, staring at him furiously while she pushed against his shoulders. "Why in God's name have you come back to torment me! Isn't there a whole country out there to pillage and ravage and burn?"

"Ah, but why would I seek a whole country when there is so much land nearby to be laid waste? There are churches and chapels still, and farmers' daughters by the score. Nay, I need not travel far, I think."

"Damn you!" She struggled fiercely against his hold,

then went still and stared into his eyes. "Could you please, then, leave me in peace and go about it?"

"My lady, I cannot! Every pillager must have a refuge, and this I have chosen as mine. Even barbarians need a place of rest and peace."

"Peace!" she snapped, trying to free her arms. "You seek peace—from me?"

"Aye . . . that I do," he said softly. He released her and leaned against the mantel, watching her. "Hearth and home," he murmured. "When I grow weary of the world around me, I crave the same things any man seeks. A warm bath to draw away the evils of the road, good ale and good food, and a soft bed to lie upon. And a gentle voice to whisper gentle words."

She stared at him incredulously, her eyes sparkling like sapphires, her lips slightly parted, so beautiful that he nearly forgot himself and swept her into his arms. It could be so easy. He was among the conquering host; he needed only to force her into his arms and nature could do the rest, for he was aware that the slow fires still burned inside of her, no matter how she denied them. He could let the passion burn and flow, and pray that it would reach its peak, burn out, and become cold ashes. He could pray that it would be so. Pray that he would cease thinking of her and remembering that the fulfillment had been greater than the promise that had teased and taunted him forever.

"Gentle words!" she repeated incredulously. "You want gentle words from me? You are insane!"

"You are my slave."

"I am your prisoner. I will not serve you food or warm your bath or your bed—"

"My bed? I do not recall asking."

She let out a furious oath and spun around to stare out the window again.

"Was that an invitation?" he asked her pleasantly.

Her answer was quick and sure, and he laughed, finding it curious that a woman who looked so fragile could swear with such heartfelt vigor. "So it was not an invitation." He shrugged. "Still, my lady, we do have a few things to straighten out between us. I do crave a certain amount of peace."

"Then sleep where you have ravaged, sir," she advised him.

"Umm," he murmured thoughtfully. He watched her where she stood, refusing to turn to meet his gaze. "But I have ravaged here, have I not?"

Color flooded her cheeks, and she tried not to respond, but she could not remain still. She swirled about, and her hair sailed in a circle while her skirt swept about her feet, and again he was tempted to step forward and prove himself the barbarian in truth. He had been a fool to have her brought to Haselford; he should have had her sent to Normandy and cast into some deep, safe dungeon where she could not plague him. He was not so much a fool that he would love again, and yet he had erred greatly in coming too near to her, for she was a flame that heated his blood; she had ruined another woman for him.

"Alaric, the battle at Hastings has been lost, and I was captured there. You have the strength to do what you will; you have the power to hold me. But you are insane if you think I will serve you! Take what you wish, but I swear I will give you nothing."

"Take what I wish?" He arched a brow in mock-surprise. "Why, Fallon, that sounds like another invitation."

"Oh! I wish to hell that some Saxon blade had split your Norman skull in twain!"

And that, he thought, was probably true. But he shrugged away her words and leaned against the mantel, idly rubbing his chin while he pretended to survey her in grave thought. She was growing more and more anxious, though she tried to hide it. She gripped her fingers tightly, lest they betray her with a tremble. She moistened her lips frequently and stared about desperately, ever seeking escape.

"You will serve me," he said softly.

"I will not!" she swore.

"What if I choose to beat you into submission?" he queried lightly. He pushed away from the mantel and walked toward her. She looked as if she wanted to shrink from him, but she caught the glimmer in his eyes. She stood still while he walked around behind her. "Aye, Fallon, perhaps we know each other too well. You call me barbarian, but in your heart, you know I will not tie you to a whipping post and slice open your back."

"Why—why would I be so certain?" she retorted, but he stood behind her now, and he heard her voice quiver. "I thought you meant to slit my throat when you . . . when you came to the tent."

"I seldom lose control so completely," he assured her. He remained behind her. "Alas, though, I am an invader, a pillager, rapist, and robber, I detest unnecessary violence. I have learned, however, that one must often be cruel to be kind. But still . . ." He tapped his chin idly and continued around her. He felt her eyes upon him warily; he felt the very beat of her heart. "You are Harold's daughter," he murmured. "You've his tenacity and his pride—but not a whit of his good sense."

"You son of a—"

"Careful!" he warned, circling her. Her lips clamped together tightly and he saw the sizzle that touched her eyes at his warning. He was too close for her to openly defy him, or so he thought.

"I want you to know, Alaric," she promised him with soft vehemence, "that you will pay! The English will rise against William; they will never have him for their king, and when you are cringing before some Saxon swords-

man, begging for mercy, I will insist that they remove
your head from your body with the oldest, rustiest double-
edged ax that can be found!"

He laughed, but his smile did not touch his eyes. "If
your fantasies amuse you, Fallon, then you must cling to
them. But we're not discussing fantasy here. Nay, we
speak the truth, and the truth of it is that you are here,
Princess, and you are mine. Don't tempt me—I have
thought since you were very small that a good beating
would do you wonders. As a child you lacked discipline.
Making up for that now could test any strong man's arm.
But then again, I am not eager to see you mauled or
harmed—not because of your sweet temper, but because
I don't like my property mangled. Still, you refuse to yield
to the simplest of requests and therefore something must
be done."

Ignoring her, he returned to the fire. Standing on the
bearskin there, he crossed his arms and watched the
flames.

Then he spun suddenly. "Fallon, I am asking you to do
no more than serve me as any slave serves her master.
The simple, peaceful pleasures in life are all that I ask. A
meal in our chambers; ale when I thirst. That is all. Will
you comply?"

"You must be mad!" she whispered, her blue eyes
immense.

He shook his head and sighed. He walked across the
room and threw open the door. "Richard!"

The boy appeared a little too soon, as if he had been
waiting there. He tried to smile reassuringly at Fallon,
Alaric realized, but Fallon was now too confused to take
any comfort. "Richard," Alaric said, "bring me ale and
something to eat."

The boy nodded and turned about. Alaric closed the
door, sat down in the chair before the fire, and propped
his feet up on a leather footstool. He said nothing, and he

felt the silence stretching out between them. He sensed her movement and turned to see her eyes dart toward the door.

"Don't even think of it, Princess," he warned her quietly. She threw him a furious glare, and then Richard tapped on the door and entered with the tray, which he set on a trunk near the window seat. He glanced at Fallon who stood silently waiting. "Shall I pour your ale, my lord?" Richard asked.

"Nay, Fallon will do it."

"Nay, Fallon will not do it!" she grated out between her teeth.

Alaric sighed, putting his feet on the floor. "Richard, you must go below to Roger. Tell him that he may as well burn the mill tonight. And he has had his eye on the steward's youngest daughter. Tell him that I give her to him. Aye, wait—Warren has asked me for her, too. Tell them that they must share her, but remind them that I will want her alive for work within the manor, too."

Richard glared at him, blinking. Alaric smiled. "Well, boy?"

"Aye! Uh, aye, my lord! As you command!"

"Wait!" cried Fallon.

Alaric dared not look when he heard her strangled plea. He lowered his head for a long moment so that when he stared at her, his features were hard and set and showed no hint of humor.

She pushed furiously past Richard and stood over Alaric. "You bastard!" she breathed. "You would burn a mill and debase an innocent girl—simply because I will not pour you ale?"

She was breathing fire over him, he thought. Her breasts heaved, and he longed to touch them.

He forced himself to gaze up at her with little interest and to answer her calmly. "Nay, not because you will not pour ale, but because you have sorely tested my temper, and I am weary of surly and sullen serfs! Richard, do as I have told you, and be aware that if you test my temper, I will gladly flay your back open."

"Aye, my lord!"

"Nay, wait!" Fallon fetched the tankard of ale and held it out to him. "Take it!"

Slowly, he looked into her eyes. He did not move. "That, *mademoiselle*, is hardly what I call good service."

"Oh!" She stamped her foot and turned her back to him. Tendrils of her hair, soft and perfumed, fell against his shoulders as she spun around. His fingers itched to touch it.

Her shoulders stiffened. Slowly she turned around, bowed her head, lowered herself on one knee, and silently offered him the tankard of ale.

He took it from her. "Thank you, my lady. It is really all that I ask. Richard, that will be all."

Richard left the room. Fallon heard the door close behind him. She did not look up, but remained before Alaric, weary and near tears. She did not know what to believe about him and what not to believe. He had been gone, and what she had heard from the guards had not been good news. Romney had been devastated, they said, and countless other villages had fallen. She had heard nothing about the English forces, nothing at all. She knew nothing of her brothers or the northern earls or Edgar the Atheling. Nothing of Delon—if he lived or if he had died.

"Get up, Fallon," Alaric said softly. She lifted her head and looked at him. Firelight played over his features, and for a moment she wondered how he could be so ruggedly handsome and so cruel. Yet she could not fathom what thoughts lay behind the steel of his cool gray eyes now, and she thought he studied her, too.

He rose himself and helped her up. He pressed the tankard into her hands. "Drink it," he said softly. She wanted to refuse, but she took a sip, then another. It filled her body, and she was warm. He watched her, then ordered her, "Now eat something, lady."

She shook her head. "I am not hungry."

He pressed her into the chair and with his knife, stabbed a portion of meat, which he offered to her. The aroma assailed her senses, and beneath his penetrating gaze, she took several bites.

He took the tray away, leaving it outside the door. Staring at the fire, Fallon heard the door close.

Where were they now, she wondered—Delon, Galen, Aelfyn, Tam? Her little cousins, Gyrth and Leofwine's sons and daughters. Had their homes been laid waste? Had the Normans taken them? Or were they running proud and free, Saxon still? Were they even now forming a new army to march against William?

She thought of Delon, of his soft beard and gentle eyes, and she smiled sadly, for even as she prayed that he might live, she knew that love was over between them. It had not been strong enough to survive this scourge. Delon was a good man, gentle and brave. But he hadn't the fire and the passion to incite men. She prayed that he was safe.

She started suddenly as Alaric's fingers moved lightly, almost tenderly, over her cheek. Her fingers wound around the lion's-head arms of the chair and she swallowed, holding still as some deep liquid heat assailed her. Dear God, no! she prayed. Do not let his slightest touch affect me so! Don't let us wage this war further this night, for I am sorely weary of it.

"The hour grows late, Fallon. I wish to go to bed."

Her head jerked up, and a blush spread over her cheeks while her mouth seemed to go dry. She shook her head wordlessly.

"Now," he commanded her. He walked over to the bed, pulling his chemise over his head. He laid it on the foot of the bed, sat down, unlaced his leggings, and pulled off his boots. She turned away as he stripped off his chausses, and her knuckles whitened against the chair.

"Fallon, now."

"Nay!" she cried.

"That gown is lovely, but if I remove it, it will surely come off in shreds."

She met his gaze. He was naked, tall, and undaunted in all his warrior's steely splendor, and she fought to keep her gaze on his eyes.

"Now, Fallon, or so help me God, I will take care of matters for you, and you will not be pleased."

She leapt to her feet, swearing. With trembling fingers she worked open the hooks on her clothing and, turning her back to him, removed her bleaunt. She stepped out of her leather slippers and stripped off her hose. In her chemise, she turned to him imploringly and was startled by the naked heat in his eyes as he stared at her. He held the soft braided belt with which he had bound her before, and she cried out, seeing it. "Alaric—"

"The chemise, too, Fallon. I do not enjoy using force."

She turned her back to him again, still swearing beneath her breath. She gave up and, in a fury, removed the garment and heedlessly swung around to face him once again. "You say that you do not enjoy using force! Then leave—"

"Lady, I do intend to leave you be. But I do intend to live to see the morning. Now, get over here."

Miserably she lowered her head. Something inside her balked. "Nay—I cannot."

She gasped as his strides brought him to her, as his arms swept around her with ill-concealed impatience. She started to fight him, but his naked flesh, hot and pulsing was against her. She closed her eyes and clenched her teeth, then went still.

She landed on the soft mattress. She dared to open her

eyes as he slipped the soft braided belt around her wrists, and tied them fast to the headboard. "Alaric!"

"What?"

"I have been here this week; I have slept in this bed, and I have not been able to elude you and Richard *and* the guards. Why are you tying me?"

"I don't think that you would kill Richard. But I am not certain that you would not murder the guards and slit my throat. As I told you before, Fallon, I do not underestimate you."

He pulled the knot tight and climbed into the bed. The room was cool with autumn's chill, and he was careful to tuck the covers warmly about her. Then he turned his back to her, and she shivered until sleep finally claimed her, keenly aware of how close he lay, and of the burning warmth that could be found in his arms . . .

When she awoke, her arms were free. Holding the covers to her chest, she blinked sleep away and saw that Alaric sat before the fire, and a plate of bread and cheese sat upon the footstool. He was studying a leather-bound book while he idly chewed on a heel of bread. He was dressed already for his trade—war. He wore chain mail beneath his tunic and mantle, heavy leggings, and knee-high boots. His helmet, shined and ready, lay by the door.

He turned to her, as if sensing that she was awake. "Good morning, Fallon."

She didn't answer him, but lay back, staring desolately at the ceiling. He had humiliated her, and now he would ride out to decimate her people. And she could do nothing to help them, because she could not escape. Surely there was a way out of this nightmare! Surely, somewhere in England, men worked against the duke. If she just had some way to communicate with them!

"I said, good morning, Fallon."

In all his mail, she hadn't heard him move, and now he was standing over her, wrenching the linen sheets and the warm furs from her. She grasped for the covers, swearing.

"You are the worst of Norman pigs!" she told him.

He lifted her up, and his mail touched her bare flesh. It was freezing and she swore at him again. "Out of bed, my lady, unless you're inviting me to rejoin you in it."

"Never!"

He gave a throaty laugh. "I wager, Fallon, that you will change your tune."

"Never," she repeated, and quickly eluded him to race to her trunk and procure clean clothing.

"Wear riding clothes," he told her.

Holding a soft white chemise, she paused. What now? she wondered? Where would he take her? Her heart began to thud. If they sent her to Normandy, all would be lost . . .

She slipped into the chemise. Not looking his way, she pulled on soft, warm hose made like men's riding chausses. She felt him watching her while, in silence, she donned her high boots and a yellow bleaunt with slit sides.

"There's milk and bread and salmon and cheese," he told her.

"I am not hungry."

"You will eat."

With an impatient sigh she swung about, but then she worried that he might be shipping her across the Channel, and so she lowered her head quickly. Remembering his manner of the previous night, she meekly walked over to the footstool, sat on the floor beside it, and nibbled upon some of the fish. He stood looking down at her. She looked up into fathomless gray eyes. "Aren't you supposed to be off devastating more of the country?" she asked him nastily.

"Not today." He bowed abruptly. "There's water to wash; I leave you to your ablutions."

He left her, and she was grateful. Alone she used the chamber pot, then washed her face and hands. When she was done she went to the door and discovered it open. Alaric was outside it, idly leaning against the wall as he waited for her. He took her arm.

The hall was silent as they passed through it. Fallon wondered where they were, and how the people fared. She had seen so little of the place when she had been brought here. The only people who had come near her were Richard and a mute boy who carried water pails.

They walked outside into a glorious autumn day. There was no sign of privation or bloodshed. War might have never touched the land. Fallon could see a team of oxen in the field, and sheep on a far meadow. Color still touched the leaves, and the sky was endlessly blue. The only signs of invasion were the Norman guards, Alaric's men, who stood about the courtyard.

There were only two horses in sight—Satan and a chestnut mare. Richard held the reins. He bobbed a cheerful good morning to them both, and Fallon greeted him in turn. Alaric helped her onto the mare and mounted his own stallion. Richard stepped back, his dimples showing as he waved.

"Where are we going?" Fallon asked at last.

Alaric glanced her way. "Romney," he said curtly.

This was the last thing she had expected.

"Romney," she repeated.

When could she get away? That was the question. She could not seek to escape him now, for too many of his men were about the manor. Nor would the town be safe, for surely soldiers hovered closely there, too. All of this area was dangerous, occupied by the Normans, but she knew the land well.

Alaric rode ahead of her; he rode hard, without stopping. Several times they passed downtrodden refugees, men and women with hopeless faces, wearily traveling inland with their few remaining possessions loaded in carts. They stared at Alaric in his mail, on his war-horse, but they made no move to challenge him, so thoroughly had they been beaten.

Once, when she looked ahead, Fallon saw that they approached a group that included two women, several children, and three men. The tallest of the men was well muscled, hale in appearance. Fallon thought that perhaps this could be her chance to escape.

"I can read your mind, Fallon. Are you so ready to risk their lives?"

She glared at him. "Are you so very confident in your sword, sir?"

He smiled, and it was a smile that chilled her. "Aye, my lady, I am. I have wielded this steel since I was a lad of twelve. I have fought since that time to keep what is mine, and I will continue to do so now."

"And to take what is *not* yours!" Fallon snapped.

But he did not rise to the bait; he shrugged. They came nearer and nearer to the party of refugees. In sudden desperation, Fallon raced toward them, drawing her horse up before them on the path. Dismounting, she approached them on foot. "Please!" she cried. "Help me!"

One of the women rushed toward her. "Why, lady! What ails thee? We run ourselves from the scourge at Romney, but—"

"Marla, leave her be," the tall, muscled man said suddenly.

"Why, Heath! Are ye daft? What has come of us, indeed, if we cannot help one another?" The woman demanded.

"Look yonder. There rides the Count of Anlou."

Fallon stared, incredulous that this man should recognize Alaric. Was he not afraid? Would he help her escape?

"Dear people, I am desperate! I am a captive, and I must escape. I—"

"Heath!" the woman persisted, staring from her husband to the massive war stallion bearing down upon them. "We must help this child if we can."

The man kept staring at Alaric.

"Please!" Fallon persisted. "Just cause some commotion; I don't believe he would hurt anyone. If I can just escape into the forest. I am Fallon, Harold's daughter."

"Harold's daughter!" the man thundered, staring at her. Fallon held silent, shocked by his reaction. Men had loved her father.

He stepped forward, staring at her in fury. "I fought in your father's ranks, lady. And I tell you he led us into death! He saw the papal banner and he gave up!" He spat on the ground. "We'd have gone on and on, but he had already lost the fight. He sold us all; he sold generations of Englishmen into heartache and bloodshed and servility."

"Heath!" the woman cried.

Fallon was stunned and defenseless. The man grasped her arm and would have tossed her cruelly from him had it not been for his wife's cry.

And then she heard Alaric's voice, and she knew that he had sat astride Satan behind her for some time. "Leave her be, good fellow. She is wearisome trouble, but she is my trouble, friend."

The man released Fallon and looked up at Alaric. "I meant no harm," he mumbled, and stared down at his feet.

"Fallon, mount your horse," Alaric told her.

Still stunned by the man's hostility, she obeyed. She hadn't cried in days, but tears were welling in her eyes at the knowledge that anyone could hate her father so.

The man was staring at Alaric again. "You are the Count of Anlou," he said.

Alaric, who had been watching Fallon, turned to him. "I am."

"I thank you for my life. For all our lives. A troop of Bretons would have slain us all. Someone stopped them with the order that no slaying of innocents should take place, and he pointed to you, where you stood atop the ridge. I recall the crest upon your shield."

Fallon turned to stare at Alaric, who did not appear overjoyed by the man's grateful words. He nodded, then said, "You speak French well."

"I intended to be a cleric. Then my brother died of the pox, and I took my father's trade."

"You're a smith?"

"Sir, I am the finest ironmaster this side of the Channel."

Alaric laughed, enjoying the man's confidence. "Go on, if you've an interest, to the village beyond called Haselford; it is under my protection. If you've a mind to ply your craft, we've surely a need of your prowess."

The man nodded. "I accept gratefully. England has been sold out to new masters—I will gladly live with the best of them." He cast Fallon a curious glare, then paused. "My lady, I am sorry. You've a daughter's grief. King Harold was a good man, but he failed us in the end. He fought when he shouldn't have fought, and he died a martyr's death when he should have stayed a soldier."

He and his wife moved on along the road, and Alaric snatched the reins from Fallon's hands.

"Let's go," he said dryly.

Silent and despairing, she rode along as he led.

They came to a ridge from which they could see Romney. Alaric stayed silent while she gazed down upon the scene.

There was nothing left of the town. Nothing but smoldering fires, and the ragtag ends of the people's lives. The land, homes, churches, shops, fields, livestock . . . all were gone. All that remained were these blackened ruins.

Fallon dismounted and stumbled along the ridge to

look down. Pathetic bands of survivors were grouped together before open fires. They poked through the ruins for food. They huddled together against a stone wall that remained standing.

Grief welled up in Fallon's heart. This was the Norman curse that she had feared all her life; this was the reason she despised the Normans so. This blackened, terrible desolation. And this would soon be the fate of her whole homeland.

Tears rose in her eyes, tears that were no longer hers alone. She did not cry for her father or for others of her own blood. She cried for the land swept ragged, the land torn by fire and demons. She cried at the fulfillment of the prophecy of Edward the Confessor.

Then she whirled on Alaric, hating him with all her heart, despising him for bringing her here. The man on the road had thanked him for his mercy; she despised him for his cruelty—he had no right to demolish her country.

"Bastard!" she shrieked. He still sat astride Satan, cool and aloof, very much aware of the effect of the place on her—he had planned it. "Bastard lackey!" Hysterical, she raced for him, pitting herself against the horse and the armored man, determined to hurt him. She leapt at him with force.

"Fallon!" he said sharply, for Satan was beginning to rear and snort. Alaric quickly dismounted, pushing Fallon from him. She fell, but she was instantly up again, blinded by her tears. She flew at him in a mindless fury, but her hands pounded against chain mail, and she could do him little harm. Choking, incensed, she flung herself against the length of him, and they went down together. He braced himself over her, catching her flailing hands at last.

"Why?" she shrieked. "Why did you do this to me? Why did you bring me here?"

"Because you had to see. You had to understand," he

told her, and his voice was curiously soft, but emotionless. "This is the worst of it; but this is William's wrath. Fallon, you seek to continue this war when you should be seeking peace."

She shook her head, unable to believe that the sky could still be so blue and beautiful, that the grass beneath her could still grow spongy and green. Hell had come to England.

Alaric rose and reached down to help her to her feet. She ignored his hand and stood on her own to stare down once again at what had been Romney.

"It will grow," Alaric said. "It will grow again. The people will return. They will build houses. Women will bake and sew, and in time, they will laugh as they purchase baubles and ribbons and lace in the square."

"And the maids will bear Norman bastards," Fallon spat out.

Alaric was silent for a moment. "They will bear life," he said quietly. "And isn't that the one thing that cannot be rebuilt? The life of each one of us is special and unique."

Fallon turned on him. "Nay, sir, you have destroyed a people! An entire people!" She walked past him and mounted the mare.

Alaric was silent, thinking about his captive as they returned. He was glad she was distraught, for he'd had to make her see the fallacy of fighting William. He knew that when she had a chance, she would seek out her brothers, the northern earls, or the Atheling's supporters, and try to make war.

At least he had made her docile. She did not try to escape him on the silent ride back. In the courtyard she ignored his hand, and she ignored Richard, Alaric's men, and the Saxon people, and walked straight to the room they shared. She slammed the door with strength. Staring up the steps after her, Alaric sighed wearily.

Chapter Eighteen

Fallon threw herself on the bed and closed her eyes and shivered. How could any kind of God allow her father to die—and William to live? To live and to seek vengeance so horribly? Surely there had to be an escape from this nightmare!

She exhaled slowly, realizing that some poor fools considered Haselford a haven. Men worked and laughed, and women sang; she had heard them below while she had paced this floor, wondering what lay in wait for her. He had made her bow down to him last night by making threats against the people here, and he had made a fool of her, for he had not meant those threats. This place was his—by forfeiture! But he seemed far more protective of this manor than he did of his land at Elwald, and so there must be something exceptional about it. The people here did his bidding.

The door opened. Alaric had come. She did not move, but she realized that he was not alone. Richard was with him, bearing food and ale, and two more lads, freshly shorn and shaven in the Norman fashion, were behind him, awkwardly balancing a wooden tub. She turned her back to them all, and listened idly while Richard possessively gave instructions as to how hot the water should be and just how much to use.

Fallon ignored the confusion and closed her eyes. In time the noise died down, and the door closed, and still she kept her back to the room. Alaric didn't speak to her, but she heard his heavy mail clanking as he removed it; then there was silence. She wondered if he had ordered a bath simply to torment her, but he hadn't said a word to her and seemed unaware that she was even in the room with him. But then, who could have taken her to the ridge above Romney except a man who was totally devoid of feelings?

She listened to the silence in the room, then finally rolled over to stare at Alaric. He was in the tub. His head was back, and a small wash towel was pressed over his face, just as he had that night in Rouen when she stumbled into his room by accident.

Her eyes drifted to the fire and she saw that another kettle of water rested there. Tonight she was ready for battle. He had deceived her last night; he would not do so again this evening. He deserved to be hurt, and she was determined to see that he was. If she courted danger, so be it. What did she have to lose? What could be more humiliating than the nights she had spent with him already, naked and bound to his side?

She slipped off her shoes and silently moved across the cold stone floor to the bearskin before the fire, and stared at the kettle of water.

She lifted the kettle from the fire, eyeing Alaric carefully. He had not moved. She walked over to him and held her breath.

He sensed her presence and pulled the towel from his face, then moved in a swift and sudden blur. He was up on his feet and out of the tub, and his eyes were lethal with fury, like twin swords. "I thought you might like more water now—" she began but his hands fell upon hers, wrenching the kettle from her. He dumped the water in the tub, and then returned his attention to her. She backed away farther, finding it horribly disturbing to be stalked by him, wet and naked and furious, and still so silent.

She backed into one of the trunks, and her knees buckled. She sat down hard, then realized that she was beside the tray. She lifted the tankard of ale to him. He ignored it, and in sudden panic, she thought to use it as a weapon against him. He caught the tankard, and his eyes remained upon her like blades. A smile twisted his lip as he knelt down in front of her. She leaned nervously against the wall, aware of his temper, and painfully aware of the gleaming bronze breadth of his shoulders and the water droplets that glistened there. A vein at his throat pulsed like rapid thunder, and she swallowed, feeling as if her blood raced in torrents in answer to his.

"You thought that I might want some more water?"

"Aye," she answered quickly, her eyes caught by his.

"Aha. And then, I assume, you thought that I might like some ale with my water."

"Aye."

"You were eager to serve me?"

"Aye."

"I think not."

She lowered her lashes, then shot him a sweet smile. "Why, my lord! Why not? Don't the people clamor to be under your protection? Wasn't that your lesson this day? Fall down upon your knees and be grateful that you have been attacked and imprisoned by the great Count Alaric!"

She watched his jaw harden and his eyes grow as cold as ice, and she began to wish she had not spoken. "Nay, my love," he said quietly. "The lesson today had nothing to do with me, but with William and his policies. He frequently believes that one sacrifice creates several mercies. Today I wished to prevent your becoming one of the sacrifices, Fallon, and that is all." He did not give her a chance to respond, but rose, pulling her to her feet along with him. "You were anxious to serve me *mademoiselle?* Well, I am most anxious to be served. Yet let me be a gentle lord here this night. The host, milady, rather than the dungeon master. Ale, *mademoiselle?* Please, do imbibe."

He slipped his arm around her, his fingers twining into her hair at the nape of her neck. He brought the tankard to her lips, and she parted them as the ale spilled over her. She sputtered and coughed, and he instantly drew back. "Ah, milady! How clumsy, how oafish, how very barbarous of me! Forgive me."

"Alaric!" Fallon protested desperately, aware that silver heat simmered in his eyes and that his hold upon her, though painless, was also merciless. "Alaric, I shall serve you! I will—"

"Nay, lady, nay! I have vowed to serve *you* this night. And alas, see what I have done. Ale seeps into your clothing, against your skin. And I have done this. But have no fear, lady; I shall rectify the matter." His hands fell upon her bleaunt, and she gasped as she felt the wool torn from her body. "Alaric!" she protested. But he moved too fast, and she was in his arms, then quickly tossed upon the bed. She tried to scramble away, but only served to assist him as he stripped her hose away. Clad in her soft white chemise, she scrambled over to the other side of the bed, her heart racing wildly. Why had she provoked him? she wondered desperately. He taunted her endlessly, but it was true that he had used no force against her, until now . . .

"Alaric, I was angry! Nay, I was hurt, I meant—"

"You meant to scald my nether parts, milady, and I do not appreciate the intent." He suddenly lunged across the bed, and she screamed as he caught her and dragged her across the room. She wondered in earnest what punishment he intended for her, then screamed again as he plucked her up and tossed her into the tub, still clad in the chemise.

Fallon grasped the edges, determined to arise. But she could not, for his hands were upon her and he lifted her again. He held her against himself as he stepped into the tub and sat, bringing her down upon him. She opened her mouth to scream, but he caught her lips with his own, and her scream faded against the fierce intensity of his kiss. There was hunger there, brutal and bruising, demanding, as he held her tightly and freely sampled her lips and her mouth. She could not breathe, and she could not escape the breathless sensation of burning excitement that swept through her. She had known him, and he had taught her well. His kiss was like a shaft of hot steel that soared and pierced deeply into her, low into her belly where it throbbed and pulsed. She gripped his shoulders, not knowing if she fought his touch or held him to her. His mouth parted from hers, and his eyes, alive and softly glimmering silver, were full upon hers. He swept a tendril of hair from her face, and he spoke to her in tones both tender and hoarse.

"I can never forget the first night that I held you so. I had always known you were an extraordinary child, bound to taunt and tease and seduce some poor man. Until I touched you, I had not known that I would be that man. The very act of touching you was lightning that coursed through my body and tore at my soul. There was no child there anymore, but a woman grown. I touched her breast . . ."

His words faded as he acted upon them, his palm falling against the fullness of her breast, his fingers curling gently around it over the slim barrier of her chemise. The fabric was gossamer and worthless then, for her flesh responded to his touch, and the crimson swell of her nipple hardened against the caress of his palm. She wanted to speak, to stop him, but she had no voice and no will, for his eyes still fell upon her. Where he touched, she burned; and where he did not, she ached that he should.

"I always knew you were beautiful," he murmured. "I simply denied that I could be held by that beauty."

His mouth crushed hers again as he continued to stroke her breast. Then his hand moved down upon her in a trail of practiced seduction, and it was all too easy for her to forget everything, all of her anger and pain, and thrill to the quivering sensation. His lips touched hers, played upon them, left them, returned to them. The kiss alone was plunder and rape, savage and sweet, and with a shudder, she began to return it twofold. She caught his lip between her teeth; her mouth molded itself to his. She tasted him fully with the sweep of her tongue, and she felt the fierce shuddering of the man beneath her.

She gasped as the hem of her soaking chemise was pushed high, and his hand wandered and roamed boldly over her thigh. Against her soft woman's triangle he stroked and probed with bold command and tender finesse, and the heat that had come to her there swirled in a searing, liquid fire. He murmured low against her lips and caught the gasp that escaped, and touched her freely, touched her deeply. He set up a rhythm that seared her, and he stroked with the pad of his thumb against tender flesh that left her gasping again and weak, and pushing against him because the sensation was such sweet, honeyed agony.

She did not realize that he had ceased to touch her. She opened her eyes to meet his and saw that they were nearly black with passion. She flushed and her eyes fell from his. "Nay! Look at me!" he commanded her hoarsely, but she could not. She choked and tried to slip away from his touch, but in doing so she arched against him and the feelings that swept her ran deeper and she cried out softly. Capturing her eyes with his own he smiled with triumphant male pleasure. She returned his gaze and swore softly.

He rose, bearing her with him. He stepped out of the tub and laid her on the fur before the fire. He did not hesitate or falter, but ripped her sodden chemise away from her breast. She saw his eyes again, the dark heated passion within them. She saw the tension that twisted his face, and she knew that he would have her then. It was wrong, but her heart hammered fiercely. Nay, it was not her heart that plagued her so. It was the hunger that dwelt inside her. It was the desperate ache and longing he created, now needing to be assuaged. She felt as if she had drunk long and deeply. The mist and the clean male scent of his body had intoxicated her. She had to find release.

She heard the fabric rip, and she weakly tried to protest as he bared her body to his view.

"I will lick the bathwater from your skin. All over."

Nay . . .

She formed the word, but no sound came. The firelight played over their bodies, laps of flames rising to coat them in gold. She longed to touch him. To reach out and press her fingers against the hard-muscled, living wall of his chest. To tease the springing mat of hair that curled and swirled there.

She dared not look down. Down upon the taut, lean hardness of his waist and the long sinewed power of his legs. Down upon an arousal grown hard and swift and sure.

He leaned over her and spread her hair out on the rug. She could not move; she could not protest or cry. She lay still and damp and felt the blaze near her as it dried her body.

Then his lips found hers and drank passionately. But his mouth did not remain upon hers. His lips trailed away and moved over her flesh like a searing tongue of flame. Over her throat, and over her breasts, pausing to suckle and savor, tease and arouse. His touch was light, so light she longed to crush him to her. Then it was fierce, so fierce that he suckled her nipple deep, deep into his mouth and slowly released it.

She twined her fingers in his hair. The very pulse and blaze of the fire seemed to be a part of her. She murmured things—she knew not what. She twisted and writhed, and his tongue touched another droplet of water and lapped in a swirl against her abdomen.

Suddenly he was gone, and she was left to cry out as he gripped her ankles, parted them wide, and knelt between them. She saw his eyes, and the burning shaft of him, and she moistened her lips to stop him. She could not. He stretched out above her, there with the firelight playing upon his golden muscled shoulders and the passion in his face. He stared at her, not releasing her gaze. She closed her eyes in a sweet agony.

"All over." He whispered the words against her flesh as he slid his hands beneath her buttocks and buried his head against her. She cried out, jerking in spasm as he teased her with the first touch of his tongue. She felt his throaty laughter and knew his eyes were on her face again, watching her response. She writhed and twisted and then arched against him. A moaning began in her throat, and she began to toss in wild abandon. Her body surged against him even as some rational place within her heart and mind sought to fight this extreme intimacy. There was no help for it, for he was determined to have all of her, and despite the flames in his eyes and the raging passion within his own body, he was determined to seduce her with leisure. He teased and probed and sought and found the tiny pebble of greatest pleasure. He wedged ever deeper into her, and fire was the stroke of his tongue. Everything within her pulsed and throbbed, and she cried out, begging him to cease, praying for mercy.

Then it burst upon her. As if a log had fallen, as if a star had shattered. Hot and wet like burning oil, she flamed and burst and shattered, and the sweet feeling of absolute pleasure shook through her with a shattering volatility.

She cried out then in dismay, for his weight was still upon her and he was laughing with ultimate triumph. Crying out with incoherent desperation, she surged against him to escape him and the sense of shame that filled her, but he held her tight. His weight remained between her legs, and his laughter faded and the tension returned to his face as he rose over her. He caught her hands, lacing her fingers with his own, and her words died on her lips as she felt the huge hot shaft of him, probing hard against her.

"I cannot" she whispered pleadingly.

"You can," he assured her.

She swallowed and twisted her head, and then she gasped out softly—for though she had been sated to near exhaustion, a quiver shot through her as he filled her. Stroked and filled her . . . and began to move with hot and swift power. There was nothing slow or leisurely in his movements now, just burning, demanding passion that thundered, pure and pagan.

But the quivering grew and blossomed inside her, and as he thrust against her in his driving rhythm, she felt her flesh and blood burn and soar again. She moaned softly and met his thrusts, and she did not protest when he whispered hoarsely that she should lock her limbs around him.

It came again. She arched her back deeply and pressed herself against him as burning heat filled her; he rose above her, taut and hard; he thrust hard, and held. It seemed to scald and sear her, to swamp her with a potent elixir from the burning place between her thighs, along the entire length of her limbs, and even into her heart and her mind.

He rolled from her then and lay back, panting as she

had. The firelight still burned over their bodies, which were slick and wet again. Fallon stared at him, at his shoulders and arms, bulging with muscles so adept with a sword and with the other instruments of death.

She swallowed and gazed at his hands and thought of the tender way they had touched her. Then her gaze fell lower to the whipcord leanness of his waist and hips, and the long bulging muscles of his thighs.

Her eyes fell upon his male sex, sated now, but long and proud still, and she shuddered again. Hot, quick tears stung her eyes, and she wondered in absolute confusion how she could know this man for the enemy he was, how she could long with all her heart for freedom, and still tremble beneath his touch. It was a marvel, she thought. It was a horror. He had told her she would beg for his touch, and so she had.

His hand rested against her breast. Idly he stroked her flesh, and teased the nipple.

With a harsh, furious cry she tossed his hand from her and tried to rise. He caught her, and when she struggled against him, swearing, he straddled her, and their naked bodies became a painful embarrassment for her.

"What now, *mademoiselle?*" Alaric demanded harshly. "Are you going to call that barbarous force?"

"Get off me!" she demanded, refusing to meet his eyes. He said nothing, and at last she looked at him miserably. It was impossible, as always, to read the message in his slate-gray eyes. "Please!" she said at last, biting her lower lip.

He stood, completely at ease with his nudity, and held out a hand to her. She looked away from him, away from the slick moisture that gleamed on his shoulders, away from the evidence of what they had done together. He caught her hand, and drew her up and against him. He threaded his fingers into her hair at the nape of her neck. "I asked you, Princess, will you call that rape?"

"Nay!" she shrilled, and tears stung her eyes as she tried to escape his hold. "Aye—it was! Just as you can hold me, you can twist my will! It is my will to be quit and free of you!"

"Lady, I felt the sweet woman's wealth of your body, and I know that I pleasured you well."

His words gave her horror, and she flushed. "By God, I do not want to be pleasured!"

"There were times there, my writhing beauty, when you had me well deceived!"

"You've had your fun! Will you not let me go now?"

He released her so abruptly that she nearly fell back upon the fur rug. Then he stepped back into the tub, swore that it had grown so cold, and rose to dry himself with a linen towel. Seated on the rug, sorely wounded, Fallon watched him sullenly. Men! Conquering bastards—how she hated this one in particular. She remembered his whispers; she remembered the tenderness in his eyes; she remembered, with shame flooding through her again, the absolute intimacy they had shared—and her temper raced and soared. He had forgotten her already. He had shattered her world and her belief in herself, and he had forgotten her already. Her hatred for him filled her with keen and deadly rage.

"Come to bed," he commanded her.

"The hell I will, you bastard!" she spat out. She rose and shivered and then stepped into the cold tub herself, eager to rid herself of his touch and his scent. She scrubbed herself furiously, ignoring him.

Arms crossed over his chest, he awaited her with a semblance of patience. But when she had scrubbed herself, she did not want to rise. She felt his eyes upon her, and just his gaze caused her throat to constrict and her blood to boil, and she could still feel him within her body. Feel his touch, remember his way and his will.

"Towel?" He stepped toward her, politely offering her his own.

She snatched it from him without a word and wrapped it around herself. He gave up his vigil to walk over to the tray and take the tankard of ale from it. He lifted it to her. "I salute you, *mademoiselle*."

She swore at him, stamping a foot, and he laughed at her. Then the laughter faded, and his gaze grew hot and tense. She lowered her eyes miserably, thinking that he was very much the superb figure of the knight, even disrobed—nay, especially disrobed. Tall and towering and fine in every sinew and muscle, in flesh and blood and bone. She thought of the years that she had known him and the things that had come between them, and suddenly she wished he were not the enemy.

But he was. He had already stolen from her. He had taken her innocence, her pride, and her will. If she was not careful, he would steal her soul, and even her heart. And that would be foolish, for all those years ago when his wife had died it had seemed that he lost his own soul. He had no heart.

She turned her back on him suddenly. She did not want to remember the promise that had been in his eyes when they shared a goblet at a banquet. She did not want to remember that he had always made her tremble, and even when she had promised that she would marry Delon, it had been Alaric's kiss that she had recalled.

He had come to England with the men who had killed her father. Harold had been dead only a few days, and already she had lain with this enemy.

With a furious growl she spun around and sought something, anything, to throw at him. His boot lay nearby, and she tossed it with a will. His other boot soon followed. She caught him in the chest with the first—and dangerously lower with the second.

Alaric thundered out in response, striding toward her

even as she picked up her own smaller shoe to send it flying. He caught her wrist and the shoe fell, and then her towel fell. Tears choked her, and she tried to kick him.

"Damn you, Fallon! Cease this! Stop, now!"

She couldn't stop. She writhed and twisted and swore at him, and she kept trying to kick. He swept her up and carried her to the bed, then dropped her and fell down atop her. She still struggled and he shook her. "Fallon! Cease! Lie still, else I shall tie you again."

Exhausted, despairing, she lay still. She met his threatening gaze in silence.

She wanted to speak; she wanted to explain the misery of her situation. Absurdly, she even wanted to lie softly against him, to feel his touch.

She could not speak, and he did not seek to soothe her.

Chapter Nineteen

Sometime during the night, Fallon became aware of a rising, frightening heat. She was only halfway awake when Alaric flung an arm her way, and she fumbled to rise, slowly becoming aware that something was very wrong.

If she had ever truly wanted to slit his throat, her opportunity had come. Indeed, he lay in such fevered torment that she wondered if the deed would be necessary.

Fallon pulled away from him and leapt to her feet, and from the dying embers of the fire, she lit a candle. She came up beside him and touched his brow. His hair was soaked and his skin blazed. He tossed and turned wildly, muttering deliriously.

"Dear God," she murmured softly. She stared at him one moment longer, and she thought that if ever she were to get away from him, the time was now. She could dress and quietly slip by the guard and seek refuge in the forest. She knew the forests well and could reach London through the Andredeswald. Within two days, she could easily be in London, among friends, among the remainder of the Saxon forces. But if she left him, he would die.

She paused, aching, choking down a cry of anguish. For once, he was powerless. His body was gleaming and

soaked in sweat; his muscles were contorted in spasms of
agony. He was with her, so it was highly probable that
there was no guard at the door, such was his confidence
in himself. She could run; she could so easily be
free . . .

For a moment she allowed the dream to seize her. But
she could not leave him. He was her enemy, but he was
flesh and blood. She had known him too many years—
too intimately, and too well.

She cast aside the vision of freedom—of herself racing
upon a Norman steed to the very outskirts of London—
and hurried to the washbowl. She soaked a cloth and laid
it on his brow. "Bastard!" she whispered to him in an
anguished voice. "I should be willing to hang you by your
toes for the torment you have caused me! But I cannot
leave you lying ill. And yet, sir, I swear, I shall one day rise
against you!"

He could not reply. Fallon turned from him and
dressed quickly. She drew the sheet up to his waist and
went to the door. It was not locked, and she had to
swallow back her bitterness, for again, she saw the way to
freedom.

There was no guard at the door, but Richard of Elwald
sat slumped over his master's shield, his oilcloth still in his
hand.

"Richard!"

The boy awoke and stared up at her as if she were an
illusion. Then he bolted to his feet. "My lady!"

"He is ill," she said. "I need water—cold water, as cold
as you can find it, lots of it, and quickly.

Fallon heard footsteps against the stairs and thought
fleetingly that the guard had not been so far away after all.
But it was Roger Beauclare who appeared at the landing,
looking more alarmed than anxious. Had they decided
that she was not so dangerous after all? Or was Alaric

simply convinced that she would not escape with him there?

It did not matter now. He burned so hot that she thought fever might well take him down where no sword arm could. A curious chill of fear began at the nape of her neck and snaked its way along her spine. She should not care! She should pray for him to die, as so many Englishmen had. But she could not pray for his death any more than she could wonder why she had not tried to flee, and why even now she stood and gave out rapid instructions.

"Roger, I shall need you. If I can't cool him down, I must give him something to purge his system, and he will fight me."

The young Norman was staring at her, and she wondered if he was weighing her words, if he perhaps thought she intended to poison Alaric. She lowered her eyes, remembering a long-ago time when she had manipulated him into doing her work. He had grown into a handsome and powerful young knight, and it disturbed her anew to feel his eyes upon her.

She lifted her eyes again. What did it matter? If she did not move quickly, Alaric would surely die.

"Richard, do as the Lady Fallon has asked you," Roger said, pushing past Richard and coming into the room. He hurried to the bed and stared down where Alaric tossed and turned feverishly. The cloth had fallen from his brow, and Fallon quickly retrieved it, soaked it, set it on his brow once again.

" 'Tis the same fever that has taken half our army," Roger said harshly. He turned to Fallon. "What can I do?"

Alaric chose that moment to kick the bedcovers from him. Fallon colored as he lay naked between them, but then she raised her eyes to Roger's. "We have to cool him down."

Richard came up the stairs with buckets of icy spring

water. Fallon tore one of her chemises into strips and ordered that they should cover him with water-soaked cloths. She then began to bathe his brow and torso and shoulders and under his arms. Then she asked Richard and Roger to help her turn him, and they set grimly about the task of cooling the rest of his body. Still he raved and talked, and as dawn began to break, he suddenly sat up and seized Fallon by the shoulders.

"Good God, why? As God is my witness, madam, you have slain an innocent! And I am cast into this trail of blood. May God forgive you, for I do not know if I can! You have slain her, and I have slain him, and now the babe, and you, oh, God!"

He shook Fallon with such a vengeance that she cried out. Roger and Richard both rushed forward, trying to ease his hold upon her. His fingers stroked her cheek, and fell to her throat. Had he wished to kill her, she realized, he could have done so with a snap of his fingers, the power of his hands was so great. Yet he stared past her and beyond her.

"He does not seek to hurt you!" Roger assured her. "He—he must be dreaming of the past."

Alaric stared at her blankly, and his eyes closed, and he pitched back to the bed again.

"Dear Lord!" Fallon whispered, her fingers fluttering to her throat. She gazed quickly to Roger, and she knew that he had understood what had happened, though she could not herself. She turned from him and caught Richard by the shoulders.

"Richard, you must go to the steward. I will tell you what I need." She gave him a list that included eggs and honey and herbs and mosses, and Richard went running down the stairs to find Hamlin. Roger kept changing Alaric's cloths, and Fallon, working silently across from him, watched him curiously, fervently hoping he would say something.

"He wanted to kill me," she said softly. She caught his eyes, and he flushed and shrugged.

"Nay, he did not wish to harm you."

"What happened?"

"I cannot tell you; it was not my affair. It all took place so very long ago."

"I know that he was married," Fallon said.

"Aye."

"And that he lost her. And that she was very beautiful."

"Too beautiful," Roger murmured. He gazed at Fallon again, and his shoulders rose and fell. "The demons must haunt him now, for 'tis not his wife causes nightmares but the memory of the girl. He meant to protect her, and she died by her own hand."

"Why? What happened?"

They broke off as Alaric began to toss and turn more wildly. His eyes, deeply glazed, fell upon Roger's and he began to speak. "He does not understand English law. He is all-powerful in Normandy and he does not understand that no king is all-powerful here."

"He talks about William," Roger said softly. Then Alaric screamed, as if in the throes of some ungodly nightmare. Richard came racing back up the stairs, and young Jeanne, the steward's daughter, was with him. "We had all but three herbs." Jeanne told Fallon, setting a tray before her. Her eyes, deeply distressed, fell upon Alaric. Tenderly, she set to the task of cooling him, and as her hands moved gently over his body, she was stunned by the emotions that swept through her.

"I shall send for a physician," Roger said, and he went to the hallway to call below.

"He will not live until a physician arrives," Fallon insisted softly, "unless I can mix him this potion." They all paused and stared at her, and she felt again the terrible mistrust, even from her own people. Hamlin and Jeanne spoke no French, Roger's English was weak, and though

Richard understood them all, he, too, seemed ready to band against Fallon in fear that she would harm Alaric. "If I can find the herbs I need, I can make him an elixir that will purge him of the infection that breeds the fever."

Roger stared at her long and hard. She knew he wanted to relent but felt he should take care.

No one had forgotten that she had stabbed Falstaff.

Roger caught her arm. "I will come with you. I will let you make your brew. But, oh, lady, let it be good, for if he dies, I will be bound to hand you to William with that offense upon your head!"

She drew her arm from his. "I do not intend to poison him, Roger," she said softly. She turned her head and took a leather bucket from the doorway. As she hurried down the steps, Roger was behind her.

Alaric's men had awakened, and they were quickly alert. Whispers and gazes followed her as she hurried out the door. She called to a stable boy for a horse.

"Where would you ride?" Roger demanded, standing behind her.

"Out by the marshes!" she snapped. "If I walk, he could well die ere I reach the place where the herbs grow!"

Roger ordered that the boy bring only his mount, then lifted her up before him. They galloped to the marsh, and Fallon gathered herbs for her tonic while Roger watched and waited nervously. He wandered away from the horse, and she saw that his sword was thrust through a saddle-bag and not around his waist.

She felt bitter and resentful. No one realized that she was defending herself when she stabbed Falstaff; no one believed she had a right to that defense. It rankled her that even Roger—who had once been her most willing slave—could think her so eager to poison a man.

She hurried back to the horse, and in silence she drew the sword. Morning birds whistled softly; then a soft hush seemed to settle in the morning mist. Fallon came up behind Roger and pressed the sword to his spine. He stiffened, instantly aware of the lethal threat she offered.

"Sir, when you escort women of my dangerous nature, I suggest you take care of your weapons."

"Fallon, don't." He stood with courage, but she heard the crack in his voice.

"Turn around, Roger, slowly, carefully."

He did so. She kept the blade against him. She raised it to his throat, and he paled. Then she cast his weapon aside and stared at him furiously. "Roger, one day I will see you all driven from England. From my land. I will gladly fight you again myself. But not by treachery or by cold-blooded murder—though there are many of your number who deserve betrayal. Sir, had I craved Alaric's death, I'd have run long ere this! Now, if you would follow me about, then pay attention and give me aid, for we must get back quickly."

She swung about, and searched carefully for the mosses and the other herbs she needed. Roger, she noted, gathered some herbs for her. She turned quickly when she had enough moss. "We must get back."

Roger set her upon his horse's back and leapt up behind her. They raced back to the manor, and when they burst into the room, they found Alaric no different. Jeanne and her elder sister Mildred sat at the bedside, cooling him as best they could with cloths. Richard stood by his side in anxious vigil. Two of Alaric's men, armed and armored, stood by to protect him. But their swords were useless against the fever that tore at him.

Fallon ignored them all and stoked the flames in the hearth. She set a kettle over the flame and added herbs and stirred the mixture, and she heard someone whisper that she must be a witch. One of the guards—the gigantic bald man who had dragged her up the stairs—stepped up to Roger, and she heard him whisper heatedly that she should be stopped—she meant to kill Alaric. She locked her jaw and kept her attention upon her task.

She rose at last, tossing a strand of her hair from her eyes, to face the men. She longed to speak in English, but she dared not, for Roger's command of the language was not good, and she did not want to lose his confidence now.

"I worked with the finest physician of the old English king at the battle of Stamford Bridge. Where there is warfare, men will have fever."

"The English water gave him his fever!" the bald knight swore.

Richard must have understood something in that French statement for he flared to the defense of his country. "The water here is good! Alaric is sick because he joined the rotting army in Dover!"

"It doesn't matter why," Fallon said. "I am aware that this creature will flay me alive if his bastard master does not live, yet I stand here taking this chance! Haunt me no more with your fantasies about witches and demons. His fever must break!"

Roger breathed sharply, knowing he held Alaric's life in his hands. Then he stepped back and indicated to Fallon that she should give Alaric her brew.

Richard watched her, and she nodded at him encouragingly. "Help me, Richard, help me to hold him."

She prayed that Alaric would not fight her then, for neither she nor Richard could begin to match his strength. But he did not, and between them, she and Richard were able to lift his head and pour some of her evil-smelling brew between his lips. She thought ruefully that she could not blame the knight for thinking she meant to slay him with the stuff, for it smelled vile.

Alaric's lips were nearly white; the proud, handsome lines of his face were ashen. She pried open his lips and carefully forced more of the liquid between them.

She stroked his throat, nodding to Richard as he strained beneath Alaric's weight. Alaric swallowed, then choked. He went stiff and rigid, and then he shuddered. "Drink, drink, more!" Fallon urged him. "Come, you must . . ."

She doubted that he heard her, but he continued to swallow. He shuddered and opened his eyes, to stare at her in horror. "My God!" he thundered hoarsely. "A pail, for the love of God, a pail!"

Alaric pushed Fallon from him and started to leap from the bed. His eyes widened as he saw that the room was filled with people. Swearing, he flung the covers from the bed and raced across the room to the chamber pot. Then he was voilently ill. He gasped for water, and Richard hurried to oblige him. He doused it over his face and head, and was suddenly overcome with weakness again. He sagged, but Richard caught him and, with Roger's help, led Alaric back to the bed.

Fallon heard a hissing sound. She turned to see that the bald knight had raised his battle-ax high. She screamed in terror, for he meant to strike her through.

"Stop!" Roger commanded sharply. "Stop, friend, stop."

"She has killed him!"

"Nay, nay, see?"

The knight stepped forward and Alaric dazedly opened his eyes. He was warm still, but the fever had broken. He tried to smile, but his eyes fell closed, and almost instantly, he slept.

"You see, he but sleeps," Fallon said dully, still stunned by the threat with the battle-ax. "He sleeps, and he will sleep for hours and hours to come. We need to keep him quiet now, and he will live."

Smiling at the bald knight, she closed her eyes and thanked God fervently that she had done well. Then she sank back on the bed and fainted.

* * *

Alaric lay ill and barely aware of his surroundings for nearly a week. In that time, messages came back and forth at a steady rate from the duke's army. William himself had been felled by the fever; he lay immobile at the broken tower and sent his men out to claim the surrounding countryside.

In London, the earls, the clergymen, and the high officials of the kingdom had proclaimed Edgar the Atheling king of England. William was in a rage over the news. No great army marched south to challenge the Normans, however, and though Edgar had been proclaimed king, there seemed to be no immediate plans for his coronation.

It was Jeanne who kept Fallon informed of events in the world. Since Alaric's illness, Fallon had discovered a certain new freedom. She was allowed to enter the hall; she was even allowed to leave the house. She had watched the harvest, and she had seen that ironmonger Heath and his family had settled in Haselford; this giant Saxon was engaged in building additions to the manor, with other refugees at his side. Fallon had spoken with his wife, Marla, who had assured her that Heath was not a cruel man, but a bitter one. "There was something of fate about Hastings," Marla said with a sigh. "Heath was the king's greatest champion, but Harold was like a man in a daze once that battle began."

"I think he believed that God had turned against him," Fallon said, and she had to swallow, because it was still so easy to cry for her father. Nay, it was still too easy to cry for all England.

Jeanne was sensitive to her position, but as time passed, it was Marla who became Fallon's closest friend. She told Fallon once that she had no idea why she should want to escape, and when Fallon stared at her in confusion, Marla told her, "I watched the rape and fall of a city. I saw beautiful young girls each taken by a dozen harsh and horrible men. I saw fighting men slain, and women taken until they were close to death. You are the king's daughter, my lady, and surely you are no ordinary girl. But neither is Alaric an ordinary man, and if he has offered you his love and protection, then it is perhaps something that you should not be fighting."

"You have given up England, Marla," Fallon told her. "I have not. My father would not give his country to a foreign king, and I will not bow down to one."

"I don't see where you suffer unduly," Marla said quietly, and color flooded to Fallon's cheeks. Alaric's men, in truth, treated her with a certain amount of courtesy and respect now. They watched her, though; she had some freedom, but there was always someone at her heels. If she walked outside, a Norman guard was there. She longed to escape, yet she needed to take great care. She needed a horse, too, for it would take her forever to walk to London. But the stables were most carefully guarded— she would never manage to steal a horse.

The people were free to travel from village to village, and Fallon wondered if Marla and the others had information that she lacked. Haselford grew daily, and refugees who were willing to work for the new Norman lord were welcome.

She gripped Marla's hands suddenly. "Marla, please! Perhaps Heath cannot understand, but my father felt that he had to fight, and when he fell, he must have believed that it was God's judgment upon him. But he was killed by these people. Count Alaric is a just man, I have known him many years. But don't you see? I am Harold's daughter, and I am bound by honor to reach my people, my brothers, my aunt, perhaps. I am desperate to reach London, Marla. You can send and receive messages. Oh, Marla, if ever there is a way for me to escape, please! Help me."

Marla sighed and looked miserably about. She knew her husband's opinion on the matter. "I doubt if I will ever be able to help you. But if I ever can, I will try."

This was the best answer that she could expect, Fallon knew.

A curious relationship had grown up between Fallon and Roger. Alaric had still barely opened his eyes, and Roger was in command. A truce existed between them, and sometimes, when she listened to the English that was spoken all around them, she recalled the time when he had come to visit her father with Alaric. She and Roger had liked each other then; they were close in age, and Roger was always soft-spoken and courteous to her.

The tales came in endlessly about the devastation wrought by William's army as it passed through the countryside. Once, watching Fallon turn pale as the news came in, Roger had tried to speak with her.

"It isn't that William intends to lay waste all the land, Fallon. But he moves with an army, a large army. Men must eat. You will see that the damage is restricted to the path that he travels." He hesitated. "I have seen William use destruction as a policy. He used it to lure your father here, to battle him quickly, before Harold could add power to his force. And I have seen him do it in Normandy, Anjou, and Maine. But if he meant only to destroy England, all England would look like Romney by now."

Fallon's lip curled derisively and she turned her back on him. "The men must eat, so they slay every animal in sight, they rob the manors and steal from the merchants, and they seize any woman older than twelve and younger than eighty!"

He turned away and did not answer her.

In those days, she often thought of running. Every night she stayed with Alaric, sleeping before the fire, rising frequently to check upon him. But he breathed easily, and though he did not wake or speak, she knew that the healing was upon him and that he would be safe. Sometimes she sat beside him with cooling cloths, and she thought that in sleep he seemed vulnerable. He was accustomed to command, and when he was well, it showed in his face. Then he was competent and confident. Even now those qualities were sometimes apparent in his features when he was awake.

Although she did not admit it to herself, Fallon liked to admire his body. His shoulders were golden and sleek. Even in repose, his muscles rippled and bulged, and his waist and abdomen were so taut that little ridges formed a pattern like a living wall.

Although attuned to the business of war, his body was still beautiful, she thought—and she bit her lip, for the idea had escaped from her heart unbidden, and she did not want to dwell upon it. She moved quickly away from him, and she was glad when Richard came to relieve her.

On the first of November Alaric opened his eyes and looked at her, really looked at her. She was busy mending a chemise, but felt his eyes upon her, and her hands fell still.

"You didn't run," he said. His whisper was hoarse and ragged. She shook her head.

"Why not?" He asked her. She didn't answer him, and he smiled slowly, closing his eyes.

That brought her alive. She set her sewing aside, and knotted her fingers together, staring down upon them. "I didn't want you to die of fever," she told him.

His eyes opened again and a small smile played at the corners of his mouth. He met her eyes gravely once again. "Thank you."

"Don't thank me. Someday a brave Saxon is going to skewer your heart, and I did not want him deprived of such a privilege."

"Does this Saxon have a name?"

"Nay, my lord—but surely, sir, you and your invaders will be caught in the end."

"Lady, you live in fantasy," he said dryly. He tried to rise, and found himself too weak. Gritting his teeth he pressed his fingers to his temples, then he lay back with a sigh. "How long have I lain here?"

"A week."

"A week!" Startled, he tried again to get up. Fallon put her sewing down and rose. There was something frightening in the absolute concentration and determination that knotted his features. Sweat beaded his forehead, but he sat up, and then his shoulders slumped and he inhaled sharply. "Jesu," he muttered, "but that fever has taken its toll!" His eyes shot to her again, and the hint of a smile returned. "So that potion you gave me—which smelled of sewer dung and tasted even worse—was not poison."

"Of course not."

"Again, thank you."

"Again, please don't bother. I cured you only because your balding friend would otherwise have cheerfully given me a most severe headache."

He laughed and the sound grew stronger. "Rollo." His eyes played over her curiously and he still smiled. "Rollo is half pagan himself; he's a Swede, a Viking. He says that we Normans are Vikings, too—but you would not have thought so if you'd seen us building our ships. Rollo has been convinced from the start that you are a witch or a child of the ancient pagan religion. He says that you are too beautiful to be a mortal woman and that we should send you back to the dark world from whence you have come."

"Tell him I am merely a Saxon, and not a witch."

"Aren't they one and the same?" he queried.

"You seem quite well recovered," she murmured, and spun around to head for the door.

"Fallon!"

Command rose in his voice, but she ignored him.

"Fallon, I am talking to you—"

"So you are," she interrupted pleasantly. "But as you see, I've little interest in listening!"

Despite his weakness, he leapt from the bed and strode to her side. He clutched her wrist with a surprising power. His eyes pierced into hers. "Why didn't you attempt to escape when you could if you hate me so? Why didn't you let me die?"

"I told you—"

"Ah, yes. So that some Saxon lad could later slit my throat. What is the truth?"

He was too close to her. She was frightened that he might read the weakness in her soul. She wrenched away from him with all her strength. "Don't imagine that I forget who you are!" she snapped. "And don't imagine that I can in any way tolerate you or any other Norman in my kingdom! I despise you, but when I best you, my lord, your eyes will be open to see it!"

She turned to flee.

"Fallon!"

She continued on out, slamming the door. When she heard him struggling behind her and swearing vociferously, she smiled despite her sudden anger.

It was enjoyable to have had the last word for once.

"Fallon?"

She heard Richard calling to her just as he hurried up the stairs. He looked at her anxiously. "He is awake," she told the boy. "Weak, though. I imagine he will be hungry. Tend to him, if you will. I'm sure he'll be very anxious for your services." She pushed away from the wall and started down the stairs.

"Where are you going?" Richard called to her.

"Out for some air!" she called back. She felt curiously light, and she wondered why.

Down in the hall, she found Roger Beauclare trying to

communicate with Hamlin. They seemed to be doing fairly well, each testing out words in the other's language. Roger looked up as Fallon appeared. "We've been hunting. Boar and venison and quail this evening, and plenty to salt and smoke and save for the winter."

Would she be here for winter? Fallon wondered dismally. Her heart sank as she thought about her other choices. She was constantly afraid that Alaric would tire of keeping her and ship her to a dungeon in Normandy. If she had any honor, she reminded herself, she would prefer that to her current fate.

She sighed softly to herself and looked up at Roger. Nay, she would not be here for the winter, no matter what Alaric's plans were for her. "He is well, he is talking, he even managed to get up and walk."

"Thank God!" Roger breathed. He kissed her cheek and hurried past her.

Hamlin stood there, his white hair sticking out in tufts, and he nodded in acknowledgment. "You look pale, milady. We've wine newly arrived. Will ye have some?"

"Aye, thank you, Hamlin," she murmured.

She sank into one of the window seats that looked over the outbuildings and fields behind the manor. Dusk was coming. Men were walking in from the late harvest while the stonemasons and carpenters finished with their labors on a rising wall and fortress.

Richard came running down the steps, shouting for a tub and water and food. Hamlin brought her wine and listened while Richard joyously told him all that Alaric had ordered. "He says that he is hungry enough to eat the whole boar!"

"Fine, fine!" Hamlin assured him. "Tell my lord Alaric that my wife and I will provide a fine meal and that we are heartily glad that he is about again."

Fallon watched, keeping her thoughts to herself as she sipped her wine. They were all so anxious to serve the

Norman bastard. She turned to the window and stared
out longingly. Then her heart seemed to skip a beat, and
a gasp escaped her.

Three young men were approaching the manor.
Dressed in coarse linens and wools, they appeared to be
coming to work in the kitchen and serve the meals to the
Norman host who dined in the hall each evening.

Delon was among those men.

Fallon's heart somersaulted. He was alive! She longed
to rush out to him, embrace him—but why was he here?
Perhaps he had a plan in coming here, and any recognition on her part might ruin his careful maneuvering. But
how could she just sit here while Delon approached? She
looked more carefully at him. He had shaved his beard,
and his beautiful golden hair had been cut. Where the
Normans ravaged, they cut the men's hair and shaved
their cheeks to humiliate them. Here in Haselford, the
men had adopted the style in honor of their Norman
protector.

Briefly, shame snaked a hot trail through her body. Her
betrothed was coming to rescue her, and she had dishonored him. She was sure that Delon would not hate her for
it—he knew that few innocents would be left where the
conquering army had been. Yet it was not the lack of
innocence that she deplored in herself. It was the hunger
that Alaric stirred—so different from the simple affection
she felt for Delon.

Fallon watched as the men disappeared around the
back of the manor house.

She jumped to her feet and strode hurriedly toward the
kitchen, desperate to meet Delon. She burst through the
door, and there he stood behind the chopping tables near
the central fire. They were alone. "Delon!" she said eagerly. "Oh, Delon!" he stretched out his arms to her, and
she ran to him happily. "You are alive and well!"

He nodded, holding her face tenderly, searching out

her eyes. "I've men with me in the forest—good Englishmen, who abhor the Norman yoke! We've a plan to help you escape. You must meet me here at midnight. Your brothers plan to rebel, and they need you. I, dear Fallon, need you, too. For I love you. We are lost without you."

Hearing the kitchen door swing open, Fallon quickly pushed away from Delon.

"Fallon!"

She spun about in horror. Roger Beauclare stood behind her. "Fallon, Alaric insists upon talking to you immediately. Ah, you there, boy, bring that kettle of water." Roger looked at Fallon. "Does he understand me? Tell him in English, please."

She couldn't tell anyone anything. Her voice caught in her throat.

"Fallon, what ails you?"

She shook her head. "Roger, tell Alaric I will come directly."

Roger frowned. "Immediately, Fallon. He says that if you give me an argument, I am to bring you bodily."

He would do it, too, she thought bitterly. Delon had turned and was attempting to disappear through another door—but his way was suddenly blocked by massive Rollo, his double-headed battle-ax swung nonchalantly over his shoulder. Delon stopped, his eyes wide at the sight of the ax.

"Rollo!" Roger said. "The count fairs well; he is up and shouting out orders. We will ride to the duke soon, I do imagine!"

"That is good news, is it not, lad?" Rollo said, turning to Delon and giving him a mighty, cheerful clap on the shoulder.

Fallon thought bleakly that Delon would be as insulted by being called "lad" as he would be nervous about the weapon.

"Tell him to take the water upstairs, and go with him, Fallon."

She stared at Delon, aware that he had understood every word. She desperately tried to remember how many times Alaric and Delon had met face to face. But Alaric was ill, and Delon looked very different with all his golden glory shorn. They had no choice. She spoke quickly to him in English, hoping she wouldn't be understood by Rollo and Roger.

"We must do as they say. Be quick about it, and avoid Alaric! I will meet you outside as soon as possible!"

He nodded. Neither of them had a choice.

Chapter Twenty

More water was needed for his bath, but Alaric crawled into the half-filled tub as he waited for it to arrive. He listened to Richard's version of Fallon's care as he did so. "She was tender, and so anxious!" Richard claimed. "She pined for you!"

Alaric eyed him skeptically. She had probably sat there praying that his fever would plague him until it was time for him to leave again.

"Ah, here she is!" Richard murmured nervously, and Alaric opened an eye to see that Fallon had indeed returned, with a lad who carried water.

Not a lad. Alaric tensed, but was very careful not to move. 'Twas no boy who carried the kettle of steaming water, but a man full grown. Blond and tall and well muscled, and obviously a master at arms. It was Delon. One of Harold's housecarls. Fallon's betrothed.

Alaric made a pretense of closing both his eyes, but he continued to watch the young man. Did they think he was blind? Or were they convinced that the fellow's naked cheeks and cropped locks would fool him? And what was this? Was there an army lurking in the forest, or had the man come alone?

Had Fallon been waiting, knowing that a plan was set in action? Had she kept him alive only to slay him now?

"Boy, set the kettle down," he said in a leisurely drawl. "Ah, and wait there a moment. Richard, come here!"

Fallon stood silently in the doorway. From beneath his lowered lashes, Alaric watched her. She was desperately nervous. She moistened her lips every few seconds, and she clasped and unclasped her fingers continuously.

The boy stood before him, uneasy himself. Alaric wondered momentarily if Richard knew what was afoot, but decided he probably did not. Richard was determined to be a knight in the Norman fashion. He had not been disloyal to the Saxon cause, for he had never embraced it.

"Go below and find Sir Roger. Say to him for me that I have heard wolves howling. They are hungry, and we must take care."

Richard nodded, frowning. Was Alaric still fevered? He hadn't heard wolves howl, but he would convey this strange message anyway.

"As you wish, my lord!" he promised Alaric, hurrying from the room.

When the door closed, Alaric called to Fallon. "Come, will you please, my lady, and pour some of that water into the tub?"

Fallon moved in silence to obey his command—a circumstance that would have put Alaric on his guard even if he hadn't recognized Delon. Fallon poured the water carefully into the tub.

Ever wary of the man who waited tensely near the door, Alaric reached out and caught her wrist. She dropped the pail and stiffened.

"You should have heard Richard," he said, smiling to her. He reached up to touch her cheek, drawing a wet line across it, allowing his finger to fall down the length of her throat and hover over her breast.

She wrenched her hand free and backed away from him. "What do you want?" she demanded hoarsely.

He shook his head, maintaining a leisurely, pleasant

smile. "I am curious, Princess, that is all. Richard swears that you were eager to save my life. Even Rollo is now convinced of your saintliness. Why?"

Her eyes darted to the blond man at the door.

"Why?" Alaric repeated.

"I—I don't know. I'll get the rest of the water for you, and this young man can return to his duties."

"Oh, I'm sure his duties can wait a moment. I am talking to you, Fallon."

She was close enough that he could grab her again, and he jerked her down to her knees at his side. She stared at him in fury, but couldn't resist throwing a nervous look Delon's way. There was a plea in her eyes; she begged Delon in silence not to move, not to intervene.

A certain pity filled Alaric's heart, for the blond man stood as still as a statue and as pale as snow. He would break soon, Alaric was certain. And he was sorry, in his way—for were he in Delon's shoes, he would surely be suffering the torments of hell.

"I want to know the answer, milady," he repeated softly to Fallon. "And yet I think I know the truth myself. Did you dream of the nights we lay together, and of all the intimacies we shared?"

She tugged at her wrist and her eyes flashed with fury. "Gutter rat!" she seethed, struggling against him.

He laughed and threaded his fingers through her hair, turning her face to his. "Have you forgotten already?" he taunted.

His lips had barely touched hers before he felt the movement. In a second he had thrown her from him and snatched up his sword. The blond Saxon, wielding his knife, came up short when he saw the blade of the heavy sword pointed at his throat.

There was no fight; Alaric had been too swift. Fallon tore across the room, intent upon attack, but he stopped her, too—not with his sword, but with the savage chill of his words. "One more step, milady, and this sword will pierce his throat. I would prefer not to kill him. I pity him too deeply for loving you."

Delon would have spoken, but the steel blade at his throat made him silent. How many times, Alaric wondered, had he sat in Harold's hall and watched this young buck adore Fallon with his eyes? He had pitied the man then, for he was certain that Harold, after he became king, had harbored other ideas for his daughter. Still, he admired the courage of the man.

"Alaric, please . . ." Fallon whispered. Alaric ignored her, keeping his attention upon Delon.

"Was that knife for my back?" he asked Delon softly. But weakness swept suddenly through him, and he broke out in a sweat.

All of his strength was seeping away from his muscles. Darkness was cascading in upon him; he was going to fall.

He looked at Fallon's face, into her glorious eyes. She was backing away from him; had he the strength, he would have laughed.

"Kill me, Princess," Alaric warned her hoarsely. "Kill me, for I shall hunt you down."

"Delon, we must run. Now!"

"Perhaps we should—"

"Stab him in the back?"

"You are right, we cannot. We must run now!"

She grasped Delon's arm, pulling him desperately away. Bless Fallon—for calling attention to the weakness of the man, Alaric thought. Then he fell to the floor, the blackness about him complete.

Fallon rushed with Delon down the stairway. Already, in the great hall, she could hear the clash of arms. Alaric had told Richard that he must warn Roger about the "wolves."

The wolves were in the hallway: two Saxons had fought their way into the manor house, but from the landing

Fallon could see that the Norman knights were stronger.

"Dear God, more men will die!" Fallon cried out.

Delon took hold of her then and dragged her toward the doorway. "I've the princess!" he called out. "Come, men!"

Her heart soared in gratitude toward her people—they had come to save her. Delon took her hand, and they ran across the hall. A cheer went up among the Saxon warriors, who covered her retreat.

Outside, a mare awaited her. Fallon leapt upon the horse. Delon mounted a bay behind her, and they raced for the forest.

She felt the rush of the wind on her face and hair, and the powerful beat of the mare's hooves beneath her. Her heart took flight as Saxon men fell in behind them, riding behind the daughter of Harold, the late Saxon king.

"Are we pursued?" Delon twisted and looked back.

A dark-haired fellow who still bore a full beard shook his head. "Not yet."

"We will be," Delon murmured.

"We must reach the forest," Fallon called above the wind.

They pounded onward along the old Roman road, their party of fifty or so. Dust rose around them. Fallon felt that she flew on the clouds. She was free.

For a fleeting moment, the exhilaration of her sweet victory left her, and the image of Alaric flashed through her mind. He could have slain Delon quickly, but he had not.

We should have killed him! A small voice taunted her. No, she couldn't have murdered him; she did not wish him dead. He had humiliated her, but she could not lie to herself: He had not forced her to taste so sweetly of love. She had come to him as if under an ancient spell. She could not wish him dead. She wished him long life and health—preferably upon Norman soil.

Triumph! Victory! Oh, dear God, she was free! And still, even as the horse moved beneath her, even as birds trilled and dusk came sweetly all around them, she knew that she would miss Alaric, his taunting grin and the soft stroke of his warrior's hands upon her.

She swallowed, forcing herself to cease her thoughts of him. These men of England had come to her aid.

The horses began to slow, and everyone soon came to a halt.

"Here!" someone called. In the gleaming, men and riders seemed suddenly to be swallowed up by the earth as they moved, wraith-like, into the dense forest. The man with the full beard respectfully moved ahead of Fallon, leading them onward. They came at last to a large clearing where a number of women waited; burning campfires, roasting venison, and pitchers of good English ale were at the ready.

Amazed, Fallon looked at Delon. A cheer went up as she rode into the circle of fires and thanked them all. "To the king's daughter!" someone called, and cheers went up again. Then Delon dismounted and came around to help her down from the mare.

Tonight's feast could have been a grand dinner at Winchester. Men laughed and talked, and then the night grew sober again. The bearded man, whose name was Frasier, had been near Harold's side when he was killed. Fallon had to know the painful truth.

"Was—was the duke in on the savagery?" she asked.

The young Saxon shook his head. "Nay, it was rumored, but that is all. As much as I loathe the Norman bastard, I will tell you he took no part in that infamy."

"And what of the count?" Fallon asked. She felt a flush come to her cheeks, for she knew that Delon watched her.

Frasier shook his head. "Nay, lady, Count Alaric was not among those butchers."

After dinner, the band of warriors and their ladies

turned seriously to making plans. Fallon's brothers were to meet them half a league to the north in the morning. Delon told her they would hurry to London and try to raise an army there. She nodded. Delon was still watching her, and she lifted her eyes to meet his.

"If anything happens, Fallon, you must not forget our dream of freedom from the Norman yoke."

"What do you mean?" she asked sharply.

He smiled and sat down beside her, taking her hand. "If something should happen to any of us, as long as there is a prayer, you must go forward. Your brothers need you."

"Delon, nothing is going to happen."

They were deep in the lush woods, and the moon rose high, casting a benign glow on the land, on the many men who slept beneath the trees, on the fires, now dying low.

Delon smiled at her. He touched her cheek, and he looked at her with a certain wonder. A trembling started within her. He loved her even though he knew she had been the mistress of a Norman. What would he demand of her this night? she wondered. To her horror, she realized that she did not want him.

"Delon?" she whispered softly.

"Hush," he told her. "You must get some sleep. We shall rise at dawn and leave as quickly as possible. We are not safe here."

In the end, he merely slipped his arms around her and held her. Fallon stared at the moon. For the longest time, she was still. She could not sleep, for she was beset by mixed emotions. Escape was sweet—but some part of her had been left behind. In spite of herself, she could not forget Count Alaric.

She had barely fallen into a doze before she was rudely awakened. Delon was pulling her to her feet. "Run! You must run, into the forest."

"What in God's name is happening?"

She had awakened to madness. Men were shouting and drawing their swords; the women cried out and tried to run for cover among the trees. Fallon stared at Delon.

"He has found us! Alaric has found this place!"

Alaric had come for her! A chill raked her spine. She saw them now, the Norman knights, clad in armor, descending upon their campsite from the forest.

"Run!" Delon insisted.

"Nay! You came for me; I'll not desert you!"

Fallon ran to the horses, searching through the saddles and the gear. By the time she found a sword she could handle and extracted it, there were Normans everywhere. Men cried out and sought the safety of the woods; many of those who ran survived the onslaught. A horse was racing toward her and Fallon turned, choking back her fear and raising her sword in warning. The warrior paused. It was Roger. He rode on.

"God help us!" Fallon prayed. She worked her way back to Delon.

But God turned as deaf an ear to Fallon as he had to her father. As she stood there, her sword outstreched in warning, she saw Alaric. She saw the steel of his eyes as he rode toward her and Delon.

He dismounted and strode into the clearing where Delon and Fallon stood. Around them, the fighting went noisily on, but here it was all deathly still. As Alaric lifted his sword in a challenge, Fallon's heart stopped, for she loved both of these strong, proud men. Delon raised his sword in return, and the blades met with an angry clash.

Again and again, the mighty steel blades came together. A thrust, a parry. Deadly force against cunning and guile, swift agility against the weight of the swords. They moved behind a tree, and Fallon began to follow.

A sword flew up, and her heart seemed to stop. She came tearing around the uprooted trunk of a great oak.

Alaric stood, his sword at Delon's throat. Delon lay still.

"No! No!" Fallon screamed. She rushed at Alaric, holding her own sword high.

The Norman turned, meeting her sword with his in midair. Fallon staggered at the strength of the blow. Then he turned on her in a rage, battering down upon her. She gritted her teeth, certain that he meant to slay her, and fought with all her might. But he was too much for her. He backed her up against a tree, brandishing his sword before her.

"Kill me, lady!"

Tears stung her eyes. She warded off his blade, but she knew she could not hold out much longer. After all this, he had not slain Delon, who lay, barely conscious still, on the ground.

"Alaric—"

"I am not so weak this morning, lady," he said. His eyes were silver flames of hatred. He pressed against her, and she hadn't the strength to hold him off. With the flick of a wrist he sent her sword flying.

She grasped the tree and stared at him. They were surrounded now, she realized. Someone dragged Delon to his feet and brought him to stand beside her.

"Fallon, it seems you are bested once again," Alaric announced.

A strangled sob escaped her.

Alaric looked at Delon, his eyes flashing silver fire.

"I should kill you," he told the young Saxon.

"No!" Fallon screamed. "No, please!" She had never seen him so furious, so merciless. She pitched herself forward and landed on her knees at his feet. "I beg of you, let—"

"Fallon, my God!" Delon swore hoarsely. "He has stolen your honor!"

"What means honor now, Delon?" she spat out bitterly.

"I would like to know," Alaric put in.

Fallon turned and stared at him—this cold, distant stranger made of steel. Only the lethal anger in his eyes touched her. All else about him was ice.

He stepped forward, gripping her by her hair. "Are you a whore?" he demanded softly. "Available to the highest bidder?"

"Bastard!" she hissed, reaching out to scratch his cheeks. He caught her wrist quickly and held it tight. Delon stepped forward, saying words she could never have uttered herself. "I never touched her, Count Alaric."

"Am I to believe that?"

"Aye, sir, you should. For I love her."

Alaric was still.

"Delon!" Fallon cried in anguish. She loved him for his words, but wished that Alaric had been left to believe that she cared not a whit for him—that she had fallen into the arms of her betrothed with sweet relish.

Alaric arched a brow as he watched them. "This is really touching. But it is also over, I'm afraid."

Just then Roger came riding through the trees. He glanced briefly at Fallon and Delon, then spoke one word to Alaric: "Wolves."

"How many do you think?" Alaric queried.

"Near fifty, but most are in a sad state. The dregs of Hastings."

"How many dead, how many wounded?"

"Near twenty killed." He paused. "We lost Étienne and Walter. We've ten captives, and another twenty-five have fled into the woods."

Alaric could not look at Fallon. He had wanted to believe in her, had wanted peace between them. He was not such a fool as to love her, but he could have kept her alive and well through this blood conquest; and in the midst of it, he could have explored the magic alchemism between them.

He still could not forswear her. But she would pay for this treachery.

He turned around and stared at the pair of them coldly.

"Delon, I pity you, sir. You are a slave to this maiden, and I tell you this not with malice but with truth: The lady accommodated herself with me. I offer you the greatest mercy when I assure you that you'll not set eyes on her again." He could barely endure watching them together—the young man's arm around her, her face as white as death.

"Please," she whispered. She hesitated, then moved away from Delon; he reached out to grab her, but Roger was quicker. He leapt from his mount, his bloody sword raised before Delon's face. Fallon went to Alaric. She lowered herself to her knees and whispered softly, "For the love of God, I beg you—don't kill him. I'll do anything you want, I'll be anything you want."

She thought that he meant to slay the lad, Alaric realized. He tightened his lips grimly and set his own sword against her chin, raising it. "Don't plead like a beggar, Princess. He deserves more than this. Get up. I have already decided what I shall do. No action on your part will sway my judgment, so do not play the humble plaintiff." He wrenched her to her feet, pulling her close for one bittersweet moment. He saw the fear, the pride, the hatred, that flashed in her deep blue eyes, and he longed to shake her. He felt ill all over again. Delon denied that he had touched her, but they had been together all night. What had taken place between them? he wondered.

He shoved Fallon toward Roger. "Get her back to Haselford and put her under lock and key. Keep her out of my sight!" he said softly.

Fallon screamed in protest, but Alaric ignored her. And

long after she had been taken away, he could hear in his mind her pleas and the thunder of her fists against a locked door.

Alaric stared at Delon and set his jaw. He had to get this over with quickly. He had managed to ride out here, and he had managed to fight well. But he was losing his strength again now. If he didn't return home quickly, he was going to collapse any moment. "As for you, my fine Saxon friend . . ."

Chapter Twenty-One

Fallon's screams and pleas were ignored. She was tossed before Roger on his horse, and they raced back to the manor at Haselford, where she was bolted into a small, crude bedchamber. Terror tore at her heart, and she paced the confines of the room wildly. A single candle burned atop a round oak table, and the fire in the hearth was dying out, but the bed was covered with a shaggy fur. There was nothing else in the room, not even a poker for the fire. Fallon turned back to the door, slammed her fists against it, and screamed.

Delon! Poor, honorable Delon. She had failed him so miserably. He had believed in her; others had rallied to her support. And now Delon was going to die for her. That he should die in a bid to save her suddenly seemed like too much to bear.

She turned her back to the door, slid down its length, and sank to the floor. She pressed her palms to her eyes in despair. Alaric had been so cold to her; as she recollected the words he had spoken, chills swept through her. She had not been able to reach him in any way; now he was pronouncing judgment upon Delon. Dear God, what had happened? Had hope come to her, just to be dashed away? It couldn't happen; he could not kill Delon, he could not . . .

She rose and pounded her fists against the door, screaming and pleading to be released. No one came to her, and though her heart continued to beat raggedly, fearfully, she was at last overcome by exhaustion, and she slumped to the floor.

A commotion in the courtyard seemed to stir Fallon from her exhausted daze. She hurried to the window and stared out. For a moment, she saw nothing but the dawn mist shrouding the landscape, swirling heavy and deep upon the ground. Then she could see Alaric's Norman henchmen walking through it. They carried some burden, and as the mist began to clear, she could see it.

They carried Delon. Blood streamed from his forehead, from which a double-headed ax protruded. His sightless blue eyes were fixed upon the sky.

She began to scream in horror.

Distantly, she heard a voice calling her name. Something shoved hard against her body, and she was being moved. Arms, warm and strong and curiously tender, circled her, and she was lifted.

"Shush, I had to push you; you had fallen behind the door. Hush, now, it's all right."

She opened her eyes. Alaric carried her across the room and put her down on the bed. She shivered and stared at him in shock as he pulled the fur over her. He found her hands and warmed them with his own.

"Leave me!" She slammed her fists against him. He held her tight. His armor was gone and he wore silk and velvet. She still could not fight him. He would not loosen his hold on her.

"Fallon—"

"Nay!" she cried weakly. "Nay, I'll not have you touch me, by God. Not after what you did to him!"

"What I did to him?" Alaric stared at her in confusion. It was another morning, Fallon thought, and he was up and bathed. He looked well. His color was returning, and his eyes were bright and alert. He was slimmer, but not much so, and he was striking in a blue chemise and a soft doeskin tunic. He was not dressed for war this day.

"My God!" she repeated, and tears welled in her eyes. His frown deepened; then he smiled suddenly, and with a startling tenderness. "I think you were dreaming, Princess, and such a dream that the visions seemed to be true."

"What?" she whispered.

He stood and reached out a hand. She stared at it blankly. Alaric emitted a little oath of impatience, then picked her up again, sweeping her easily into his arms, and carried her to the window.

A group of his men were below. They called out to one another, laughing, as they loaded supplies on the backs of several fine English ponies.

Delon, too, was below. No battle-ax cleaved his forehead—no injury seemed to have been done him at all. He sat upon a horse, a coarse shepherd's cloak about his shoulders, and waited. She held tight to Alaric and watched as someone shouted an order. Roger was down below, too, near the steps to the manor house. He waved, and the party started off.

"Where—where are they taking him?" she asked, moistening her lips. She had indeed been dreaming, for Delon lived.

"Normandy. They will take him across the Channel, where he can cause no more trouble."

She lowered her eyes and started to tremble. She felt his gaze upon her, and his arms tightened about her. "Do you wish to accompany him?" Alaric asked gently.

Why could she not answer, Aye! Gladly! But Fallon knew that once she was a captive in Normandy, all hope would be lost.

She had to find her brothers, she assured herself. Delon

had told her that she must remain and continue the fight for England.

Was it just that, or something more?

"Never mind," Alaric said wearily, "I shall not ask you to answer that. But you will tell me honestly how he came to be here."

Her eyes widened and she tried to think quickly. Delon must have had a message from Marla, but Fallon could never admit such a thing. If Alaric did not find some punishment for the woman, then her husband Heath surely would. Fallon did not know which would be worse. She shook her head. "I—I don't know."

"You don't know?" His brow arched. He carried her across the room with long steps and set her down on the fur-strewn bed. She stared up at the ceiling, shielding her eyes from his gaze with an arm. "Speak to me, Fallon," he whispered softly.

"I swear to you, I don't know how he came to be here."

He put his hands on her shoulders and leaned close, growing angry again. Had he sensed that she did not want to be sent to Normandy? Was this a deceitful lull before he exiled her?

"Fallon, I want to know when he came and how you spoke and where he stayed and—"

"He did not stay," she told him nervously. "He had just come! I saw him first in the kitchen, just moments before you bid me come to you."

He held perfectly still above her. She trembled beneath the force of his eyes, and her lashes fell. Please, God, she prayed, let him be happy with this truth. Let me not betray Marla for her kindness.

"He said that he did not touch you. Is that the truth?"

"What difference does it make?" she asked dully.

"It might make a difference one day, Princess."

She stared at him, wondering at the sound of his voice. She smiled with a certain malice, glad that, for once, he might be the one to suffer and wonder. "It will be difficult, won't it? You will always wonder. Did Delon tell the truth, or did he not?"

She did not receive the reaction she wanted. He smiled slowly, leaning back to watch her. "I can summon your dear, brave betrothed. I can force him to tell the truth, and I can sever his head from his body when he is done."

"You would not!"

"I leave *you* to wonder, Princess. In fact, I leave you to pray."

He rose as if to leave. She did not believe him for a second. She had known him too long. He was a man of honor. He would not kill Delon. Surely . . .

"Stop!" she cried.

He turned politely.

"We were never—together," she said haltingly. "Your men came upon us where we awoke, where we had slept, among all the others. Every Saxon who survived your massacre knows the truth of it."

"That is fact?" The warmth of his whisper touched her face. He stretched out beside her, leaned upon an elbow. He reached out and brushed her cheeks with the back of his hand.

To her horror, Fallon felt a quickening heat within her. She didn't move. She met his eyes, feeling her heart race.

"I hate you, you know. I will rise against you again and again. As long as there are Normans in England, the Saxon people will rise."

"Be that as it may, Princess, I care not. I wonder about you and Delon. Have you told me the truth? Or should I—"

"Aye, I have told you the truth!"

She could not believe it. He touched her, and she trembled. He knew she spoke the truth, and he played with her! He teased her, taunted her . . .

And still, when he touched her, she was glad of it. Oh,

not with her mind! But her senses came alive, her body ached, her heart was swayed!

With a light stroke of his hand, he smoothed a stray hair from her forehead. His fingers traced gently over her lips, and he watched her with a rueful smile. "That's what your young swain told me, yet I wished to hear it from your own lips." His thumb lingered on her lower lip. He stroked it lightly, and she was stunned by the reaction that so small a caress caused in her. She wanted to touch him—to move her fingertips over the planes of his face, to trail them over the muscles of his shoulders. How could she feel so? She did not hate him; she craved him. Deep within her secret self, she felt the aching need to hold him and to be held in return. It seemed so long since they had met and touched on a plane where their allegiance was meaningless; where "Norman" and "Saxon" were just political terms, where man met woman, in an instinctive surge of raw and unbridled longing. She, who had loved knowledge and wisdom and her country so dearly, had never guessed that this passion could come from within her.

Never . . . until he touched her. Even now, as Delon was being taken to exile in Alaric's distant country, she felt the need to touch her Norman lover. She fought the desire desperately, but her breath came quickly, and she could not tear her eyes from his.

"Bastard!" she whispered to him.

"Be glad, Princess, that you did not play the lover."

"Why not? Shouldn't I crave the touch of an honorable man?"

He smiled at her. "Honor, love? Your honor will be seen in your ability to name the father of the child you might well bear."

She inhaled sharply, growing pale. She realized that he was right. She could already be carrying his child.

He laughed at her stunned expression, though his laughter carried a tinge of bitterness.

"God will not let it happen!" she decreed angrily.

"I am no more eager for bastards than you," he told her. And for a moment, his anger was greater than hers. She thought that he hated her again.

"If you do carry my child, lady, you will do nothing to harm it."

"I—"

"If you do, lady, you will know wrath that lies beyond any other paltry hatred or revenge!"

She trembled; she believed him, and was suddenly afraid of his anger. Even more, she wanted to assuage it, to ease the tempest that raged in him. She cried out, "I would never do such a thing—I swear it!"

"I shall lock you in a tower, Princess, should it come about."

"I am not one to—to slay an innocent."

Perhaps he was satisfied. He kissed her suddenly, savagely. Then he gazed at her and at the torment in her eyes, and some tenderness touched his face.

He leaned over her and touched her lips lightly, so lightly, with his own. He kissed her gently and quickly, and rose above her to study her eyes again. "Poor fool!" he murmured, and he stroked her face again tenderly. "Poor young Delon—casting himself headlong against a conquering army, just to have you by his side. He risked his life for you; he was willing to move heaven and earth to have you. And I blame him not, my love, for your beauty is maddening, and the sultry fire of your kiss can steal a man's senses away."

His fingers played with the hook on her bodice. She made no move to stop him, but felt sweet, burning anticipation at the apex of her limbs. Already her breasts seemed to swell to his touch, and she ached to know his gentle soothing against the cruel cauldron of her life.

Suddenly she gave in to temptation and allowed her hand to fall upon his hair, her fingers to tease the satiny strands. He caught her eyes with his own, exhaling softly. Then he parted her bodice and lowered his head to her bared breasts. The warm whisper of his breath fanned the sparks inside her to a raging fire, and she moaned softly while he hovered there, breathing in the sweet, clean woman's scent of her, holding her close. Then his tongue teased and laved her, and he sweetly sucked hard upon her nipple, filling himself with her, and slowly, slowly released the budding pebble to lave it softly again.

As she clutched his hair and tugged fiercely on it, she caught his eyes.

"Tell me, my lord, if Delon were such a fool, where would the quest end? Would you, too, move heaven and earth to have me?"

He stared down at her for a long time. Firelight seemed to play against the gray slate of his eyes. "No," he stated flatly, simply.

"Knave!" she charged him, longing to strike him. But he caught her hands and kissed them. "Calm down, my fiery witch, I pray you. Indeed, you are everything that a man could desire—I know that far better than your friend Delon. I have indeed been drugged by the sweetness and fullness of your beauty. Aye, you ravage my mind. Is that what you wish to hear? Had young Delon touched you, an ax might well have cleft his skull. You wish to hear that you are beautiful? You know that well, my princess. You wish to hear that I desire you? Well, that I have proven time and time again. Would I move heaven and earth for you? Aye, my love, I would. You are mine. I will never let you go."

She stared at him in wonder. She felt the full force of his body upon hers, and even as they lay there fully clothed, she felt the pulsing shaft of his sexuality throbbing against her. Aye, he desired her, as she needed him.

At this moment he was air to breathe; she needed him to survive. Yet she could not believe his impassioned words. He was a warrior first, William's man, henchman to the Conqueror.

His lips came down on hers, and she could not deny them. His kiss was hard and punishing, and still she cried out and wrapped her arms around him, and she tasted the textures of his mouth. With a sweep of her tongue, she dueled with his, cherishing its force, arching against him; she whimpered as his palm closed over her breast, and she shivered with delight when his hand made free with her, roaming where it would.

When he rose above her to discard his clothing, she saw him all too clearly. Daylight bathed his rugged male body in splendor. His shoulders rippled and bulged, and his arousal was evident. She suddenly felt shy.

"The sun is up," she murmured nervously.

"The sun, my lady, ever lives within that bounteous golden blaze that you ignite within me," he whispered. His hands fell upon her again, seeking fervently to disrobe her. Soon they lay crushed against each other, naked and free. Quickly, anxiously, he played against her. Soft sounds escaped her while his whispers urged her on. She buried her head against his throat, and she touched his shoulders with her tongue, then kissed his chest, tasting him, drawing wet lines and circles upon him, eliciting more heated groans and hungered commands. She crawled atop him, exploring, learning, playing. But in the end he caught her hard and swept her beneath him with a guttural cry. Her jaw was tense with the need for him as he cupped her buttocks in his hands and lifted her to the fever of his thrust. He held himself above her for an instant, and Fallon stared up at him, a small sound escaping her. She bit her lower lip when he wrapped her in his mighty arms and began a slow, steady thrust, designed to sweep her away. He told her she was beautiful everywhere, and as his movements grew stronger and faster, she clung to him desperately, arching and writhing and thrusting, reaching for the sweet and elusive splendor that he managed to keep just out of her reach until she thought she would go mad.

Suddenly he pulled away from her. She cried out and tried to draw him back. But he would have none of it. He rained kisses over her again, on her face and her lips and her breasts, on her belly, her thighs, and then on the throbbing point of desire at the juncture of her limbs until she screamed in ecstasy. Only then did he come back to her and plunge slowly within her.

The shattering climax burst within her, stealing her breath, and while stars exploded around her, beyond them the world went black. She wondered if she was dying amid the splendor, for she was certain that she lay in no earthly place. For seconds there was nothing but the blackness, yet then she felt his body spilling into hers, and she was back on the bed, and birds were singing, and sunlight still played in through the windows.

Neither of them spoke. He held her tenderly against him and she dozed, awaking to find him moving against her again. She was but half awake, yet he seemed aware enough himself. He aroused her slowly and fully again, made love to her again, and when that was over, she shuddered and fell into a deep, tranquil sleep.

When she awoke again, he was gone. She heard horses in the courtyard below, and she pulled the fur about her and rushed to the window.

Alaric was there, dressed for war again; his mail shone beneath his long tunic, on which his crest and his coat of arms were emblazoned. He wore his helmet, which shielded all but his eyes. His great stallion, Satan, was decked out in all his plumage—the plumage of war.

Alaric raised his sword high and shouted to his men, "We ride! For God, for the duke! Hail to the Lord our

Father, and hail to Duke William—nay, hail to our king!"

A great cry went up, and the horses clattered out of the courtyard.

There was a knock at the door. Fallon turned in terror, wondering who might have come for her. Alaric had left her without a word. Was her punishment to begin now?

She was Harold's daughter, Fallon reminded herself. She drew the fur more tightly to her and lifted her chin. "Come in!"

Richard nervously opened the door. "My lady?"

"I am here." She breathed a sigh of relief.

He smiled at her, but she was wary. "Count Alaric has gone to join the duke," he said. "Coventry has fallen, and William moves inland. You're to dress, my lady, and pack."

"Oh, God!" she whispered, staring at him in horror. "Where—where am I going?"

"Why, to Bosham, my lady. He has ordered Roger and Rollo to stay there with a small company of men. They will take you to your lady mother."

She licked her lips. "Bosham?" She repeated. "To my mother?"

"Aye, milady!"

" 'Tis no trick? They'll not—they'll not take me across the Channel?"

"Nay, milady." Richard frowned. "My lady, the count adores you! He speaks often of your beauty, your gentleness—"

She hushed him, for the boy was such a dreadful liar. Then, for a brief moment, relief and happiness swept through her. But suddenly blackness began to engulf her. She was about to faint, she realized. King Harold's Fallon never, never fainted. But the world was slipping away, and she was about to fall. "Richard!" she called, and she did, indeed, fall.

Chapter Twenty=Two

Alaric caught up with William at Canterbury. From there, the main Roman road of England, Watling Street, ran straight through to London. Alaric sat in council with the duke, Odo, Robert, and various barons, and it was decided that they would take the pilgrims' route, skirting the city.

William's army was growing smaller. Wherever he built fortresses, he left some of his men behind. Alaric had left a number of his own knights in Haselford and had sent others to Bosham, where William had also sent men to keep a steady eye on Harold's old homestead. Nearly a third of the main army had remained in Dover, for William was determined to keep that city under his control. In the unlikely event of a crippling defeat, he could, even in winter, escape with his troops across the Channel from there.

As the days passed, Alaric had little time to think of Fallon. As their troops moved through villages and towns, they faced the never-ending task of finding food and shelter. The soldiers swarmed over the land, and though he could control his own men, he had little power over the others. Even the duke could not stop the pillaging.

William sent a spy to London, and the news he brought back was interesting and varied. A sheriff, Edegar, had been horribly wounded at Hastings, but had managed to return to the city, and he was now acting as some sort of a war chief. The spy, who was dressed as a peddler, told them more of what he had gleaned. The good news made the duke smile.

It seemed that the papal banner and blessing that William had obtained were his most formidable weapons. The churchmen in London were beginning to waver. People whispered that Edward the Confessor's deathbed prophecy had been fulfilled: Demons had come to England, and fire was ravaging the land. By striking Harold down, perhaps God had thus delivered his judgment upon the land. Perhaps they should submit to William, who claimed to be their rightful king.

But although everyone talked, nothing actually happened. So William moved forward again.

Alaric rode forth with a contingent of five hundred horsemen to challenge the city's defenses. They made their camp in the village of Camberwell. The people put up a strong fight, and though Alaric despised wanton destruction, he was obliged to burn many of the homes in the town. They moved on to Southwark, from where they could see London Bridge. Here Londoners came out to fight them, but Alaric's men, a mixture of his own knights and William's personal retinue, pushed them back across the bridge. The Normans did not cross the bridge; they burned Southwark and then marched back to rejoin the main army.

William awaited them at Nutfield with his largest force. When Alaric reported on their progress, William listened gravely, then told him that they had acquired an intriguing ally.

He pointed at a map of the area surrounding London and indicated Winchester. Alaric arched a brow. Winchester, the ancient capital of Wessex, had once been the center of the English kingdom. Now it was held by Edward's widow, Harold's sister, Aedyth, the dowager queen.

"The lady has declared that she wants me as king," William told Alaric, smiling. "She has submitted to me. Fresh troops have just arrived from Normandy, and with the queen's consent, I intend to take the city. You will meet with the new contingent here." He paused to point at the map. "Then you will ride north and meet me at the Thames."

Alaric studied William's plan, pointing out barriers and cover that he knew. The duke nodded, his excitement evident. Harold's sister, the Confessor's widow, had accepted him. The rumors were also coming in that the churchmen were growing more and more nervous, and their influence over the men who now held titular power was strong. Morkere and Edwin were reportedly planning to leave London and travel north, in the hope that William would leave their distant earldoms intact.

Alaric felt some of William's optimism when he led his horsemen into Winchester, Aedyth spoke with a surprising eloquence to the people gathered before her palace, and Winchester was taken with remarkably little violence.

That night Alaric dined with the dowager queen. By candlelight, she seemed once more like the pretty girl who married the old king, and they passed a pleasant evening. They dined alone, and when their laughter faded, Alaric asked her why she had decided to support William of Normandy.

She fingered her chalice absently and stared into the flames. "Harold could have held England," she said softly. "Perhaps even Gyrth or Leofwine could have done so. But they are all dead, and their children are too young to wield power and command respect. Harald Hardrada is dead; Tostig is dead. Edgar Atheling is just a boy." She stared into Alaric's eyes. "We have no one who can best William, and as long as we keep trying, we will bring more devastation on this land. There is nothing to stop William. He is too powerful for us." She hesitated. "I believe in fate," she murmured, shivering. "I'll never forget the day Edward died, the way he held my hand, the way he entrusted us all into my brother Harold's keeping. He said then that fires would rage over the country and demons would come. It has all happened, hasn't it? The comet foreshadowed doom, and doom has fallen upon us. We must bow before our fate."

The words reminded Alaric of Fallon, and a pain pierced him. He prayed that he hadn't been a fool to send her to her mother. He and the duke both had men there, but if Fallon chose to escape his protection, Bosham was a likely platform from which to do so. He ached, too, missing her.

"Not everyone will bend," he murmured softly.

Aedyth laughed, and Alaric looked to her quickly. "My niece," she said. "Fallon."

Intrigued by her reaction, Alaric pressed her. "Aye, Fallon."

Aedyth wagged a finger his way. "You'd best be wary of the girl, Count Alaric. If you have her, hold her tight."

"It sounds as if you mistrust your niece," he commented lightly.

"Fallon?" Her eyebrows rose with surprise; then she shook her head, and a smile curved her lips. "Nay, I adore her, I have always adored her. She is fire and passion, and I always dearly wished she were my own. I say what I do only because I know her so well. She has my brother's pride and my father's thick-headed tenacity, and she adored my brother. People love her easily. She can sway crowds when she chooses. She is the fairy-tale princess, you see, so very beautiful and loyal." She paused to finish her wine. "I hope I have made my peace with William."

He assured her that William bore her no malice, and would surely honor her as Edward's widow. They talked a while longer, and then Alaric told her he was weary and would retire.

She had prepared for him a suite of rooms, and she had forgotten nothing. Wine for the night awaited him, as well as a steaming bath. His bed had been aired, and his linen was fresh, and soft fine furs awaited him. One vaulted room held the bed and a wardrobe and several trunks, while a second chamber housed a large bathtub, a huge fireplace, a table, and several chairs. This room looked out upon a garden, bleak now, in early winter, but still offering a view of the night and the city lights in the distance. It was a very comfortable place, he thought, as well it should be, for Winchester was beloved of the ancient race of Anglo-Saxons. It was the seat of Alfred and the other ancient kings, and the English loved it well.

Alaric lowered himself into the tub and allowed the warm water to ease away his weariness, the result of many days spent in the saddle. It seemed obvious that London was about to submit to William. Alaric didn't know what demands William would make, but he grew ever more tempted by the dreams that filled his nights. By day the duke's business claimed him. But by night, he longed for Fallon. When he closed his eyes he saw the thick mane of her ebony hair, soft and sleek, tangling about him. He saw her eyes, blue as the noon sky, softened and hazy with passion. Dreams came to him so hauntingly that he could nearly smell her sweet scent; he could almost reach out and trace the curves of her body, feel the pulse of her heart.

He clenched his jaw as he remembered her attempted escapes, wondering now whether she lay in her old bed in Bosham, plotting new insurrection. Winchester would be a good place, he thought suddenly, a very good place to keep Fallon. She just might get into trouble in Bosham.

She'd be better off here, with him and her aunt. Perhaps Aedyth could make her see the sense of submitting.

But of course none of that really mattered, he realized. He wanted her here because he needed her. Because he missed her sorely. Despite her threats and rebellious acts, he wanted her with him.

She was wearying, he reminded himself. She was an endless battle.

He smiled slowly, his decision made. He was willing to fight the barbs in order to pluck the flower.

Fallon rose from the table and kissed her mother's cheek. Then, as she had every night since she returned, she hugged her tightly and whispered how much she loved her. Edith returned the whisper and tightly hugged her daughter in return.

Fallon smiled sweetly at Roger and Rollo, who always dined with them. Or, she mused, perhaps it was they who dined with Rollo and Roger, for there were as many Normans here as Saxons. Twenty of William's men spent their days and nights teasing the young girls and eating up all the food that was to last them through the winter. Roger was in command of a score of Alaric's men, and although they managed to behave with a bit more dignity, it was obvious that they were weary of this dull activity while the treasures of a whole country awaited them. The only saving grace was that the knights were skilled hunters, and they were adept at fishing, too. Also, for their pleasure, vast quantities of wine had now crossed the Channel, and so there was meat and drink for all.

That evening, Fallon was anxious to quit the hall and reach her own chamber. She hurried up the stairs, closed the door to her room, and listened. Footsteps followed her. She did not know if it was Roger or Rollo; she did know that they took turns guarding her, that one of them was always near.

She pressed her ear against the heavy door and faintly heard her guardian settle against it himself.

"Good night, Rollo!" she called sweetly.

" 'Tis Roger. Good night, milady," he returned.

"Ah. Good night, then, Roger." She paused a moment, then hurried behind the tall wardrobe in the corner of her room, where she sank to her knees and pushed open a panel. A small tunnel was revealed, and two young Saxon men—dressed as cotters, yet still proudly wearing their long curls—crawled out of it to meet her.

"Fallon, we must settle this tonight—" the elder began.

She brought her fingers to her lips. "Shush!" She indicated the door. They both shivered from the bitter cold of the December night. She smiled then, a warmth of love filling her, and she threw her arms quickly around her brother Galen, kissing him hastily, and then repeated the same action with Aelfyn. "I love you both so much!" she whispered.

Galen led her to the fire, and the three of them sank down before the blaze.

Edith knew her sons were living quietly as cottagers in Bosham. They pretended to speak no French, and the townspeople played out the charade so willingly that no one suspected that Harold's young sons might be about. Young Tam was not with them, for Galen had ordered him to London, and from there he sent reports of everything that was happening.

Galen reached out to touch her cheek tenderly. "Fallon, we are leaving tonight."

She caught his hand and tears scalded her eyes. 'I'm so afraid for you! Let me come with you! I'll—"

"Nay, Fallon. I know how desperately you long to escape, but you would endanger us. No one will note two cotters walking from one conquered village to another.

But the guards will know instantly if you have gone."
Galen told her.

"Of course."

Aelfyn gazed at Galen. "What we need from you, Fallon, must come later."

She sat back unhappily, winding her fingers tightly together. She knew what they wanted, and she was afraid. It was evident now that Edgar Atheling would not be crowned; no one felt that this boy had the power to fight William.

But there was one very powerful man who would gladly, eagerly, move against William. The boys had been in contact with their distant cousin, Eric Ulfson. He had sworn that he would fight any battle for Fallon, Harold's daughter.

Aelfyn knelt down beside her. "Fallon, think of Father. You must help us win Eric's support."

She shivered. "I don't like it. He is a berserker. What difference will it make if we are ravaged by Vikings or Normans?"

"Eric can be controlled. 'Tis true. He *is* a berserker, mad for battle. But no matter what, he would leave England to us. Saxon rulers for a Saxon land."

Galen paced the narrow space before the hearth, gazed toward the door, and came back to take Fallon's hands. "I have heard that Alaric is sending for you. I imagine the messenger has not yet come, else one of your keepers would have mentioned it tonight."

Fallon stared down at her hands, afraid she might betray some emotion with her eyes. She plucked nervously at her skirt and said nothing.

"He is going to have you taken to Aedyth."

She stared up at them, startled.

"Surely, you can get away from her. If you'll just meet with one of Eric Ulfson's men and assure him that you are anxious for him to come."

She shook her head. She didn't like Eric, she did not feel comfortable near him, and she sensed that he was the most barbaric man she knew—Saxon, Norman, Dane, Swede, or Norwegian. "Father is dead," she said softly, "and so the crown belongs to Edgar the Atheling."

"Aye! But he has not the power to take it! You can bring Eric here with a Viking horde. William cannot fight forever. His men lie scattered across the countryside already. His numbers grow fewer. Some knights guard you here, others fill Dover; many sit in a fort at Hastings. Eric has no scruples about any papal banner. Some say he is a Christian. But we know he worships Woden and rides for Thor. He exults in death and destruction."

"And you want me to bring him here," Fallon said wearily. "Exchange one monster for another."

Galen pulled her to her feet. "Have you forgotten our father?" His voice rose dangerously and she again pressed a finger to her lips. Galen lowered his voice, but he was still bitter as he spoke. "I have not! I was there. I was just paces away when they stormed upon him. Have you become such a traitor that you have forgotten?"

Her hand cracked across his face, but shame and anguish filled her, and even as Galen reddened and the mark of her fingers came alive across his cheek, she sank down to her knees, fighting nausea and tears. Galen knelt beside her. "I am sorry, Fallon. Truly I am. Can you forgive me?"

She shook her head, and she could not answer him, because she was afraid that his wild, angry accusation might be true. She did not understand her feelings, a tangle of pain and regret and anguish. But neither did she hate all of her enemies. With all of her heart she wanted William beaten. But she wanted Alaric spared. While she prayed earnestly for deliverance from the Normans, she prayed more fervently that one particular Norman might live.

She had sworn to do battle, but she was afraid; and no matter how bravely she might speak, she longed for peace.

"Fallon?" Galen said to her softly.

She sat back, shaking her head again. "Galen, is there no other way? Surely—"

"There is no other way. Not if we wish to win. No one but Eric Ulfson has the strength. I'll get a message to you. Then it will be time for you to escape. Fallon, you are the only one who can convince Eric that he must help us defeat the duke of Normandy."

Slowly she nodded.

"We've got to go!" Aelfyn warned Galen.

Galen nodded, still looking at his sister. He kissed her forehead, and she hugged him tightly. "Take care, Fallon. Take care. I love you."

She kissed Aelfyn good-bye, and her two brothers escaped through the hidden tunnel. When they had gone, she stared after them, recalling what fun the tunnel had been when they were children. She replaced the panel and went to sit before the fire, determined not to cry.

Whatever their sources, her brothers had their information right. The next morning, a young blond squire arrived. He stood joking with Roger and Rollo in the hall when Fallon came down.

"We're to escort you to London, milady," Roger said. "Young Steven has come to tell us so."

Silently she gazed at Steven. "When are we to leave?"

"As soon as you can prepare to ride," Roger told her.

"I shall make ready," she said, "and say good-bye to my mother. Then I'll be ready to ride for my dowager aunt's palace."

She turned away from them. Roger watched her, frowning, wondering what she had just said that had disturbed him so.

Her aunt's palace . . .

He hadn't told her that they were going to the dowager queen's residence, had he? He had said that they were riding for London.

Roger shook his head and shrugged. Someone must have said something to her. How else would she know?

"Beg pardon, sir, but am I to come?"

Roger turned around and saw that young Richard was eagerly watching him. "Count Alaric said that I might begin to train as a squire once the duke had been duly crowned king!"

Roger clapped him hard on the shoulder. "Aye, lad. He's not forgotten. You are to come. Go with Steven and prepare the packhorses for the trip. We'll spend the night somewhere along the way, and by tomorrow, lad, you'll be in training."

Richard thanked him profusely, his eyes alight. Roger looked back at Fallon, who was heading up the stairs.

What was the lady thinking? he wondered. She had given no hint of emotion. Was she dismayed that her chaste interlude here with her gentle mother was being interrupted? Was she disturbed to be dragged back to Alaric's side? Did she still hate all Normans? Or was she bowing to the inevitable?

Don't fight him again, Fallon! Roger implored her silently. Don't fight him again. I love you and would not see you harmed.

Perhaps Alaric even loves you, too . . .

Nay, Roger thought. Love died for him many years ago in a heap of dry and bitter ashes. Yet what he claims as his, he cares for with tenderness.

Roger shook his head, still disturbed. He couldn't put his finger on what had bothered him about the morning. It didn't matter, he told himself; they would soon be in London. The coronation would be grand, the feasting a marvel, and all of England would bow down before the Conqueror.

Determined to ignore his misgivings, Roger started out.

Upstairs in her mother's chamber, on the bed where she and her brothers had been born, Fallon hugged Edith fiercely, with tears in her eyes. It had been good to be home. She had run across the fields where she played as a toddler and dangled her bare feet in the cold water. She had sat before the fire where her father had told them tales of ancient Camelot and of the great king Alfred. She had felt warmth touch her face as she remembered the stories Harold himself had heard from his Danish mother, stories about Woden and Thor and chariots that rode across the sky. Stories from his father about the Druid priests who had read messages on the air, who had talked to the deer and the squirrels and even the trees.

Now she would leave her memories behind. She looked at her mother and knew that Edith was remembering, too. Now, too, Fallon understood the love between a man and a woman, and her heart broke for her mother, who had loved Harold so truly and so well. Fallon was certain that her mother would never want another man. She had loved Harold, and no man could match him.

Fallon, trembling, realized that she felt the same way about Alaric. She had no love to base her feeling upon, no shared years, no whispered dreams. But Alaric had touched her. He had awakened her. She would never have been with him if disaster had not seized them all, but she could not change that now. She would fight him, as she had vowed to Galen. She and her brothers were Saxons, they were Harold's cubs, they were bound by honor to repel the Normans.

Edith pulled away from her. Tears glittered in her eyes as she studied Fallon's face. She smoothed her hair from her cheeks and her forehead and whispered softly, "Fallon, lay down your weapons, I beg of you. Fight no more!"

Something clutched at Fallon's heart, and she wondered what her mother knew. "I don't know what you mean, Mother," she murmured innocently. "What power have I?"

Edith smiled. "More power than you will ever know. But, Fallon, please, wage war no more for us. Your father is lost, and his brother, too. The finest of our Saxon warriors. Your brothers have gone, I know, to gather men to rise against William. They are quickly growing to manhood, and I cannot stop them. Possibly, I shall lose them, too. So, Fallon, please, fight no more."

"They killed Father!" Fallon whispered.

Edith rose and moved restlessly around the room; then she swung on Fallon. "Harold chose to do battle that day. You say, '*They* killed Father.' *They*? What *they*, my love? Alaric would not have killed him. Fallon, I tell you this now so that you won't deceive yourself: If Alaric had been open to a proposition of marriage, your father would have wed you to him no matter what your wishes."

Fallon gasped, stunned. "Nay!" she protested. "I was betrothed to Delon; we would have wed—"

"Never." Edith shook her head with finality.

"Father liked Delon!"

"Aye, he did." Edith almost smiled. "But you were not meant for him. He hadn't enough strength for a wife who could wield a sword and rouse a crowd."

"So now he languishes in a Norman dungeon!" Fallon cried.

"Perhaps, yet perhaps he is not so confined," Edith murmured. "But I care not—"

"Mother!"

"Nay, Fallon, I have lost too much, and I look to my own, and I beg of you, fight no more! Alaric is a good man; your father admired him above all others, including the English. Give way, and you could love him."

"He does not love me."

"He feels something for you. He holds you dear."

"Mother!" Fallon cried suddenly. " 'Twas you! He swore to *you* at Hastings that he would keep me from trouble!"

Edith shrugged. "He honored me for your father's sake. So save us heartache, Fallon, and bow to him. I have seen you flush when his name is spoken. I know that you have felt the sweet breath of fire, and I have been glad to imagine you in the protection of so fine a knight. Please, Fallon, take care!"

Fallon lowered her head, trembling. Her mother wanted her to be his willing mistress lest she find a harder bed elsewhere. Her brother called her traitor; yet he, now, wanted Fallon to remain in Alaric's bed so that she could help to bring him down.

Pain stole into her heart, and she was suddenly aware that she was falling in love. Perhaps she had always been a little bit in love with him. Perhaps that was why she had goaded him over the years, teased him, taunted him . . . kissed him.

She was in love with him. But she could never let him know it. She could not give up her pride, her dignity. Nor she could abandon her hatred, for he was her enemy.

And by her own avowal, she was honor bound to betray him.

Chapter Twenty=Three

The trip to London proved to be torturous. They rode where the conquering army had passed, and all along the way there were the signs of devastation. Where William's men had not burned, they had pillaged. The winter would be harsh, and the armies' theft of foodstuffs would condemn many people to starvation. Along the way they met beggars who did not hesitate to approach well-armed Norman knights. Surely they must have felt that a swift blow from a sword would be a far more merciful death than slowly freezing and starving through the months to come.

Fallon quickly gave away the food that she had brought for herself; Richard, watching her, did likewise. Roger made no comment. They passed through one village where the remaining people sat together in abject despair. Here Roger called a halt and he and his men combed the forest and brought back several rabbits, which they gave to a woman who sat huddled with her children. Watching him, Fallon was touched. He asked Fallon to tell the woman that those who could not eke out an existence should travel to Haselford where there was food and where they could find work.

As they rode on, Fallon touched Roger's sleeve. "Thank you," she told him.

"Don't thank me, Fallon. 'Tis Alaric's order, so if it sits well with you, thank him."

She shook her head. "Alaric did not catch rabbits for the woman."

He stared at her for a moment. "Do you remember, Fallon, when we were young? You were out to plague him, and when you were caught, you but smiled at me, and I was willing to do anything for you. I had fallen in love." He paused for a moment. "I still fall in love when you smile, Fallon. But I am not a lad anymore; we are all older, and life is sadder. I have learned everything from him. What courage I have, he has given me. What temperance I have learned, he has slowly worked into me. Mercy and judgment and wisdom are virtues I have learned from walking where he has walked. He is my liege, and though I still love you, lady, I want you to know that loyalty is another quality I have learned from him."

"I know you are loyal, Roger. And, nay, we are not children. I still say you are a fine knight and a fine man, no matter your nationality. This ride has pained me greatly, for these are my people. You have shown kindness, and I am grateful."

He smiled. "I am bewitched," he said simply.

They were perhaps still two hours outside Winchester when Roger paused, halting the party of ten who rode with them. "Riders coming," he said tensely.

Fallon held her mare steady. Though William held London, his men were still worried about an ambush. They were all clad in armor, and they carried weapons. Rollo bore not only an ax and a sword but also a spiced mace, which Fallon was certain she could not even lift. No man was more adept at war than he, she thought.

The men riding toward them were also dressed for battle. Beneath the winter sun they shimmered and glittered, and the pounding of their horses' hooves upon the hardpacked earth was a threatening sound indeed. But

Roger lifted his hand in greeting, and he smiled at Fallon. "See the banners? 'Tis Alaric coming to meet us."

Her heart fluttered, and she was shamed by the warmth that filled her. She drew her fur mantle tightly around her shoulders and watched as the horsemen came nearer.

Alaric rode at the lead, as smooth as the wind. His mantle flew behind him, and his visor hid the planes of his face from her view. She felt herself tremble. He had sent for her; he had called her here. He wanted her here, and something within her was flooding with desire to see him.

She held tight to her reins, lest he see her shake. He raised his hand, and the men behind him paused, reining in their enormous horses. Roger called out in greeting and Alaric led Satan forward in a prance so that the two men might clasp hands. Then his eyes were upon her.

She could see only his cool gray eyes, which gave nothing away.

"Milady," he said quietly. The warmth of his breath formed a mist. A horse stepped forward and the little bells on his harness tinkled. The forest that surrounded them seemed caught in spun ice and crystal.

"Count Alaric," she returned quietly. It had been more than a week since they had seen each other. She longed for dignity, but she trembled now that he was near.

Alaric paused a moment longer, assessing her. Then he turned Satan from her, to ride beside Roger. They started off again, and she heard them speaking about the coming coronation and how the city was crowded with their own men. Some of the people reviled the Normans while others opened their hearts to the conquerors—and made a few coins for their pocketbooks.

When at last they reached Winchester, Fallon saw with a sinking heart that these reports were true. Some people muttered against the Normans sullenly, but many hawked their wares. It was winter, Fallon reminded herself. Come what may, men chose to eat and to feed their families.

They drew up before her aunt's palace in the ancient capital. Aedyth awaited them on the steps, her men-at-arms now dressed in William's colors. As Alaric swept Fallon from her horse, she felt his eyes hard upon her. Heat radiated from his body. Winter might whiten the world around them, but she felt warm when he touched her.

He led her to Aedyth, who embraced her warmly. Then she smiled, with just a hint of warning. "Welcome, my niece. Welcome to my home. I am happy to have you here, and I know, Fallon, that you will be happy residing with me."

Aedyth hugged her again. Holding her aunt, Fallon saw Alaric's eyes upon her. She was a prisoner here, she knew. Just as she had been since Hastings.

"It is good to see you, Aunt," Fallon said softly. Aedyth turned to walk her into the hall. She asked Fallon about her mother, and if she had seen her brothers or any of her cousins, and Fallon told her that her mother was fine, then sweetly lied about the rest of the family.

"They have told me, Aunt," Fallon said, "that you invited William here, that you want him as king."

They both stopped short. Aedyth stared at her niece a long moment, looking up at the tall girl who subtly reproached her.

"Aye, I wanted William to be king," she said. "My brother Harold told us when he went to battle that God must decide for him. God decided, didn't he, Fallon?"

"My father is dead; England still stands."

"Not much of it, my dear," Aedyth said wearily. "Tread where the army has walked and you will see." She smiled bitterly, then led the way again.

They came into the great hall where a fire burned brightly against the winter's chill. Servants tended a great kettle over the fire and even as Aedyth grandly indicated several fine high-backed chairs with rich tapestry covers, steamy chalices of mulled wine were brought forward to them. A sudden silence, fraught with tension, fell around them. Sitting, Fallon saw that only Alaric and Roger and the squires, Steven and Richard, had come into the hall. Alaric stripped off his helmet and Roger did the same. Steven, well trained, stepped forward to collect the heavy metal weaponry and assist Roger with his mail. Richard did the same, yet even as he took Alaric's helmet, it slipped through his fingers and crashed to the floor. The metal clanked noisily, and poor Richard stared up in dismay. Fallon felt a smile play at her lips, and Alaric burst into laughter. Soon Roger did, too, and suddenly Fallon felt merriment well up within her. The hostility faded as Alaric and Roger teased young Richard.

Aedyth leaned toward Fallon. "I loved my brothers, all of them, Fallon. I loved Tostig and Leofwine and Gyrth—and Harold. But Harold is dead, Fallon. No vengeance can bring him back. I do not embrace William to dishonor Harold. I do so that the curse upon us can end and people can begin to live again."

"Now, my good lad, have you got it this time?" Steven said to Richard, and they laughed again, and the squires then quit the place while Roger and Alaric came to sit before the fire and drink their mulled wine.

They sat there for some time. Roger talked about the coast and about the few ships that were coming and going across the Channel. Alaric talked about the city and the battle at the bridge, and as he did, his eyes fell upon Fallon and grew warm. He was restless; he rose time and time again to grip the mantel, and stare down at the blaze. He drank several cups of the wine.

Watching him, Fallon grew warmer and warmer. He said something about armor, yet she felt his eyes strip her. Aedyth talked about the West Minster and coronations, and Fallon barely heard a word, for she could not turn away from Alaric. He stood at the fire, his elbow on the mantel, idly dangling his cup in his hand. His eyes did not leave her. The fire grew, the blaze heated, and she saw its glow upon him and felt it against her cheeks, burning. Words around her faded. Servants came and went, and she was barely aware of any of it, for she was held there by the power of his gaze.

"Alaric? What do you say to that?" She vaguely heard Roger ask him. But he didn't seem to have heard that himself. He did not look at Roger, but gazed at her. He set his cup down and briefly excused himself to Roger and her aunt. He came before her and took her hands and drew her to her feet, still staring into her eyes.

"I shall show Fallon to her quarters," he said.

She felt a tide of crimson rise to her cheeks.

His fingers curled around hers. She could not resist him there, before her aunt, she told herself. But it was a lie, for she trembled and burned with the wanting of him.

Candles seemed to spin before her eyes as he pulled her along with him. She tripped upon a stair, and he lifted her into his arms. They came to a door, and he opened it with his foot, still staring into her eyes.

"You've no right to do this," she said.

"You are mine. And I will have you now."

"I am your avowed enemy."

"I suggest you think of peace this hour."

"I suggest you remember—"

"I feel you tremble. Deny me, Princess, if you can. Fight me, if you have the heart."

The wine had taken hold of her. She burned, and yet she felt lethargic. She did not wish to be released from the strength and heat of his arms. Aye, she would fight him, she swore to herself—but later . . .

They entered a suite of rooms, but she barely looked about her. She was afire with the wine and with his touch and with the sweet, honeyed longing that seemed to course through her veins and fill her limbs and her heart and her very womb.

A small fire burned in readiness for them in the beautiful chamber. But she was aware of nothing but the sight and the feel and the scent of him, and the overwhelming hunger that filled her. She touched his hair as he carried her to the massive bed. He laid her there with tender care, and his fingers seemed to tremble as he stroked her cheek. "I have missed you. Like the sun, like the moon, like the stars."

She could scarce breathe; she could only feel him, so hard and masculine. When had she fallen so completely beneath his spell?

"Tell me," he said hoarsely. "Have you missed me, Princess? In any small way at all?"

"You are my enemy," she reminded him, but her eyes fell. "I must fight you."

"Do you hate me so, then?"

"Nay, not you. But I despise the world from which you have come to steal away my own."

He groaned slightly, burying his face in the silken spill of her hair, lifting it in his fingers, pressing his lips against it. "My world, love? For the mere sight of you, I would cast it aside. Yet I cannot. Not in truth. I am no magician, no alchemist, to take away the past or to foretell a dazzling future. Yet I would give it to you."

She reached up and stroked the finely chiseled lines of his striking face. A thousand candles seemed to gleam around them; golden fire breathed and danced on the air. Outside, the world was white and cold with snow, but here it was all magnificent heat.

"If only . . ." she heard herself whisper.

And he caught her fingers, kissing each one. "If only, aye! If it were possible, I would build you a crystal palace, and you would reign there as snow queen. No death or danger would ever touch you there, and no devils or demons could come. And I would love you there so sweetly that you would forget the dark world beyond and embrace me with your radiance."

His whisper fell against her lips, and then his mouth descended, and with a soft, glad sigh, she gave herself to his kiss, and to the intoxicating blur of his whisper and his urges. The light that bathed them was golden, and she did not look away when he took off his clothing. She trembled as he stripped her own clothes off. Softly, softly, swirling upon the clouds that created her crystal palace, she reached out and touched him. Then her snow-white world of wonder seemed to fade, and everything was fire. The gleaming slope of his shoulder and the contours of his chest. The shadow of his hand against her, and the color and taste and texture of his kiss. She rose with him to her knees, and they laced their fingers together while their lips melded again in hunger. Gold filled her and burst inside her; she stroked the golden shaft of him and melded to his strokes within her. While the fire rippled and burned and blazed, he lay back and she rose above him, daring to meet his eyes. Then he claimed her, and she let her head drop back and felt his hands enclose the weight of her breasts. She soared, and he led her. He caught the roundness of her buttocks and led her in an ancient rhythm.

Alaric savored the passion, luxuriated in her beauty. Today she had given him everything. Raw, sweet hunger had been satisfied, and she had denied nothing in her quest to meet his needs. She fulfilled all the sweet and wild and wanton promise she had ever given. Her dance upon him was as erotic as her beauty, as sensual as the promise that lay in the ripened beauty of her breasts and the curve of her hip.

In all his wanderings, in love and in lust, he had never known so great and erotic a mating as this, a love that transcended time, and in which he thought he could die, the explosion of his seed was so great.

When it was over he lay beside her, holding her close, stroking her damp flesh.

He knew that he was falling in love with her. And to love Fallon would surely be fatal to both of them. He closed his eyes tight and told himself he was being foolish. It was not love, but an incredible lust—and why not? Nature had bestowed upon her some incredible gifts, and each time he touched her, more of her bounty fell his way.

The fire died low, and Fallon slept. Her hand, fragile and slim, lay on the dark breadth of his chest. The soft sweet heat of her breath warmed his flesh, and her hair fell over him like an angel's wing. Her knee was thrown over his, and she lay against him with the greatest ease, vulnerable and yet secure beside him.

He clenched his teeth and closed his eyes, and the visions he had seen a million times came back to haunt him—images of death and treachery. Don't love her! he warned himself.

She sighed and shifted, crushing the fullness of her breasts against the hard muscles of his arm.

It was too late, he thought wearily. Maybe it had been too late for years and years and years.

He dozed. In time, they both awakened. In the dim light, their bodies were intertwined, arms and legs tangled, her hair wrapped about them both. She smiled at him, still half asleep, and turned over, bumping him with the smooth, round contours of her behind. He felt himself aroused anew at the feel of that soft flesh hard-pressed against him. He put his arm around her waist and pulled her tight to him and gently entered her, then slowly, slowly picked up his tempo. When it was over he held her still and did not withdraw. He stroked her hair and the slope of her back. The fire still burned. They dozed again, and he was still inside her.

When they awoke again, the room was cold and the fire had died. She was shivering, but gazing at him wide-eyed. "I suppose I should fix the fire," he said lazily, and she nodded. He rose, feeling her eyes on him, and he was pleased that they could be so natural with each other.

He poked at the fire, then added a log. Resting on the balls of his feet, he watched the new wood slowly catch fire. He turned to see her studying his features. Caught, she flushed, and he reached out an arm to her. "Bring those furs," he said huskily, "and come here. This may take a while to burn warmly again."

She hesitated, then came to him, with a blanket of pelts around her shoulders. He found a skin of wine and offered it to her as he shared the fur with her, sitting on it, and drawing it high around their shoulders.

"It must be night," she whispered, and he gazed down at her face, at the fine and delicate beauty in it, and the haunting courage that never quite left the depths of her blue eyes.

"Aye, I'm sure it's night." He smiled, prodding the fire and laying another log on it. He kissed the top of her head. "Perhaps it's almost day again."

She leaned against him, and they were silent for several seconds. He ran his hand protectively over her shoulders, then idly cradled her breast beneath the blanket, awed again by her power to arouse him.

"Are you sorry that I sent for you?" he asked her very softly.

Color filled her cheeks. It seemed that ages passed, and darkness fell between them. She sighed softly.

"Alaric, I . . ." She paused. "I do not deny the magic," she whispered.

He caught her fingers and kissed them. "Yet we are enemies."

"Yet we are enemies. Truly, Alaric. Neither of us can forget that."

His arms tightened. "You are mine, Fallon, and yet not even in fantasy had I imagined that you would come to me so exquisitely—not captive, but lover. Some magic does reign there. I wonder sometimes if that priest of yours—"

"Father Damien?"

"Aye, that strange man of your father's! Sometimes I think he sees magic, or truly knows the ancient ways of wisdom. I wonder if he did not cast a spell upon us, for I swear I am bewitched."

She shook her head and smiled up at him. The soft yellow gold of the flames played against his face, and he was young and striking and beautiful. He was not a Norman now, but a man—the fine and valiant man her father had always admired.

But it could not be, she knew. She was Harold's daughter, and ashamed to be thought a Norman's whore. And that was all she could ever be to him, she knew. Some sinister memory haunted him, and he trusted no woman. He would never marry her, but that was just as well. To marry a man who daily killed scores of her people would surely be the greatest treason.

She meant to betray not her country but Alaric, she reminded herself. She would rise against him again and again. Yet she sat here with him now, craving his intimate touch. She loved him not as a Norman, but as a man.

If she failed in her attempt to betray him, she would pay. She didn't want to think about the future, for now he gazed upon her with tenderness. They had seldom in their time together shared such a gentle moment.

She sighed miserably. "There has been so much between us, Alaric. I am not sorry for this . . . this magic— nay, but I am still your prisoner and your sworn enemy."

He nodded. "I know," he said softly. "You are the finest cub of a proud king. Ever his proud, invincible defender." He leaned down to kiss her, and when his lips rose from hers, he said, "But we have this night, another day, and another night in which to be together."

She threw back her head to gaze at him curiously. Might they seize this interlude of peace? "Don't you have to be gone with morning's light?"

He shook his head. "For what?"

"To do whatever knights do—when they're not ravaging the countryside."

"Ah, love, it seems that this country has ravaged me," he murmured. "Nay, I have no business tomorrow. The world will encroach upon us soon enough." He picked up a piece of kindling. "Tell me, love, what is it you hate the most in this world that I have wrought?"

She watched him, still curious at his mood. Then she said, "Hunger! I hate the hunger I see in the people's faces, I hate it that they starve."

He cast the stick into the fire. "Begone, hunger!" he ordered, and the flames burst higher.

The furs fell from her shoulders and she, too, cast a stick into the fire. "I hate the dishonor that has come to good men!" she cried. "That they should be slaves!"

The fire crackled and snapped. Alaric moved forward, entwining his fingers with hers. "I hate the death, and the blood!" he cried. "I hate it that my good friend died. I despise it that Gyrth and Leofwine fell."

"Aye!" Fallon cried, tossing another stick. "I hate it that my mother should be alone with her dreams."

Alaric tossed a handful of dry twigs upon the blaze. It burst high and beautiful. "Begone, I say! 'Tis Fallon's crystal palace where we abide, and no evil, no pain, may enter here!"

Watching her eyes, he brought her hand to his lips and kissed the palm very tenderly. Naked and unashamed, she wound her arms around his neck, pressing her body to his. She opened her mouth to his hungrily, and together they sank back down onto the furs. He laid her back and he kissed her arousingly from head to toe, fascinated by the beauty of her form as it caught the light.

When they were finished, Fallon thought a world of color—gold and crimson and beautiful pink—had burst upon them.

It was the dawn, she realized. Dawn had truly come upon them. She was falling asleep again. She was barely aware when he lifted her and carried her to the bed.

She did not need the softness of the mattress. She had the taut golden warmth of his hard body. She loved the feel of his muscled arms around her, the curve of his stomach at her back. She loved the rough texture of his chest and legs and she loved having their limbs entwined. She loved the feel of his breath against her cheek and her earlobes, and she loved him rising and rousing and slipping inside her. It was like a dream, but surely it was not a dream. She was destined to wake from it, yet while it went on, it was beyond beautiful.

Cast the nightmares to the blaze! she thought, curling into the softness of the bed with him beside her. 'Tis Fallon's world, a crystal palace, and no evil may enter here!

His arms encompassed her, and she gave herself entirely to the wonder of the man.

They did not rise at all that day. Servants brought food, and they ate it lazily before the fire. They drank wine, and they made love.

The only note of dissension came when they spoke about William. Resting her chin on her knees, Fallon thought miserably about Christmas Day. Only a year ago, Edward had lain dying, but her world had still existed.

"So William will be king," she muttered dryly. "God help us all."

"You will be there to see the coronation," Alaric told her.

She shook her head furiously. "Nay, I will not!"

"Aye, you will. For he has ordered it."

"I do not take orders from William."

"You will take them from me."

"Nay!" Her temper flaring, she stared at him.

He strode to the mantel, then turned on her. "You will be there, Fallon, and you will be silent and respectful."

"How can I?" she cried, jumping to her feet to face him. "How can he expect that?"

"Come what may, lady, you will be there! Edgar the Atheling will be there, as will the northern earls. Aedyth and the churchmen will be there—and so will you."

"I will not!"

"Bend or break, lady!"

"Bury me, my lord. You know that I will not bend."

"Damn you, Fallon!" he swore heatedly, striding over to her. But when he reached her and pulled her to him, he whispered huskily, "Nay! Into this world of our making no discord may come!" And he kissed her.

She did not think that discord could be denied. She slammed her fists against his chest, but his kiss was too hungry, and too sweet. Discord was cast aside. She fell to the heady power of his caress.

When the second night had passed and another dawn came, he left her to wash and put on his mail and his armor and his implements of war. Only now did she realize that he had spun that fantasy for her because he wanted her. But reality still awaited them, and he was equally determined to have his way with it.

She was determined not to attend William's coronation. She would fight Alaric, kicking and screaming, all the way there—unless she should somehow first escape him.

When he left her, she feigned sleep. He kissed her brow

and lips softly, but she felt the barriers between them keenly again. There he was in his armor, with the cold slate color already falling over his eyes, as if it, too, like his sword or his shield, was something he donned for battle. Then he turned and left the room.

Rising, she called for a servant to bring water.

An old, gnarled woman appeared, and Fallon asked her to send for another servant. She was too old to lift heavy buckets of water, Fallon said. But the woman insisted, and finally Fallon permitted the toothless crone to assist her.

When Fallon finally was settled in the tub, she closed her eyes and leaned back into the encompassing heat and steam. The old woman suddenly moved close to whisper in her ear. "Tomorrow morning, milady. The count will be with the duke, the guard will be drugged, and the south door to the street will be open."

Fallon's eyes flew open and she sat up quickly. "You've come from Galen!"

The old crone smiled, then lowered her voice still further. "There's a meeting at the Irishman's tavern, the Seafarer, down the river. Your brothers are in hiding, but they're to meet you there if they can. If not, a big Cornishman named Alfred will meet you at the door and take you to your Danish cousin, Eric Ulfson. Have you understood it all, my lady?"

Fallon swallowed. If her brothers were not there, she was supposed to persuade Eric to bring a fleet of Vikings to fight for them.

And then they would all be free from William's yoke. She would never have to see the bastard duke crowned. Fallon herself would be free from Alaric and from the desperate web of love and desire that gripped her ever more tightly.

Her hands were shaking. She pressed them against her face. "Aye, I understand," she said softly. The time had come to fight again. She had warned him that she was still his enemy.

The old woman left her, and the bath grew as cold as the dreams of her crystal ice palace, where no evil could come.

She was determined, but very much afraid.

Chapter Twenty-Four

Fallon had been to Winchester many times as a young girl, for it was one of King Edward's favorite places. She knew the palace very well. She could find the kitchens, the audience chambers, the ladies' solar, the music room, and the scores of bedchambers. She felt almost as free here as she did in Bosham. Despite the presence of guards, she could roam the palace, walk to the stables, and even visit the merchant stalls by the river.

It was very late when Alaric returned. Fallon had spent the day alone, feeling curiously numb and reminding herself how fiercely she hated Duke William. She lay, feigning sleep, when he entered. If all went well, she thought, she would never see him again after tonight.

Thinking her truly asleep, he moved silently about the room, shedding his clothing, then carefully slipped into bed beside her. She threw her arms around him, and he apologized for waking her, and she caught his words with fierce kisses that surely surprised him—yet he was quick to take advantage of her mood. She loved him, fiercely, savagely, tenderly, and all the while, hot tears stung her eyes. Later, she again feigned sleep, lying with her back to him, feeling his fingers on the curve of her hip. She told herself viciously that she was indeed a fool. She was Harold's daughter, about to escape the yoke of the conqueror.

She had sworn again and again that she would fight, and now her chance had come.

But there were certain things that she could not escape, she knew. She could not escape her memories, or the emotions that swept through her.

Fallon knew now that their passion had borne fruit. She was certain that she had conceived on the night he first came to her, when Falstaff had lain wounded. The night of the battle at Hastings, when Harold died.

She clenched her teeth so as not to groan aloud. She turned, and in the dim light beheld his features. She reached out and touched the planes of his face, thinking that she would like their child to be a boy who resembled him—strong, slow to anger, resolute. It would be a beautiful child.

He would be Harold's grandchild. Where would his loyalty lie? Half Saxon, half Norman, grandson of a slain king, child of a legendary knight of Normandy. Which side would he claim?

She trembled suddenly, remembering Alaric's anger on the night Delon had tried to rescue her. Alaric had reminded her that she might have a child, had thought that she might actually harm her child. Their child. Had he no faith in her? Would he wonder again if she had been with Delon on that one sweet night of triumph when she had thought herself free?

Did it matter? For England's sake, she had to leave on the morrow.

Swallowing back tears, she placed a kiss on his forehead and touched him one last time, memorizing with her heart and hands everything about him. She held still then, waiting. She could not sleep. Thus she lay throughout the night, watching him.

In the morning, when he kissed her softly on the lips, she was barely aware of it. She smiled at the gentle caress and sank into the covers. When she did rouse herself, it was only to realize that he was gone.

There was a soft, urgent pounding on the door. Fallon flew to it and found the old crone of the night before standing there. Two guards were stretched out upon the floor nearby.

"Drugged only, and I don't know for how long!" the woman told her. "Come, Princess! You are our only hope!"

Fallon dressed quickly and with care. She wore thick woolen chausses and a dull gray bleaunt over a soft chemise. She did not take her soft fur-trimmed mantle, but a heavier one in simple wool with rabbit trim and a giant hood to pull low over her face. When she was ready, the old woman nodded grimly. "You look like a maid about to take religious vows. That's fine. Now, come."

As they hurried along the cold and silent halls, they heard a servant humming, and ducked into a room. Footsteps rang out, and they stayed still once again. Then rushed to the southern servants' door, and Fallon bowed her head low as she left, folding her hands as if in prayer. Her heart took flight, for people were all about them now—servants and merchants. An old man stopped them and Fallon's breath caught; but all he wanted was to sell his apples. She shook her head without revealing her face.

"Come!" the old crone said.

Fallon looked around her as she walked. Outside the walls of the palace, morning activity went on. One woman cleaned fish, another chamber pots. A group of men polished harnesses. Fallon felt as if someone was watching her, but when she turned, she saw no one looking her way. A youth in heavy dull wool was bent over with his back to her, rewrapping his leggings.

"My lady, haste is needed!"

When they came to the river, the old crone was quick to turn Fallon over to a solid boatman, who bowed quickly and low before her. "My lady!" he murmured reverently.

"This is Alfred," the woman said. "He will stay with you."

Fallon thanked him as he helped her aboard. There was a low fog on the river, and as he pushed the boat away from the riverbank, Fallon felt as if she moved through a nether world. She pulled her mantle more tightly around her. She felt that she should pray, yet she wondered just what she should be praying for. In her father's name, these loyal people had come for her. They wanted her to strike a bargain with a Viking prince, who would bring more death and devastation upon them all.

But that had been Edward's prophecy, hadn't it? she asked herself. Fires and demons raging across the land. They were all doomed to pay for their sins.

The morning was very silent. She heard the oars fall against the water, and that was all. It was cold on the river, and her cheeks burned. She shivered against the wind, and she began to pray that she would see her brothers soon. They believed in her strength, but she was very much afraid.

It seemed that they traveled for hours. Finally Alfred drew the boat against the opposite shore. He hopped out, secured the boat to the dock with a line, then reached down to Fallon. "My lady?"

He helped her ashore, and they hurried along the mist-veiled road. It seemed quiet even here, Fallon thought. Men and women and even children moved through the foggy street, and a great wall of mist rose above the river. An occasional oxcart careened by them, but despite that noise, the silence weighed down upon them.

At last they came to a door, and Alfred pushed it open. They entered a room where a poorly vented fire made the air seem as thick as that of the world beyond. It was a crude inn, Fallon saw quickly. The rushes were dirty, as were the tables that crowded the room. There were many men here, and few women. Yet she was safe, she thought, for though all eyes fell curiously upon her, no one wanted to come near the giant at her side.

"Are my brothers here?" she whispered.

"Nay, lady," Alfred told her. "They could not risk it." He pointed across the room. "There! The Viking has come. You go to him, and I'll guard the door."

In the far corner, a man in a cape and cowl much like her hooded mantle raised his head. She was quick to recognize Eric Ulfson. A smile slashed his handsome, cruel features, and his blue eyes sparkled. A full golden beard covered his chin, and a mustache curved above his thin lips. He lifted a tankard of ale to her, staring at her with fiery purpose as she crossed the room. Miserable shivers raced up and down her spine.

Eric rose, clasped her hands, and quickly drew her down to sit across from him. "Fallon!" he breathed against her hand, and his eyes fell upon her again, greedy and determined.

"Eric." She had to fight to keep from wrenching her hand away. "Eric, my brothers believe you can raise an army. They say you are willing to fight."

"I will do anything for you, lady. Anything."

Fallon's blood ran cold. Her stomach tossed and turned, and she thought that even the tiny infant growing inside of her must be repelled by his familiarity.

Eric was their only hope, she knew, but she would promise him nothing. She would ask for his help, but this was one battle she would not attend. If and when he came with his army, she intended to be far, far away.

"Eric, England needs your help. And now, I believe, is the time to strike. Few people realize how very weak William is. Aye, a few more of his ships have arrived with reinforcements, but his numbers remain weak. It is his cruelty, not his force, that has caused many people to surrender."

"I will fight him." The blond with the cool Nordic eyes watched her with intensity. He picked up his tankard and swilled some, then took her hand and opened it. He smoothed his thumb over her palm. "I will open you like this, like a flower," he murmured. "I will fight the Norman usurper, and when I have cast him back across the sea, you will be my prize."

She sat there shivering. "Eric! Take care," she warned him softly. "William is weak, but he is no fool."

Eric smiled and watched her. He lifted her hand and gave it a curious kiss—more like a lick. "I am anxious," he said. "They tell me that you have been mistress to Count of Anlou."

She started and pulled back. His smiled deepened. "Don't fear, Harold's daughter. It adds to the fascination. His reputation as a warrior is legendary. I will enjoy killing him, and I will be pleased to see what he has taught you when we lie together. Virgins, milady, are something to be taken in the heat of battle. For pleasure a man desires a woman to thrust and rise beneath him."

She stared at him blankly, gritting her teeth in fury. If only her father lived, Eric would never dare to talk to her so. But the king was dead, and so she sat here weaving a deadly bargain with him. Her stomach was in open revolt now. She would readily die before she would ever let Eric touch her so. "Eric, as yet you've still to raise your army. Defeat the Norman conqueror, and then we will talk again."

She started to rise. He caught her hand and pulled her back. "I will kill the conqueror, and I will kill Count Alaric. And when I do, milady, you will be my prize."

The stench of the tavern—from the unwashed bodies and stale ale—made Fallon queasy. Eric leered at her.

" 'Tis a pact, Fallon." She held silent, and he smiled

and stroked her cheek with his fingertip. "And to seal it well between us, I will take a kiss now."

She closed her eyes. She felt his lips touch hers, felt the coarseness of his beard against her cheek.

Then a cold wind rushed between them, and a brutal, thundering sound erupted. She opened her eyes in horror. A knife had been thrown between them; it had sliced through her sleeve and pinned her fast to the wooden table. She gasped, and saw the surprise in the Viking's face.

Eric rose, casting back his hood and reaching for his sword. Another man strode toward them. A man with fury in the hot steel fire of his eyes.

It was Alaric. He bore down upon them in long, swift strides as Eric bared his sword. Alaric did the same. Above the table, their swords clashed, coming dangerously close to Fallon's face. She did not cry out; shock kept her silent.

Parrying a blow with his sword, Alaric used his free hand to seize his knife, freeing Fallon. "Go!" he ordered, not looking her way. She had barely moved when Eric kicked the table over, shouting as he lunged at Alaric. "It's been a long time, Count!" Eric said. "What a pleasure!" He went for Alaric's throat. But Alaric easily parried the blow and returned it. As their swords clashed and caught, Alaric frowned grimly. "Eric Ulfson, I believe."

"Aye, come a-Viking, my lord. And what will you do?"

"Why, slay you, of course!"

Again their swords clashed. Fallon scurried away as their fury rose, and tables and benches were shoved and kicked about. Men fled the tavern, crossing themselves. Flattened against the wall and still stunned by Alaric's appearance, Fallon watched the fury and strength of the two men who battled. There was a deadly beauty to it all, for they were so powerful and well trained. It was nearly a dance. Now and then when their great broadswords crossed, they taunted each other, only to start anew in earnest.

"Your whore shall be mine!" Eric told Alaric.

"I believe not," Alaric said smoothly. "For I do not share, and if I did, Viking, she'd have no interest in a corpse."

"A corpse, Count, is what you shall be! And I tell you, sir, when she is mine, she'll not escape me to run to another. Perhaps you have not kept her warm enough, eh?"

"Sir, you will freeze in eternity this night!" Alaric promised.

"Damn you both!" Fallon swore. She struggled toward the door. Alfred was gone; indeed, most of the patrons had fled. The few white-faced onlookers who remained were caught behind overturned tables.

Tankards flew, ale billowed and blew, and wood cracked as the warriors' swords met and struck again and again. Breathless, Fallon reached the door. Don't let him die, God, she prayed silently. Please don't let him die! And it was a conquering Norman she prayed for, not the man who had come to help her free England from bondage.

As she flung open the door, her eyes widened. Two blond giants pushed past her. They had come with Eric, she realized. They were disguised as monks, but they planned to deal out death.

She fell back, staring at them. The one grinned at her with blackened teeth, then seized her and tossed her toward his comrade, who held her. She screamed, and Alaric swung around at the sound of it, and saw the danger at his back.

Eric charged. Only with swift agility did Alaric avoid the deadly blow that came his way. He countered, carefully watching the two newcomers. One heavy Viking threw himself toward Alaric with wild, screaming berserker rage. Alaric lifted his sword and ran the man through.

But Eric had the advantage. He lifted his sword while Alaric struggled to retrieve his blade from the body of his fallen enemy. For one brief moment, Alaric's eyes met hers. And inside, deep inside she quivered at the depth of hatred she saw there.

She screamed, certain that Eric's sword would fall upon his neck. In the nick of time, Alaric's sword came free and he countered the blow.

Suddenly the Viking who held Fallon called out something to Eric Ulfson. Eric spun around, and his friend used Fallon as a shield, throwing her with tremendous fury toward Alaric. He caught her against his chest, then swore and pushed her away from him, heading after the retreating enemy.

Fear spurred Fallon to her feet. Alaric would go after Eric, but then he would come for her, and he would no longer be her tender lover, that she knew. She had to get outside, escape into the mist.

But even as she staggered to her feet, Alaric reappeared. His eyes beheld her with a cold, controlled rage. He closed the door and leaned against it. Watching him, she felt ill. When he entered the inn, she had been sealing the bargain with a kiss, and he had seen it. He felt doubly betrayed, she knew. Yet she had been his prisoner, and he must realize that she was bound to fight to the bitter end.

But he couldn't know how much his anger hurt her, how deep the anguish lay in her heart! He could not know that she loved him and that it was harder to betray him than it would have been to turn her back on her father's memory and her country.

"An old friend?" Alaric queried sardonically. He came into the tavern and leaned against one of the fallen tables, crossing his arms over his chest.

"I warned you that I would fight," she said quietly.

He moved away from the table and walked around her, and she felt the full force of his fury. "I should have asked just how many men lurked in your past. Eric Ulfson, milady, is more dangerous than your young swain, Delon. Ulfson is a berserker like his distant kin, Harald Hardrada, and they are always dangerous. Not a man with whom to seal your fate, *chérie.*"

Fallon's blood seemed to freeze and congeal at his casual yet menacing use of the endearment. He did not touch her, and she thought perhaps he was afraid to do so, lest he strangle her where she stood.

The door opened, and two knights she did not know entered. "We've taken the big man, but Ulfson has escaped us," one told Alaric. Alaric nodded in acknowledgment, watching Fallon. "Word came that they caught the old woman," the knight continued, "and the fellow who brought Harold's cub down the river. It was easy, for it seems that the entire city knows what has happened."

Alaric paused for a moment, his eyes still upon Fallon. "That is too bad," he said softly. "An example will have to be made."

Her heart skipped a beat and then thundered. Would William really go so far as to slay her as an example? she wondered. Nay, he was no murderer, she thought. And yet, in his eyes, this was treason. Soon he would be the annointed king, and to fight him would be treason for any English subject.

"Take her," Alaric said softly to his men. He looked at her with cold-steel eyes, but did not touch her himself.

When the men moved toward her, she screamed and, in desperation, raced to a corner of the room. The good and hearty Saxon men were returning to their ale tankards, righting the fallen tables—and swearing beneath their breath about the Norman hordes. Fallon gripped the shoulder of the biggest, heartiest fellow she could find. "Sir, help me, please. I beg of you. I am Harold's daughter! I was promised to the nunnery at Saint Mary's on the Rye, and I was on my way there. I have taken certain vows, and if these men try to take me back now, God will condemn us all."

Murmurs went up. These English were a superstitious lot, very worried about defending their God. Despite the weapons and prowess of the Norman knights, the good Englishmen started to form a wall around her.

Alaric did not move, and she breathed a great sigh of relief even while hope began to bud inside her. He did not want to slay these innocents. Perhaps she would escape.

But a smile played on his lips, and he lowered his head. When he looked up, she saw that his smile was a lie, and the steel in his gaze registered an ever-growing fury. "Good friends," he addressed the workmen and fishermen around him. "Tell me—have you ever heard of the Saxon king's daughter being promised to a nunnery?"

"It was a deathbed request!" Fallon called out. "Good fellows, Harold lay upon the battlefield, a Norman arrow in his eye and the knowledge in his heart that they would hack him to pieces!" She spoke with passion. Alaric grew tense, and she knew she was gaining ground. "Please, just stand between us until I can reach the street—"

"I tell you, friends," Alaric said, "that she is no virgin who has sworn a vow of celibacy. I can prove it to you now. We need only a physician or a midwife to examine the girl and tell you she is no nun. She is Harold's daughter, aye. But she is also my mistress, my property, my slave. If you wish it, good friends, I will see that it is proven to all."

The men murmured. Fallon bit her lip, and she knew that he would do it: She saw sheer ruthlessness in his eyes.

"Fallon?"

She lowered her head in defeat. He strode through the crowd and took her elbow. Barely suppressing his fury, he dragged her out of the tavern.

The mist still remained on the street. Fallon was glad of it, for it hid the torrent of emotions that gripped her as he roughly grasped her hands and tied them together.

He pushed her forward, and one of his men caught her by the shoulders. "For now, return the princess to her aunt. I will search for the Viking and discuss this with William later."

He barely glanced her way as he leapt upon Satan and galloped down the street. His man turned and lifted her up on his mount. There was a clatter of hoofbeats on the road. With a sinking heart Fallon saw that the new arrivals had come directly from Duke William. They wore his colors.

"Where is the count?" Alaric's man was asked.

"Gone after the Viking."

"This is the Saxon vixen?"

Fallon lifted her chin. "Princess," she said. The duke's man ignored her. He was assured by Alaric's men that she was indeed King Harold's daughter and that she was being taken to her aunt at Winchester.

"Nay, I'm afraid not. The duke demands that she be brought before him. Now."

Fallon's heart began to flutter. She kept her head high as panic rose within her. William would have no compassion whatsoever. Courage! No matter what they did to her, she would not falter.

Nay . . . but she would beg William to uphold the law. By English law, the life of an unborn child was not forfeit with that of the mother. They could not slay her until the child was born. A sheer, weakening terror swept through her. She did not want to die.

Alaric's men did not seem pleased, but without their count among them, they could not refuse the duke's order. They began to ride. Soon they crossed the tributary on a barge and headed toward London. They were making for the wooden fort that William had ordered

built there. Nearby, men were already at work digging.
She had heard that he meant to build a fortress there in
stone, a great tower, right on the river Thames.

They rode to the fortress. Men-at-arms parted before
them, and she saw how very well guarded the duke's
stronghold was. Soon, she knew, he would go to West
Minster. He would be crowned there, as Harold had been
before him.

They rode past the gates and into the bailey. Fallon
clenched her teeth and tried to keep from shivering as
they arrived, for William was there. The rumor of her
escape and assignation with the Viking had traveled very
fast, she realized.

The duke came toward her and lifted her from her
mount.

"Lady Fallon," he murmured in greeting. "Is our hospitality so poor that you should be so eager to escape us?"

She stood as tall as she could. "Duke William, you will
forgive me if I find my father's murderers to be a group
of churlish men."

"I am sorry we cannot make you happy," William told
her softly. "And I am very sorry that I have to prove to
you that we cannot tolerate your treachery, my dear."

"You are a loathsome usurper, William."

He digested her words with no comment. "Fallon, I am
still loath to slay a woman. I pray that it will never come
to that." He turned away from her, calling to someone.
"Twenty lashes for the princess. Perhaps she will think
twice before plotting against me again."

She choked back a gasp as a man stepped forward and
took her hands.

The man assigned to administer the lashing did not
look cruel. Fallon realized that this was his duty, not
something he enjoyed. She heard the duke and others
walking behind them, their footsteps crunching on the
snow-packed earth.

The man whispered to her. "I will be gentle as I can, but the whip she cracks and hisses. Try not to tense against it, and forgive me my duty. You will not be scarred, I promise you."

She stumbled and faltered as she crossed the muddy ground. A tall post rose in the center of the duke's training yard. There were spectator stands, and wandering merchants hawked their wares to the knights who came to train here. Though the fortress was gated, many people milled about within its walls.

The man quickly led her forward and hooked the rope that bound her hands over a spike in the post. Fallon bit her lip to keep from crying out as she pressed against the pole. The man took her mantle from her and tore her chemise and bleaunt to bare her back.

With bitter dismay, she heard shouts of encouragement from the crowd sitting in the stands, eager to see the lash bite into her.

And bite it did. Fallon choked and convulsed as the lash stung her back and the pain streaked through her. He had warned her not to tense, and yet she could not help it as the pain seared into her.

The whip cracked again, and she screamed as it tore into her tender flesh. She sagged hard against the ropes that held her, and she wondered if, mercifully, she just might pass out. She did not want to scream, but this was agony.

The whip fell a third time, a fourth, a fifth, a sixth.

Then suddenly it was over. She was dimly aware of the sound of hoofbeats, and she heard shouting, and then a determined argument. She could not catch the words, for they spoke very rapid French, and she was drifting in and out of her world of pain and blackness.

Then fingers tore into her hair, pulling her face from the pole. She cried out softly at this new anguish, but sound died upon her lips as she stared into Alaric's eyes, silver and harsh.

"Alaric," she whispered, "you came to stop them. I— I thank you."

"Don't thank me, Fallon. *Mademoiselle,* you deserve fifty lashes, and William would have had his way with or without my agreement this time. A Saxon fellow came riding after me to tell me that the duke's men had taken you. Still, for yourself, you deserve this. But I demand an answer, and I will have it now . . . Is it true?"

She did not understand him; she did not understand anything but the pain. He jerked on her hair again and she thought he must truly hate her. "My God, answer me, and answer me now! Are you with child? The priest says you are with child."

"The priest?"

"Damien met me upon my arrival."

"Oh!" she gasped, shivering. How could he possibly know?

"Damn you, answer me! Are you eager to lose the child? Or is it your own life you seek to forfeit?"

"Neither!" she screamed, and she prayed that tears would not spill from her eyes, that she would not betray her weakness. But her flesh burned as if a thousand demons seared it, and his eyes bore into her like blades of condemning fury.

"I repeat, my lady, are you with child?"

"Aye!" she said. "Aye! Please . . ."

Suddenly her hands were free and she was falling. She was caught by strong arms. A mantle was thrown around her shoulders; she cried out as the material touched her raw back. She opened her eyes, and Alaric was there, staring down at her. No mercy yet touched his gaze. He had come and saved her, and she wanted to thank him, but the words died on her lips, for he seemed to hate her more than ever.

She swallowed and closed her eyes. He lifted her into his arms and began to walk, and she lost all thought as she swam in the pain. He carried her into a room in the fortress and put her down on a slim pallet. Unable to talk, she closed her eyes against the pain. Moments later she felt a touch and opened her eyes. Alaric stood at the back of the room, arms crossed over his chest, eyes fierce as he stared out to the fortress yard beyond.

Fallon choked back a scream. It was Father Damien who had touched her. He held an urn of yellow salve, which he was rubbing on her back. She bit her lip, trying not to cry out, and she stared at him in amazement.

"Father?" she whispered. "Ah. So you serve William now, too."

"I serve God," he told her.

"You knew!" she whispered to him. "How could you know what I have only just realized myself?"

He gazed at her, giving nothing away. "A green tree grows together of its own accord," he said very softly. "My lady, let it grow!"

Nothing that he said made any sense to her. He continued to smooth the salve over her wounds, and when he was done, he forced her to drink a green liquid. "You will rest," he promised her. And she would, she knew, for the sweet void was beginning to claim her already.

But she did not sleep for long. Hands fell upon her shoulders, and she was shaken roughly. She opened her eyes, and Alaric was there. His eyes were still like ice, and he stared at her with greater anger than she had ever seen. "Tell me, my lady, what was your plan?"

She shook her head. "There was no plan."

"No plan!" The thunder of his voice raged into the drowsy forgetfulness that had claimed her, and she winced. "No plan, my lady? I saw your lips against his. You went to him to sell yourself to him. For England—and bloodshed!"

She tried to shake her head.

"Knowing you carried our child! Or *is* it our child, milady? Perhaps we'll never know. Mayhap it is a Saxon whelp of young Delon's. Maybe you lied to me then, too."

"I did not lie to you. The child is yours."

"So you knew that you carried my child, and yet you went to that Viking—" he began hoarsely, closing his fingers around her arms.

"Count!" Father Damien interrupted him, and Alaric's hold upon her eased. "She is hurt, and I have drugged her. She cannot understand you. Leave all this until later."

"Nay! Not this!" Alaric was seated beside her. "Fallon!" It was a command to open her eyes. As she did, she was startled by the anguish within his.

"Fallon, why didn't you tell me about the child?"

"I wasn't—sure," she murmured. "Not until the last few weeks."

"And you did not tell William when he had you dragged to a whipping post?"

Amazed, she widened her eyes. "Had he meant to— kill me, I would have spoken."

He lowered his dark head for a long moment, then raised it and looked at her again. His features were as hard as stone, and his eyes were filled with anguish. She fought to understand, but the drug was claiming her too quickly.

"You did not seek to rid yourself of the child?" he demanded.

She stared at him in confusion, then shook her head. "Nay," she said softly. "Nay, I want the babe. I want it because—because I am the hope of England. Didn't you know that?" She could speak no more. Her eyes fell shut, and oblivion claimed her.

Chapter Twenty-Five

Fallon awoke to discover that she was back in the palace at Winchester. She lay on the bed in a soft linen gown, and a fire burned gently in the hearth. Someone sat before the fire, quietly polishing something. Fallon blinked to clear her vision and wondered how long she had lain asleep, and how she had traveled from William's fortress back to Winchester. How had Alaric even known that she had escaped to meet Eric?

She must have made some slight noise, for the person before the fire turned, and she realized that it was Richard. He rose quickly and came to her. She was touched because his concern for her seemed so great.

"Hello," she murmured softly.

"My lady!"

He poured her some water and she sipped at it, watching him.

"Thank you," she told Richard. She gazed about, wondering where Alaric was and what he might be feeling. He had repudiated her, she thought, and yet she felt so very weary that it did not seem to matter. She had done all that she could. She had followed her father to two battles, and lost. She had tried to join Delon, and succeeded only in getting him exiled to Normandy. For her brothers she had tried to engage the aid of a foreign prince, and that, too, had ended in disaster for her. Now she was so tired.

"I'm sorry, milady," Richard said. "I'm so sorry!"

Puzzled by his words, she stared at him.

He shook his head mournfully. "I—I sent Count Alaric after you. I saw you leaving, and I was afraid for you. I rode out after Alaric. I thought he might reach you before the duke."

She leaned back painfully. So Richard had betrayed her. One of her own kind.

"He did find me first," she said ruefully. "But then he set out after Eric Ulfson—"

"A Viking, milady?"

"Aye, a Viking," she agreed softly. "I thought it a mistake from the beginning, but there was no other choice. Anyway, it is over. And it's all right," she said softly. But it wasn't over, was it? Galen had wanted her to lure Eric into the fray. Well, she had done that. He had escaped and could still gather his army to ride against William. She didn't know if she cared or not. She was weary of it all. William would soon be crowned; he would be king, whether devils and fire and demons roamed the land or no.

"I swear, I never meant to hurt you!" Richard repeated.

She smiled and lay back weakly. All of her energy seemed to be gone, stolen from her. "And I swear, Richard, it is all right."

"You forgive me?"

"With all my heart." She reached up and touched his clean-shaven, boyish cheek. He caught her fingers and squeezed them.

"That is the greatest gift I could receive this day, lady."

She frowned. "This day?"

" 'Tis Christmas Eve, Lady Fallon."

"Oh!" Tomorrow would be Christmas . . . and William's coronation. How much her life had changed in just one year!

Richard smiled and reached into his pocket. He produced a little brooch for her. It was neither gold nor silver, but some harder metal. She looked at him.

"It's not much," he murmured. "I made it from a broken knife. A smith here helped me with it. See that design engraved upon it? 'Tis the dragon of Wessex."

"It is beautiful. I thank you so much. But I have no gift for you."

"You have forgiven me. That is my gift. Oh, lady! I had to send him after you. He loves you."

But Alaric did not love her; she knew that now. She was surprised that she had been brought back here, rather than put into a dungeon somewhere, so great had been his fury.

"Richard, please—" she murmured, but he interrupted her.

" 'Tis true, I swear it—though perhaps he does not know it yet! But, ah, lady! You should have seen his face! It was wretched with pain when he brought you here. Father Damien was with him, and he was actually swearing at the priest. The good father assured him that you slept peacefully, that you would feel no pain. And do you know what else he said?"

She arched a brow to him, easing back upon her pillows and plucking at the covers she held to her breast. "What who said, Richard? Alaric or Father Damien?"

"Well, both, I suppose!" Richard claimed. "It was a beautiful, passionate moment. Alaric swore that Damien would be his first clerical victim if his drugs hurt you or the baby. Damien warned Alaric that he should take care, because God would take offense at his treatment of a man of the cloth. My lord Alaric swore and said that he wasn't in the least sure what god Damien was talking about, but then the priest laughed and told him that you would be fine and that his son would be fine and that he had nothing to worry about. Then Alaric grabbed the priest and told him he'd best know the truth of it, for by the honor of his sword, he would have it so."

Richard stood, and Fallon had to smile. The audacity of his lies was enormous, but the dramatic appeal with which he acted out his words was contagious and charming.

"Then Alaric carried you here," the boy said, "and he would not leave when your aunt came with her women to cleanse your wounds again and take off your ripped and bloodied clothing. He demanded to know each ingredient in the salve the priest rubbed on your back. And when they were all done, milady, he sat here holding your hand and gazing down upon you."

He nodded to emphasize his point, and then he went deathly silent. Fallon followed his gaze, and she, too, froze for Alaric stood in the doorway watching them, and he was not amused. No sign of a smile broke the grim line of his lips, and his eyes were cold and gray.

"I was—er—just finishing with your bridle, my lord," Richard said, his cheeks burning.

"So I see," Alaric offered. His glance fell upon Fallon.

"I was just leaving," Richard said.

"There is no need," Alaric interrupted. "Fallon, I see that you are awake, and you look well enough. We leave this afternoon for the city, to be there early tomorrow for the coronation. You will be dressed and ready, and you will stand by my side. And, lady, you will stand silent, except to hail your new king. You may wish to have some things packed for the banquet, which will run late. We'll not be returning here this night."

He bowed low, a lock of his dark hair falling over his forehead. Then he turned on his heel and left them, slamming the door in his wake.

Richard glanced at her. "I—I'll send someone to help

you bathe and dress, and to bring food. I must take his armor to him now."

She smiled. "You're his squire now, aren't you? Just as you wished to be."

"I'll be a knight one day, my lady. And I shall ride to your defense and the defense of your babe, I swear it!"

"So everyone knows now," she murmured. She lowered her head, smiling at his passionate outcry. She wondered if this boy was not her best friend now. She loved her brothers deeply, but they did not seem to care about her welfare, and they would not be here to pay the price of treachery with her.

She bit her lip. She had no choice but to attend the coronation, she knew. She could go willingly or be dragged there, but she would attend. She rose carefully, clutching the bed to keep her balance. She should refuse to walk or move, she thought dismally. She could not rejoice at the banquet and swear her loyalty to the Norman usurper. She could not do it.

Suddenly, there was a knock, and the door opened. A line of people seemed to stretch down the hallway. Two maids, two hefty serfs with a bathtub, a dozen boys with water. Fallon sighed softly and lowered her head, and when the tub was filled, she stepped into it. She determined then that she would hold her head high. She could not acclaim William, but neither could she fight. She would stand silent, and her silence would condemn him.

She dressed carefully in her finest silk chemise, soft beige with Flemish tatting at the sleeves. She donned a rich purple bleaunt with ermine at the cuffs and collar and all along the hem and train. She dressed her hair with pearls, and when she was done, the women helped her into her fur mantle, and she clasped it about her shoulders, fastening it with Richard's brooch. She stood and waited. In moments, Alaric came for her.

He stood in the doorway, staring at her. Surely she was

the finest, richest gem that the country possessed. She stood so still, so tall, so proud. Her long hair fell over the beautiful gown in vast ebony waves that glowed blue in the firelight. She was so silent and still awaiting him, her eyes like sapphires in the night, her swan's throat a pure cream with an erratic pulse dancing against it. She was ready; she would be there. And every man would see her, for what man could not gaze upon her?

His mouth tightened at the thought of her most recent betrayal—enacted knowing that she carried his child. She had seduced him into a lull of peace and trust while she spun her webs of deceit. She would have run with the Viking and called him lover.

She owed him no explanation. She was property—spoils of war. And he had known, as no man did, that a woman could be cherished but not loved.

He reached out a hand to her. "Come," he said simply. Trying not to shiver, Fallon obeyed.

Alaric did not speak to her as he led her from the palace or during the long ride to West Minster. Richard was at his master's side; Roger was in their company and Rollo, too, and another score of Alaric's retinue. The day was icy and cold, the ground was hard-packed. The horses snorted and their breath misted on the air, and their trappings jingled loudly as they moved over the snow-covered land.

At midmorning, they stopped at a manor to eat, and though Richard remained at her side and Roger and even Rollo came to ask after her welfare, Alaric did not come near her. Fallon was hungry, for she had eaten almost nothing in the past two days. But as soon as she tasted the salted meat, she felt queasy. When they started to ride again, she knew she would not hold her food. "I must get to the woods," she told Roger.

"Fallon, no tricks, I beg of you."

" 'Tis no trick; I must get by!"

He gazed at her with alarm, and so she nudged her horse and burst into a canter, seeking a small road into the forest, where she could be alone. She had barely reached a copse and dismounted when her stomach completely revolted. She gagged and gasped, and fell into the snow, eager for the icy stuff to cleanse and cool her face.

"Fallon!"

She turned and Alaric was there, feet wide apart, hands on his hips, towering against the backdrop of crystal trees. He strode toward her angrily then, but she rose and backed away from him, nearly tripping over a root.

"Damn you! Leave me be! I am not running anywhere!"

He paused and seemed to reflect upon the way he had found her, on her knees in the snow. "All right. Let's go."

"I'm sick. I cannot go on."

He shrugged. "Such illness is common with women when they breed, milady. You will be well when we reach the city."

"Women when they breed!" she railed, her fists clenched at her sides. Had he forgotten who had put her in this miserable predicament? Or did he still wonder if the child might not be his?

Fallon stood her ground stubbornly for a moment, determined to irritate him. "What is it, Count? Do you still have doubts?"

His voice had a ragged edge when he spoke. "I have no doubts whatsoever, milady."

"I can't imagine that you would trust me so."

"Milady, I do not trust you a single bit. We've taken a number of captives who were in on your first attempt at rebellion. Their stories of the night all match. Your betrothed it seems, is a man of honor."

"You didn't believe me. You went to others—" She broke off, seeking terms vulgar enough to describe what she thought of him. She started past him, but he caught her arm.

"You should be glad, *ma belle*. I will claim the child."

"I'd rather the devil claimed it!" She wrenched her arm free. He stiffened and offered her a cool smile.

"*Mademoiselle,* now, if you please . . ." He lifted his arm, indicating the road. She hurried to her horse, wanting to mount alone, but he was there beside her, lifting her. When she had mounted he led her from the trees, and they rode again.

The streets of London were in chaos. People thronged everywhere, anxious to be near the new West Minster, even if they could not enter into the festivities. The riot of human life gave Fallon new hope—if she disappeared into this crowd, all of the new king's men could never find her. But Alaric seemed to read her mind, and as they entered the teeming mass, he called a halt to lift her from her mount and set her before him on Satan.

He still had nothing to say to her. She felt his arms around her and the protective wall of his chest behind her. There was no warmth there, and as they hurried toward their destination, she felt ill all over again.

They were to lodge, she realized, at the palace. Alaric set her down in Richard's care, warning her only that there would be a guard at her door.

Richard took her to her own room—the chamber that had once been hers. Then he departed, offering apologies, for he had to serve Alaric.

Fallon spent most of the evening pacing the floor. Finally, near crazy with restlessness, she tried the door. It opened, and she choked back a scream. Her guard was none other than Falstaff, the huge bear of a man she had stabbed in the tent at Hastings.

"Oh, God!" she breathed.

"Lady," he bowed to her. "I am well, *mademoiselle*, and I bear you no grudge."

"I did not wish to kill you," she whispered miserably.

"And I am not dead!" he returned cheerfully, "so all is well."

She nodded, feeling ill all over again, and closed the door.

When night fell, Richard brought her food. It was not the dried meat they had eaten on their journey, but fresh stew and a mound of bread. She was ravenous. "Alaric said to make sure you ate the bread," Richard told her. "He said it would help."

"Has he had so much experience with 'breeding' women?" she snapped.

Richard colored and busied himself with picking up the tray. Alaric did not come, and in time, exhausted, Fallon curled up on her bed and fell asleep.

Alaric did not come to her at all that night. She awoke before dawn, still alone. She lay in a tempest, unable to control the misery—and the desire—that swept through her. She wanted him beside her. She had fallen in love with him, and she was going to bear his child.

She closed her eyes and tried to recall what had happened when he had taken her from the whipping post. He had been furious with her, because he thought that she hadn't cared about the baby. Did he care himself? She had been so immersed in pain and then in drugs that she did not know.

She admitted to herself that she was afraid. She had been willing to run, so what would it matter if he cast her aside now? She could go north, as she had always planned, and find refuge with Malcolm, King of the Scots.

Nay . . . William would not allow that, she knew. If Alaric had tired of her, she might well be locked into a dungeon in the bowels of one of the stone castles William saw fit to erect all over the countryside.

She closed her eyes and drifted back to sleep. When she

opened her eyes again, she panicked. She was not alone. William, partly dressed in his coronation regalia, sat by her on the bed. Fallon stared at him in alarm and inched back into a corner of the bed.

He smiled at her. "I believe, Fallon, that I am, in truth, a demon to you."

She didn't answer him; she could only stare. Had conquering this land given him any pleasure? His face appeared old and tired.

"I came to tell you that I am sorry for what you forced me to do. I did not want to hurt you. But by rights, lady, after your child is born, I will still owe you twelve lashes. Please don't ever remind me that it is so."

Fallon breathed slowly, watching him.

He rose, looking weary. "Eric Ulfson," he murmured. "Lady, you do not know your man. He is cruel and vicious in ways even I do not know, yet you would loose him upon your people."

"Where your armies have trodden, William, no greater cruelty can follow."

"You are misled," William said simply. He reached for her suddenly and pulled her forward. In panic she cried out, wondering what he intended. "Easy, girl!" he warned her. "My God, lady, but you are a spitfire! I only wish to look at your back."

Her teeth chattered. "It is fine."

But she found herself facedown upon the bed, her chemise pulled low. She gritted her teeth, but his fingers moved over her flesh, with startling tenderness. "It is healed—just pale lines remain. Do you feel pain any longer?"

"No," she said quickly.

He rose, and she spun, wrapping the bedcover about herself. "Fallon," he said softly, "I am no demon, I swear it. I would have peace between us. Now, dress. Alaric will come for you shortly."

He left her then, and she sat trembling a long while. wondering what lay ahead. Finally she rose and dressed very carefully.

It was not long before Alaric came for her. She caught her breath and lowered her eyes when she saw him, for she thought that he was surely more noble than any king. He wore scarlet and blue, and his hair was a deep contrast against the colors. His shoulders were vast beneath his fur-trimmed mantle, and he was lean and whipcord hard about the waist and hips. His features were striking and handsome, his eyes slate-gray and powerful. He opened the door without permission and spoke curtly to her, ordering her to take his arm. Fighting a sudden sting of tears, Fallon did so. And as they walked along the hall, she raised her head high. She prayed that all Englishmen would know that she was still one with them, a prisoner here, and no lackey to the enemy.

It was Christmas Day, she reflected, as they entered the church. The beautiful voices of the young choristers were raised in song, and the church was aglow with candle-light. Wedged between Alaric and Roger Beauclare, Fallon could scarcely move, much less resist.

Aldred, archbishop of York, was to perform the cere-mony in English—just as he had for her father. Thinking of that, Fallon lowered her eyes and began to pray. The rite would be nearly the same now as it had been a year ago. But Geoffrey of Coutances was there, too, to repeat the ancient English words in French, so that all men could understand them. It was the same. William was given the scepter and the crown and the mace, and he was sworn to the people, as the people were sworn to him. Then the cries went up: "Vivat! Vivat!"

Suddenly a different kind of noise was heard—first a murmur, then screams. Smoke billowed through the church, and chaos broke out. "Christ's blood!" Alaric swore. In alarm he rose, pushing Fallon into Roger's arms. "Guard this one!" he cried. People were hastening out of the church in panic.

Duke William still stood at the altar. The archbishops and other clergy tried to restore order.

In the near-empty church, the ceremony continued. The smoke dissipated. Fallon felt her heart race. What was happening? Alaric did not return, and a guard had formed around the duke.

Frightened, she jumped up and, moving so quickly that Roger could not catch her, ran from the church. When she reached the street, she cried out. All around her, houses were ablaze, and panic had taken hold everywhere. "Oh, God!" she breathed. Across the way, a young woman tried to beat down flames that threatened to consume her home. Fallon rushed to help her, grabbing a heavy woven rug to beat the blaze. "What happened?" she demanded, gasping for breath in the choking smoke.

"I don't know, I don't know!" the young woman wailed. "When the people hailed the new king, the stupid foreign mercenary army thought we meant to revolt! They set fire to us. Oh, God, my home, 'tis all I have, my husband dead at Hastings, and seven little mouths to feed. Oh, God!"

Fallon continued to beat furiously at the flames. She did not notice as a man upon a huge black horse rode over to them. He watched for a moment and then dismounted. His hands fell upon her shoulders and he jerked her around to face him.

Fallon could not comprehend his anger. She had indeed left Roger, but only to help save this woman from what his people had done.

Alaric shook her. "What do you think you are doing?" He demanded.

"The flames!" she cried. "They will consume this house and burn the next and the next—"

"I've men here to stop the fires, little fool!" he railed.

"I will help!"

"Nay, you will not. You will hurt the babe!"

He swung her around and pulled her away from the fire. Snatching the heavy rug from her hands, he set to work himself. In seconds the fire was out, and the woman knelt before him, thanking him. He tore a fine gold brooch from his mantle and gave it to her. "Perhaps this will pay for the damage, madam. My deepest apologies for what has happened here."

He turned from her and took Satan's reins; then he reached for Fallon and dragged her back to the church. His cheeks were black with soot, and he looked more formidable than ever.

At the entrance he called to a groom to take Satan. Then he and Fallon entered the nearly deserted church just in time to see the end of the holy rite linking the king to the people, and the people to the king.

King William of England. The crown was placed upon his head, and the final words were spoken. Fallon saw that William trembled, and she wondered what he was feeling. She lowered her head as the mass began. When the service was over, a hand grasped her by the wrist.

"The banquet will begin soon, Fallon." She started as Alaric reached for her cheek. He raised a brow and wiped away a smudge of soot with his thumb. "Lady, you, too, are slightly the worse for wear."

As he led her from the church, she saw that the fires were dying and that order was being restored all around. Alaric found Richard and Falstaff and gave her over to their care. By the time she reached her room, she found that a bath and a young serving girl already awaited her. She was eager to rid herself of the soot and smoke, and glad, too, for this brief private time before she would have to bow down to William as king.

She took as long as she dared, richly lathering her skin,

sudsing the smell of smoke from her hair, then drying it before the fire. Then she put on a white gown of silk and wool and soft white mink, and her hair fell against it in midnight contrast. She tried to fathom the tempest in her heart as she waited. Not so long ago she had been eager to escape Alaric. But now that he seemed not to want her, she felt bereft. She was ashamed, too, for she longed to touch him just one more time like a lover. She wanted to feel his heartbeat against her breast, the ripple of his muscles beneath her fingers. She wanted to feel his passionate gray eyes upon her and to know the intoxicating magic of his fingers moving over her. Agitated, she rose and paced the room, trying to hold fast to her father's memory against this surging tide of passion and longing.

There was a knock upon the door. Holding her eagerness in check, she tried to answer it with dignity.

It was not Alaric who stood there, but Roger. She swallowed down her disappointment as he bowed to her and offered her his arm. "Alaric is—engaged. He has asked me to escort you to the hall. And I beg of you, Fallon, seek not to elude me again. Have you no kindness in your heart for me? I swear, I'd not like another tongue-lashing such as the one I received after you left the church!"

"I am sorry, Roger. I didn't mean—"

"I didn't think you meant me ill. But I suppose you must wish us all to go to hell."

"I'm sorry, Roger," she repeated. He touched her cheek very gently. "Beauty such as yours needs no apology, lady." He shook his head. "How he can bear it . . . ?"

"What?" Fallon demanded.

"He has said nothing to you?"

She shook her head. "About what?"

"Oh, God," Roger groaned. "Now I have truly slit my throat."

"Roger, tell me! I beg of you! I swear, what you say to me, I will not repeat." He held silent, and she swallowed nervously. "Roger, I beg of you, don't do this to me! Tell me, what has he planned?"

"I—uh—I think he intends to send you to Normandy."

"Oh, God!" she breathed, clutching her stomach, nearly doubled over with sudden pain.

"Fallon, not for long, I am certain. Just until some of the trouble here dies down."

"Until the trouble dies down! Why, William will face trouble in England for years—for a generation!"

"Well, you are a part of that trouble, Fallon," Roger said unhappily. "Yet perhaps he will not send you away. Convince him that you will make no more pacts with the Vikings, and perhaps he will keep you here. God knows, Fallon," he swore softly, taking her hand, "I could not send you from my sight."

He stared at her entreatingly. "Show no temper today, Fallon. Bow to William, and maybe Alaric will forget your pact with the Viking."

"I did not run to one man in order to escape another," she whispered. "I merely tried to fight anew." She gazed at him sorrowfully. "Roger, all England should not have been lost at Hastings! It was a battle, and other battles could have—should have—been fought."

"Fallon, who would you have as king? Edgar is just a boy."

"An English boy," she told him. He did not answer her, and they started forth again.

A rich assemblage had gathered in the great hall, and Fallon saw that she was not the only representative of the old Saxon nobility. Edgar Atheling himself was in attendance, looking sad and drawn, as a young boy should never be. The northern earls, Edwin and Morkere, were there, and Fallon remembered how they had danced and laughed not so long ago. Aedyth was there in splendor, and even her father's dear old friend, Wulfstan of Canterbury. The Norman barons, of course, outranked them all; Fallon was painfully aware that she and her Saxon brethren were merely elegantly clad prisoners. The earls, she was certain, were desperately praying to be left to their earldoms. She and Edgar wanted escape. The churchmen had decided, it seemed, that William's victory was God's judgment, and they were resigned to accepting him as king.

Fallon saw Father Damien and she asked Roger to take her to him. To her surprise, Roger did so and then left her there, alone with the priest. Father Damien gravely asked her how she felt.

"Very well, thank you, Father. The wounds are well healed."

"And your soul?"

"It can never heal, can it?" She gazed up at him and tried to still the quivering inside her. He knew so much! Like Edward the Confessor, this man saw things. It was frightening.

"Aye, it can. It takes time."

Alaric finally appeared at her side. He greeted Father Damien, who bowed to them both and left. Alaric watched him crossly, then turned to Fallon. "It is time to join the king, *mademoiselle*," he told her. He awaited no reply, but led her across the room, and she discovered with a sick heart that she was to sit between William and Alaric at the head table, visible to all.

William, it seemed, was determined to be charming. Since his wife was still in Normandy, it was proper that Fallon should sit by his right side, and her aunt at his left. His barons sat at the high table, too—Alaric, Odo, Robert—and a number of church officials. As the food was served, William turned to Fallon. "White becomes you, lady. You appear as sweet and saintly as any angel, yet so lovely as to bring out the devil in any man."

She lowered her eyes and murmured a word of thanks.
He bent low to her. "You must bow to me, lady. I am
your king, by English law. Can you deny that now?"

She reached for her chalice, but Alaric's fingers were
already around it. She looked up at him. Both men
awaited her reply.

She withdrew her hand and placed it in her lap. "You
are king," she said to William. "You wear the crown.
Before God you have been proclaimed monarch. What
would you have of me?"

It was an unsatisfactory answer and she knew it. William laughed, but she did not like the sound of it. And
Alaric pressed the chalice into her fingers.

"We have shared a cup many a time, milady," he told
her. "And yet you find difficulty now."

"I have always found difficulty in sharing a cup with
you, my lord."

"When we have shared so much else?" he queried, and
she flushed.

William chose that moment to rise. He thanked his
supporters, and he spoke of a better England, a better
Normandy, and a great union of both. He spoke long,
and Fallon's attention wandered. With dismay she realized that he was looking down at her, his chalice raised
high.

"And so, my friends, I salute the lady Fallon, for in her
lies the very foundation of our future. She carries in her
womb a Norman babe, the seed of my greatest and strongest champion and the fruit of this great venture. Harold's
daughter will bring to life the first of a new generation. To
your health, lady!"

Every eye was on her, and Fallon felt the shame of the
moment deep in her soul. Her fingers gripped the chalice,
and she rose in fury, determined to splash the blood-red
wine on the taunting face of the bastard Norman duke. As
she rose with the chalice in her hand, someone seized her

arm. In a fury she threw the wine to the right—into Alaric's face. He rose and wrenched the goblet from her hand. A hush fell over the room. She trembled, watching as he wiped his face clean, as his jaw locked and his eyes blazed. He would surely strike her, she thought, or else appear a fool before all who had gathered here. She would not cringe. A chill seized her as she stared into his eyes, waiting.

But he did not strike her. He grabbed her and pulled her into his arms. His lips descended on hers, consuming and brutal; his hands moved over her.

A cheer went up, and taunts flew in the French language fast and heavy—ribald jokes about the Norman blade that had tamed the Saxon vixen.

His kiss was cruel; there was no tenderness behind it. She could not breathe, and she could not move, and though she had longed for him to touch her again, this cruel mockery was not what she had craved. When he released her at last, her knees buckled beneath her.

She nearly fell, but Alaric swept her into his arms. "If you'll excuse us, sire?" he said to William. "I believe the day has been too much for the lady."

"By all means, Alaric," William said, giving him permission to leave. Fallon burned with shame at the taunts that followed them from the hall.

Alaric carried her swiftly to her room. The door shuddered as he slammed it with his shoulder. He tossed her down on the bed, where she lay, stunned and aching. He turned away to wash his face. Fallon stared up at the ceiling.

"That was stupid," he told her at last.

"I meant to hit William."

"That would have been very, very stupid." He kept his back to her. "Fallon, you are not some luckless farm maid I stumbled upon. You are Harold's daughter, and William has a vested interest in your behavior."

"I thought I was your property," she taunted him wearily. She ran her tongue over her swollen lips.

"You *are* mine, my lady. And I am answerable for you."

She hesitated, then propped herself up on an elbow to question him softly. "There is no further problem, is there? You are sending me away."

He spun around, his eyes hard, then walked slowly to the bed and sat, staring down at her.

She was silent, staring up at him. She would not beg to stay, she promised herself. He reached out to touch her cheek, and his knuckles grazed her face and her throat and then her breast. "You are beautiful, Fallon. Every time I look at you, you dazzle me anew. Dressed in white you carry a virginal beauty that I know to be a sham, and still your loveliness seeps into me, and I long to touch you. You are radiance in white. Softer than winter fur, brighter than crystal. Your eyes are an enigma, like the ever-changing sky—clear at times, stormy at others, often threatening a tempest to roil into my very being."

The tone of his voice lulled her. She closed her eyes against hot tears and savored the tender touch of his fingers. She longed to reach out for him, but forced herself to lie still.

He did not continue speaking, and she opened her eyes at last.

"Tell me, Fallon, would you stay with me wherever I was sent and seek no more revenge, seek no other man?"

She tried to speak, but her lips were too dry. Disavow him! she ordered herself, but she moistened her lips, and all that she knew was that she loved him. She lowered her eyes. "Aye!" she admitted softly.

"You love England so very much," he murmured. "Would that you could love a man so much."

She stared at him, but his handsome features were a grave mask. Then he stood sweeping his mantle aside, and leaned against the hearth, staring at her. "Come, Fallon. Persuade me to let you stay in England."

"What?" she gasped.

He lifted a hand. "What is difficult in that, lady? Come, show me that you wish to stay."

"But I have just told you so."

"Surely you can do much better than that."

She bit her lip furiously. He wanted her to play the whore. She hated the indignity of it, but she longed for him desperately. She had ached to touch him and plead her cause. Here, then, was her chance.

She swore softly, but his eyes were hard upon her. So she rose at last. She walked to him and stopped before the fire, meeting his eyes with her own in brilliant defiance. There, with the glow of firelight on her flesh, she stripped away her clothing and stood proudly before him. The pulse in his throat took flight, and she heard the rasp in his whisper as he bade her come closer. He kissed her tenderly, erasing the memory of his earlier harshness, and he touched her naked body, murmuring hoarsely of her beauty. He turned her over and pressed his lips against her back, kissing the stripes left by the whip, and then he turned her again and began to caress her breasts. They were heavy in his hands, the nipples dark and full. He murmured that he should have guessed about the babe, since she had changed and ripened.

He picked her up in his arms and carried her to the bed. He asked her if she was well, and she nodded, then buried her face against his neck. When he continued to caress her, she rose up on her knees and freed him of his sword, then his tunic, hose, and chemise. When his shoulders were bare, she pressed her lips against them. Fever grew deliciously within her, and to her amazement, she found that aggression came easily to her. She eased herself against the length of him, kissing and nipping, touching. She stroked his manhood and reveled in the power of it. She cast her dreams and heartaches to the wind and luxuriated in the clean male scent that was uniquely his, and, dizzy with euphoria, kissed him to the rhythm of his heartbeat. Suddenly she felt herself swept beneath him and cherished from head to toe. And then he was imbedded inside her and she was arching hungrily to his every thrust. When they lay still at last, he stroked her breasts and laid his head against her belly. "Damien says you carry a boy," he whispered warmly against her flesh. She shrugged, not wanting to talk about it. He rose above her suddenly, harshly, swiftly. "It will be a boy. It will be a son. You will bear a Norman boy. A Norman bastard. Yet you tell me you want the child. Do you lie? Is there anything about you a man can trust?"

She shook her head and smiled bitterly. "Perhaps Damien is right, and it will be a boy. But he will be an Englishman."

He laughed and fell beside her, yet there was still a restlessness about him and little humor. He lay beside her, caressing her breasts, cupping the fullness in his hands, stroking her nipples. Finding sweet comfort in the gentle and tender touch, Fallon slept.

In the morning he was behind her, awake and aroused. He ran his hand over the smooth curve of her buttocks, then around her waist and down between her legs. She awoke quickly with the shattering sensation as he moved into her and swept her away in quick and heady passion.

When he was done, he arose quickly and began to dress. In moments she felt a sharp slap against her backside and she rose with protest, holding the sheets to her.

"Get up," he told her, "and dress quickly and warmly."

"Why?"

"Do as I say."

She washed as best she could with the water in the room, aware that his eyes remained keenly upon her. She dressed, still feeling his gaze as she stood with her back to him, feeling as if he would devour her, as if he memorized every curve of her. Color rose to her face, and finally she turned to face him, but just then there was a knock on the door. He answered it.

Falstaff was there. "We are ready, Alaric. 'Tis best we leave at once."

Alaric nodded.

Fallon looked from one to the other, and when Falstaff stepped outside and closed the door, she realized what it meant. She flew across the room at Alaric, ready to rake his face and chest with her nails. "You bastard! You filthy bastard! You made me—you made me believe that I could—that I could—"

"Persuade me to change my mind?"

"You bastard! I never had a chance, and you let me—"

"I let you take what you wanted, Fallon, and that is all." He grasped her hands and held them behind her back. "I told you once that I would not base my decisions on the effects of your charms and beauty. Aye, lady, you're going to Normandy. I am not being cruel, merely practical. I've no time to be distracted by your schemes. I do not know where Eric Ulfson has gone, and I do not trust you!"

"I have no schemes!"

"Ah, but I can't believe you, can I, Fallon?"

She couldn't move; she was caught in his arms. Moisture glazed her eyes and she spoke in a rasp. "You bastard! If you're done with me, let me go!"

He held her fast with one hand and cradled her cheek with the other. "But I am not done with you, lady. I'll be with you again soon enough, I swear it."

"Doomsday will be soon enough!" she choked out.

He sighed softly and wearily. "You forget, Fallon. The babe you carry is mine. I pray you, keep him well."

"And I pray you—"

"Think, Fallon, before you speak," he warned her. "Take care what you say to me, for I have power over you. You should wish to appease me now."

"Appease you!"

"Would you have the babe born on Norman soil, Fallon?"

She hesitated, staring at him, and they both knew that she was beaten.

He whispered against her ear. "Then behave, milady, and I will come to you when I can." Slowly, he released her. She lowered her head and would not look his way.

"The lady is ready!" he called, and Falstaff entered the room and bowed to her deeply.

Chapter Twenty-Six

It was not so cruel a banishment as Fallon had expected, for the weather turned exceedingly bitter, and she spent the month of January with her mother at Bosham. She was curious that Falstaff would make such a decision, but he was quick to tell her that Alaric feared the crossing might be rough and did not want any chances taken. Falstaff also told her that he was wise to her tricks. They would all be safe a while at Harold's old home.

Edith had heard nothing about Fallon's abortive meeting with Eric Ulfson, and Fallon chose not to say anything. Edith was very excited about the baby, and Fallon did not want to ruin her mother's happiness by reminding her of the circumstances of the child's conception. Once, however, while her mother sat knitting a tiny garment, chattering contentedly about the child, Fallon did remind her bitterly that the baby would undoubtedly be a beautiful bastard.

"Maybe Alaric will marry you," Edith said softly, and a single tear ran down her cheek. "Few understood our Danish law here. The new breed of men taking charge regarded all of you as bastards. But William is a bastard; Alaric, too. What matters it if the child is also a bastard? He will be your father's first grandchild. How could you ever begrudge this baby life?"

Fallon ran to her mother and knelt down by her side. "I am so sorry, Mother. I love you. I did not mean to hurt you. I want this baby very much."

Her mother smoothed back her hair, holding her. "And you have fallen in love with its father."

Fallon pulled back, looking at her mother. "How did you know that?"

Edith continued stroking her hair. "Your father always swore that you and Alaric would be a match one day. He wanted it, you know."

Fallon rose and walked away. "Father's wishes have little power now. Alaric will not marry me. He has little real affection for women, I'm afraid, and for me least of all."

"But he does recognize the child as his."

"Oh, aye," Fallon said bitterly, remembering the night of William's banquet. "They are all quite amused that Harold's daughter will so quickly give birth to the proof of Norman supremacy."

"Count your blessings, then, daughter," Edith said softly. "Many a Saxon maid will soon bear Norman fruit and not know which of the conquering soldiers is the father. So many raided our villages one day and disappeared the next."

He has sent me from him, Mother! she longed to cry out. I have fallen in love, and he does not even want me!

But Fallon could not open her heart to her mother. Instead, she shrugged and said casually. "I could not marry him anyway, Mother. It would be disrespectful."

"Disrespectful? To whom?"

"To my father's memory. To the memory of my uncles. To all those I held dear who died to defend this realm."

Edith stood and walked over to her, shaking her knitting beneath her nose. "Don't you ever say that, Fallon. Your father would have chosen Alaric himself, if he'd had the power. Hard times are upon us, but Alaric is a good man; he has always behaved with courage and honor. He was your father's friend, despite his loyalty to the duke. Fallon, you are going to bear his child! Forget what you have heard from others—aye, even your own brothers! If Alaric will wed you, then you owe it to your father to marry him!"

In all her days, Fallon had rarely seen her mother in such a passion. Surprise kept her silent for a long time. "He has not asked me to marry him, Mother, and I doubt that he will. But perhaps he will let me come here to you when it is time for the baby to be born. I—I am praying that he will."

"And if not," Edith whispered, "I shall come to you."

They hugged each other and then sat silently before the fire.

During the second week of February, Fallon and Falstaff made a safe crossing to Normandy, and by the twentieth she was at Rouen where, to her surprise, she received a warm welcome. Matilda seemed to understand how sorely it had hurt Fallon to lose her father and her way of life. Tiny and swathed in fur, William's wife braved the wintry day to greet her.

"Come, and be warmed by the fire," Matilda said. "The children are anxious to see you. I swear poor Robert is in love with you. And the girls are so eager to see you." She hesitated. "And your uncle, of course—Wulfnoth has been most excited ever since he heard you were coming."

Fallon bowed her head, dizzy with the emotion that swept through her. The only remaining son of Godwin survived. He lived because he resided in the duke's household—as a prisoner.

As she was herself now.

"I would dearly love to see my uncle," Fallon said.

She was led to the pretty chamber where she had once

stayed as a guest. She wondered briefly why she was not given the room where Alaric always stayed in Rouen, but she was too exhausted to care.

When she saw Wulfnoth, Fallon cried. For a long time he held her and soothed her, reminding her wearily that he had been the duke's hostage for over a decade, and would surely never know freedom now. "But I am happy enough, Fallon. I am not bound or tied or locked in a dungeon. I spend time with William's family. I tell myself that I am an honored guest, and I can almost believe it to be so. I scarce remember my own language, for I speak it so seldom. Yet you and I are survivors, Fallon. We must remain so. We must remember for future generations the England we used to know."

She thought fleetingly that perhaps the lucky ones were those who had not survived. But come what may, she was glad she lived and carried life within her.

"Uncle," she asked him when they were alone, "do you know what has happened to Delon? He was sent here, and it has been on my conscience ever since. Does he suffer on my account?"

"Suffer?" Wulfnoth laughed. "Nay, child, rest assured on that matter! He is not here. He fell for the pretty young sister of an ambassador from Sicily, and he is now in the service of the Sicilian king."

"Oh!" Fallon said, startled. For a moment it hurt that he had forgotten her so quickly. But it was only her pride that was stung—for in truth, she hardly ever thought of the young man who had risked so much for her. She was glad, heartily glad, that he was free and happy. She laughed with Wulfnoth.

Life in Normandy was not so bad, but Fallon missed her home. She missed the beauty of winter, when ice covered the land, and the welcome resurgence of life in spring. She loved the English holidays and the dances around the maypole, and she loved hearing the serfs and servants and cotters speaking in her native tongue.

But she was not miserable. Matilda was a dear woman, and unerringly kind. She not only managed the children's lives, but acted as regent of Normandy, with her son Robert, in William's absence. Her court at Rouen was always busy and crowded. Women abounded here, a circumstance that pleased Wulfnoth no end, but somewhat disconcerted Fallon. There was one redhead who watched her constantly. Each time Fallon's eyes fell upon her, she saw a derisive curl come to the woman's lips. One evening as Fallon walked back to her room from the hall, the red-haired woman suddenly stood before her.

"You're beginning to show—my *lady.*" The last was said with a sneer. "He'll never marry you. He'll never marry any woman. He has tired of you already, that is plain. You sought to trap him, but you've only encumbered yourself with an unwanted babe, and marred your youth and beauty!"

Fallon stared at her, stunned. No one in Matilda's court had ever dared speak to her so. Indeed, guided by the duchess's example, the ladies had all been kind.

Her fingers clenched, and she felt her fighting spirit rekindled. *"Madame,* I believe you forget: I am a Saxon. We did not invite the Normans. They came of their own accord, and they took what they wanted. Whether I marry or not is surely no concern of yours." Fallon swept by the woman, but soft, grating laughter followed her.

"You are not the one assigned to his chamber," the woman murmured insolently.

Fallon kept walking and tried not to think of the voluptuous redhead sleeping in Alaric's arms! Fallon was aware that she grew more ungainly daily. When Alaric returned, would he find her repellent? Would he turn to the redhead for . . . that?

The idea plagued Fallon. In her nightmares, Alaric and

the woman laughed at her. In one dream, after the child was born, Fallon was cast into a stygian cell in the dungeon of the castle; then Alaric and the woman left with her child.

When morning came she awoke exhausted. She lay there, too listless to move, until Matilda came to her. Cheerfully she plumped the pillows and made Fallon drink cool milk, then demanded to know what was wrong.

Fallon said only "How can you be so gentle and wonderful—and be William's wife?"

Matilda did not take offense, but sat down beside Fallon. "I thought William was a monster myself at one time. I had sworn I'd never marry the bastard—and he burst into my father's house and beat me."

"And still you married him?"

"Umm. I feared not to! I knew that he wanted me badly and that I would find him strong enough to love and respect forever. And we have had a good marriage. Beautiful children, and a solid union. He does not roam, he loves me still. Passionate men are like that. They can be fierce and brutal, but when they love, they do so deeply, and they cannot be swayed. Alaric is like him."

Fallon did not respond.

"Ah," Matilda said, "I see. Margaret has been talking to you."

Fallon looked at her quickly.

"The redhead with the mountain range upon her chest."

Fallon had to laugh, and the duchess laughed, too. "She feels she has some claim upon him," Fallon murmured.

The duchess shrugged. "Well, on again, off again."

"She says he'll marry no one."

Matilda sighed. "Has he never spoken to you of his past?"

Fallon said no, and Matilda told her the tragic story of

Alaric's marriage. "I think that now Alaric is *afraid* to love too deeply," Matilda finished.

"Do you think . . . do you think he really wants this child?"

"Aye, that I do, for he bade me take special care of you. You mustn't be afraid of those who are jealous of you." She started to leave, but paused at the door. "Don't hate my husband overly, Fallon. He truly believed that he was the heir to the crown. He and your father were very much alike. They both did what they had to do."

"He had me whipped," she told Matilda softly. "And he humiliated me before his barons and my own people. He is not easy to love."

"He admired Harold greatly. He thought that if they ruled together—William as king, your father as subre-galis—they would have been truly great. Your father died in battle. Give William a chance. I assure you, your father would not have wanted you to battle William." She left. For a long time, Fallon lay on the bed, reflecting on what Matilda had said. Fallon herself could remember that Alaric had changed. As a young man, he had been full of fire—a cavalier out to right the wrongs of the world and defend the liege who had stood by him. But a part of him had grown hard and cold, and she wondered how he had felt when his wife had died. Aye, it must have hurt him; it must have changed him.

But then, she loved him. It was easy to bleed a little bit inside for the tragedy that had befallen him.

In London, Alaric was thinking of Fallon. But his thoughts were not so tender. It had been a long day in which he and others had sat with William and painstakingly gone through the names of men who had fought at Hastings and who deserved compensation. They had allotted land grants and titles and dispensations, trying to be fair to all concerned. Almost everyone should be happy, except for the English peasantry, Alaric thought. They were accustomed to being ruled by thanes who held their rightful places at the hundred moot. Now strangers—men who did not speak their language and knew nothing of their customs—would rule them.

That night Alaric sat with Roger and Rollo, and even young Richard, and proceeded to drink as much as he could. He had spent the last months riding hard. He had visited shires and valleys and villages and towns, and he had tried to assess the mood of the country. The people were surly, at best, but the violence now seemed to be dying down. William had ordered that men who surrendered were to be treated with mercy. He knew that rebellions would rise for years, and those rebellions would be dealt with ruthlessly. But for the common man, William wanted the cruelty to end.

While they drank and stared at the fire, Roger murmured, "How strange. We have taken England, yet here we sit, dreaming of our own home. We revile the English for fighting, yet what have we always done? Why, war is our very livelihood."

" 'Tis mine, at that," Rollo agreed.

"I've a mind for some peace," Roger murmured. "A home and a hearth and a beautiful maid to come home to. One with skeins of silky soft hair to wrap around my naked frame, and eyes perhaps the color of the noonday sky—"

Richard choked, interrupting him. Roger, aware of his description then, swallowed abruptly and sat straight in his chair.

Alaric said nothing at first. Then he threw his cup hard into the fire. "Don't be deceived," he told them softly. "Soft blue eyes can be as treacherous as any others."

"She is Harold's daughter," Roger reminded him, squirming uneasily.

Alaric stood and wandered to the mantel, and looked back at his friend. "Oh, aye, she is Harold's daughter." And so, he thought wearily, he would have to fight her all his life. Was it worth it? Could things have been any different?

That night, like many nights before, Alaric wished he had not sent her away. He ached to hold her, he burned to possess her. He wondered how she looked, for that was one thing he would not ask in his letters to Matilda. Was she heavy with the child yet, or just beginning to show the babe in a soft swell?

She had left him. She had been so desperate to destroy William that she had left him and walked into the Viking's arms. Carrying his child, with his kiss still upon her lips.

There was the thorn, oh, aye! He longed to forgive her. He hoped against all hope that she was really glad of their child, that Damien had foretold the truth, and that his son would be born healthy.

"Were she mine, I'd not let her slip away!"

It was Roger who spoke. With a glance at the evil expression on Alaric's face, Rollo quickly dragged Roger to his feet. "We'll retire for the night, I think!" He led Roger out, and Alaric sank back to his chair. Richard brought him more wine, and Alaric stared at the boy as he sipped it.

"Well, go ahead, speak. You've got something to say. I don't suppose that you would let her slip away either."

"Oh, nay, sire! Why the lady Fallon is more stunning than the dawn, more arresting than the most golden twilight. She is wind, and she is fire, and she is—"

"Treacherous," Alaric interrupted dryly. He rubbed his temples, but then he smiled at Richard and raised his wine to his lips. "So tell me, lad. I knew from the moment I saw her that she was trouble. I knew that I could meet any warrior on the battlefield—but that I should turn and run from this woman. So what is it, lad? Are her lips really redder than other women's? Is her hair more beautiful, more silky? Is there really magic in her eyes? Does she move differently, is she more graceful, more sinuous? What is it that pierces the heart, and captures the soul, and taunts the mind?"

"I—er—I think it's called love, sir," Richard said.

"Ah, but I have sworn not to love again, Richard. And even if I did love, I'd have to be a fool to love her, don't you think?"

"Well, surely, not really, sir. I believe she loves you, too."

"She loves me," Alaric murmured sardonically. His eyes, like silver smoke, fell on Richard. "That is why she ran from me to form a pact with a Viking. That is why I found them embracing."

"Well, surely, sir, she was ready to throw up."

"She what?"

"I know she didn't want to kiss the Viking. But let's be honest, sir. This has been a rather—uh—brutal conquest. People don't like to be ruthlessly crushed."

Alaric stared at him, then started to laugh. He rose, giddy with too much wine—he had not drunk so much since he was ridiculously young.

He wanted Fallon at that moment, with all his heart and soul. But he was afraid, for he knew she was dangerous still, and would be all her life.

For Fallon would not bend, and she would not break.

"Richard, the king is returning to Normandy for Easter. Would you like to see my homeland?"

"Aye!"

"Then it is settled. We will travel with him."

Alaric set off ahead of the king and, with Richard riding hard behind him, went straight to Rouen. By the time he arrived, he was so eager to see Fallon that he was nearly speechless.

Matilda must have been told of Alaric's approach, for as soon as he had dismounted, she hurried out to greet him. He kissed her smartly and told her that William was well, and together they walked into the hall. Alaric quickly looked about, but there was no sign of Fallon.

"Where is she?" he demanded of Matilda. Damn Fallon! His stomach was a jumble, his nerves were twisted as if they had been braided all inside, and the woman was nowhere about. He gritted his teeth, remembering how they had parted, and a sinking feeling swept through him. He knew that no man should trust a beautiful woman, and especially Harold's daughter. She was bound to fight him, and he was a fool to think otherwise. Suddenly he thought despairingly of the years to come, and they seemed very grim.

"I told her that you had been spotted," Matilda murmured unhappily. "I'm sure she'll be here any minute."

"My lord!" Falstaff saw him, and came to him, and they greeted each other with clasped shoulders and ready smiles.

Then Margaret suddenly appeared. Alaric smiled at her coolly. Then he looked up. Fallon was there. She was perfectly still and achingly beautiful, but no smile of welcome touched her lips. She wore white again, and her hair was a black cloud around her shoulders; it curled and streamed in radiant beauty to her knees.

Suddenly his anger roiled. He was furious with himself for missing her so badly, for allowing her to haunt his dreams and his life, his every moment. She knew, the vixen, that he was in thrall to her beauty, and she dared to test his temper time and time again.

He turned his eyes away from her and reached out for Margaret, who laughed and was ready to greet him with the rest of the ladies and knights in the hall. But with

Margaret, of course, it was no casual kiss, and laughter rang out while it endured. Then others claimed him quickly, and when he looked up again, Fallon was gone.

"Excuse me," he muttered to Matilda. He extracted himself as quickly as he could from the crowd and found the stairs. He raced up the steps two at a time, and reached the top as Fallon disappeared around the corner. He followed her, making his strides longer and longer.

He caught up with her as she tried to slam her door in his face. He shoved it open, and she hadn't the strength to stop him. She backed into the room, and he followed her still, closing the door behind him. For a moment he paused, taking in her form from head to toe. He strode toward her, and she stared about desperately for some place to go, but he backed her into a corner.

"Nay!" she pounded a fist against his chest, aware of the dusky silver fire in his eyes. "Get away from me, Alaric!"

He caught her face between his hands and kissed her. She twisted and squirmed beneath him, and though her heart beat feverishly, she fought his touch. "Go down to your Norman whore, my lord!" she commanded him scathingly. "So help me, God! You'll not have us both!"

He avoided her flailing arms and her soaring temper to sweep her into his arms. His spirits soared. It was so good just to see her again. To touch her, to hold her. Her beauty was far greater in truth than in memory. "What is this? Have you forgotten that I raided and plundered and ruined your country? How like a woman, love. All can be forgiven but the kiss of another maid. And how quickly you have forgotten the injury you did me! You will recall, lady, that I came upon you with your lips melded to that Viking's!"

"Oh!" Enraged, she struggled against him more fiercely. "And you forget, sir, what you did to me!"

"Milady?"

"You tricked me, you deceived me, you—"

"I enjoyed the evening thoroughly, Princess, and I would have sworn that you did, too."

She swore at him, but he pulled her to him, securing her wrists.

"I loved you, lady. Was that so harsh a punishment?"

There was such a curious tenderness to his voice that she went still, her heart pounding. He bent to kiss her, and she could not twist away, nor, as the seconds passed and the hunger of his passion swept through her, did she care to. When he released her at last she met his eyes, trembling.

"Let me go! Now! Leave me."

He laughed, and he buried his face in her hair, breathing in the delicious scent of it. "Lady! I have ridden hard and long to get here and claim what is mine, and you would bid me leave?"

"You sent me here!"

"And I have sorely missed you, Princess. Sorely."

He spoke huskily and with a trembling depth of sincerity that left her breathless. She stared into his eyes, and she knew that the mad quivering had taken flight inside her again. Her heart pounded wildly, and intoxicating excitement filled her, rushing through her like a white-foamed cascade of water.

His mouth covered hers again in slow, sweet hunger and need this time. He savored her lips completely, and her arms came around him at last, and her fingers played with the hair at the nape of his neck. He kissed her until she was dizzy, and when he broke away, it was to carry her to the bed.

His merest touch made her writhe in anticipation, she wanted him so badly. He did not deny either of them. They met and melded like fire, and they made love quickly, swiftly, desperately, yet Fallon felt herself explode within more sweetly than ever. She could scarce believe that he was really back with her, that he lay beside her, that they both gasped for breath and touched, still damp and slick with the exertion of love.

He rose up on an elbow and studied her thoroughly. She flushed, thinking of the changes within her. She was not so slim, she thought. And not at all alluring. And yet he seemed fascinated. He touched her as she had dreamed that he would touch her, stroking the mound of her belly, leaning over to touch her breasts very lightly with his kiss. "Have you been well?" he asked her softly.

"Aye. Very. Matilda is kind." She hesitated. "And you, my lord?"

"I have suffered wretchedly," he said, and she smiled, her heart soaring, for he smiled down at her honestly. He ran his hand over her stomach again and as he did, she gasped, startled by the first movement.

"What is it?"

"Oh, feel, Alaric, feel! He kicks!"

He pressed his palm and fingertips against her, and in answer, the babe kicked fiercely again. Fallon laughed and stared at him in wonder.

"The first time?"

"Aye, 'tis the first I've felt him."

"His kick is hard and strong and sure."

"Perhaps it is a girl."

He shook his head. "Damien says that it is a boy. I'll be damned if I know how he knows, but he does know— things. It is a lad. A good strong, healthy lad." He pressed his lips against her flesh and kissed her swollen belly with tenderness. Content, Fallon lay back and smiled.

He lay down beside her, and for long moments they were silent as he stroked her hair. Then he sighed unhappily. "I have messages for Matilda, and I must see certain men."

"No women?"

He cupped her chin and drew her face to his. "Nay,

Fallon. Not since I have known you. There is no other maid to compare. I have hated to tell you so, for your beauty is stronger than any sword, or any word. You wield it well."

She lowered her lashes over her eyes, then stared at him directly. "She flaunts what she was, your old mistress, my lord. And I cannot hide the fruit of our affair any longer—even if the world did not already know, thanks to William. I—" She paused, swallowing nervously. "I did not wish to be sent from England. That is my home. But it is true, too, that I did not wish to leave you. I went to Eric, aye. But I cannot beg your pardon, for I meant it not against you, but for my country, in my father's memory. I swear, Alaric, I had no wish to betray you. And now—"

"Now?"

"I pray that what you say is true," she said softly, "for it hurts me to hear her taunts while your child grows within me."

"And what does she say?"

"That I do not even share your chamber."

He smiled and stroked her cheek. "You share my life, Fallon. Or perhaps you have become it, I do not know. Matilda put you in this room because it was winter when you came and this is a warm room. I'll not sleep away from you, and I promise, Margaret will know it."

She stared at him, dazed. He bent low and kissed her lips, and when he moved a breath away, he whispered into her mouth. "William comes for Easter. We must celebrate with him at the abbey, but when I've finished with my business here, we'll go home."

Warmth bubbled within her. "I may have the baby at Bosham?"

"Nay, love, for that was your father's home."

"In London? In Winchester?"

"Nay, not London, and not Winchester."

Hot tears rose to her eyes, for she thought that he

taunted her with a prize that she could not reach. She swallowed. "You said that we would go home. I thought—"

"The babe can be born in England. But we shall go to Haselford, for it is ours and ours alone. Taken in peace. There was no conquest there. I was asked to rule the town, and the people will welcome us both. He will be born there. Does that please you?"

"Aye!" she whispered. He smiled and rose, after kissing her forehead. He donned his clothing and went to take his messages to Matilda.

When he was gone, Fallon pulled the covers about herself. She smiled in deep contentment, and she wondered why. She had never thought she could feel so happy, though her happiness did come with a certain guilt. She should still be fighting. But she had fought nobly and well. Perhaps she deserved a time of peace.

The baby kicked again, and her smile widened.

"He does love us, little one. Perhaps he doesn't know it, perhaps he cannot say it. But surely he loves us."

Chapter Twenty-Seven

Easter proved to be a grand occasion for William and his party. When the mass had been celebrated, there was no end to the rounds of entertainment.

Edgar Atheling, Edwin and Morkere, and many other important English officials, all of them well dressed, were with the party. They were treated courteously, and yet, as Edwin told Fallon, they were like birds, trapped in jeweled cages.

"William has brought us here so that there can be no rallying point in England while he is gone. Had he been able to find your brothers, they would be here, too. We are on display before these Normans, who gawk and stare and laugh at our clothing and our language. God, how I wish to go home!"

As the days and then the weeks passed, Fallon began to feel the strain. She missed Alaric, when he rode to Anlou. She offered to accompany him, but he seemed cold and brooding and distant, and he refused her.

He did not stay away long, but when he returned there was some part of him she could not reach, and she wondered if it was not the same with her. She was glad to be with him, and she did not deny it. He was loyal to her, openly so before any who saw them. She was grateful, for her pregnancy grew more apparent daily. At night, in his arms, she was happy, but the days were a strain, and she longed for them to end.

Soon after Easter, William held a great tournament. Watching from her place in the stands, Fallon was proud to see Alaric's fine appearance when he rode in the lists. His combatant was a Hessian knight, and Alaric easily unseated him, then just as competently dealt with him in a mock swordfight. Fallon rose to her feet, clapping. But as Alaric bowed before leaving the field, she became achingly aware of the whispers behind her.

"Who is that maid?" a woman's voice demanded.

"Why 'tis the old Saxon king's bastard girl!" a man replied.

"And now a well-laid whore!" the woman laughed.

Before the next contest could begin, Fallon rose and quit the stands with dignity. She hurried to the palace and discovered Edwin there, in the hall, standing morosely before the fire. Although he was a young man, he seemed to bear the weight of the world upon his shoulders.

"Fallon!" he said startled, and his eyes took in her tense and distraught face. "What is it?"

She shook her head. "Oh, Edwin, I cannot bear much more of this!"

"They are jealous," he said quietly. "They stare at the most beautiful of the birds in the jeweled cage, and they are jealous." She was afraid that she was going to cry. He came to her and put his arms around her. She placed her cheek against his shoulder, and he smoothed his hand over her hair.

"Oh, Edwin. Sometimes it just hurts so badly!" she murmured.

"I know. I know." Suddenly he stiffened, and his hand went still. Fallon pushed away from him and turned, and discovered Alaric there, still in his mail from the joust, his helmet held beneath his arm. He was towering and straight, and she could read no message in the cold slate color of his eyes.

Edwin faced him with pride and courage, Fallon thought. He addressed Alaric quickly. "There is nothing here, my lord, except what the eyes plainly see. We are old friends, seeking the comfort of that old friendship, and nothing more."

Alaric bowed curtly to them both. "Then I leave you to that comfort," he said coldly.

He walked back to the lists in a fury. Matilda had sent a messenger to warn him that something had upset Fallon. He'd left the tournament to find her, and find her he had—in the arms of another man, the youthful earl, Edwin of Mercia. Would he never be able to trust her? Would he always harbor the fear that she sought her own kind, that she sought escape? As sweetly, as lovingly, as tenderly as she came to him, it seemed that the barrier remained. He was the vile conqueror; she was the Saxon maid. How long would she fight this battle?

He stomped back to his tent, and though the joust went on, he shouted for Richard to bring Satan to him. Old friends, indeed. "Satan," he told the horse, "now, you, good sir, are an old friend. You fight with courage, you cross the Channel in good humor no matter what the weather, and you don't seem to give a damn if you're a Norman horse or a Saxon horse!"

He was about to mount Satan when he heard his name called softly and he turned. Matilda was there by his tent, smiling sweetly.

"Where are you off to in such foul humor?"

He shook his head to her. "Just riding, Matilda."

"Come and talk to me."

He saw the gentle smile on her open, pretty face. He handed the reins to Richard and walked along by her side. She chatted idly about affairs in Normandy and reminisced about years past. He listened halfheartedly as they walked under the trees and along the brook. Spring had come with splendor. Birth and beauty were everywhere, and the earth was fragrant and rich.

"Why the temper?" Matilda demanded suddenly.

"You are mistaken. I am in no temper, lady."

She laughed. "Alaric, you forget! I have known you since you were an honorable lad, determined to speak up for William."

He shrugged. "I am in no temper."

She stopped walking and stared at him. "Marry her."

"What?"

"You are angry with Fallon. I don't know what happened, but your mood is most obvious. People speak cruelly of her. They say things that are not true. You have made her your mistress. Soothe your own soul. Marry her. Give your babe what you and William never had—legitimacy."

"William and I did quite well without it, *madame.*"

"Alaric—"

"Nay, Matilda! I will not marry again!"

"And why not?"

Alaric paused, watching William's determined duchess. "Matilda, you twist knives where no man would dare. But I will tell why I cannot marry her. I do not believe in love, *madame.* I have seen the hurt it does. I do not trust women, and most especially I cannot trust Fallon. Twice she has taken up arms against me. Eric Ulfson escaped me and will no doubt raise an army to rise against William. And as his prize, Fallon has promised herself. Then, for the last, lady, it is unlikely that she would consent to wed. She still sees us as the murderers who slew her father in cold blood."

"I believe she would marry you."

"It will not happen."

"You are a fool, Alaric. You are denying yourself happiness."

"Perhaps."

"Keep thinking about it, Alaric. For the child. For yourself. And even for Fallon. I know she is plotting nothing else against you. I believe—Why, I believe she loves you."

Alaric growled skeptically. Matilda continued to watch him anxiously.

"All right, Duchess, all right! I will consider what you have said." He meant the promise; but he doubted that he could still his own tortured fears of her betrayal long enough to make it through a wedding ceremony. He sighed. "She is mine, Matilda, and I will care for her, and I will see that she suffers no more from vicious tongues. William has work for me, and I am eager to return home."

"This is your home."

He glanced at her frowning, then explained himself to her. "I wish to return to my property in England. I have promised Fallon that the babe will be born there. I will love him, he will be my heir. It will be enough."

He bowed low to Matilda, then turned and left her. He didn't rejoin the festivities, but hurried to the room he shared with Fallon.

She was there, sitting quietly before the fire, knitting some tiny garment. When he entered, her eyes met his in brilliant blue defiance.

He cast her a chilling glare, then bellowed for Richard to come and help him with his armor. When it was removed, he ordered food and wine brought to the room. Richard gave Fallon a quick nod, and departed quickly.

She still had not spoken. He stood by the fire and watched her for a long, long time.

"We will depart tomorrow for England," he said.

Startled, she dropped her needlework and stood, and nearly raced across the room to his arms. The coldness within his gaze stopped her, and she stood watching him in silence.

"Thank you," she murmured, restrained.

Richard brought them food. Fallon discovered that she had very little appetite, and Alaric remained brooding and silent. When she had finished eating, she picked up her needlework again, ignoring Alaric. He likewise ignored her and prepared for bed. Fallon stared at her tiny stitches while her mind raced. How could he suspect her of wayward behavior, when she grew bulkier daily with his seed?

"For God's sake! Will you stop that and come to bed!" he snapped out suddenly.

Fallon stared his way, her eyes narrowing with anger. "I'll do what I damn well please, Count!"

She quickly discovered that he did not intend to take the bait. Instead he rose and swept her into his arms, deposited her in bed, then blew out the candles. For an eternity they lay there in silence, and Fallon began to think that he slept. She started to get up, only to feel his hands dragging her back down and doing so with firm intent. She cried out as she heard fabric tear, and she flailed against him in a sudden heated fury.

"Nay, my lord, you will not treat me so!"

"Why? Is it only other men you crave to tease?"

"You are an oaf!"

"Did you receive the—comfort—you craved?"

"You fool! You've women enough so that it's like a fall of apples in autumn—one never knows when one will strike! While I—"

"While you, my lady, have suitors across England and beyond, so it seems! And today you flirted with that poor boy—"

"Flirted! Oh, you ruddy bastard! What man craves a woman who is enormous with another man's child?"

He held her arms tightly, staring into her eyes with a frightening intensity. "Eric Ulfson," he said softly.

Fallon froze, looking down at him.

"Tell me, lady, what other plans do you have?"

"I—I have no plans. I swear it," Fallon said huskily.

"Would that I could believe you."

She shook her head miserably. "I didn't mean to betray you, Alaric!" she cried. "Truly. Eric Ulfson has always made me shudder. Can't you see that I sought him out for England?"

"And would you seek him out again—for England?"

She shook her head. Tears were forming in her eyes.

"Why not?" he demanded.

She could not tell him that she loved him. Such a declaration would make her too vulnerable. "Because of our child. Because I do not believe that his hordes could save England now. Because men and women are just beginning to live again. Because there is law established in London. Please, Alaric. I never wished to practice treachery."

His hold on her eased, and his eyes softened. He pulled her to him, and she willingly, eagerly accepted his kiss. He tore her clothing to shreds, but she barely noticed as she entered the magic realm where the earth spun about the two of them, and nothing but the taste and touch and feel of him had substance. Some demon held him as he moved against her, swift and driven. He shuddered and convulsed, groaning deep in his throat, falling against her, soaked and spent, pulling her hard against him again, whispering erotically of his satisfaction. She lay, tempest-tossed and drifting, in his arms, but then as they reached solid ground, she felt the brooding that haunted him once more. She said nothing, for she did not understand it.

His chin rested on her head and he held her protectively close, one hand on her belly. "If only this were always truth," he whispered, with a curious touch of anguish in his voice. She twisted from him to study his face.

"What do you mean?"

"Nothing. Go to sleep," he commanded her.

She could not fathom his mood, and so she lay silent beside him. He held her tight, and at last she slept.

He was true to his word. In the morning, they started out for England. Roger and Rollo were returning with them, as well as Steven, the squire, and young Richard and a number of other knights in Alaric's service. Matilda insisted on sending one of her women, Magalie, who was an experienced midwife. Fallon was glad of her, for though the woman was nearly toothless with wild gray hair, she was cheerful and pleasant, and had a soothing way with her, which was good—for Alaric's temper did not improve. He was angry with himself that they had not left earlier, for Fallon was now nearly seven months along, and he cursed himself for the danger in her riding. Still, they reached the coast with no incidents, and their crossing was wonderfully smooth.

He told her that they would pause for a few nights at Bosham where she could spend time with her mother.

Fallon would have stayed longer, but at the beginning of June, Alaric was determined to return to Haselford. He did not want Fallon traveling any later, and he reminded her curtly that if she did not take care, she could well bring forth their babe on an old Roman road. Fallon wanted her mother to accompany her to Haselford, and Alaric had no objection, for he liked Edith very well.

It was good to return. Alaric felt the same affection for the place that he had felt from the beginning. Hamlin and his daughters had kept the manor house in good repair. The land was rich and green with the promise of summer. The crops grew well, and sheep grazed in a meadow bright with yellow flowers.

Alaric watched Fallon carefully and thought that she

seemed happy to be here. It was a place where simple people lived, where cooking fires always blazed, where the rushes were swept, where the bedding was aired, and men and women still held their heads high.

Fallon was glad to be reunited with Jeanne and Marla, and Heath was quick to show Alaric all the work that had been done in his absence. There seemed to be children all about.

"It is hard to believe that there has been devastation at all when one sees this place," Edith commented when they sat down to their first evening meal.

" 'Tis a paradise, I believe," Roger agreed with her.

Alaric threw Fallon a smile. " 'Tis Fallon's world," he said softly. "We say begone to evil, and it is so, for thus she wills it."

Startled by his gentle words, Fallon looked his way to find him gazing tenderly at her.

It was a homecoming for them, and when they were alone together, Alaric was both fierce and tender. But when he held her that night, he thought regretfully that her time drew very near, and he should not lie with her again.

In the morning, he told her that he would order his things moved to another room.

She stared at him, startled. Trembling, she lowered her eyes. "Why?" she asked him softly.

"I'd not disturb you and the babe," he said gruffly. "Fallon, perhaps we have taken this too far already. You've little time left."

She nodded, looking up at him. "But do you have to leave the room?"

He shook his head slowly, and he felt a sweet warmth fill him. "You wish me to stay?"

"We can still sleep beside each other," she reminded him quietly. "If that means anything to you."

He kissed her hand. "Aye. It means a great deal to me.

But I shall have to leave for a few days now and then. With William still in Normandy, there is no help for it."

He did, in fact, leave within the week, for he was determined to be back from his business when the child was born. He had to go to Dover first, with messages and instructions for William's officials there, and thence to London, to make some new appointments and see to the smooth functioning of the government. Roger and Rollo went with him while Falstaff remained behind to guard the manor house.

Alaric was still uneasy about leaving Fallon. In certain ways, she was very much his—more so than he had ever expected. He had never thought such heaven could exist in a woman's arms, and no maid had ever poured her love so sweetly upon him. She spoke to him in honesty and did not deny the passion that raged between them.

Yet all the while that she had plotted against him, he had never suspected it. He could not help wondering if even now she would betray him.

He loved her; in his heart, he knew it. But he dared not trust her, and there lay the barrier between them. Nor could he forget what had once befallen him in the name of love.

Later in June he rode home from London with Roger, Rollo, Richard, and Steven. The day was beautiful and bright. Robins sang tunefully, and the trill of a thousand insects rose with the soft bubbling of a nearby brook. The burned-out villages they passed were being rebuilt. Fall and winter had truly brought death to England, Alaric thought. Now spring and summer were bringing life.

"I don't see how he can do it."

Alaric straightened, aware that Roger's loud comment to Rollo had been voiced for his benefit.

" 'Tis difficult, isn't it?" Rollo replied. "You would think that he'd wish to change the trend now, eh?"

Alaric stopped his horse and turned to the two of them.

His mood was ragged, for he longed to sleep beside Fallon again, yet it was difficult to hold her without wanting her. The babe was big now, and he loved to touch her belly and feel the movement and speculate about what angle formed what part of the body. He was glad to hold her, to smooth his fingers over her breasts, glad to hold her close. But the dilemma did little for his mood.

"If you must talk, talk. What is it now?"

"Now?" Roger asked innocently. "It is nothing now, nothing that has not been the same these many months."

Alaric stared at Rollo. "What the hell is he talking about?"

"Nothing. Except that you are indeed behaving crudely. Quite the barbarian the Saxons deem a Norman to be."

His temper was now fully ruffled. "I am a most merciful man."

"Merciful! Did you hear that, Richard?"

"Richard!" Alaric roared, staring at his young squire. "What is this? You talk behind my back, lad?"

"Nay—"

"Aye, he does!" Roger claimed boldly. "Alaric, you've borne the stain of bastardy all your life, and you would do it to your first begotten son, to your heir! Once you wed a maid who could not believe in love. Now this one—who could have never been tamed by any hatred or force—has fallen to the very tenderness she feels for you. Yet you let her suffer for what another has done to you!"

"She does not suffer!"

"She does!"

"I doubt if she would wed me!"

Rollo burst into laughter. "Why, he is afraid. This great lusty fellow, the greatest sword arm in Europe, is afraid."

"Oh, the hell with both of you!" Alaric groaned.

"You haven't any time left!" Roger bellowed.

Alaric turned and started to ride. He urged Satan to a gallop and the others fell in behind him.

They soon reached Haselford. Dismounting, Alaric felt a stifling fear grip him, for there were horses in the courtyard. He left Satan there with a pat on the rump and hurried up the steps to the manor.

To his surprise, he found Father Damien in the hall, drinking ale with Falstaff.

"Father," Alaric stated, staring intently at the priest as he stripped off his gauntlets. "What is wrong?"

The priest rose and took the hand offered to him. "Nothing is wrong. I came because I felt you might need me."

Falstaff stood and pounded Alaric on the back. "But he's come too late, eh? The priest has come too late."

"What are you talking about?" Alaric demanded.

Roger, Rollo, and the squires came into the hall. Falstaff started to answer, but just then Edith appeared at the top of the stairs. She smiled absently at Alaric and called down to Falstaff. "Tell Magalie that I need her now, please. The water has broken, and we must change the bed." She smiled at Alaric again. "The babe is coming."

He could not stand. His knees buckled and Roger was quick to shove a chair beneath him. But he found his composure quickly, and rose with new strength, glaring at Roger. He clenched his teeth hard and searched out the farthest corners of his heart. He strode on only slightly unsteady legs to the table, poured wine into a chalice, and swallowed it down. Strange. He had thought he had so much time. Stranger still, he had thought he knew his heart and his mind.

He firmly set the chalice back on the table. "Father Damien, I do need you."

Roger laughed. "Alaric, you are too late."

"I think not," Father Damien said, his eyes sparkling. "Babes do take some time to enter the world."

Magalie came out of the kitchen and hurried through the room with an armful of clean linen. Alaric stopped her. "Magalie, tell Fallon that I have come home and will be with her shortly."

Magalie bobbed a curtsy to him. "Aye, my lord," she said warily, as if she was not at all sure that Fallon would be glad of the information. She hurried on up the stairs.

Even in the summer's balmy warmth, Fallon shivered as her mother put a clean gown over her head. Magalie, with Mildred and Jeanne's help, quickly stripped the bed and put clean, dry sheets on it. Almost as soon as Edith helped her daughter back into bed, Fallon bit back another scream, doubling over. The pain was ungodly.

It had begun that morning, so subtly as to be deceptive, so slowly she thought that she imagined it.

But it grew viciously, winding around her lower back and spine like a steel clamp, constricting her belly.

It seemed that now there was scarce any time between the knifelike stabs of pain. She had never imagined pain like this.

"Breathe deeply," Edith advised her, squeezing her hand.

She tried to breathe. She squeezed her eyes closed and prayed for the pain to go away. She choked back a scream at the sheer agony of it, and when it left her at last, she lay back, panting, sweat-soaked, and exhausted. "Mother!" she cried softly. "I cannot bear this, I cannot go through with it."

" 'Tis late now to talk so!" Edith laughed, cooling her forehead with a cloth.

"Never again," Fallon vowed. "How did you bear so many of us? I swear I shall join a nunnery!"

The three women laughed, and Fallon swore, then screamed as another pain racked her. Magalie looked at Edith and nodded. When the pain ebbed she examined

Fallon and spoke to her cheerfully in broken English. "Soon, *mademoiselle*, you push. Very soon. Yes?"

Very soon. She wanted to die. Tears stung her eyes. She—who was supposed to be so courageous—was not doing well at all. She was soaked with perspiration and she felt as if she were being drawn and quartered.

Once again the brutal pain seized her. "Oh!" she cried when it was done. "May they all rot in hell, every rutting male of every nation!"

"Oh!" Magalie exclaimed. "The count comes!"

She remembered her message just as the footsteps paused outside the doorway. Fallon stared at her mother in pure alarm. "Don't let him in, Mother, please! Stop him!" she demanded frantically.

Edith shushed her daughter's frantic words. "I'll speak with him," she assured Fallon. But Alaric did not ask to enter, he just entered, and to Fallon's further dismay, he wasn't alone. Father Damien followed behind him.

"Oh! Oh, dear God!" Fallon screamed, trying to adjust her gown, desperate to maintain a semblance of dignity. "Damn you, Alaric, get out of here!"

He ignored her and strode to her side, then sat beside her and took her hand.

"Damn you!" she said again, but pain tightened around her and she twisted her face to one side, clenching her teeth. Why had no one warned her that it would hurt so badly to bring forth life?

When the pain ebbed, she was shaking and wet, and in anguish. "Please, for the love of God, will you leave me!" she begged him.

He touched her brow and held her hand tightly. When a spasm seized her again, she barely waited for it to fade to rail against him. "I hate you!"

Worried, he glanced at Edith, who shrugged. "She won't remember what she says."

"I *will* remember!" Fallon flared.

"Perhaps we had best hurry," Father Damien said from the doorway. In a haze of pain, Fallon realized that he was still standing there like a tall black bird.

She moistened her dry lips. "Hurry for what?"

"We're going to be married," Alaric said.

"Nay!" She tried to sit up, but the pain was too great. "Nay, you clod!" She was dangerously close to tears. He looked so handsome to her there, dark hair falling over his brow, his eyes dark and worried. Yet she wanted to tear him limb from limb, for surely this was all his fault.

"I'll not marry you!" she snapped stubbornly, close to hysterics. "You've had months and months to marry me, and now you're too damn late. I won't do it! Oh! Oh, God! Please let this stop!"

Her eyes watered again, the pains were coming so strong and so quick.

"I'm afraid that I didn't trust you," Alaric told her.

"And what is different now?"

"I have decided to take my chances," he told her with a tender smile. "Squeeze my hand."

"I will not—"

"Fallon, now!" he thundered. He wasn't going to leave. He would give her no peace. When she squeezed his hand with all her strength, he held tight. After the horrible pain left her, she was dazed with it.

"Marry me," he insisted quietly.

"I can't marry you. I hate you. I intend to join a nunnery, and I will love no man again."

"Fallon!" Edith said sharply. "He is the father of your babe, and you've just minutes left. Oh, let the poor babe be legitimate!"

Alaric's eyes bored into hers, silver and steel and commanding. "Now, Fallon."

She lay silent, and he nodded to Father Damien. The priest spoke the words of the marriage rite, and Alaric stated his vow with no hesitation. When she paused, he

squeezed her hand fiercely. "Aye!" she cried. "Aye . . ."
And she repeated after Father Damien, word for word,
the promises he demanded of her. To love, cherish—and
obey.

By the time it was over, she was in a sorry state, for the
pain never abated. She was scarcely aware when Father
Damien brought her vellum and a quill, and as she signed
the certificate she hardly knew what she did. The urge to
push was upon her so strongly that she could not restrain
herself, even when Magalie insisted that she wait. Edith
ushered Alaric and Damien from the room.

Fallon burned, as if she had been torn apart, split
asunder.

Then Magalie said that she might push, and push
again. The babe came gushing from her body. When
Fallon heard his first cry, the pain was all suddenly,
miraculously, lost in joy.

"My baby!" she sobbed. "Mother, is it a boy? Is he all
right? Is he fine? Is he healthy?"

Magalie cut the cord and reminded Fallon to push
again to expel the afterbirth. Fallon tried to obey her, but
she thought no more of pain as her mother reached for a
boiled cloth and cleaned his little face.

Then she pressed him into Fallon's arms. "Aye! It is a
boy. And perfect in every way! Ah, love, he is a fine big
lad with a full thick thatch of hair!"

She laughed and sobbed, hearing her mother's words,
trembling as she held the squalling infant. He was beautiful. His face was screwed up in a fit of temper greater than
any of her own, yet he was completely perfect and beautiful. She counted his fingers and his toes, thanking God in
a weak silence as she pressed a quick kiss against his belly.

"Let him suckle; it will bring in your milk," her mother
advised her.

She held the babe to her breast, and when he latched
on to it euphoria swept through her. He suckled hard and

tugged, and a tiny fist beat against her; Fallon laughed and cried. She had no memory of the anguish; all that she knew was her encompassing love for her infant son and for the abounding beauty of life.

At last he released her nipple with a little popping sound that made her laugh again. "I'll take him and bathe him," Edith said, "Magalie will help you wash, and then you must sleep."

Sighing in a deep, sweet contentment unlike anything she had ever known, Fallon lay back, closed her eyes, and smiled as she listened to her mother and Mildred gush over the baby. She felt Magalie's soothing hands on her. The sheets were stripped from beneath her, and Magalie helped her bathe and dress.

"Mother, once again!" Fallon called softly, when she was cleaned and dressed anew and her bed was white and fresh. Edith brought the babe. He, too, had been bathed, and he was more beautiful than ever. He opened his eyes and looked at her, gurgling out a small noise. She had never known love as sweet as that which thrilled through her. Then his eyes closed, and he slept.

Edith gently took him from her side. She kissed Fallon on the forehead. "Go to sleep. I'll take him to his father."

Fallon started to close her eyes. The exhaustion was overwhelming. It had been hours and hours since the pains had first begun to tear into her. She was so very weary; she could not wait to sleep, and sleep deeply.

She bolted up, staring after Edith. "Mother!"

"What, love?"

"My, God! Was that real? Did we—am I—"

"Married?" Edith laughed with delight. "Aye, my daughter. Your son is legal issue, his father's heir. And you, daughter, are now most legal, too. The Countess of Anlou."

Chapter Twenty-Eight

When Fallon awoke, the world was bright. She smiled even before she opened her eyes, for she heard her son let out a lusty cry, and her body responded instantly. Her breasts filled and throbbed, and she pushed herself up from her pillow, eager to reach for the new joy of her life.

She was startled to discover that he lay naked at the foot of the bed, and that Alaric sat there, too, exploring every inch of the infant's body, counting fingers and toes as she had done herself. The babe had now decided to protest his father's examination.

Alaric glanced her way, and she warmed to the silver laughter in his eyes. She wished that she had a comb, and she wished that she might have washed, but she was glad at least that she had donned a soft clean gown. Surely, she must be in better repair today than she had been last night. He looked so good this morning, she thought wistfully. He wore cool linen against the summer heat, and a short doeskin tunic. He was ruggedly handsome, and younger than she was accustomed to thinking him. Perhaps it was his easy, tender smile. Perhaps it was the brilliant silver in his eyes.

"I think he wants his mother," Alaric said, and wrapping him in his swaddling, he lifted the baby carefully and handed him to Fallon. He was squalling loudly by then.

Fallon leaned back to allow the baby to root against her breast. She was stunned by the pleasure she felt again when he latched on to her hungrily, and she was entranced by the eyes that met her own in soft wonder. They were blue, like the morning sky over the English countryside.

She kissed the top of his head; then her eyes wandered dreamily to Alaric's. "Do you like him?" she whispered softly.

"Like him?" Alaric queried. "He is the greatest gift I have ever received."

She smiled, and he was touched by the softness and innocence in her eyes. He had never seen her so gentle, so peaceful, so very beautiful. Her hair streamed about her soft and delicate face like black magic, and her cheeks and lips were the color of a pink rose. "He is beautiful," she said. "Exceptionally beautiful, isn't he? He is not wizened, and his color is perfect."

Alaric's lips curled in a half-smile, which he tried to suppress. "Aye, he is perfect."

It seemed that she might say more, but then she became entranced with the babe all over again. He moved closer to her and gently ran his fingers over his son's cheek and then over hers. She gazed at him again, a sweet, serene smile on her lips.

"I have something for you," he said softly. He produced a small coffer from the foot of the bed. " 'Tis a morning-after gift."

She smiled, for such a gift was a Danish custom made English, and it was not given for the birth of a child, but handed from a husband to a wife after their wedding night, if she had pleased him.

"You surely owe me no gift," she murmured.

He shrugged and grinned at her ruefully. "Well, perhaps the night came first, love, and the wedding later."

"Did we really wed?"

"Aye, Fallon."

Her lashes swept over her eyes and she pressed her trembling lips against the babe's soft curling hair. "Why, Alaric?" she asked softly. "For our son?"

"Nay, not that alone," he answered slowly. "For our lives, Fallon. For a future here. For a peace that I crave between us. Do you mind it so much? Being wed to the enemy?"

Fallon shook her head, unable to look his way. He laughed suddenly. "Well, then, I'm glad. Last night you hated and loathed me, and were most fiercely determined to join a nunnery."

"Was I?" Fallon laughed.

"Aye, don't you remember?"

"Very little," Fallon admitted.

"Then you really don't hate me so terribly?"

"Nay. I do not hate you."

He was quiet for a moment, then said, "I have given you title to the land, in your name alone, on the spit of land where your father and Edith lived together. It was mine to give through William. Now you own it directly of the king, and none can take it from you. I know it was your father's, and perhaps you feel that I give you something that was yours to begin with, but now I have done this legally. I thought of jewels, and I thought of gowns, and yet I could think of nothing that a man could hold in his two hands or purchase with any coin that could mean as much to you as the land that belonged to those you love, and so . . . I hope my gift pleases you. The deeds are in the coffer."

She stared at him, touched and amazed. Tears of sheer happiness glazed her eyes, and it was on the tip of her tongue to whisper that she loved him—that she had loved him perhaps forever. But she swallowed back her words, for despite everything that he had done for her, he had yet to whisper the same words to her, even in the height of passion. She was his wife now, she reminded herself, and a sweet warmth filled her. But still, he held something back from her, and she did not know if it was his distant past that plagued him or his more recent past with her.

"Thank you," she told him in a whisper. "Thank you, Alaric. There is nothing you could have done to please me more."

She bit her lip, curiously close to tears. Suddenly the babe emitted a loud belching sound, which provoked them both to laughter. Fallon picked him up just a bit awkwardly and held him against her shoulder, where he fell asleep. Alaric carried him to the ancient cradle Hamlin had brought from the barn, he wrapped him carefully, and set him down gently. Then he came back to Fallon's side. She stared up at him, sleepy and peaceful and still beautifully serene and tender. He kissed her fingers, then her forehead, and then her lips.

She touched his cheek, content, and dreamy. "What shall we call him?" She asked.

He hesitated a moment. "I don't think it would be wise to name him for your father, and I'm sorry, for I'm sure you would like to do so."

Fallon shook her head. "I do not want some vengeful kin of William's to harm him at some later date for bearing his grandsire's name!"

"Fallon, William bears you no malice—"

She did not wish to fight about William. "I had thought of Robert, for my mother's father," she said. "Perhaps we could call him Robin while he's a lad."

"Then Robert he is, and Robin as he grows."

She smiled at him shyly, feeling a perfect love, and a perfect peace. His eyes remained dazzling and bright as he stared at her. She dared to slip her arms around his neck and pull him down to her, and they shared a sweet and binding kiss. A knock at the door interrupted them, and they moved apart. The door opened, and Edith led Father Damien into the room.

He grinned at Fallon. "I had a wish to see the babe. A boy, I believe."

"Aye, a boy," Fallon told him.

The babe was staring at the priest and gurgling, and Fallon gave Damien leave to pick him up. While the priest held and blessed the infant, Edith told Alaric that he was needed in the hall. The door closed behind her mother and Alaric, and Fallon discovered herself alone with Father Damien.

"He is a fine and beautiful lad," he told Fallon, returning the babe to his cradle. "He will rival his father in size, and in him the might of Normandy will be combined with the ancient wisdom of Saxon England. He is the first of a new breed, Fallon, and he will bring mercy and justice to this land."

She swallowed, watching him. She wanted to know the future, and yet she was afraid to hear of it.

"The green tree," she murmured, "growing together of its own accord. The devils and demons and fire came, as Edward the Confessor said they would. The comet, they said, foreshadowed doom for my father, and he died. Tell me, Father, will this child bring us peace?"

He hesitated a long time. "My lady, peace does not come immediately after the violence of war. Peace is not a shout, but a whisper, and when the tempest is past, peace must come slowly to the land." He sighed. "Peace, for England, will be a long and hurtful time in coming, but it has begun. Cultures meet and clash; good men, who believe in God, still die. But you must not give up on peace, Fallon. It comes between individuals first, between men and women, as they seek to touch, and to understand." He bowed low to her and left the room.

Fallon lay back, watching Robin in his cradle. His eyes were closed; he slept again. For long moments she thought of nothing except how fiercely she loved him. Then she brooded over Father Damien's words, and a certain desolation settled over her. There was sure to be more warfare. She had not heard from her brothers, there were still Scandinavian kings and princes to make claims, and while Edgar the Atheling lived, men would rise to his cause. And as long as some part of England lay wasted and bleeding, she would bleed, too.

She might love Alaric; she might be his wife. But what real peace could there be for the two of them?

Robin was baptized that afternoon, before Fallon was able to rise. She was startled to learn that William and Matilda had insisted on being godparents to the boy, but since she was thoroughly convinced that no one was going to wrest England from William's hands, she offered no protest. Hamlin and his daughter Jeanne stood in as proxy for the absent godparents, and Edith assured Fallon that Robin had been solemnly and dutifully christened— and that the ceremony had been performed completely in English. She smiled at that assurance and eagerly took her son back into her arms. She took great pride in him, for he wasn't a day old, and still he stared at her with such bright and curious eyes, and when he let forth a squall, he did so with a vengeance.

Holding him, Fallon heard the sounds of revelry down in the hall, and she knew that they feasted ere Father Damien should leave them to return to Normandy, as he had promised. Someone played the lute, and hearty laughter came to her up the stairs. She smiled, for Mildred sat with her and the babe, and she knew that her mother was down there, that the knights—Roger Beauclare and Falstaff and Rollo—were there, too, and some of Alaric's other Norman vassals, as well as Hamlin and Heath and Richard. She knew that much of England still lay in shambles, and many Englishmen lived in penury. Norman castles were springing up across the land, not in fear of an enemy from without, but to protect the new Norman landlords from the hostility of the people they had defeated.

But here at Haselford, no man made a slave of his neighbor. Alaric had taken ownership of the land; but his cotters were free men. Here knight and scrubmaid alike lived in dignity.

Perhaps she could not change the fate of England. Yet here she and Alaric could create the magical world they had once spoken of, where pain and terror and tragedy should be gone forever.

She closed her eyes and drifted off to sleep. Later, when the fire had died low, she awakened again to the sound of her son's insistent cries. Just as she opened her eyes, the babe ceased to cry; there in the darkness stood Alaric with Robin in his arms.

"He has his mother's temper, I think," Alaric commented.

Fallon retrieved the babe from his father's arms. She settled him at her breast, smiled, and retorted, "I think the temper is his father's!"

"Nay, lady. I am calm. You are the vixen. His temper is English—his *reserve* is Norman." He kissed her forehead. "I'll call your mother to sit with you," he murmured.

"Must you?" She whispered.

"Aye, I must, Fallon. Robin is scarce a day old, and you should not rise so soon."

A dryness constricted her throat. She caught his hand. "Please, Alaric, stay with me."

"Fallon, I should not. You need rest. I fear that I will disturb you."

She paused, suddenly afraid to show emotion. But the darkness shielded her, and she spoke softly. "My lord, please do not leave me. I am disturbed when you are not with me, and I am at peace when you lie beside me."

He paused a long moment, then kissed her forehead again.

And in the shadows and darkness, she heard him disrobe. He crawled into the bed beside her, and while Robin nursed, he tenderly held her.

Fallon fell asleep first. Alaric took Robin from her side. Father surveyed son, and son surveyed father gravely. "I believe those are English eyes, my fine fellow," Alaric told his son. He placed the babe back in his cradle. "I wish you could have met your grandsire," he said softly. "They will revile him in things that they will write. We will have to justify what we have done here. William's historians will say that Harold seized the throne, that he was an opportunist, that he lied and broke his oath to William. But I tell you, Robin, he was brave and strong and more. He was wise, and he loved learning and the law. It was some greater force that destined this state of affairs. And you, my son, are part of this destiny. I pray that you understand it all one day."

Robin stared at him, and his eyelids grew heavy. Soon he was asleep, and Alaric returned to Fallon's side and slipped his arms around her gently.

Soon he, too, slept.

Fallon lived the first two weeks of her son's birth in a cocoon of happiness. Edith stayed with her and together they enjoyed the baby.

On her first night back at the table in the hall after Robin's birth, each and every one of Alaric's knights gallantly hailed her. Alaric watched with a tender smile, then led her with true pomp and chivalry to ·her place beside him. Once Fallon had believed that it would be a dishonor to her father to marry Alaric. But now she was deeply glad, and watching him with a mischievous smile, she was suddenly startled by his curious expression.

"What are thinking, minx?" He demanded.

"On the night before the battle at Hastings, my father told me to come to you," she admitted. "But I had too much pride to do it. Think of the heartache we might have saved had I but done so!"

He watched her for a moment and then gently kissed her fingers. "Fallon, had you come to me begging refuge in your father's name, I'd have been honor bound to see that no man claimed you, including myself, and we'd not have Robin now."

She smiled and lowered her head. He caught her chin and raised it, and the sparkling beauty of her eyes and the curl of lip gave him a heady pause. He dared not touch her yet, and still the whole of him knotted into a quiver of desire.

"You're laughing at me!" he challenged.

"Nay! I am laughing at myself. I was thinking that I'd have missed much more, besides my son."

"Don't look at me so, wife," he begged her softly. "For our time has not yet come."

She colored and reached for the chalice. Her fingers twined around his, and she flushed with countless memories, and then together they laughed. He quickly gave the chalice to her, and drank when she was done.

Their sweet idyll was doomed to end. In the morning a messenger came from William. There was an open revolt in the west where certain thanes had joined with a few Welsh princes. Alaric was ordered to subdue the rebels.

As soon as Fallon heard the message, she swirled about in a sudden flurry. "You cannot go!" she told Alaric.

His knights turned to stare at him; the messenger's brows rose. Alaric clenched his teeth. "Roger, ready the men to ride."

In silence, Fallon squared her shoulders, then turned and started for the stairs.

"Fallon!" he called. She ignored him, and he swore in anger, ordering Falstaff to see to the comfort of the messenger before he raced after his wife.

She sat by the fire with Robin in her arms.

"*Madame*, I do try to curb my temper, and I have tried in every way to treat you with all honor. Fallon, I have made you my wife! I have sought peace! But dear God, lady, when will it end? When will this battle cease to rage between us?"

She shook her head, and he saw tears in her eyes. "When you cease to fight the English!" she said, and a sob caught in her throat. She stood suddenly whirling around with the baby in her arms. "You have come, you have conquered! Yet it is not over! You will ride again and again and again, and I will never have peace. Each time I will sit here and wonder if my brothers are among the men you will fight, if you will slay them, if they will slay you! Nay, Alaric! We fool ourselves when we dream of peace! There can be no peace between us!"

Robin began to cry. Alaric stared at her in a cold fury. "Then so be it!" he said. He swung around, and then he was gone. The door slammed in his wake.

She felt its echo, and she trembled. He was going to fight again, and she had sent him away in anger. Absently, she tried to soothe Robin. Then she put the baby in his cradle and ran quickly after Alaric.

She was too late. The men were just riding away when she reached the foot of the stairs.

For the next few weeks, Fallon alternated between sweet pleasure in her son and fear for her husband. She prayed that he was not fighting her brothers. She did not realize that her mother was also terribly worried until the morning that Roger Beauclare rode into the village alone.

Fallon was in her chamber with Robin when she heard that Roger had ridden in, weary and battle-grimed. She put the baby down so quickly that he howled in protest. Pressing a kiss on his forehead, she ran down as quickly as she could. Roger, casting aside his helmet and accepting a chalice of wine from Hamlin, stared into her tormented eyes.

"Roger! Oh, please, Roger, what has happened? Has Alaric—Oh, God, Roger! Why are you alone?"

"What? Oh, Fallon, I am sorry. I had no idea that you had heard nothing! Alaric is very well. And I am happy to assure you that your brothers were not involved in the fighting. I came ahead to tell you that Alaric will quickly return. The Welsh princes have run back to their borders, and the land is safe in our hands again. Alaric has stayed only to restore order and see to the people."

"Oh!" Fallon breathed happily. She heard a sound and turned, and saw that her mother had fallen to the floor in a dead faint.

Roger was quickly at her side, and together they lifted Edith and pressed a cup of wine to her lips. She came to and smiled at them. "Thank God!" she whispered. Fallon had not been aware of her mother's anxiety. Now she knew that they both desperately feared the day when Galen, Aelfyn, or Tam would fall to a Norman sword. What hope had they for peace?

But despite her fears, Fallon was keenly anxious for Alaric's return. Robin was a healthy six weeks old. She felt her own health and youth and burning vitality, and she longed desperately to be held again in Alaric's arms, held like a lover.

It was August, and the land was fragrant and warm. One morning Fallon took Mildred with her to the stream that joined eventually to the river. There, in the sunlight and the flowers, she decided to wash her hair and let it dry with the clean and fragrant scent of the day. Mildred would guard her from passersby, and Roger Beauclare would watch from the road.

She wondered at herself as the water bubbled and rushed about her, over the pebbles and the stones in the brook. She could remember longing to escape Alaric's touch, but now she trembled in sweetest anticipation of it, longing for him to return to her. Robin had been fed, and her mother stayed with him, so she dared to take her leisure, soaping her hair and her body, luxuriating in the feel of the cold water rushing over her body. The sun was hot and high, and when she lifted her hair to it, she felt a blazing sensuality. She wondered when he would come, and she planned what she would wear. She tried to form words to whisper, to let him know that she loved him. Telling him of her love would not be easy, she knew.

If he came by night, she thought, she would greet him in the hall. She would dress in white, and she would speak softly and as sweetly as any man could desire. Hamlin had ready a deer that Roger had brought down in the forest that morning, and Roger had been through their stock with her and selected a cask of wine from the south of France of which Alaric was especially fond.

It had been so long. Yet she promised herself, she would make his homecoming very sweet. She would love, honor, obey—and seduce him, she thought with a little grin.

Fallon hoped that someday, too, her brothers would lay down their arms and embrace the peace that she had forced herself to accept. From time to time, she knew, she would probably hear tales of their derring-do, or stories of mysterious skirmishes in the night, brave Saxon battling the Normans still. But she hoped fervently that soon she would learn that they wished to build a new England from the ashes of battle.

A twig snapped and she ceased her dreaming to turn curiously. "Mildred?"

But Mildred was not with her anymore. She started to call out, but the words froze in her throat, for Alaric sat astride Satan, his head bare and his dark hair gleaming in the sun. He was clad still in his mail and a golden tunic, and he seemed as indomitable as the sun in the noonday sky. His eyes, a dark and serious gray, traveled slowly over her; she had risen, stood before him naked, with her hair a sodden black cloak around her and cold water sluicing from her body. "Alaric!" she whispered, and she thought with dismay and a sudden shyness that her plans for sweet seduction had gone awry. But what he saw there was the sweetest seduction ever. Bluebirds sang and the air was fragrant with flowers and warm with the sun.

She was more beautiful than he had remembered in his long days and nights of battle and conquest. She was something pagan and wanton, rising from the stream, her breasts taut, full globes kissed by water droplets, gleaming and tempting. Her waist was slim again, her limbs so long. She was a sprite, arisen from the water, a witch who walked the earth to steal his spirit and his soul.

He dismounted and, paying no heed to the water that swirled around his boots, strode through the brook until he reached her, and then he pulled her hard into his hands. Her lips parted beneath his, her tongue slipped into his mouth like a sweet blade of fire to duel with his own. A soft groan escaped her, and she melted against him.

He kissed her and released her, whispering urgently as he ran his hands over her in a desperate fever. He led her back to the shore and lay down beside her, spreading her hair against the earth and burning inside at the slow, welcoming smile that blossomed on her lips and sizzled like magic in her eyes. "Your mail," she whispered, and he looked down at the imprints it had made in her flesh;

he flung it aside with hasty abandon. Soon he was as naked as she, but she caught his shoulders with sudden alarm when he came down beside her again. "Mildred! And Roger. Neither of them—"

"I sent them home when I came down the road," he assured her, smiling. "No one is anywhere nearby."

"I didn't hear you approach."

"I know. I whispered to Mildred and Roger. I wanted to watch you."

"Oh, Alaric—"

"Hush . . ." His lips met hers hungrily. She surged against him in raw and savage delight, moaning softly at his every caress, touching him with wild abandon. Still, no matter how she twisted and held him, no matter what pulsing fires raged within him, he loved her slow and tenderly. She cried out his name in frustration, but he nipped her earlobe and reminded her softly that it was the first time since the babe had been born, and that he must take care.

"But I need you," she murmured.

"Desperately?"

"Aye."

"How desperately?"

"So desperately . . ."

He held her eyes with his own, and she loved the teasing smile that came to his lips, young and boyish. "And I am desperate for you. See how desperate." He pressed her hand against him, but still he would not take her. He kissed her throat and her breasts, flicking his tongue against her flesh mercilessly. He touched her where each water droplet fell, and he made love to her until he felt her body flood with warmth and liquid, and then, only then, did he cry out with his own need and bury himself within her.

Nothing in life had ever been so good, so sweet, so very right, Fallon thought later, as she lay staring up at the sun.

His arm still fell across her naked breasts, his leg was atop hers, and his breath fanned her cheek. Birds still sang, the breeze was cool, and somewhere nearby Satan grazed on tufts of rich grass.

She turned in to Alaric's arms. She stared into his eyes and caressed his cheek. "I am so very grateful that you have come home, alive and well."

He accepted that in silence for a moment, then asked her, "Why?"

"Why?" She frowned. "Because . . . you are my husband. Because you are Robin's father. Because——"

"Tell me, Fallon, do you think perhaps you love me?"

His smile was rueful, and she returned it. "Tell me, Alaric, do you think perhaps you love me?"

He started to laugh, then straddled her. Aye! The word sang on her lips, and she wanted to shout to the world that she loved him. He was her husband now and the father of her babe, and damn the world, but she loved him.

Yet even as she smiled in her sweet desire to tell him so, a scream welled inside her. There was sudden, swift movement behind them.

Her scream rent the air, but too late. As Alaric turned, the heavy oak butt of a battle-ax came crashing down on his skull.

Chapter Twenty=Nine

For the longest time all she could hear was the sound of her own scream, ricocheting around her.

Then she heard the thud as Alaric's body fell to the earth by her side, and she stared up with horror and disbelief into the berserker eyes of Eric Ulfson.

"I promised that I would come for you, Fallon. I have done so," he told her. Then he fell to his knees before her, and she realized that he meant to take her right there by the stream, by her husband's body. And if he did, she thought, she would surely die, for she could take no more. She threw back her head and screamed again in terror. Half a dozen Vikings instantly appeared. Dazed, she understood some of their words, and she knew that they were warning Eric not to tarry.

Eric stood, and Fallon tried to crawl to Alaric, but the Viking caught her by the hair and dragged her to her feet. She was too numb to care that she stood naked before him and his men.

She was too despairing even to care that they might all rape her. In those first few minutes she cared for nothing at all. If Alaric lay dead, then she would gladly die, too.

"Come, Fallon." Someone brought Eric a mantle, and he swept it around her. She threw back her head to scream again, and he did not even try to stop her. "Your lover's men are far behind—he rode ahead in his hurry to reach you. You disarmed him well for me, Princess. We will make a fine pair."

She shook her head, still disbelieving. "Nay, nay. Let me go to Alaric! He is my husband now. I have married him. William holds England; there is nothing that anyone can do—"

"You will not go to him," Eric said. "William holds England; I hold you. Svein, cleave the bastard's head from his body, and we'll be on our way."

"Nay!" she shrieked. "Touch him and I will fight you with the last breath in my body, I swear it! I will kill you, Eric, or I will kill myself!"

Eric stared into her eyes and seemed to believe the violence in them. He shrugged. "I strike well. He is probably dead now. Leave him whole, then, for the carrion crows." He looked past her to another of his men. "Did you take her brat?"

The man shook his head. Eric went livid. "I ordered you—"

"The woman escaped with the boy into the forests. We hadn't the time to follow her."

Bless her mother! Fallon thought. She had saved Robin.

But then despair filled her again. She couldn't bear any more. If Alaric was dead, she wasn't even sure that she would want to keep living for her son's sake.

With a savage oath, Eric pushed her toward his men. She grasped the mantle against her, stumbling.

"Get her on a horse," the Viking said flatly.

The men caught her arms, and she did not resist. There was the hope that Alaric lived, and she needed to lead them away from him before someone did take a blade against him.

She was set upon a small English pony; Fallon assumed that they had come ashore in their Viking boats and raided a village for the animals they rode. Eric came up beside her and took the reins to her mount. "I've admired you for a long time, Fallon, Harold's daughter. I have admired your spirit, and your ability to fight. And I know that you will run if I do not stop you."

She tossed her hair back and prayed that Alaric lived. "I will run, Eric."

"We have a pact."

"We have no pact. William is king of England. You have done nothing. I owe you nothing."

"I have come a-Viking, Harold's daughter. I care not for pacts or for England or for anything else. I wanted you, I have taken you. England may rot beneath the Norman, and I care not. I am taking you with me to the kingdom I have claimed in the Scottish islands, and you will learn to love and obey me there, and you will bear fine strong Viking sons!"

"No!" she whispered. His hands on her pony's reins were slack. She slammed her knee against the beast's flanks, and the animal reared and plunged. She leaned against its neck, and prepared to ride.

But one of Eric's men veered forward, cutting her off. The pony reared again, and this time she was thrown. Dazed, she could not move when Eric strode before her and stood staring down at her. "You will learn to love me," he assured her. He lifted her in his arms and cruelly tossed her over his own horse, then mounted behind her.

From which village had they stolen the horses? she wondered. And as they passed through the woods near the manor, she tried to twist her head to see. There was no smell of smoke from Haselford, so they had not burned the thatch and wattle cottages, nor had they burned the manor. But Eric's man had said her mother had taken Robin into the forest, and so she knew they had been to the manor house. They must have come in by the coast and raided some village there.

She swallowed down her misery and thought that she really wanted to die. But then she imagined that she heard Robin's cry, and in response her breasts became engorged and ached. Her heart cried out for her son, and in silence she prayed that William would honor his duties as godfather and care for the boy.

Fallon prayed that Alaric would live. She begged and bargained with God. She had lost so much already—her father, her uncles, her family, her country. Not . . .

Alaric, too! Not her infant son!

Hanging miserably over the horse, Fallon realized that if Alaric did live, he would surely despise her now. He had seen her with Eric once, and now he would surely damn her a thousand times over for seducing him to destruction.

Alaric awoke to thunderous pain that seemed to bind his head like a band of steel. He blinked and tried to focus.

"He lives! He is back with us!"

Faces swam before him. Then he saw Roger and Falstaff staring down at him. A cool cloth moved over his head, and he looked to his left, wincing at the pain that slashed through him at the movement. A pair of concerned blue eyes stared down at him, and through the fog of his vision, he thought for a moment that it was Fallon.

But it was not, of course. It was Edith.

He exhaled, and it all came back to him. It was the berserker, Eric Ulfson, who had looked down at him in twisted vengeance, swinging his ax.

When he had lain with Fallon, when he lain with his wife, the Viking had come up behind him and—

"Damn her!" he swore savagely.

He tried to sit up; his mantle fell from his shoulders, and he realized that he was still naked beneath it. He swallowed down his pain and shook his head, and his vision cleared. He stared at Roger and then at Hamlin, and he realized that he was in the hall. It had been torn apart. No tapestries lined the walls, chairs were tossed hither and yon, and broken trunks and discarded linen lay everywhere.

"Ulfson came here?" he rasped out.

Roger nodded. He helped Alaric to sip cool water. "They were here when I came back. I saw them while I was still in the shelter of the trees. I heard the men riding behind me, and so we thought to surprise them, but they had slipped out back."

"We thought it a random raid," Hamlin told him, "and so we all took to the forests. We have been savagely looted, but no one of us died."

"Robin!" Alaric screamed out harshly, paralyzed by the fear that flooded through him.

But at his words, the babe began to cry. He pushed himself to his feet, and the warm, living bundle of his son was placed in his arms. He looked at Edith, whose blue eyes were red-rimmed with tears.

She had read his mind, and she stared at him with reproach. "You have to go for her, Alaric! You have to find Fallon, and you have to bring her home."

Robin was howling with a ragged fury then, his face red. Alaric touched his cheek and the baby tried to root onto his finger. "Find a woman in the village to nurse him," he said quietly, handing his son back to Edith.

Fear froze her features. "Alaric, you must go for her! You must!"

"She betrayed me again!" he snapped.

Edith seemed to crumble and break. She sagged against the wall, hugging the baby to her.

Alaric swore. "I am going after her, Edith. I am going after her because she is Robin's mother, and because she is my wife. Edith!" He caught her shoulders and shook them. "Edith, stop crying! Tend to the babe. I will bring her home."

Edith nodded and turned away, leaving the hall with the baby. Alaric shook the dizziness away. "We ride again," he told Roger.

"We'll warn the knights." Roger nodded to Falstaff, and the two hurried to their task.

"You'll need wine and food for the ride," Hamlin said, and hurried toward the kitchen.

Alaric looked about, and found that they had retrieved his clothing. Still wincing against the throbbing pain in his skull, he reached for his chausses, then fell back weakly. He strained again before he realized that someone was still with him in the hall. He turned to see Richard standing there, staring at him sullenly.

"God's teeth, boy! Help me!"

Richard did not rush with his customary zeal to aid his lord. Indeed he planted his hands on his hips and stared at him in a cold fury. "You *must* ride for her, because she's Robin's mother because she's your wife. Because after dishonoring her the very night her father died in battle, you found that she was left with your child, and only when she lay in agony to bear that child did you condescend to marry her!"

"Watch your tongue," Alaric warned him, gray eyes narrowing.

"Nay, my lord, not this night! You may beat me or hurl me into a Norman dungeon or throw me to the wolves, but tonight I will speak the truth! If you ride for her, my lord, ride for her because you love her! Ride for her because she loves you."

"She betrayed me again!" Alaric roared. Then he clutched his hands to his temples. His head pounded as if it would split, and Richard was not making things any better.

"Why should she have done so? She was your wife."

"Boy, I caught her with the Viking once. You do recall it—you sent me after her!"

"And once, my lord, you sat at her father's table and called him friend," Richard said very softly. "Then you came with an army, sire, and fought savagely against him. So, my lord, if you do not intend to love her, if you cannot believe in her, then leave her to the Viking. He wants her, too. And if lust is all that either of you feels, then what is the difference between one rutting lout and another?"

Alaric drew back his hand in a seething fury, but Richard stood his ground.

Alaric's hand fell. "Rutting lout!" he muttered. "Saxon, I should cut out your tongue."

Richard hurried forward to help Alaric dress. "I have always known that you loved her, sir."

"How long a start have they on us?"

"Not an hour, my lord."

"The Vikings will head for the coast. They will be easy to follow. But we must move quickly. We must get ahead of them and cut them off on the old Roman road."

"Aye, sire!"

It was dark when Eric Ulfson called a halt. He lifted Fallon down, but she had ridden so awkwardly for so long that she fell, and he helped her up. The mantle cloaked her well, but as he carried her he ran his hands over her breasts, and the way his eager eyes fell upon her made her cringe. She had always sensed evil in Eric; now she felt it.

She clenched her teeth and struck out at him. Still laughing, he set her down before a heavy oak and left her there, then called to his men. Fallon swallowed and pulled the mantle around her and leaned her head back wearily against the tree. Her breasts burned with pain, she was so far past Robin's feeding time. Her back ached and she was thirsty and parched, and she felt truly beaten.

Alaric was dead, she thought dully. If not, he would have come for her. He would have, surely!

And yet he might not. He might be damning her this very moment, swearing that she and the Viking deserved each other. They were kin, after all, weren't they? The Norman aristocracy had been bred from the Norseman Rolf, and her grandmother had been an Ulfson. But now she was English, and Alaric was Norman . . . and he would never believe that she loved him far too much to betray him, even in her father's memory, even for her country.

"Fallon, Harold's daughter . . ."

She jerked up, chills creeping along her spine at the way Eric spoke her name. He stood before her again, and his smile was sly and lascivious. "Now," he murmured, running his tongue over his lower lip. "I will have you now."

Nay . . . Not while life remained in her. She looked about quickly and saw where the Viking's men had laid their packs and weapons. It mattered not that she hadn't held a sword for nearly a year. She was desperate, and she was determined.

She gazed at Eric weakly, then she pushed herself away from the tree trunk, lunged across the clearing, and snatched up a sword that lay against a pack of looted goods. Eric was quick behind her, but she spun with the blade pointed upward, and though he laughed softly, his blue eyes grew wary. His men jumped to his defense, but Fallon backed away from them all, waving the sword. She could not hold the mantle closed, and so she stood nearly naked in the cool night, facing them all with the blade. If she fell, it would not matter what happened to her.

Eric ordered his men away from her, then drew his own sword and raised his free hand in a challenge. "So you will fight me, Harold's daughter? You will lose, but I will enjoy the play, and then perhaps I will enjoy you more fully."

"I will thrust this blade through my own heart should it come to that."

He shook his head. "You are too strong to die, Fallon. You will give in to me because you are a fighter and you do not know how to surrender. But fight me if you will. I will give you swordplay."

He took a step toward her, swinging his broadsword hard. She parried his first blow easily, but he moved like the wind, and she found herself growing breathless as she fought. Still, she held him off. She tried to recall every word that Fabioni had ever said to her. She was thin, and Eric was heavily muscled, but she had the advantage of speed and agility, for he was bulky and quite slow. For all his strength, he had not managed to dislodge her sword from her grasp.

"Fallon, you are well worth the fight!" Eric called to her, his eyes gleaming with lust and the pleasure of the battle.

"I pray that I slay you, Eric. Then I shall happily surrender to death!"

Dancing, spinning around the fire, she took on the attack, and to her everlasting surprise and triumph, she was able to bear down on him, bring him back, force him into the trees.

But when he leapt back toward her, her flying mantle caught on a branch. Crying out, she fell hard on her back, losing her sword. It skidded against the soft earth, and landed just beyond her reach.

Eric walked toward her, his handsome face split into a cruel and savage smile. "Now you are beaten—" he began.

"And now, Ulfson, you will engage in battle against a man your own weight and size, and you will die this night."

At the sound of the deep and ringing voice, Fallon gasped and turned, and to her astonishment she saw Alaric standing behind her.

He was alive! Joy soared through her.

How had he come so silently through the trees? she wondered. Then she realized that she had been so fiercely engaged in combat that the earth could have moved without her knowing it. She remembered suddenly that she had to warn Alaric that Eric was not alone, that he had a score of men with him.

But even as the Viking went to their leader's aid, more men appeared from the woods, silent as wraiths. They stood arrayed around Alaric.

Eric Ulfson was his. She saw it in the fire in his eyes. She saw that they were meant to meet, to battle to the death.

Alaric threw back his head and let go with a fierce and furious battle cry. Eric answered the shout with his own and stepped forward. Swords clashed. Cries echoed on both sides, and Norman knights stepped in to battle the Viking host.

Someone rushed forward and grasped Fallon's shoulders. "Lady, come, into the trees, I beg of you!"

It was Richard. He helped her to her feet and wrapped the mantle tightly about her. She smiled at him weakly, then saw over his shoulder that one of Eric's men was racing toward them with a battle-ax raised high. "Richard!"

"Jesus, Mary, and Joseph, help me!" Richard shouted. He waited until the man was almost upon them; then he jumped forward with a simple hunting knife. Dodging the ax, he thrust the blade home into the attacker's heart, and the man fell.

"Oh, my God, lady, we're alive!" he said in amazement, staring down at the dead man.

"Get her out of here!" came a shout.

Fallon's head jerked up, and she saw that Alaric still battled Eric, who tried to take advantage of his momentary distraction by delivering a savage battery of blows.

"Come, Fallon!" Richard begged her.

"Nay! I cannot leave him!" she cried. "Oh, dear God!" she breathed, for suddenly it was so like Hastings. All she could hear was the terrible clang of steel, and the more awful sound of swords and axes sinking into flesh and bone.

Suddenly she screamed, for Ulfson was backing Alaric toward the trees. One of his berserkers was behind him with a battle-ax, silent and waiting.

"Nay!" she shrieked, and she rushed forward, pitting herself, weaponless, against Eric Ulfson. Surprised by the flurry of movement, he paused.

Alaric spun around, alert to the danger behind him and slew the giant berserker with a single blow to his throat.

Eric pushed Fallon savagely from him. She struck the earth hard, and the world seemed to spin and fade and be swallowed in mist.

Eric rejoined his battle with Alaric, but the end had come. Fury, soaring and deadly, swept through Alaric and he stepped forward, and brought down the death blow upon the Viking, cleaving his skull. Eric stared at Alaric in hideous surprise, then fell to the earth without a sound.

Alaric dropped his sword, for he quickly saw that his men were more numerous and quickly dispatching the few survivors of Eric Ulfson's Viking party. He dropped to one knee beside Fallon's fallen body and swept her quickly into his arms, wrapping her tenderly in the mantle. His heart beat in a painful staccato rhythm, and he thought suddenly that he could not stand it if she did not open her eyes, if she did not live.

"Fallon! Fallon! Love, I beg of you, speak!"

It seemed to Fallon that he was calling from a long way

away. She opened her eyes, but they fell shut again. He lifted her and held her tight. He looked around and saw that dead men lay everywhere. Falstaff, Rollo, Steven, and Richard were backing carefully toward him, looking warily for some further opponents. More of his men joined them.

A victory cry went up among the men. "Have we any dead?" Alaric asked hoarsely.

"Two, my lord," someone replied. Two of his young knights had fallen. Alaric ordered them buried quickly, and he held his wife tightly against him.

Richard stood anxiously before him. "The lady Fallon . . ."

"She lives, Richard. She lives. Take her while I mount, then hand her up to me, so that we may start for home."

So it was that when Fallon opened her eyes again, Alaric's arms were around her and he held her tight, and the moon was high above them. He stared down at her gravely, and she tried to reach for him, but her hand fell.

"Alaric!" she whispered brokenly. "Alaric—"

"Hush."

"But I must tell you—"

"Hush."

"Nay, Alaric. Whether you believe me or not, I must tell you. I love you. You came and you conquered, and I swear, Alaric, I had given up the fight!"

He smiled very tenderly. "Nay, Fallon, you have conquered. I did not know how to love or how to trust. You fought me with honor, and you gave me peace with honor. I was almost fool enough to lose it all. I was afraid that you could not love me enough to hold the peace between us. But that little scamp"—he nodded toward Richard—"told me then that I must love you—or let you go. I could not let you go."

"Oh, Alaric! I do love you, so much. I have been trying to tell you."

He drew up on Satan's reins. The party moved ahead of them with silent understanding, and beneath the moon, he kissed her with tenderness and hunger—and the promise of all his love. Then he brought her hand to his lips and kissed the palm.

"Love, believe me," he said, "you have conquered this heart and this soul. I am ever your most ardent slave."

A smile tugged upon her lips, and she found herself able to giggle even after the horror of the night.

"Don't laugh at me, Saxon wench!"

"Princess," she reminded him sweetly.

"Countess," he corrected her.

"Whichever, my lord husband, I do find it hard to imagine you anyone's slave."

"Well . . . perhaps," he admitted arrogantly. But then he added in a deep and husky whisper, "Still, Fallon, I shall love you. Most gladly and freely for all of my life. God knows that the world we live in will be hard for us, yet I swear, come what may, lady, I love you with all of my heart."

She touched his cheek. "Come what may."

Alaric nudged Satan, and they started off again. Fallon stared up at her husband's handsome features and fine gray eyes, and she sighed in sudden contentment.

"Father Damien says that this is how peace begins. War may plague the country, but peace comes between men and women."

He looked down at her again and smiled. "Aye, love. For where we live, there will be peace. We will reside in Fallon's world, and we will let no horror or bloodshed enter. We will make our world strong; we will work at it."

"Aye, love!" she agreed, and she cuddled against him. "Alaric!"

"Aye?"

"You must see that Richard is knighted. He saved my

life tonight, too. He slew a berserker with his little hunting knife."

He kissed her. "He will be knighted, lady. Now, tell me, do you request that honor yourself?"

She laughed again. "Nay, my lord! My sword is laid at your feet, husband, I swear it."

"And my heart, lady, is laid at yours. I swear it."

It was near dawn when they returned to Haselford. The hall was still alive with people who most eagerly awaited their return. Edith cried out her joy, Mildred anxiously hugged Fallon, and even Heath came, with his wife at his side, to welcome her back with a relieved smile.

Fallon looked at her mother eagerly. "Where is Robin?"

"In the arms of our guest," Edith said happily.

"What?"

She looked by the fire, and then she cried out gladly, for a tall figure in the dark robes had stood and turned to her, her sleeping babe in his arms. "Father Damien!"

"God's blood!" Alaric swore, coming forward. "Damien! What do you do here? I thought you were in Normandy!"

The priest shrugged. "I knew to come, though I did not know the danger. I was too late, and yet now that I am here, I am content."

Alaric arched a brow at him. A silent question passed between the two, but Fallon scarce noticed it as she eagerly took her son, and quickly excused herself to feed him.

It was full morning, and as Fallon returned Robin to his crib there was a knock on the door. Answering it, Fallon smiled to see Father Damien there.

"This time, Father, I have the second sight. I knew you were there."

He stepped inside and silently blessed her sleeping son. "I am leaving. I came to say good-bye."

She cried out softly in protest. "You have just come—"

"But William is not aware that I left him. I, too, am a Saxon, Fallon. I, too, must work to earn his trust."

She smiled at him and gave him a quick hug. "I don't understand anything about you, Father. But you cared for my father, and you care for Alaric, Robin, and me. I am grateful."

"Aye, Fallon."

"Am I at peace yet, Father?"

He smiled at her gravely. "Aye, Fallon, you have found peace within your heart, and that is all that any man or woman may seek."

"We fought, and we lost. They conquered."

He shook his head. "Nay, Fallon, though it may seem so. Your father fought a glorious battle. He was valiant and brave. But believe me, Fallon; he sits in a higher court, and he, too, knows peace now. This generation will not know it, and perhaps not even the next or the next. But we have won, Fallon. We, the English. Time will tell the tale. We will be a greater people for it, for the Normans bring us much. In the end, we shall conquer. We shall remain English to the heart, to the soul, to the very core. In time, the conquerors will speak our language. They will even claim to be English. And they will be."

He kissed her cheek, and when she would have spoken, he pressed his fingers against her lips.

Then he bowed and left her.

Fallon sat down and gazed at her sleeping son. Fervently she thanked God for her life, and for her son. And for Alaric's life. For when she thought that she had lost him, she felt that she had lost her reason to live.

She heard the door open and close. And then she felt his hands fall gently upon her shoulders, and she touched them reverently with her own. "Father Damien was here," she murmured.

"I know."

"He said we have come through very well."

"Aye, I believe that," Alaric agreed softly.

She turned and buried her head against his hard belly, and he moved his fingers gently through her hair.

"I do love you so very much!" she whispered. "I thought they had killed you, and I—"

"Hush, love."

"I did not want to live myself."

He lifted her chin and smiled tenderly into her eyes. "Fate has stolen much from you, Fallon. But she has given to us richly, too. Let us question no more. I am alive, and you are here, safe with me. Our son sleeps sweetly, and will grow healthy and strong. We have come through the savage tempest, and what is left is our ever-conquering love. We must believe in that."

She rose against him and kissed him sweetly. Her arms curled around his neck and she smiled radiantly for him, warmed by the tenderness in his gray eyes, secure in the sweet possessive strength of his arms.

"Then come, my lord, and hold me, and fill me with that all-conquering love, as I would fill you."

"Aye, my wife, and gladly," he said softly, and sweeping her from her feet, and with a beautiful new dawn bursting through the windows, he proceeded to do so.

WHAT'S LOVE GOT TO DO WITH IT?

Everything . . . Just ask Kathleen Drymon . . . and Zebra Books

CASTAWAY ANGEL	*(3569-1, $4.50/$5.50)*
GENTLE SAVAGE	*(3888-7, $4.50/$5.50)*
MIDNIGHT BRIDE	*(3265-X, $4.50/$5.50)*
VELVET SAVAGE	*(3886-0, $4.50/$5.50)*
TEXAS BLOSSOM	*(3887-9, $4.50/$5.50)*
WARRIOR OF THE SUN	*(3924-7, $4.99/$5.99)*

Available wherever paperbacks are sold, or order direct from the Publisher. Send cover price plus 50¢ per copy for mailing and handling to Penguin USA, P.O. Box 999, c/o Dept. 17109, Bergenfield, NJ 07621. Residents of New York and Tennessee must include sales tax. DO NOT SEND CASH.